THE HEATHERY ISLE

HOME BY CHRISTMAS

IAIN STEWART

 FriesenPress

Suite 300 - 990 Fort St
Victoria, BC, V8V 3K2
Canada

www.friesenpress.com

ISBN
978-1-5255-3494-2 (Hardcover)
978-1-5255-3495-9 (Paperback)
978-1-5255-3496-6 (eBook)

1. FICTION, WAR & MILITARY

Distributed to the trade by The Ingram Book Company

Dedication

From 1914 to 1918, some 59,544 members of the Canadian Expeditionary Force out of a total of almost 63,000 Canadians died as a direct result of the Great War. This book is dedicated to them.

WE WILL REMEMBER THEM

CHAPTER 1

FORT WILLIAM 1909

*
* *

"Ewan Duncan MacBride! Whar' are ye, ye wee scunner?" Called Ma MacBride at the top of her formidable lungs. Ewan had vanished in the afternoon after promising to help his mother with the chores. Mary MacBride was not all that surprised but was put out by this blatant disregard for her welfare, or so she said … with a wink. Boys will be boys after all.

"Och, Ma, what dae ye want now?" replied the exasperated Ewan for what seemed like the hundredth time. When his Ma used all three of his names, though, he knew he'd better answer.

"It's time to fetch yer Da frae his work."

"Oh, all right, I'll be hame shortly." Unfortunately, Ewan was in the middle of an argument with some of his friends. They were talking about immigrating to America. It was an argument rather than a discussion because Ewan was trying to be against the idea and his friends were for it. He thought he could make a go of it in Scotland, maybe not Fort William, but definitely without leaving his country. He wanted to work on the railways like his Da, maybe an engineer or maybe a conductor. Or maybe the shipyards in Glasgow, which were booming, the only bright spot in an otherwise dull economy. He was good with his hands.

His friends wanted to be free to wander and pick what jobs fancied them at the moment. Ewan didn't think that was a very productive life. He wanted a family, a wife, children, a house. Maybe even one with an indoor toilet! He could dream, couldn't he?

Dreaming ... gah ... he'd forgotten his Da again. His friends had gotten bored and had wandered off, which was apparently *their* dream! He had started daydreaming again and had forgotten to fetch his Da. Gah ...

*
**

Hamish MacBride worked for the West Highland Railway as a conductor. He thought of it more as being a shepherd, conducting the sheep onto the trains bound for Glasgow and further, taking them from the Highlands forever ... being led to the slaughter as it were.

It was 1908 and Scotland was being bled white by the waves of emigration to the cities and the colonies in search of jobs and better lives. He didn't blame them, but it didn't gall him any less to think that they had little choice, it was that or starve. Scotland's greatest export has long been Scots, and it seemed that it forever would be.

So, when his fourteen-year-old son, Ewan, came to fetch him home for supper he couldn't help but wonder how much longer before he would lose him to the rush to leave the Highlands. Ewan had been making noises about emigrating for a couple of years now. Two of his best friends were in Canada and one had gone to Australia. He'd just have to make the most of the time he had left with his only son. His two daughters, Moira and Shona, were quite a bit younger than Ewan and destined for the factories of Glasgow, or emigration, themselves.

"Ewan, where have you been, you were supposed to be here half an hour ago!" Hamish, scolded him, with a knowing twinkle in his eye. He knew Ewan had recently discovered that the fairer sex was not just for throwing mud at and had a particular interest in one red-haired lassie in town.

"Sorry Da, I got distracted along the way," said the somewhat shamefaced young lad.

"I'll just bet you did!" laughed his father. "No matter, we'll be home for supper in no time. So, what's distracted you so badly then?"

"Oh ... nothing," he hedged.

"Nothing eh? You're a half hour behind your time because of 'nothing'?"

"Well, nothing important anyway."

"You've been mooning over young Heather MacLeod again haven't you?" Hamish said with a laugh.

"What? No nothing like that, I swear!" he scrambled to reply. Although if he'd had time to think before answering he most likely would have said yes. He knew how worried his Da was about him leaving Fort William. A pretty girl was a much easier reason to explain away than thinking about leaving home.

"Well, then what? You have piqued my curiosity lad, and you know I'm like a dog with a bone when there's an interesting secret to be had," he said.

"Well ... "

"Come on, out with it then." Hamish was apprehensive about this line of thought though, because he knew that if it wasn't a young lassie that had Ewan so flustered, then it must be the subject he didn't want to think about.

"Well, Rory and Sandy are talking about going to America to seek their fortune ..." he said, rather lamely he thought.

"And you think those two layabouts are going to become millionaires in New York or California eh?" came the somewhat derisory, yet tentative reply.

"Not exactly ... no ... not as such ... no ..."

Hamish could tell he was trying not to answer. "Then what, precisely, *does* that mean?"

"Well, no I don't think they're going to make a fortune in America ... probably not anywhere else either when it comes to that ... it's just ... well ..."

"It's just that you're ready to start your own life and there's nothing for you in Fort William. I know ... believe me, I know. There's talk of selling the West Highland Railway or maybe even closing it, so I can't guarantee even I will have a job this time next year. I feel your pain, I really do," his crestfallen father replied. "I don't want you to leave. You're too young."

"I'm a year older than you were when you went to sea!" protested Ewan. Then kicked himself because he didn't want to go anywhere and here he was pleading his case to leave. Plus, he knew what a sore point that was with his Da.

"Aye, and see where *that* got me?!" Hamish said, waving the empty sleeve of his left arm at his son. He had lost his arm at sea when he was just two years older than Ewan, thus condemning him to non-physical jobs in an era when industrialization was driving people to the cities in droves.

"Aye, well, I don't actually want tae go anywhere. It's just that a' my friends are either leaving or talking about it, and it's got me thinking."

"Yer far too young to be thinking about that, you need a trade before you even consider emigrating." Hamish hoped that aside from keeping Ewan in Fort William for a while longer, the lad might find something that would keep him here permanently.

"Aye, I suppose yer right but what kind of trade would I get? There's nothing here that I would fancy … or be good at, come to that," Ewan despaired.

"Well, yer good wi' yer hands and Angus Mhor is always looking for good lads to fetch and carry at the smith, maybe he'll apprentice you. Would you fancy that?" Hamish hoped.

"I suppose. Would that get me on at the railroad? I'd like that!"

"If you were a journeyman blacksmith, you could write your ticket any-where, Ewan."

"I'll give it a try then. Rory and Sandy are already working there after school sometimes, it might be a lark too!"

"Well, let's see what Angus has to say, he'll no like yer scrawny arms lad that's for sure!" Hamish teased his only boy.

"Och, they are not, look at that!" he said flexing his biceps with a smile.

Hamish had overheard two Englishmen joking on the train the other day, *"The muscles on his brawny arms stood out like sparrow's ankles!!"*

"That settles it then, here we are at hame anyway. Yer mither will be in a ripe old mood!"

*
**

Ewan was the typical young teen of his time, or any other time for that matter, concerned about, but also excited for the future and what it might hold. He was a diligent (sometimes) student at school, only receiving the "tawse" every other month or so, more interested in the physical subjects such as mathematics and geography and, mostly ignoring the "softer" sub-jects like English, Latin and especially, Religious Studies.

He was, however, a smart lad who was always curious about how things worked, most particularly the trains that his Da worked on. He was also a well-built boy with dark blond hair and piercing blue eyes which were, by far, his best feature. He was slim and relatively short, only five foot five, but very muscular and quite fit. Much of his time was spent wrestling or playing Shinty. He had an aptitude for mechanical things and, when Hamish took him up to see Angus Watt, the local blacksmith, known as Angus Mhor or "Big Angus" he wasn't the least bit intimidated by this gentle giant. Angus Mohr was fully six foot seven inches tall and not an ounce under twenty-two stone! And none of it fat!

The young lad walked right up to Angus, looked him straight in the eye, well, at a pretty steep angle but he tried not to make it all that obvious, and said, "How do you do, sir?" Of course, Ewan knew Angus, everyone did, but this was a more formal occasion, and he thought he should use his best manners.

Hamish introduced them. "Angus, this is my boy, Ewan, he's almost finished school and is looking for a position, he's quick with his wits and a fair dab wi' a spanner too!"

"And what would I do with this scrawny whelp? He hasnae any muscles!" Ewan didn't see the fat wink that Angus gave his Da and was mortified. He looked around the smithy and saw a small anvil, which he thought he could lift and went right over to it and grabbed both ends of it and tried to hoist it in the air. It seemed like it had been welded to the floor, that's about how much it moved. Angus and his Da were both watching and when they saw the look of sheer dejection on Ewan's face they burst out laughing. At first Ewan was even more dejected but then he realised he had been had and joined in.

The ice was broken.

"Well, I guess I'd better hire him, if only to keep him out of harm's way!" Angus was still laughing.

Ewan finished school in June. After that he took the apprenticeship with Angus Mhor. He worked only four days a week, as there were three other lads who were also apprenticed there and there wasn't enough work to keep all of them on full time. Also, because he was the smallest of the four he drew the short straw when it came to the larger jobs. Still, he was a hard worker, learned quickly, and had soon become an experienced apprentice blacksmith.

Rory and Sandy were two of the other lads who worked at the smith. They were both smart, hardworking young lads, despite Hamish's dislike of them, and they were likeable fellows to boot, and he spent much of his free time with them. They were fast friends and had a generally happy time of it. The three of them played Shinty together, wrestled together, went hunting rabbits with their slings together and, now that they had discovered that girls were, in fact, the same species as them, went girl "hunting" together as well, though Ewan was better at that than the other two.

Ewan had started noticing that certain young lassies were no longer the same nondescript shape as everyone else and were starting to develop certain bumps and curves which, for some reason, he found pleasing to the eye.

One in particular, young Heather MacLeod, had caught his eye. She was the same age as he was. Born on precisely the same day as him. Or so he told her, with a wink. She believed him too, for about ten seconds. In fact, he was about a month older. They were in the same year at school and had many of the same friends and had played together as children.

Then one day they had been roughhousing after one of the boys had "accidentally" pulled the hair of one of the girls. After a few minutes they were all out of breath and giggling like girls ... even the boys ... when Ewan found himself lying on the ground underneath Heather MacLeod. Their faces were only inches apart and on an impulse, Heather kissed him. Just a light peck and a little off centre of his lips but it was definitely a kiss!

Ewan was mortified! This was the most awful thing that had ever happened to him! What if his friends had seen it? He would be too ashamed to ever show his face in the town again. He would have to go somewhere and live as a monk. He'd heard of a place called Tibet, maybe that would work?

But then, about three seconds later, he realised that it was also the most wonderful thing that had ever happened to him.

From that moment on he was Heather's dog; he followed her everywhere and made sure that she got what she wanted and that no one got in her way, *or there would be HELL to pay!*

Heather thought this was no less than her due because she was a *girl* after all, and weren't all girls better than any boy? At least that's what she had *meant* to think. The fact of the matter was that this was a first love for her too and it had taken her by surprise just as much as it had Ewan.

After that they were inseparable (when he wasn't working) – always together, giggling to each other and holding hands. All of their friends found this just too amusing for words, and they tried to make fun of them but just couldn't be serious about it because the truth was they were jealous. Ewan and Heather were the first of their group to fall in love.

But, teenagers being teenagers, by the end of the summer most of them had paired off and they all had a very, *very* interesting summer!

All except Rory and Sandy, who were simply too shy to make that sort of friend very easily, or at least that's what everyone else thought, when they thought about it at all.

The two lads spent a lot of time together, going on long hikes in the hills, playing conkers and marbles and other games as well as spending hours talking. Ewan didn't think much of it before he met Heather, and nothing at all after. If he had, maybe things would have turned out differently.

Rory Sinclair was a shy young Catholic lad who lived with his parents and fourteen brothers and sisters. Needless to say, he spent as much time as possible with his two friends, if only to get away from home. Alexander (Sandy) Stewart was an orphan who lived on charity, or on the street when he wasn't working. He was also quite shy and timid and spent as much time as he could with Ewan and Rory, for much the same reasons.

That was before Ewan "found" Heather. After that, Rory and Sandy spent much of their time alone or with each other. Nobody seemed to care. There were rumours of course, but there are *always* rumours in a small town. And they seemed happy enough so what of it?

The only fly in the three friends' particular ointment was the fourth apprentice at Watt & Son, Smithing and Metalwork. One Herbert Wadsworth Henry Chelmsford by name, an English boy whose father was one of the chairmen of the North British Railway. They were in the process of absorbing the West Highland Railway. Herbert's family was living in Fort William to take stock of the WHR and to observe its operations. They were what became known as nouveau riche, having made their fortune off the backs of those who rushed to the cities to cash in on the industrial revolution. Herbert was, very much, cast in that mould.

He was older than the other three, having reached the dizzying height of seventeen years of age. Quite the old gentlemen by their reckoning. He was also arrogant, brash, and unfortunately, very good at his job, as he had apprenticed to a large blacksmith in London before coming to Fort William.

Herbert, as he preferred to be called, (Herbie to Ewan, Rory and Sandy) took it upon himself to give orders to the three friends because he was bigger, older, and more experienced. Fortunately, Angus Og (wee Angus), the 'Son' in Watt & Son, didn't see it that way and made sure that all four had equal say in what went on because, as he put it: "You're all fookin' useless buggers and you will remain such until I, and *only* I, say different."

That being said, Wee Angus was tough but fair, which was just as well because he was built like a granite statue. At almost twenty-three stone, without a single ounce of fat, he was just thirty years old, but had been a smith since he was ten, having apprenticed to his father, Angus Mohr, instead of finishing school. Wee Angus owned the smith now since his father had signed over title when he became able to run things on his own. He was the only man that Ewan ever met who could carry a ten stone anvil around like it was a puppy and put it down just as gently. Needless to say, he was the local Highland Games Champion and could toss a twenty-foot caber around as if it were a stick.

Big Angus wasn't around much anymore. He was in his late fifties and figured he had earned the right to take some time for himself. He was still able to lift ten stone anvils, but he had to put them down again quickly. He still weighed twenty-two stone, but some of the muscle had eroded off his shoulders and was collecting at his waist.

It was Angus Og who stepped in whenever Herbert started throwing his weight around.

Life went on like that for a few months and got into a sort of rhythm. Herbie imperiously giving orders, and Ewan, Rory, and Sandy ignoring them and Wee Angus stepping in when he needed to. Then after work Ewan and Heather would disappear and Rory and Sandy would wander off on one of their hikes. And Herbie would do whatever Herbie did.

Scotland being Scotland though, there wasn't always good enough weather to go hiking so sometimes Rory and Sandy would stay in the workshop and talk for hours.

One day in late August, it was warm but raining cats and dogs. No-one felt much like going anywhere so after Herbie wandered off they started chatting. After a few minutes, Heather arrived; she had agreed to meet Ewan there. She looked a little perplexed.

After giving her a passionate kiss, well passionate for fourteen anyway, Ewan asked her, "What's wrong with you? You look like you've seen a ghost!"

"I think I have. I just walked past Herbie on the way here, and he gave me the most peculiar look," she said puzzled.

"He didn't touch you did he? If he did I'll thrash him!" Ewan said flaring.

"No, no, nothing like that, it was just an evil sort of look. Maybe it was just the light caused by the rain." She shrugged, dismissing it.

"Well fine, but if he says or does anything …"

"I know, I know … you'll 'thrash' him!" she turned to Rory and said, "He's my protector you know!" and winked at him. Rory winked back.

"Bah, I've just niver liked yon loon, he rubs me the wrang way." Ewan said.

Sandy said, after watching this, "I wish I had a relationship like yours, happily being with the one you love, in the open for all to see."

"Och, but you will someday, ye're a fine looking lad, you and Rory both, ye're bound to find someo..." And then she stopped. She had just seen the look that Rory and Sandy had passed between them. It was the same look that she and Ewan shared whenever they were alone.

"Sandy … you and Rory …. you're not …. Oh my God, you are!!" she was shocked but when she looked over at Ewan she could see that he wasn't. "You knew about this?" she said to him, not accusingly, it was just a question.

"I didn't know but I suspected, I just figured it was none o' my business so I didn't ask."

Heather came to a decision, "You're right, it harms no-one, it's none of our business, so enjoy your love as long as it may last, which I hope is a long time!"

No longer shocked but not wanting to take the thought any further she continued, "Well, the rain has stopped, and we should be off. Ewan, let's leave these two alone and go!"

So, Ewan and Heather went off, hand in hand and left Rory and Sandy alone.

What they hadn't seen was Master Chelmsford lurking in the dark as they walked down the road from the workshop. He was returning to retrieve his coin purse, which he had left there that afternoon. He didn't particularly want to talk to the "lovebirds" so he ducked into a dark doorway as they went past.

He scowled as he always did when he saw that cocky brat, Ewan MacBride or any of his ilk. They were too full of themselves by half. They thought they knew everything. The irony was completely lost on him, of course. He'd love to show that little slut, Heather MacLeod what a *real* man was like!

So, with that pleasant thought in his head he walked into the workshop, not even pausing to wonder why a light was on.

What he saw before him staggered the imagination. What he saw was Rory Sinclair and Sandy Stewart standing and embraced in a passionate kiss.

Herbie lost his mind, "You filthy, disgusting, arse licking, little fairies," he grabbed a nearby broom and started beating them with it.

The shock woke them out of their blissful reverie and brought them back to reality. Realising what was happening first, Rory fought back. He grabbed the end of the broom handle and tried to wrest it out of Herbie's hands.

But Herbie was bigger and stronger, and his ire was up, and Rory realised that he was out matched and tried to back away.

Sandy came to his aid just then, but Herbie simply swung his arm and caught Sandy in the temple at full reach and he dropped like a sack of potatoes. "You bastard!" as Rory tried to counterattack, but Herbie easily held him off.

Still angry, though calming down, Herbie said, "Right, you little buggerers, that's a beating for both of you. And if you say anything I'll tell everyone what I saw just now! You'll be run out of town!"

"You can't do that!" cried Rory.

"Oh, but I can, and I will … sweetheart!" sneered Herbie. He'd been waiting for an opportunity like this – a chance to get rid of two of the three fleas on his back. That would just leave one, and he would enjoy bringing him to heel soon enough. One thing at a time …

Sandy was coming to at this point and had caught that last exchange. "You can't do that to us! It's heartless!"

"Heartless, you say? Well, perhaps it is a bit extreme." Hope was beginning to return to Sandy. "I've always wanted a personal slave … or two."

Herbie was thinking how much fun this would be.

*
**

Life became a living hell for Rory and Sandy after that. Herbie was as good as his word making them into personal slaves. At first, he wasn't too bad, he wanted to probe the waters before getting his feet too wet.

Little things like sweeping up his work area as well as their own, fetching him water when he wanted it, bringing him food. But then it became increasingly ugly.

It escalated quickly, to licking his boots, top and bottom and laying their coats down so he wouldn't get his feet wet walking through puddles, anything to humiliate them. If they didn't do exactly as he asked, and quickly, he would smack them on the ear or punch their shoulder or stomach or make them cry out in pain some other way. Never in front of Wee Angus or Ewan though, he didn't want his fun spoiled after all!

Their shame was complete. They managed to keep it from Ewan, though how they did they didn't know. The recently happy lads were now miserable and downtrodden again.

The morning of October 5, 1909, started off like any other day. There were only two boys working that day, Herbie and Sandy. Wee Angus had them fabricating an engine hoist for one of the newer garages in town. There was a growing trend in motor cars. And although that resulted in more metal being available to them, it had not worked in the smith's favour, as cars rode on rubber tyres and not on steel shoes. All the metal used for automobiles was made in factories and there wasn't much use for a traditional blacksmith anymore.

Watt & Son was struggling and would take on whatever work came their way, such as their current project, an engine hoist. The frame of the hoist was somewhat simple, which is why Wee Angus decided to assign the task to his two apprentices. He put Herbie in charge, not only because he had built one previously, but also because it was his turn to supervise. Unfortunately, this turned out to be a fatal mistake.

Herbie had told Sandy to sling the horizontal crosspiece of the hoist from one of the roof trusses in the shop, so they could work on it while it hung in the air. Slinging it like that was a two-man job however and Sandy asked Herbie to help.

"Oi, Herbie" Sandy called out, "Give us a hand slinging this I-beam. I can't do it by myself."

Herbie had a quick temper. "I told you to hang that steel," he growled "so you'd better bloody do it, or you'll be sorry,"

"I'll try again" said Sandy rather angrily, "but I don't think it will work."

So, Sandy tried to hoist up one side, then move over and hoist the other side, in kind of a sawing motion. It almost worked. But right at the last moment, right as the steel was seven feet in the air, one side slipped out of its lifting harness, swung down and caught Sandy square in the crotch. The end of the beam hit both thighs, severing both of his femoral blood vessels.

Although Sandy had only seconds to live, Herbie spent those seconds raging at him for dropping the beam and causing him extra work.

Angus rushed in when he heard Sandy's screams. He saw the tableau in front of him. One of his apprentices, Sandy, was on the ground screaming in mortal agony and the other one, Herbie, was standing over him raging at his incompetence.

He had seen similar injuries before, but never that bad. He knew he had only seconds and began to work on a severed vein. Suddenly, he realised that the other one was severed as well. He knew he couldn't work on both at the same time and hollered at Herbert to assist him. Unfortunately, Herbert was still screaming at Sandy.

Twenty seconds later, Sandy was dead. Every drop of blood had pumped from his body like a firehose, twin hoses in fact. It didn't take long. Mercifully, Sandy died quickly. He was just one month to the day short of his fifteenth birthday.

Angus stayed on his knees for another minute, hanging his head in shock. He then slowly and deliberately stood up and walked over to Herbert who was still raging and screaming at Sandy and proceeded to break his jaw.

Once Angus had recovered sufficiently from his own shock he went to the police to report that one of his employees had been killed due to the callous incompetence of another. However, Herbie had beaten him to it. He had immediately gone to the authorities and reported that Angus had broken his jaw because Herbert had witnessed him killing another of his employees in a murderous rage.

There were no witnesses to interview so the only statements were those of Angus and Herbert. The only parts of which that agreed were the parts about Angus breaking Herbert's jaw.

When Herbert's father learned that his son had been so badly abused by a local 'tradesman', he immediately filed charges of assault against Angus Og. The fact that a local homeless boy had been killed in the exchange was all but ignored. It was, after all, the word of a 'tradesman' against the word of the son of an upstanding citizen. Almost as an afterthought Angus was also charged with Sandy's murder.

The result was a foregone conclusion.

Ewan and Rory meanwhile were in shock. The day after the death of their friend they went to see Wee Angus, who had not yet been arrested. He told them what happened and what the likely outcome would be. He was under no illusions as to the chances of a common tradesman winning against English money.

He told the boys where certain valuables were hidden and asked them to look out for his father as best they could once he was gone.

"Ewan, you've got to promise me you'll look after Pa as well as you can. They'll likely put me away forever. Probably a dozen or more years at hard labour, and I know what hard labour means. Slow death. Even for me," Angus said more calmly than he felt.

"Don't even think that Mr. Watt! You'll be out in no time!" Rory was beside himself with grief.

"Aye, ye'll see to him yoursel' soon enough!" cried Ewan.

"Well, we'll see," Angus knew better but didn't want to depress the lads any more than they already were, "in any case can ye do a few things for me?"

"Of course, anything at all, we owe you a huge debt for giving us a trade," an emotional Ewan said with as much dignity as he could muster.

"Under the floor in the shop, under the anvil is a steel box with almost one thousand pounds, mostly in sovereigns. It's mine and Pa's life savings. It's yours on condition that you take care of my father first. I need you to swear to me that you will look after my Pa," a very plaintive request but one that could have only one answer.

"Of course, you have my solemn word as a true Scot and as a blacksmith," Ewan couldn't think of anything more binding.

"And I swear by almighty God that I will honour your father as long as he lives," added Rory.

"Well, that will have to do then," was Angus's reply spoken very matter-of-factly. Later that day he was arrested, and they thought they would never see him again.

A month later Angus was sentenced to fifteen years at hard labour and all of his property was forfeited to the crown. Angus Mohr was heartbroken.

*
**

Ewan and Rory then found a quiet place to discuss what the hell had just happened.

"That bastard has not only killed our friend, but he might as well've killed Angus Og; he's as good as dead. Not to mention our jobs and, likely, Angus Mohr," facts stated bluntly by Ewan.

"Aye he has, not to mention my first love, now what do we do about it?" came Rory's equally blunt, and increasingly angry, response.

"Well, we need to think carefully," said Ewan.

"From Exodus: 'And if any mischief follow, then thou shalt give life for life, eye for eye, tooth for tooth, hand for hand, foot for foot,'" quoted Rory.

"If that means what I think it does …"

"It does," confirmed Rory.

"Then we have to plan this and make sure we can cover our tracks and be prepared to leave Fort William forever," Ewan stated, not repelled by the thought of killing Herbie because he really thought that it was justified.

Though they didn't really mean to murder Herbie, they were just so emotional over the loss of one of their friends and the condemnation of two others that they had to vent their frustration somehow.

"We were planning on doing that anyway, weren't we?"

"Leaving Fort William? Aye, but not like this. This means leaving our families, possibly in the dead of night with the authorities right behind us."

"What choice do we have?"

"You're right. Sandy must be avenged. Wrongs must be righted. But first we have to get the gold before Chelmsf … *fuck* … I can't even say his name I hate him so much!" Ewan exploded.

"We'll go for the gold tonight."

"Right."

Six hours later it was dark enough and late enough to enter the blacksmith shop but still light enough to see what they were doing. They entered the shop through the farriers' door, which was closest to the big anvil. This was the thirty-five stone anvil used for making large parts for trains and ships and the like. They stood and looked at it for a couple of minutes wondering how the hell they were going to move it. It had taken four of them to even shift the thing last time they had done that and one of them was Angus Og.

After looking around the shop in growing frustration they realised the solution was right above their heads. Since they had last shifted it, Angus had installed another crossbeam directly above the anvil for moving bigger pieces of steel. This should have been obvious as Angus would have used that to move it any distance, but they were so panicky that it was a wonder they didn't make any more mistakes.

There were a couple of blocks and all the required tackle nearby, so it shouldn't be too hard.

They had set up the gear many times so, even in the near dark, it was easy for them. Then, out of the corner of his eye, Rory spotted a light moving towards them. They immediately dropped to the floor to wait until whoever it was went by. No such luck, Rory had left the farriers' door open to let in some extra light. The light stopped right outside the door, then slowly moved towards it. It then paused and the person carrying it said "Who's there? Show yourself! I'll call for the police!"

Ewan immediately recognized the voice, even though it was heavily muffled by bandages. It was Herbie! What the hell was he doing here? The light started moving again, paused, then came on again. At that point he had to see the tackle rigged up on the anvil and the beam. Sure enough: "What are you doing? You can't steal an anvil!" he said through his bandages and a crushed jaw, so it was hard to understand.

"We're not stealing the anvil," Ewan said as he jumped out of the shadow and tackled the light.

"*You*!" Herbie said as the light fell to the floor. Ewan noticed in passing that it was one of those fancy new electric torches. "What are you doing here?"

"We're takin' what rightfully belongs tae Angus Mohr and Angus Og. And which you shall'na have," Ewan said with conviction.

"We'll see about that!" said Herbie as he swung wildly with the torch, which he had picked up from the ground.

He landed a glancing blow on Ewan's head, which made him see stars. Then he grabbed at a large spanner that was hanging up behind a bench and managed to swing it at Ewan's head, just missing and connecting with his left shoulder instead. Then he swung it again, and this time connected with his solar plexus, knocking the wind out of him. He meant business and Ewan knew he was in a fight for his life.

Herbie rushed at Ewan wildly with the spanner, once again connecting with his shoulder.

Ewan managed to dodge him the next time, but only just. Herbie went flying past Ewan and straight into the arms of Rory who chose this moment to make his presence known. Rory and Herbie were rolling around on the ground each trying to get on top of the other. At first, Herbie got the better of him because he was bigger and stronger. He got his hands around Rory's throat and started to choke the life out of him. Then Rory's wrestling experience started to tell and, even though he was smaller and younger he started to get the upper hand. In wrestling, smaller often worked to your advantage and Rory now played that card.

They rolled around trading positions with one getting the upper hand then the other. Rory was tiring fast, though, and Herbie's stamina started to come to play. Ewan rushed at them and crashed into Herbie's back with a thump. He managed to twist him around so that Rory was out of reach.

Ewan got hold of Herbie's torch, which he broke over his left forearm, shattering both bones.

Through waves of agony, Herbie saw his tormentors trying to pin him down so with one massive heave of his back he threw Ewan off and heavily to the ground. Unfortunately for him that left his head exposed for just a few seconds. More than enough time for Rory to get around behind him.

Rory got him in a headlock and drew his head back so that it was presented to Ewan. By this time, he had searched for and found the large spanner, which Herbie had tried to crush his head with. He then smashed it into Herbert's skull saying, "This is for Angus Og!"

Then Rory got a better grip on his head and with a burst of adrenaline he twisted it until he heard the vertebrae pop saying, "and this is for Sandy!"

And then it was over.

They were stunned.

They had killed a man.

It ended up as self-defence but it had been their plan all along, hadn't it? Kill Herbie for what he had done to their friends. Thinking about doing this, deliberately killing a human being was one thing. Actually following through with the thought was a completely different matter. Ewan didn't believe they'd actually do it when it came right down to it, but here they were with a dead body at their feet.

"What have we done? What the fuck do we do now?" Rory said almost in tears.

"There's nothing for it … it's done." Ewan replied. "We have to follow the plan."

"We should tell the police what happened!" Rory said.

"And end up like poor Angus?" Ewan said. "No bloody fear. We won't be walking away from this when the dust settles, and that's for bloody sure!"

"You're right, of course, but what do we do with him?" he said, pointing at the mortal remains of Herbert Wadsworth Henry Chelmsford lying at their feet.

"He should fit into whatever box the gold is in." Ewan hoped.

"With our luck the gold is just Angus dreaming." Rory dejectedly replied.

"It can't be, Angus was so anxious about it, it has to be true."

They finished setting up the block and tackle and strapped up the anvil with it.

"OK, let's shift this bloody thing and see what's there," Ewan decided.

Moving the anvil turned out to be anticlimactically easy. The steel box was right where Angus said it would be, so they dusted the soil off of it, opening it in situ. Ewan noticed that it was, indeed, a big box and that it would hold Herbert's body quite handily. The gold was in several separate canvas bags, which they quickly removed from the box. Then they stuffed the body inside, filled the hole back in and lowered the anvil back into place. They then loaded the gold into the two haversacks they'd brought for the purpose. Finally, they made off with it as quickly as possible. Nearly two thousand five hundred gold coins, mostly sovereigns and half sovereigns, in ten canvas bags, is nearly thirty pounds, which is heavy but not when you have that much adrenaline pumping through your veins!

About then the shock of what had just happened started to set in; they consoled each other and convinced themselves that it wasn't actually murder. Though that's what they had planned to do, it ended up being self defence. That's what they told themselves anyway. The nightmares would come later.

They hid for the rest of that night in a barn on the edge of town, holding each other and shivering from the shock and the cold. The light rain that started after midnight seemed to set the right tone for the night. They caught what sleep they could, which wasn't much and made it to the next morning.

At first light, they woke themselves and considered what they were going to do next. The police hadn't found the body right away, but it seemed obvious that they soon would. It seemed equally obvious that even though there were no witnesses to the 'event' (they didn't want to call it a crime) that they would be the prime suspects. They had to get out of Fort William before he was found and as soon as possible. But where to go?

"We can't stay here," Rory said.

"Of course not, ye gawp!"

"Well then, where?"

"South, it'll have to be south. Glasgow maybe?" Glasgow was where Ewan had been planning to go anyway.

"Aye, we can disappear in Glasgow, lay low for a while."

"We have to go see our folks before we leave, I'll have to see my Da, see if he can get us on the train."

"Aye, I need to say good-bye to my parents at least," said Rory sadly.

"We'll give my Da enough of Angus's money to set up Angus Mohr for the rest of his life. Half of what he left us."

They agreed to meet later that afternoon at the station. Hopefully Ewan could arrange rail passage to Glasgow.

But, more importantly right now he had to say good-bye to Heather. He couldn't just leave without saying something to her. She had supported him through all this and was just as devastated by what had happened to Sandy as the boys were.

He found her at home, crying her eyes out. Her Da met him at the door. "Hello lad, this is not a good situation." He was just talking about Sandy's death, he didn't know about Herbert yet, neither did Heather so when he told them what had happened they were in shock. He didn't go into all the details, just that Herbert was dead and that, although it had been an accident, or at least unintended, they were going to be blamed for his death and they had to, essentially, run away.

"I'll come with you!" cried Heather in anguish.

"No, you won't," stated her father firmly but rather calmly and kindly Ewan thought.

"He's right, Heather, this is nothing to do with you, you mustn't get involved."

"But I love you!" she cried again.

"I know you do, and I love you, but you can't come with me, not right now. Maybe I'll send for you later," Ewan said while looking at her father. He was met by a firm and determined shake of the head and a gaze 'no you won't' it said, and 'you're only fifteen' it implied. But he was not unkind, and he left them to say their farewells.

They stood and held each other, vibrating but not saying a word for an eternity, or so it seemed. Then a final passionate kiss and Ewan was gone.

*
**

"Where the bloody hell have you been?" was Ewan's greeting from his Da on coming home. "There've been police and lawyers and Chelmsford's Da looking for you for two days!" Apparently, they had found Herbie's body already.

"I'm sorry, Da. You heard about Sandy?"

"Aye, and I was right sorry to hear about that, he was a nice lad. What the hell happened?"

So, Ewan give him the short version of what had happened over the last two days … and nights, leaving nothing out. He waited for his Da to explode.

"So, that's the way of it then?" Hamish said, entirely too calmly for Ewan's comfort.

Hamish knew that at his heart Ewan was a decent, honest lad and that he could trust him to be telling the truth now. He also knew that Chelmsford had raised such a storm over the death of his son that Ewan would be unlikely to escape it. Angus Og hadn't and there was no more honest a man in the Highlands than him.

Ewan just sat there with his head down and his hands in his lap.

Hamish said, "What now?"

"I was going to ask you that," came the plaintive reply.

"Well, you can't stay here."

"I know." Head hanging.

His mother and sisters came in at this point, and she ran to him and took him in her arms. He started crying, he was only fifteen after all, still a child in a lot of ways. Though those days were now, irrevocably, over.

Moira and Shona were crying as well, though they didn't know why.

Hamish waved to them to just stay where they were, and he'd explain the situation later. His Ma didn't say anything right away and just nodded resignedly.

But she couldn't hold it in for long so, finally, "Where are you going to go, what are you going to do?" she said with a knife edge of panic in her voice.

"Rory and I are going to go to Glasgow," he said.

"Aye, I think that's best for now." Hamish agreed. "I can get you on the train tonight. Where's Rory?"

"Saying good-bye to his family."

"That'll take some time!" Hamish tried some humour to lighten the mood. He got two weak smiles for his efforts.

"Aye, we're going to meet at the station this afternoon. I was hoping you could get us on a train. I promised Wee Angus that I'd leave money here to look after his Da. Here's almost five hundred pounds in sovereigns," he took four large canvas bags from his haversack and gave them to his Da.

Hamish was taken aback, Ewan had told him what Angus Og had left for them but seeing it, or part of it, was still a shock.

"That will definitely be enough to keep old Angus comfortable for the rest of his days." Hamish said with a slight tremor in his voice, not from avarice but from worry as to how he was going to keep this secret from Chelmsford. He'd worry about that later he decided.

Most of both families, the older Sinclair children anyway, were there to see the boys off. There were many tears, all round, because they knew they'd most likely never see each other again.

"This isn't how I wanted to leave," Ewan said, crying like he was two years old again.

"I know that my poor wee lamb!" cried his distraught mother.

Ewan gave his sisters one last hug and cried even more.

Hamish didn't say anything, he was too worried about what was going to happen in the coming days. And he was even more worried about what his only son would be doing for the rest of his life or even if he'd have one.

As for the boys, they just waved and cried as the train pulled away knowing that, for good or ill, this part of their lives was over forever.

*
* *

Arriving in Glasgow on the 19th of October 1909 they set about finding a place to live and work. They didn't want to use the money that Wee Angus had bequeathed to them for frivolous things such as food and shelter. They went down to the waterfront because they thought that the best chance of a job that either of them had was either at the shipyards or the docks.

First things being first though, they had to find a place to stay. Glasgow at this time was a boom town, with new shipyards and docks being built all the time and existing ones being expanded constantly. This meant that they probably wouldn't have much problem finding a job of some sort, but lodging might be an entirely different matter. They spent the first night huddled together for warmth underneath one of the many new railway trestles leading to the docks.

Much of the next day was spent searching for a room in one of the new, but already run down, tenement blocks springing up all through the industrial parts of the Clyde. Between being chased off by dogs and propositioned by whores and thieves they were pretty discouraged by the end of that day and another cold night was spent in the open – this time in a new warehouse still under construction. In the wee hours of the morning they were sent on their way by an angry night watchman who wondered how they dared to invade his domain with their filthy bodies.

Eventually they found a space in a newer block where an older couple had an extra room. The woman took pity on the boys when she recognized their accents, they being from Oban themselves and only being in Glasgow a few months.

"Och, you boys look like ye've been dragged through a hedge backwards, dunked in a muddy puddle and then chased by the hounds of hell through the Highlands all the way to Glasgow!" exclaimed Mrs. Moira Duncan when she set eyes on them for the first time. She said it in a concerned tone but with a grin and a twinkle in her eye. These weren't the first starving waifs looking for a job she had seen since coming south.

She and her husband, Jock, had come to Glasgow to run a tailor's shop, which Jock's cousin had bequeathed to him when he'd died of consumption the previous year. It had been a successful shop catering mainly to shipyard executives and staff, and Mr. and Mrs. Duncan had every intention of making it even more so. Their only son had immigrated to Australia three years previously and their two daughters had married and moved to Edinburgh and Stirling, so they were able to transplant to Glasgow quite easily.

Moira still had the nesting urge, though, so when she saw these two half-drowned rats at her door she swept them up like stray puppies. She knew better than to enquire too closely into their pasts. She suspected it would be something they weren't proud of or happy about or generally just something they wouldn't want to talk about.

She was a good judge of character though and quickly figured these lads were naïve but trustworthy and could be safely taken in.

"You'll be wanting a room I expect?" she said to them.

Ewan spoke up, "Yes, missus, we'd be right obliged if ye would be so kind," he was fairly tripping over himself to be polite!

"Well, I've got a spare room at the back, there's no bed but I can give you an old mattress, which you'll have to share," she offered. "I'll feed ye if you help wi' the housework! Pay me what you can until you get jobs, and then it'll be three bob a week for the both of ye."

"Oh, aye, that's more than fair missus, thank you very much!" Ewan said elbowing Rory at the same time.

"*Ow*, oh, I mean, aye … err … yes very kind indeed," stammered Rory nervously.

Once they'd had time to eat and get cleaned up they could finally relax a bit. Enough to put some serious thought into their predicament.

"What do you think our chances are of getting a job at the shipyard?" Rory asked. "We are blacksmiths after all."

"Och, well we're apprentice blacksmiths, and I don't think there'll be many horses need shoeing at Lithgows or Yarrows! Not to mention we can't very well ask for a reference."

"Aye, maybe so but we could ask to try out!"

"We're not even sixteen yet and don't look older either."

"Well, how about the docks then?" Rory tried again.

"Same thing, we're no even sixteen and we're no verra big."

"There's lots of ships comin' in, maybe they're desperate?" Hope springs eternal!

So, the next morning they went down to the dockyards and watched the ships coming in and unloading for a while.

They didn't see anything too promising the first day, so they went back to their lodgings to think the matter over. One thing that worried Ewan was that where they were staying was none too safe to leave Angus's money while they were looking for work. They still thought of it as "Angus's money" and they didn't want anyone to find it and steal it. So, they each bought a waistcoat which would go under their jackets. They spent the rest of the night sewing half of what was left, about four hundred and fifty coins, into the linings. A full stone of gold in total. This was actually not that heavy and even less so once they had evenly distributed the coins over the breadth of the coat.

Little did they know how good an idea this was going to be.

After a couple of days, they were drawn to a particular dock area. The sign on the dock said, 'Hamburg South America Line'.

"That sounds fancy," Rory ventured.

"Aye, too fancy for the likes of us I'll bet."

"We don't want to *go* there; we just want to unload their ships!"

"Go on. What are you seeing that I'm not?" Ewan thought Rory was ill in the head!

"See there, they're unloading sugar from that ship, it probably came from South America. That doesn't look too hard, most of the lads look around our age too, maybe a bit older," said the ever observant Rory.

"Well, what have we got to lose?" Ewan agreed.

So, they went down to the dock with the German sign. They saw a big, jolly looking man who appeared to be in charge.

"Excuse me, sir!" ventured Ewan nervously.

"*Jawohl! Meine kleine boychik?* Vot can I do for you? Hmm?"

"We're looking for work, sir."

"Verk! Ha, two *kleine jungs* like you! Vot can you do?" he laughed.

"We're hard workers, sir! Give us a chance, sir! Please!" not quite whining but very close.

"*Ach so!* Very well zen, help those two *jung* unload those crates of sugar and we'll see what you can do! Break even one and I'll throw you off the dock myself!" he chuckled to himself as if he'd just made the funniest joke in the world.

Four hours later the exhausted boys were finished. The large German man, whose name turned out to be Ludwig Weber, was laughing at them. "Never have I seen such small boys work like such big men! How can I turn down such *mensch*? Welcome to the *Sudamerikanische Dampfschifffahrts-Gesellschaft!*"

"Did he just say 'fart'?" whispered Rory out of the side of his mouth.

"I think so, but whatever you do don't laugh, I think we just got a job!" Ewan grinned in return.

So, there they were unloading sugar, coffee, and something called guano, for a German company on the dockyards of Glasgow with no families and no friends and, for all they knew, a price on their heads. Just a week before, they had been apprentice blacksmiths without a care in the world.

CHAPTER 2

HAMBURG 1909

*
**

"Good morning, sir, may I help you?" As always, Peter was polite to potential new customers.

Peter Baum had recently been promoted to serve customers directly at the company's shop front, which was remarkable for a boy who had just turned eighteen. He missed making barrels himself, but he thought he could help his friend, uncle, mentor and boss, Joseph Schulmann, more if he worked directly with the clients.

"Good morning, is Herr Schulmann here?" asked the rather austere looking gentleman.

"I'm afraid not, sir, perhaps I may be of service?"

"Perhaps, are you authorized to take orders?"

"Certainly sir, what did you have in mind?"

"I am Herr Wagner, I represent a large brewery here in Hamburg, which is expanding its facility by a considerable volume and we require an additional two thousand of your two hundred and fifty litre barrels for our growing export market. The Americans have taken a liking to good German beer! We will require this quantity on an annual basis." The fellow looked rather like a beer barrel himself and seemed eminently qualified to order barrels!

Peter had to swallow a couple of times before replying. "I think, sir, that I will have to consult with Herr Schulmann before taking such a large order. He will be in this afternoon."

"That will be fine," the client allowed. "I'll return after lunch. Good day." He then left.

Peter was elated, this one order was more than the total number of barrels that he had made since he started in the cooperage when he was eleven.

His parents had died in a train accident when he was just six years old. He had no formal education to speak of beyond being taught to read and write and basic arithmetic at the local Lutheran orphanage. His parents had been Jewish, but the Lutherans took him in, a fact for which he would be forever grateful. He left to work for his uncle Joseph when he was almost twelve. His first job was sweeping the floors in the factory. This was, he was told, an important job because wood shavings were a horrible fire hazard, and it was vital that he keep the floors clean. Whether true or not it resulted in him being a hardworking and generally diligent lad.

Joseph Schulmann had been born in Munich into a brewing family and had been put to work in the brew house at about the same age as Peter. He knew the benefits of hard work and the character that it would bring.

Joe had lost his wife, Inga, to consumption five years earlier and needed someone to keep him company. The boy's parents had been his boyhood friends, as well as relatives, and he felt an obligation to them.

Peter soon graduated to making barrels and by the time he was fifteen he was a fully qualified cooper.

He was also big for his age. At eighteen, he was already 1.8 metres tall, large framed and unusually strong. His dark handsome features combined with his jet black hair and green eyes made him popular with the young *frauleins* of Hamburg, who found him exotic and mysterious.

Earlier that year, Peter had been called into the Infantry Reserve of the Imperial German army, he was required to train two or three times during the year. He flourished in the rough camaraderie and discipline of army life. And the uniform didn't hurt with the frauleins either!

He acquired some new skills and discovered a love for living and working outdoors.

All things considered, when he thought about it, life was good, and he was doing rather well. Peter could not understand why his uncle had taken him from the factory, which he loved, and put him in the shop. It had its benefits, to be sure, but it didn't allow him to work with his hands. He loved all the processes of making barrels and enjoyed the work itself. It was seldom boring as every piece of wood was different, and every barrel had its own challenges.

What he didn't know was that his uncle Joe had to move him to the shop for his own safety. He was *too* good at building barrels. Several of the older, bigger men who had been there for more years than Peter had been alive, resented the fact that this young, handsome, pipsqueak was hired because he was the owner's nephew. The fact that he was better at their job than they were just rubbed salt into the wound.

Joseph had heard rumblings about how some of them wanted to rough him up a little, just to teach him a lesson, show him who's boss. So just in case there was anything to these rumblings he moved him into the shop. He convinced him it was a promotion and paid him more, so he wouldn't mind as much.

At first this was a wonderful change and Peter was able to travel throughout Europe, he made several business trips to towns like Paris and Zurich which were both beneficial to the firm and personally very enjoyable. This made everyone happy, the coopers had this younger, better looking, more talented owner's pet out of their hair and Peter got a more important (he thought) and better paying job … for a while. Peter missed the factory floor though and still wanted to work with his hands, but he was too grateful to his uncle to complain.

This went on for a number of months, with Peter getting better at running the shop and with Joseph giving him more authority in the business. It seemed that Peter was set for life, and he adjusted nicely to his new routine.

Sometimes life has a funny way of playing that game though.

*
**

Joseph met with Herr Wagner that afternoon. After some negotiations he concluded that his facility could make the required quantity of barrels at a fair price. The deal was done.

What that meant for his factory, though, was that it needed a twenty per cent increase in production, which meant hiring more coopers and all the other trades associated with barrel making, blacksmiths for the hoops, cartwrights for the wagons, etc., etc.

The upshot of all that was that Joe couldn't afford to keep a talented young cooper in his shop when he desperately needed him in the factory. Furthermore, since most of these twenty per cent new coopers needed to be trained from nothing, he needed Peter to help run one of the shifts while he pulled more experienced men to train the new hands.

This did not go well right from the start.

Peter was already disliked for all the reasons noted earlier and now he was one of their bosses. This combined with the fact that the most experienced men, who had been more accepting of him, were now off training the new men. This left Peter in a very precarious position.

The worst part of all was the fact that he was only the number two man on the shift. There was another man above him. And he was the worst of all.

His name was Rudolf Schmidt. He was an arrogant Prussian who had been invalided out of the German army after losing a leg to an artillery carriage, which had run him over on manoeuvres in northern Germany.

He was fifteen centimetres shorter than Peter, hampered by a false leg, fully twenty kilos lighter, ten years older and had a face like a squashed sausage. It was hatred at first sight. And the fact that Peter was Jewish was the cherry on top.

The rot started immediately. When Peter gave an order, it was routinely ignored. If he gave it again it was ignored again. If he got forceful the man would go to Schmidt and get the order rescinded. If he faced Schmidt about it, he got yelled at and threatened. He wouldn't go to his uncle Joe, it was a pride thing.

Peter got more and more irritated by this situation until eventually it came to a head.

One day in late fall 1909, soon after his nineteenth birthday, Peter saw two of the men, who hated each other, the one man having gotten the other man's sister pregnant, fighting on the shop floor. He waded in to stop it. The men were fighting with barrel staves, which are sturdy enough to be used as pretty effective clubs and, when broken, can be sharp enough to use as stabbing weapons.

By the time Peter waded in both men had beaten each other pretty badly, they were covered in blood and one man had a broken arm. Peter grabbed the other man and tried to pull him off. This had the effect of pinning the man's arms behind his back for a few seconds. Long enough, unfortunately, for the other man to grab a broken stave with his good arm and thrust it into his antagonist's belly and then yanking it out again.

Pulling a thick piece of wood out of a man's belly has the same effect as pulling the cork out of a barrel … the barrel empties quickly.

As luck would have it, the man who died was Schmidt's brother. Schmidt finally showed up at the scene and what he saw was this. He saw his brother lying messily dead on the floor with Peter standing over him covered in blood. He didn't immediately see the other man, the one with the broken arm and also covered in blood. When he did it didn't matter because he had already decided what had happened.

In his mind Peter had killed his brother for no-one knew what reason, the other man had tried to intervene and had had his arm broken for his trouble.

It was a slam dunk in Schmidt's piggy little brain. And none of the witnesses would back up Peter's story because they all hated him too.

It was open and shut: Peter was guilty of murder.

*
**

Herr Schulmann, of course, didn't believe a word of it but he had to act fast. The *polizei* were, undoubtedly, on their way. He quickly pulled Peter into his office ostensibly to get his side of the story.

"What's going on?" asked his incredulous uncle. "What the hell happened?"

Peter told him what happened but then added. "That Schmidt and his cronies have got it in for me. They're going to blame me for this," he warned.

"OK, I need to talk to Schmidt. Let me deal with this. Make yourself scarce for now, but come to the house tonight. I have to think about this. And be quick. The police are already on their way."

He then dismissed Peter and brought in Schmidt to get his story.

"That Jewish swine Baum has killed my brother! For no reason at all!" Schmidt raged. "What are you going to do about it eh? Protect your little pet nephew I bet!"

"Stop screaming Schmidt, the police are on their way, what more can I do?" The police arrived a few minutes later.

They found a total of twelve "witnesses" whose stories varied hardly at all from each other. Peter had started beating Schmidt's brother, probably to get him to keep quiet about Peter having raped his sister, then when the other man tried to intervene Peter broke his arm with a stave, which also broke, and then he grabbed one of the broken ends and stabbed the brother with it.

One of the more experienced policemen, Johan Becker, who had been a policeman all his adult life, thought that the stories were far too similar to be believable, witness statements are never that accurate. But having nothing else to go on and, coupled with the fact that the suspect had fled from the scene, they were left with little choice but to charge Peter Baum with murder.

Now they just had to find him.

*
* *

Peter had run from the cooperage in a panic. He caught his breath and slowed down and eventually was able to think rationally.

He thought about his situation. He was charged with murder, probably, and he had lost his job, certainly. He couldn't bear to contact his friends because he didn't want to get them involved.

Uncle Joe would know what to do. He had always helped before.

Peter hid out at the docks for the rest of the day. They were only a block from the cooperage.

He then went to uncle Joe's house after it got dark and timidly knocked on the door.

Uncle Joe lived alone, his wife had died five years earlier and his two children now lived abroad, one in America and the other in South Africa.

Joe answered the door after the first knock. He had been expecting him. For Joe's part, Peter was the last of his relatives that lived in Germany. He would do much to help the boy.

"Come in, come in, quickly now," they had to be very careful. "Come into my library. Now sit down."

Peter sat down but he didn't say anything.

"Well, say something for God's sake! What are you thinking?"

"I'm thinking that I'm in trouble," Peter eventually said.

"Yes, you are," came the blunt reply, "but nothing that can't be dealt with."

Some hope maybe? Peter thinks. "How?" he said. "I could join the French Foreign Legion, I suppose," he added, only half-jokingly.

"Pah! Don't be an idiot! There are always solutions."

"OK, I'm listening."

"As you know, in this business you make a number of contacts in the shipping business over the years. I have a friend at Hamburg South America Line who will help me out. They have ships going to South America every month."

"I don't want to go to South America!" Peter was aghast.

"No, no, no … the ship they have leaving tomorrow from Hamburg will be stopping in Glasgow to pick up some more cargo and he's willing to take you as far as that," Joe explained. "Once you're in Glasgow we'll figure something else out."

"Glasgow? But that's in Scotland, I don't speak English!" he complained.

"Don't worry, boy, neither do they!"

*
**

Two days later, Peter was outfitted for a sea voyage, though hopefully a short one, plus a stay in Glasgow of who knew how long.

He boarded the SS Cordoba at Hamburg dock and set sail for Scotland.

The sea passage from Hamburg to Glasgow took two interminable weeks. He was told it would take less than one, but they made an extra four stops before getting there – Rotterdam, Calais, Liverpool, and Belfast – to pick up further cargo. Plus, he had been told that the North Sea and the English Channel were two of the roughest seas in the world, and after this trip he had no reason to argue with that.

He paid his way by working in the boiler room. It was hard work, but he was no stranger to hard work, so it was no real problem. The only problem was that every time he ate he ended up throwing it all back into the sea!

It was a good job they were only at sea for two weeks; he would have starved if it had been any longer.

The captain knew he was related to Joe Schulmann who had given HSDG (*Hamburg-Sudamerikanische Dampfschifffahrts-Gesellschaft*) a lot of trade over the years, so he was treated well.

All in all, rough seas and no food notwithstanding, he didn't mind the trip. Being a young man, it was all an adventure. Maybe not the circumstances he'd liked to have seen this part of Europe in but considering what he had just been through not so bad.

Thus, Peter arrived in Glasgow on November 27, 1909 without a single piece of solid anything in his belly. It was all in the Irish Sea.

* * *

It seemed that when Joe said the Glaswegians didn't speak English he wasn't kidding. They said it was English, but it didn't sound like it to him.

Joe had given him the name of one of HSDG's employees who had been working in Glasgow for a while, an old friend of his, Ludwig Weber. He had met Ludwig many years ago when he had come to the house before heading to Argentina to work for the company. Now, it seemed, he was in Glasgow, a small world indeed.

Peter found Ludwig down by the docks where his crew of wharf rats had already started unloading the Cordoba.

"Hallo, Herr Weber, how are you?" he said formally.

"Well, well, well, Peter Baum! It's been a long time, lad. What are you doing here? This is the last place I would have expected to see you."

"I don't want to go into too much detail, but I need to lay low outside of Germany for a while," came the cryptic reply.

"Ah! Say no more! How do you think I ended up here?" Ludwig thought Peter meant girl problems.

Peter thought it best to let him continue to think that. "It should all blow over soon. Uncle Joe will send for me when I can return to Hamburg."

"Splendid! I suppose you want a job while you're here eh? How old are you now?"

"Nineteen, Herr Weber."

"Pah, you'll be the old man of the crew, you're bigger than most too! You'll be running them by the end of the year I'll just bet!!" Ludwig laughed.

* * *

So, Peter went to work unloading cargo. It was interesting, if hard, work. All kinds of exotic things were coming in from South America, from sugar and coffee to textiles and even bat guano! It was never a dull moment.

He met lots of interesting people too. Several of the lads he worked with were from South America, some were from Germany, but most were from Scotland.

Peter picked up English fairly quickly (it turns out Glaswegians *do* speak English after all). He met two young lads from Fort William who were happy to trade him English lessons for German. Ewan and Rory were their names, they were younger than him, but not by that much and they were friendly enough. They obviously had secrets of their own, but he didn't want to pry lest his own secret come out.

They quickly became best of friends. Young men tend to gravitate towards like-minded individuals and once the language barrier was removed the camaraderie of youth asserted itself. Peter recognized in Ewan a kindred spirit and a mutual trust grew up, quite naturally, between them. Rory was friendly enough, but he didn't have Ewan's intellect. He was more of a follower than a leader.

Peter saw that Ewan was far more mature than his fifteen years would allow. He realised that they had both shared similar experiences that had driven them to where they were.

*
**

Christmas came and went. Without their families there wasn't much to celebrate. Though Mrs. Duncan did the best she could to brighten the season for them. So, 1909 became 1910 without too much fanfare though the Scots do celebrate 'Hogmanay', as they call it, *very* enthusiastically!

Even though he was still only fifteen, Ewan introduced Peter to scotch and Peter returned the favour with schnapps. Not much work was done on January 1, that's for sure!

Throughout January and February and into March the three became inseparable, Peter's English got better and better, likewise Ewan and Rory's German. They made it a game, each trying to outdo the other in pronunciation.

They worked hard and laid low; it behooved none of them to stick out in the crowd.

March 10, 1910 started out as just an average Thursday, a typical Glasgow morning: dull, dour, and raining. An HSDG ship had just left port bound for Buenos Aires with a cargo of machinery and manufactured goods. The biggest ship in port was the *SS Canada* taking emigrant children to her namesake country. Bound for Halifax, Nova Scotia … New Scotland. Ewan took note because he had a couple of friends in Canada, and he started wondering …

It was then that he heard a commotion coming from the other end of the dock. It seemed that two private detectives, hired by Chelmsford, had tracked Rory and him to Glasgow, and they had Rory cornered at the end of the dock.

He hesitated not at all and went to his friend's aid, despite the danger to himself.

Peter had seen this disturbance as well, from a different part of the dock and, not knowing why these people had surrounded Rory, he rushed to help his new friend.

One of the detectives, seeing two angry men rushing at them from two different directions drew a gun and pointed it at Peter shouting, "Stop or I'll shoot! I swear to God I will!"

Peter, by this time convinced that Rory was being robbed, kept coming. The man panicked and fired wildly at him, narrowly missing. This enraged Peter even more, and he charged at them. The man kept shooting but his aim got wilder and wilder as his panic grew. Rory, trying to save his friend's life jumped the detective before anyone else could react and took a bullet square in the chest … and fell … dead, in the water, his gold-filled vest dragging him straight to the bottom of the Clyde.

Enraged, Ewan and Peter reached the detectives. The unarmed one fled but the one with the gun stood his ground. Maybe it was his fear that rooted him to the spot or maybe he was just a bad shot, but he missed with all of his remaining bullets. They hit him almost at the same instant, from slightly different angles, and they both heard the crunch as his spine snapped. The momentum carried them all into the water right behind Rory.

Sputtering to the surface they looked at each other and realised they were in trouble … a *lot* of trouble. They knew they had to do something drastic at this point.

Ewan knew that he had seen Rory for the last time, but he also knew that if he took the time to dwell on that fact he would either drown or be caught.

They were both good swimmers and the *SS Canada* was only about a hundred or so yards away, so they decided to swim for the ship.

A couple of the ship's officers saw the boys swimming towards them, but they hadn't seen or heard the fight. All they saw were two young boys swimming for a ship full of other young men escaping to a better place. They lowered a rope ladder and helped them on board.

Laying there, on the deck, gasping for breath, they looked at each other and realised that their lives had taken yet another turn.

Another adventure had begun.

CHAPTER 3

HALIFAX 1910

*
**

They lay there, gasping for breath like newly-caught fish, fighting to get their breath back. Something fundamental in their lives had changed … permanently.

As luck would have it they came aboard just as the ship was about to sail. No one on the shore had seen them board the ship, few had even seen what had happened on the dock. The two young ship's officers who'd pulled them out of the water weren't much older themselves. They were used to destitute young people fleeing Europe to a better life in the New World. They quickly squirreled the boys away below decks where they merged, fairly seamlessly, with the young people already aboard.

Ewan had almost been dragged under by the weight of gold he was carrying … like Rory had … and only the adrenaline of the moment had carried him through. After recovering his breath, he instinctively checked to make sure his waistcoat with its almost 400 gold coins was still in place and intact. It was, but he took little pleasure in that fact either, it was just a piece of information to take note of for now. Nothing to rival the loss of his best friend. That, of course, would change in the days ahead.

By lunchtime, they were passing by the shipyards of Clydebank and by the next morning they were heading into the Irish Sea. Heading for Canada on the *SS Canada*. The coincidence and irony of that fact occurred to Ewan but he was still too depressed about losing Rory to take any real notice of it.

He had lost his two best friends, his first love and, most likely, his family in a very short period of time and he was ill-prepared for any of this.

Peter had his own thoughts. So much for lying low in Glasgow for a while and then going back to Hamburg. His life had taken a very unexpected, and complicated, turn. Two men had now died in incidents he was involved in. He couldn't go back home because the police would arrest him; he couldn't go back to Glasgow because the other private detective had gotten away and could surely identify him. Maybe it was best to head to Canada for a while and see how that worked out.

So, resigned to their respective fates, the two young men, they weren't really "boys" anymore, made the best they could of the situation.

Their bond of friendship became even stronger over the course of the voyage. They offered to help wherever it was needed and ended up spending much of their time in the galley helping the cooks feed all the other young emigrants who were on board.

These young people were in very similar straits to Ewan and Peter. Most were orphans from Britain and Europe who were escaping to a better life in Canada. Some were going to jobs that had been arranged before they left home. Others were entering into positions little better than slavery: indentured servitude. But, they reasoned, it was better than what they had left behind, and, with the resiliency of youth, they too made the best of their situations.

Seven days later they spotted land far in the distance to the north. It was Cape Race, Newfoundland though they didn't know that. Forbidding looking but land nonetheless. Peter's stomach wasn't doing any better on this trip than he had on the earlier one and he was pretty hungry by this time, despite working in the galley. Ewan was in a similar case and also hadn't managed to keep much down. He may have been born and bred in a fishing port, but he'd never been on a boat of any kind, much less on a large passenger ship on the sometimes violent North Atlantic. The crew kept telling them that this wasn't a bad trip, hardly any storms but that was of no consolation whatsoever.

It was with much relief that they sailed into Halifax harbour on the morning of March 18 and saw Canada for the first time.

Halifax was, of course, the first non-European city that either of them had ever seen. They landed at Pier 21 where generations of immigrants to Canada had and would come ashore. The two young officers from the ship made sure that they were part of the throng of young people who were arriving, and that they were properly treated.

But once they were ashore they were on their own. Here, at least, they were in a friendly foreign country. With nothing but the clothes they had on their backs, Peter didn't know about Ewan's waistcoat yet.

Peter was stricken. He had nothing. New to the English language, no family, no friends, no money except a few coins that he had in his pockets, no baggage … nothing. All he had was Ewan.

Ewan was a little better off, he had read about Nova Scotia, New Scotland it meant, everyone here spoke English with a vague Scottish twang, the town looked like a cleaner, prettier, less depressing version of Fort William. He knew he was home, for better or worse. Plus, he had his waistcoat.

At Pier 21 they were processed just like any other immigrant. Of course, in reality, they were immigrants now too, whether or not that had been their intent. After that whirlwind they wandered into the town proper. Ewan's first impression was reinforced here, the people looked and sounded familiar, he even saw some men in kilts which was not very common in Scotland anymore. The place had an enervating spirit to it, a feeling of hope.

He saw though that Peter did not feel the same way, he was wary, constantly looking over his shoulder to see who was watching him. He was even more depressed than he had been on the ship. It became his mission to cheer his friend up.

Eating some food on solid ground seemed like a good place to start. He had spotted what looked like a German café as they were leaving the harbour area, so he went looking for it. Sure, enough there it was, the Halifax Hofbrauhaus two blocks from the harbour. Seeing a German restaurant immediately cheered Peter up, but he said to Ewan. "How can we eat here? We have no money?"

It was time for Ewan to reveal his secret, he took one of the sovereigns into his hand and showed it to Peter. "I have quite a lot of these, almost 400, we'll eat verra well wi' that!" By this time, he knew he could trust Peter, he had, after all, sacrificed much to end up in Canada with him.

"*Verdammt!*" was the astounded reply.

Ewan told him the quick version of the story. "I'll explain it in more detail later, for now let's just eat some real food … wi' luck, we may even be able tae keep it down!"

Peter was astounded that he could get real German food in a British colony. There was certainly nothing like this in Glasgow!

"Canada has immigrants frae every country in Europe, some ye've never even heard of I bet."

"You'w pwobabwy wight," he said through a mouth full of bratwurst.

They felt the strength flowing back into them, the resiliency of youth working in their favour once again.

So, they told each other their stories, the complete stories, not just the abbreviated versions they had told each other when they met. All the nasty details that they had told no-one else. They both, at some deeper level, knew that from now on they were all each other had in the world. For the foreseeable future they couldn't even write to their families. They would never know when it was safe to contact them, and their families didn't even know they were in Canada.

For now, they would just take a few days to recover their strength and then they would start their new lives … whatever that meant.

A few days later, they felt much better about their lot in life and they started to plan a future.

"Peter, you're a cooper aye? I heard you talk a lot about makin' barrels," Ewan asked.

"That's right, in my uncle's cooperage. What do you have in mind?"

"Well, I'm a blacksmith and you're a cooper, there must be some way tae combine oor talents," Ewan wondered.

"What about automobiles? They use both wood and metal," mused Peter.

"True, but the autos are made in big factories and that kind of metal work is beyond my talents."

"Plus, you don't have that kind of money, I guess. Hmmm."

"OK, what about boats, they're really just big barrels cut in half aye?" Ewan was reaching at this point.

"Do you know anything about boats?" Peter asked, not expecting a positive response.

"No, I suppose not, I grew up around them but was never much involved in working wi' them." They were back in the Hofbrauhaus for lunch, Ewan looked around for inspiration, and he noticed that the tables and chairs were made of wood and metal. He started thinking.

After a period of silence Peter said, "What are you thinking about? I know you've got some scheme in mind."

"We could build furniture! I could build the iron frames and you could build the wooden bits, we could even make barrels our theme! What dae ye think?" Ewan's enthusiasm was infectious.

"*Ausgezeichnet!* Zat is brilliant!" Peter reverted to German when he got excited.

"We would have tae start wi' a blacksmith's shop because I need special machinery and tools. I should hae enough money tae dae that." Ewan was definitely caught up in the concept.

They spent the rest of the afternoon looking around for suitable premises and, in fact, spent several days looking throughout Halifax and even into Dartmouth across the bay before finally settling on a small blacksmith shop on Robie Street almost in the centre of the industrial part of Halifax, immediately north of the Exhibition Grounds. They figured they'd get some business from the fairs and such.

The owner was over sixty and had built up a small but successful business catering to people who needed everything from carts to steam engines repaired. He'd had a good run at his shop, but felt he was getting too old and wanted to retire back to Antwerp. That was where most of his family still lived.

He and Ewan settled on a fair price and that was that. Ewan and Peter now owned a blacksmithing and cooperage shop. It never once occurred to them that they were, essentially, still children and that children simply didn't do such things. They were in need of work so if work wouldn't come to them, well then, they'd bloody well go to it.

Peter came up with the name 'MacBride & Baum – Ironwood Creations.' Ewan thought it was a good name, one that would make them comfortable, or at least put a roof over their heads. Hope springs eternal.

The blacksmith part was already established, so Ewan just had to learn the peculiarities of his new equipment. Most of it was older but still quite serviceable. On the other hand, Peter spent many weary days building up the woodworking part of the business, the cooperage. Ewan helped where he could. He found it interesting. He'd never worked with wood before.

The hardest part was in coming up with ways to incorporate barrels into furniture, but it was also fun coming up with new ideas. Weary but happy, Peter became more and more at ease with his new situation.

Their first big contract, well, big to them, was from the exhibition grounds, as they'd hoped. They wanted twenty-five benches to be spread around the grounds. This allowed them to work out the kinks of their new partnership and make a name for themselves. Ewan was the front man, knowing the language and being familiar with the culture, more or less. Peter knew the business side of things having virtually run his uncle Joe's cooperage. That all seemed like a lifetime ago now.

Spring became summer and summer in its turn became fall and then, inevitably, fall became winter. Not as bad a winter as they had feared. In fact, they both remarked that the winter was very similar to their homes. They had heard how bad Canadian winters could be but not, apparently, that bad on the coast.

By the summer of 1911 they had completed their first year in Canada, they had made a favourable name for themselves in the manufacturing industry and they were making unique furniture that had caught the eye of fashionable and traditional folk alike. Ironwood Creations was becoming a household name ... at least in Halifax!

*
**

Peter turned twenty-one that year, June 21. That was also the day a ship from Hamburg came into port, the *SS Bremen*. She was a passenger ship on her way to New York, she had experienced engine trouble and had put in to Halifax for repairs.

This wasn't particularly unusual; ships broke down all the time. What *was* unusual was the commotion coming from the ship. Peter had been down at the port that day picking up a load of English Oak for bench slats.

He had just finished loading the material on to their donkey cart to take back up to the shop when he heard a loud noise. Apparently, all hell had broken loose on board, and it sounded like a full-blown riot had started.

Naturally he went to investigate. At first, he couldn't see what was going on but then he saw smoke billowing from an after compartment. Shortly after that he saw people ... lots of people ... boiling from that same compartment.

They came swarming en masse down the companionway onto the docks where they were met by the police. A number of police officers were already there to meet them. At that time, he didn't know why the police were there. Later he found out that they had been tipped off as to what was going to happen.

It turned out that the ship was bringing German immigrants to the US and not all of them were there of their own free will. Some women, all of them young and pretty, had been "sold" into what amounted to indentured servitude, prostitutes in effect, by a Hamburg court. Basically, it had been, either go to the USA as servants to some wealthy Americans or go to jail. The charges had all been trumped up so that these girls would get caught in this net.

Some of them had decided that they would jump ship at the earliest opportunity. The engine trouble seemed to present the perfect cover. One of the girls had started a fire in the galley in some cooking oil, which resulted in dense acrid smoke pouring from the portholes and creating a panic.

Fire is never a welcome thing, but it's particularly feared on board a ship because there's usually nowhere to flee to. In this case there was the dock.

The problem was that word of their planned escape had gotten to one of the ship's officers. He didn't like the thought of a fire on his ship for any reason, so he had alerted the Halifax police. They were on the dock in some force in case something happened. They weren't really expecting anything though and were not at all well prepared for what did happen.

Initially, there was a certain amount of confusion and panic on the dock before the police got organised. Most of the girls were recaptured soon after they fled the ship.

Peter was watching all this, not really understanding what was going on but not too alarmed because everything seemed to be relatively calm and orderly. Except for one young lad who had jumped ship with the girls and was not about to be recaptured at any cost. He got into a struggle with one of the policemen and Peter saw him pull a knife and slash the cop across the throat. Fortunately, the blow didn't go very deep and the cop was able to staunch the bleeding quickly but assaulting an officer of the law was not on. A big chase ensued, most of the police ignored the girls and went in hot pursuit of the lad.

They spent fifteen minutes hunting for the boy, but he was younger, fitter, and frightened. That combination got him away before he got caught. One policeman would have a nasty scar on his throat, but no real harm was done.

That excitement eventually died down, so he turned his attention back to the people on the dock, he caught some motion out of the corner of his eye. He had seen three girls duck behind some crates at the end of the dock.

He kept one eye on the struggling mass of people who had come from the ship who were sorting themselves out into two groups, passengers and crew in one group and police and runaways in the other. His other eye was watching the crates where the three girls had hidden.

Remembering his and Ewan's own, less than conventional, entry into Canada, he didn't want to pass judgement on the girls until he had heard their story.

So he cautiously and, he hoped, not obviously, walked over to the crates in question. He stopped on the opposite side to the girls and waited until the furore had died down. As it turned out the police didn't know exactly how many girls were involved and the girls didn't rat on their friends, so everything went back to normal fairly quickly, the runaways were led away, the crew put out the small galley fire and everything calmed down.

At that point Peter moved slowly around the crates until he was around the other side.

He was confused at first because he had expected to find three frightened girls cowering there, but he saw nothing. Then he noticed a gap between two stacks of crates and very carefully approached the gap.

Not knowing the girls were German at this point he said, softly in English. "You can come out now, they've gone."

No reply.

He tried again. "I saw you three hide behind these crates, I know you're there."

Still no reply.

"I won't turn you in." He hoped that would work.

It did. "Who are you?" came the timid and heavily accented response.

"A friend … I hope."

"Well, we need a friend." He heard some shuffling around and then one by one the girls came out of hiding.

The first two were teenagers, about sixteen and quite pretty. Obviously scared but still quite poised, carrying themselves confidently.

When the third girl came out he felt his heart stop. He had never seen such a gorgeous creature in all his life. She was older than the other two but not by much, she was about 1.7 metres, quite tall for a girl, slim build and had the blondest hair and bluest eyes he had ever seen, it cascaded down onto her shoulders and framed her exquisite face perfectly.

Peter Baum was in love!

He determined right then and there that even if these girls were murderers he would help them … well one of them anyway.

Discovering that they were German was just a bonus, it made it much easier to communicate with them and made things easier for the girls too.

The younger two were sisters, fraternal twins named Anika and Agathe Bauer. They might almost have been Siamese twins though, they were never apart. The blonde girl was called Elsa Franke … the most beautiful name in the world. Peter was smitten.

Once he learned their stories he was even more determined to help them. Anika had been "caught" shoplifting, turned in by someone in the pay of the human trafficking ring that was rounding up girls for export. Agathe, of course, had refused to be separated from her sister and so she too had been caught in this web, a nice bonus for the man who trapped Anika.

Elsa had been lured a little more deviously. She had been offered employment by her uncle as a nanny for a wealthy industrialist's family to look after their three children. She was, almost immediately, implicated in the "theft" of the wife's jewels which, of course, weren't missing at all, and ended up on the *Bremen,* bound for America. There, to be sold into what amounted to white slavery as an indentured servant to a rich American banker.

Instead she, and the twins, were able to jump ship in Halifax.

Where she met Peter Baum.

It was love at first sight for her too.

Peter took them to the shop to meet Ewan, who was more than a little surprised to see what else he had picked up at the dock when all he was going for was some wood!

"Peter, what have you got there? You've been picking up strays!" he joked. "And what are we meant to do with them?"

"Well, they're all looking for jobs, they were on a boat down at the harbour," he told Ewan the story, "and the long and the short of it is, now they live in Halifax! Oh, and the pretty one is mine!" He gave the twins a wink and laughed. They laughed back at him.

"Yours, am I?" Elsa exclaimed, in passable English, "we'll see about that!"

"So, what can you do?" Ewan enquired. "What sort of job do you want?"

Elsa said, "The girls have just finished school and don't know what they want to do." Anika stuck her tongue out at her.

Agathe replied, in English, "well it's true enough sister, we don't have a trade. I like sewing and you like ... what is it you like ... boys isn't it?" Anika hit her.

Elsa added, "all I know is that you can't separate them with a team of oxen! So, they'll have to find a job they can both do. I was working as a nanny, but I didn't much like it."

"Well, there's an exhibition ground right near us, they're always looking for people to help with the animals – horses, cows and the like. We've been shoeing the horses. Do you like animals?" Ewan asked.

"Oh yes," Anika enthused, "our papa owns a small farm near Hamburg, we are ... I mean 'were' ... looking after the animals," the twins got really subdued then.

"We'll never see them again, will we?" Agathe started quietly weeping.

"I wouldn't say never but it's going to be a long while." Ewan tried to sound optimistic, remembering that he and Peter were in a similar situation.

"It's only Wednesday and it's still early so let's go and ask around." Peter was keen to help them out.

They all trooped up to the Provincial Exhibition grounds where quite a few animals were kept. Ewan had a contact there that he knew from shoeing some of the horses at the grounds, as it happened the man was from Inverurie and had come to Canada ten years earlier. There were also two older German immigrants who worked there, two young women in their twenties who worked with the animals, and they took the twins on as helpers.

With them sorted that just left Elsa.

Over the next few days, they figured that the business was doing well enough that Elsa could be their office manager. She was not only very pretty (it wasn't just Peter's obvious bias!) but she was very personable and had a good head for figures and sales.

She was very good at talking to people and finding out what they needed and wanted, and she proved invaluable in drumming up new business and serving existing customers. As a nice bonus she already spoke English quite well.

Already in love, Peter and Elsa spent every possible moment together. Both in the shop and after work. They were the perfect match. Both young and smart. Not afraid of hard work and with the stamina to do it. Their interests meshed so exactly that they never argued about anything.

Peter had fallen in love with the outdoors when he was with the army in Hamburg and Elsa loved being outside too. They explored their new country every chance they could get, roaming all around Halifax and Dartmouth.

They also explored each other with a fervour born both of youth and of a little desperation. The desperation born of their mutual circumstance of being away from their homes. But that just punctuated their love and brought them even closer together.

Not wanting to waste another minute, Peter proposed to Elsa one afternoon in November and within a week they were married. Ewan, of course was the best man and Elsa had Anika and Agathe as her attendants.

The party lasted the whole weekend.

*
**

By the following year, 1912, MacBride & Baum was one of the fastest growing businesses in Halifax. In no small part due to Elsa Baum who turned out to have a head for business and figures and was a lot more organised than either Ewan or Peter.

The year started tamely enough, with the Scots and Germans, and a few others, trying to outdo themselves at New Years. Hogmanay, of course, won out, and the sore heads carried them into February.

One unanticipated consequence of Hogmanay 1912 was that Ewan got married. It didn't happen quite that fast, of course, but it certainly seemed that way to those involved.

Her name was Morag MacInnes and she was from Galashiels in the borders of Scotland. She had come to Canada with her parents three years earlier when she was fifteen. Her father owned a successful tannery at the northern end of Robie Street, near the railway line. Ewan had met her in the first week of January. He had been picking up some tanned hides they were using for upholstery on custom barrel benches they were making for a client in Dartmouth.

It didn't go quite as smoothly as Peter and Elsa's courtship.

"What dae you want?" Morag said with an exasperated sigh, to the scruffy young man who had just pulled up with an old donkey cart to pick up some hides. He hadn't washed in a several days nor shaved in a couple of weeks and it showed, both visually and via a certain distinctive aroma.

"I've come tae pick up some hides for MacBride & Baum, there's o'er a hundred ready tae pick up, or so I'm told." Ewan wasn't in the mood to play games with this silly girl. He'd been working fourteen hours a day for a full fortnight to get the frames of the benches ready. There were forty-two of them in all and he was burned and bleeding in a number of places from rushing to finish them.

"Well, who are you then? I was told that Mr MacBride his self would be picking them up and you dinna strike me as a successful businessman!"

"And what, exactly, does a successful businessman look like then?" he was tired and irritated but not actually angry yet, so he nibbled at the bait a bit.

"Not like a bloody ragamuffin, that's for sure." Morag *was* getting angry. It was probably the red hair; that did it every time.

That only made Ewan more determined to see how far he could poke her before she popped. "Then, clearly, ye're no' a successful businessman either!" he was starting to enjoy himself now.

"Why you jumped up little toad! I should gie you a thrashing you'll never forget!" she was almost over the edge now.

Just then the day was saved by Mr MacInnes who had heard the raised voices. "Hello, Mr MacBride, I see you've met my daughter Morag!" he said with a broad smile.

Morag was stunned. Her jaw dropped almost to the floor and her perfect cheeks went as red as her flowing hair. She was speechless and started to cry. Then she ran, mortified, into the back of the shop.

It was at that moment that Ewan fell in love. He had just realised how beautiful she was, and he too was speechless.

Sean MacInnes, however, was by this time laughing so hard he couldn't speak either.

*
* *

A week or two later, when he'd worked up the courage … and with Elsa scolding him mercilessly for being a coward … he timidly approached the MacInnes Tannery with the ready excuse of picking up the remainder of his hides. He had no idea if they were ready or not he just couldn't think of any other excuse, and he couldn't stay away any longer either. Visions of long flowing red hair were all that was in his head.

Fortunately, it was Sean that greeted him when he walked in. "I wondered if you'd ever be back!" his ready humour to the fore and a twinkle in his eye.

"Ermmm … I've come for the rest o' ma hides," he stammered out, rather lamely.

"No, you haven't, you wee scoundrel, you've come tae get another glimpse o' ma daughter!" Sean was no fool, he was going to have his full measure of fun with the lad, but he knew a good prospect for Morag when he saw one. Ewan was young, smart, talented, a fellow Scot and, if the rumours were to be believed, wealthy through an inheritance of some sort. Not to mention a very good client. That wasn't going to stop all of the teasing though. "So, where's yer cart then?" he laughed.

"My cart?" Ewan was confused.

"You came tae pick up yer hides, didn't you? You'll need a cart!"

"Oh, aye, my cart … ehmm … I just came tae see if they're ready, I'll get the cart if they are." Another lame answer he realised.

"Hmmm … is that right? I'm a wee bit sceptical about that." Sean feigned irritation. "Anyway, they're not so you'd best be off."

Ewan panicked, "No! … I mean … ermm … there was one other thing."

"What 'other thing', out with it boy!" Sean was enjoying this a little bit too much.

Morag had been listening from the other room, and she was getting a little tired of her father's picking at Ewan. Besides she had rather liked what she had seen of him the last time, despite all the dirt, oil and grime he was covered with. She had just been tired at the time.

She burst into the shop with all the intention of telling off her father in no uncertain terms. "Father! Stop teasing the poor ma—" But then she caught her first proper glimpse of Ewan. He'd cleaned up some. He was wearing what had once been a nice business suit which was neat, but a little threadbare and brightly shining boots, which seemed new but probably weren't. His face was scrubbed to a shining pink colour that positively lit up her father's shop. His piercing blue eyes had her staring into them like she'd been hypnotised. But what really got her heart aflutter was the brand-new straw boater that he was wearing at the perfect rakish angle. She didn't know why but straw boaters made her weak at the knees.

"By God boy, that's the second time ye've made her speechless in as many weeks! I'm going tae have to hire you to come around more often, maybe then I can get a word in edgewise occasionally!"

Sean could see the tears starting to well up in Morag's eyes. He wasn't a heartless man by nature, and he knew he'd pushed his fun far enough. Giving in he said, "Mr Ewan MacBride, esquire, of Fort William, may I introduce you to my daughter, Miss Morag MacInnes of Galashiels. My pride and joy," he was positively beaming. Sean's wife had fallen ill on the voyage from Scotland and had passed away shortly after arriving in Canada. Morag ran his household like her mother had and worked in the tannery doing the books and dealing with clients when he wasn't around.

Ewan ripped off his hat so fast that he almost tore the brim completely off. "Pleased to meet you miss Mor ... ermm ... Miss MacInnes." He was stammering again, and he felt his cheeks turning even pinker than before if that were possible.

"Please to meet you Mr MacBride." She was so quiet that Ewan barely heard her. All four of their cheeks were having a battle to see whose would be the pinkest. Morag's won but only by the narrowest of margins.

"Well, I think I'll leave you two young people to get acquainted. I'll be in the next room mind ... so no monkey business." He winked at them both.

It wasn't possible, but their cheeks got pinker still anyway.

After that they were never apart. Within a week it was like they were joined at the hip. They spent their time at either Ewan's shop or Sean's because both businesses were busy and they both wanted to help out as much as they could.

Peter didn't mind the extra work because he was happy that his friend had met someone that made him feel like Elsa made him feel.

By the end of February, it was obvious to anyone with eyes that they would be married. Except Ewan hadn't actually asked her yet.

"What is wrong with you, Ewan? You have the second most beautiful woman in Halifax tied to your hip, and you haven't asked her to marry you yet? Are you ill?" Peter was pretending to be terribly disappointed in him.

"I haven't decided how to yet."

"Well, traditionally you buy a ring, you get down on one kn— *Ow!*" Ewan hit him, but he was laughing when he did.

"I know that dummkopf! I mean I'm waiting for the right moment."

"When's that? When my children have moved out and are living on their own?"

"You don't have any chil— oh, I see yer point. Yer right, of course, what *am* I waiting for?"

So, the next day Ewan went to the biggest jewellers in Halifax and traded three of his dwindling supply of sovereigns for the biggest diamond he could get. That night, he went to Sean MacInnes's to ask for his permission to ask his daughter for her hand in marriage. He wanted to do this in the most traditional way he could.

"Mr MacInnes," he started.

"Sean, lad, we're good friends you and I." He suspected he knew what was coming.

"Not tonight, sir, tonight you're Mr MacInnes, and I'm the interloper trying to join your family."

"If it's what I think it is, my only question is: 'What's taken you so long?'"

"'So long, sir? But I've only known Morag for less than two months."

"I knew that first day, even when you were yelling at each other that you were meant for each other, and so did you."

"Aye, I did." he replied sheepishly.

"Well, then what are you waiting for? She's in the kitchen … *LISTENING IN I HAVE NO DOUBT!*" He winked.

"*I AM NOT!*"

Ewan walked slowly into the kitchen, both frightened to death and excited. He saw Morag standing by the sink nervously clasping and unclasping her hands.

When the moment came he wasn't nervous at all. He walked right up to her, dropped to one knee and grasped her right hand in his left. He pulled a small blue velvet box from his pocket and took out the largest diamond ring that Morag had ever seen. "Morag Catriona MacInnes, you are the most beautiful and perfect human being I have ever seen, I'm not a religious man but you are a gift to me from somewhere, and I don't intend to let that gift out of my sight. Will you grant me the honour of becoming Mrs Morag MacBride?" his solemnity was inspiring.

Morag took a minute to gather herself. "Ewan Duncan MacBride, you are the perfect man, you're kind, you're funny, you know how to make me warm inside, but most of all you make me happy. I can't imagine being away from you either. Of course I'll marry you, you silly man!" somewhat less solemn but no less sincere. With that he put the diamond on the proper finger. He then stood and gave her the first of what would be many hugs and kisses … well, the first official ones anyway!

They set the date for Sunday the 14th of April and started the planning right away. Peter was obviously the best man and Morag's best friend, Rebecca, coincidentally a German girl from Berlin, would be Morag's maid of honour.

They both had more than enough friends to flesh out the wedding party, but the lack of relatives was hard on both of them. They both had relations in Scotland still but no way to invite them to Halifax for the wedding. Morag telegraphed her aunts and uncles to let them know though and got happy, cheerful messages in return.

Ewan finally broke his silence with his parents. He sent them a letter detailing what had happened in Glasgow and how he ended up in Canada, also mentioning that he was getting married and he apologized that he had gone, so abruptly, without telling them and hoped they'd forgive him. The one thing he didn't do is give them the address in case someone tracked him down.

They would make the best of it and keep it as simple as possible. Ewan was officially Presbyterian, and Morag was officially Catholic but neither cared too much so they chose to keep it basic. They found a Methodist minister who was willing to do simple, non-denominational vows that would satisfy their religious friends and keep them honest.

After the service they had organized a Cèilidh at one of the local pubs which went into the wee hours. With drinking and pipers and drinking and fiddlers and drinking and singing and drinking and Bodhrans. As everyone was heading home, anticipating the nasty hangover they were sure to have the next day, Mr and Mrs MacBride went to their room at the inn next door.

That night they truly became husband and wife.

*
* *

At the same time that Ewan and Morag were learning more about each other, fifteen hundred people were drowning or freezing to death only a few hundred miles to the east.

The RMS Titanic chose that night to hit an iceberg and sink with the loss of two thirds of the people on board.

Ewan and Morag were blissfully unaware of this that night. They awoke at a leisurely ten thirty the next morning. They spent the remainder of the morning in bed exploring each other both physically and emotionally. When they finally got up and went to get something to eat, they were greeted by complete pandemonium in the streets.

"Titanic sunk with all hands!" cried one newspaper seller. "Titanic sinks, 1,500 die!" cried another.

Stunned, they wandered around uncomprehendingly. They had, of course, heard stories about the great, unsinkable ship and they knew that her maiden voyage was around now, but they had been so wrapped up in each other that they had paid little attention.

Now it was all too real. The joy of their wedding day had all but evaporated.

No one yet knew the real story of what had happened to the RMS Titanic as she was crossing from Britain to America. But the rumours were flying in all directions. Ewan knew several ships captains from dealing with various shipments coming in from Europe.

"I'll go down tae the docks and find out what happened," Ewan told Morag.

"Do you have to? Can we not just enjoy our moment together?" she pleaded.

"Do you really think we can, knowing what has just happened?"

"No, I don't suppose so," she replied sadly.

Big accidents and natural disasters weren't very common in 1912 and something like this filled everyone's imagination with all sorts of horrors. Both of them had come to Canada very recently on ships not too dissimilar to *Titanic*. They both wanted to do whatever they could for any survivors because one thing that they'd heard throughout the day was that the survivors may come to Halifax first.

So, they went to their new home, which was the house they shared with Peter and Elsa. Peter, it turns out, had been following the story for a while. Word had arrived early that morning, so he knew more of the details. He and Elsa had slept in too but had been awakened by the commotion in the street.

The newlyweds spent the first night in what was now "their" bed not joyously making love as they should have been but huddled together with Morag imagining people wet and shivering on the North Atlantic in lifeboats.

In mid-morning, Ewan and Peter went to the harbour to ask any of the ship captains they knew if they had more details. The first person they saw was Fred Larnder, the captain of the *Mackay-Bennett*, who they knew because he had just recently bought some bunks for his ship from them. He was bustling around all over the docks frantically gathering people and supplies.

"Ho Freddy, hae ye heard any more about *Titanic*?" Ewan called to him.

"Bugger off, can't you see I'm busy?" came the exasperated reply. But then he thought to himself, *Hmmm … these strapping young lads might be useful, they're hard workers.* He made a decision, "Sorry lads, I'm rather frantic right now. P&O have asked me to take my ship to where she went down and try and find any survivors." Or recover bodies he didn't add. "Are you able to come with me to help?"

Ewan and Peter looked at each other and their reply was instantaneous, "Aye, of course!", "*Ja, naturlich!*"

"Well, I'll be ready to sail early tomorrow morning, be here as soon as you can, pack for hard work and a few days at sea." And with that he bustled off to get his ship ready.

The boys went home where they suddenly remembered that they were married, and that this might not fit in with the girls' plans, Ewan and Morag being newlyweds and such.

"Morag, my love, I'm not sure how tae ask this …" he began somewhat sheepishly.

"Ask what?" was the subdued answer. She had an idea what was on his mind.

"Well, we met Freddy Larnder … you remember, the fellow who bought those two bunks last month?"

"Aye, the ship captain."

"That's right, the *Mackay-Bennet*. She's off tae look for survivors tomorrow and he asked us," pointing at Peter, "to come wi' 'im. He thinks we might be useful." Ewan tried to make it sound important.

Turns out he needn't have worried about that. "Aye, of course, you must. Just you come back to me, no risks … do you hear?" in fact the hardest part about telling Morag was in preventing her coming with them.

"Does he need any more people? I can be quite useful too you know!"

Ewan was tempted but he realised that the *Titanic* had sunk a day and a half ago and it would take them two or more days to get to the area and that there likely wouldn't be any more survivors. There were just likely to be bodies and he didn't want his new wife seeing and dealing with that.

He gently said, "I know you can but … but … no love, it's best that you don't" was all he said, and he left it at that.

Morag understood. "Aye, well, we can have our honeymoon later."

*
**

In the event it took them almost three days to get to the site. The weather had been foggy and rough and they both got fully reacquainted with seasickness.

They arrived the night of the nineteenth and began the search as soon as it was light enough.

Only the briefest search was made for survivors as, by this time, it had been five days since the sinking and the water was horribly cold. Anyone who was wet and frozen would have succumbed much earlier.

The sight that met them was beyond horrifying. There were pieces of floating debris everywhere. At first they had trouble distinguishing between pieces of the ship and the bodies. They arrived at night. The water was below freezing temperatures, but the salt content kept it from becoming solid. Not so anything above the water which had been significantly colder at night. This resulted in everything having a coat of thick frost on it, which made some things hard to recognise.

They passed a searchlight across the water trying to distinguish shapes. Sometimes a shape that looked like a piece of a lifeboat or a deck chair or a tarpaulin would be a person clinging to a piece of wood or a great coat with someone in it floating upside down. Everything was frozen solid.

As soon as it was light enough to see the recovery effort began. Ewan and Peter went down into one of the skiffs that were launched to recover the bodies. They slowly rowed through the debris that was floating on the surface. Almost immediately they came across what they assumed was a pile of clothes that was floating by itself in the way of their passage. Ewan was looking at it as they passed. When they brushed by, it rolled in the wake and he saw what looked like a person. At first he thought it was a toy, serene looking with a white face it looked like a porcelain doll. Taking a closer look he was shocked to see that it was a little baby who had been separated from its parents and who now lay, rather peaceful looking, in the North Atlantic, far from home and loved ones. The dark eyes looking right up at Ewan.

He was horrified. Seeing such a small child, lifeless and yet so peaceful looking shocked him to the core. Looking at Peter with blank emotionless eyes, Ewan steeled himself to the work that must be done. He pulled the babe from the freezing waters and gently handed him to Peter who laid him in the keel of the skiff as gently as if he had been a newborn. They didn't yet know whether the child was a boy or a girl, but it seemed so callous to say "it" so "he" was used instead.

These unfortunates, guilty of nothing more than seeking a new life, deserved at least to rest in the land they were headed for. They renewed their task with newfound energy, the kind that moved mountains.

That first trip they recovered around fifty bodies. They were all frozen solid. There had been little physical trauma to the victims and after only a few days in very cold water they were still mostly intact and mostly looked like they were sleeping. It was an unpleasant experience to be sure, but it could have been a lot worse.

It did get a lot worse. The next day they came across several horrific sights. One fellow had been cut in half, presumably by the ship's propellers, still spinning as he fell to his death when the stern rose above the water for the last time. That's the only way he could have contacted spinning propellers. Another man had lost his head, possibly in a similar way.

A young lady and an older man floated in a permanent embrace as if they were dancing. Father and daughter? They would never know.

One man was stark naked. Perhaps in the bath at the time? Another was wearing two layers of fur coats and wrapped in three life preservers. Maybe kept him alive long enough to hear the last screams of the dying.

During the following six more, increasingly grim, days recovering floating corpses and pieces of corpses, it did get very much worse.

By the time they left for home, the *Mackay-Bennett* had recovered over three hundred bodies. They kept only first and second-class passengers, like John Jacob Astor, who were then embalmed. Everyone else was buried, properly, at sea, most had no identification anyway. They still had almost two hundred bodies on board when they returned on the thirtieth.

When they docked in Halifax there were dozens of volunteers to unload the victims and take them to the curling club, which was the only place both large enough and cold enough to hold the bodies without risking decomposition and disease.

Morag and Elsa were among the volunteers and did prodigious work making sure that all respects were paid and that as many of them as possible were identified. These had been people after all.

The little baby turned out to be a two-year-old boy who was never identified or claimed so the crew of the *Mackay-Bennet* called him simply "Our Babe", paid for his interment and laid him to rest.

That little boy's face looking up at him from the cold water would haunt Ewan for many years to come.

CHAPTER 4

HALIFAX 1914

*
**

And thus it was that two years later, by the spring of 1914, that MacBride & Baum – Ironwood Creations was a thriving business with seven more employees, two blacksmith apprentices, one cooper, two delivery drivers and two helpers. Plus, their pride and joy were the two, brand spanking new 1914 Ford Model Ts, which Ewan and Peter had converted into delivery trucks! Neither of them had ever driven a vehicle powered by an internal combustion engine before, nor even seen one up close, for that matter. It was quite a thrill for all of them. Only the two drivers, Scott and Jamie, were familiar with them.

Ewan was barely twenty years old and already married and a self-made man, although Angus Og had provided the start for him, he had worked his proverbial arse off making a go of it.

He and Peter were well known and respected tradesmen in the community. Ewan appealed to the more numerous British side, and Peter to the smaller but generally more affluent, European side.

For example, with the help of the twins, they had provided the furniture for a new show at the fairgrounds. The boys had come up with a new style of folding chair made of iron and barrel slats that had become quite fashionable. They had based the design on chairs they had seen floating amongst the debris of the Titanic.

The modification they had made to their new Model Ts to carry cargo caught the imagination of some and they made several similar conversions for other businesses in town. This further enhanced their reputation for innovation.

Ewan had never really followed what was going on in the outside world, he had been too busy worrying about his own affairs to worry about what the King and the Kaiser were up to. He was aware that there was a war brewing in Europe, but that was mainly in the east wasn't it? Some place called Serbia.

Then one day in early summer a ship arrived in Halifax from Germany with some iron that they needed for the shop. As usual Peter went down to collect it. There he got to talking with one of the ship's officers. First of all, it turned out that they didn't have the iron that they had ordered. Then he discovered that it had been held back, temporarily, because it was an "important raw material" which, he was told, Germany needed.

"Why does Germany need a few scraps of iron?" he asked. "Surely there's lots to go around?"

"Don't you read the newspapers?" replied the officer. "There's a war coming, everyone can feel it."

"War? With who? Between who? Isn't that all in the east?"

"For now, but the Fatherland is being cautious and keeping a close eye on things – materiel, like wood, steel, fuel, chemicals, etc."

"But surely Britain is friends with Germany? We are traditional allies, aren't we?"

"As I say, Germany is being cautious with everyone. I'm afraid you'll have to get your iron somewhere else for now." The officer was getting a little angry with Peter, so he left it at that.

Peter thought about what had been said and, more importantly, what had been implied in his brief contact with someone who had, so recently, been in his homeland.

He went home and told Ewan what had happened.

"What dae you think is going on?" Ewan curiously asked.

"I have no idea," Peter replied. "I haven't read a newspaper in months."

They chatted about it for a while but then life took over again. They had to find a new source of iron. They could get it from America but the kind they needed was more expensive from there. Well, so be it.

A couple of weeks later another German ship came in to Halifax, one that Peter was familiar with, he had a couple of friends from Hamburg on board, so he sought them out and had a chat with them. Mostly they just chatted about news from home, how his uncle was doing and just generally getting caught up.

Then one of them said. "The army is starting to bring reservists into the regular army, Peter. Aren't you in the reserve?"

"Yes, I am, or I was." That seemed like a lifetime ago to him.

"You are still liable to be called up protect the Fatherland!" his friend said somewhat indignantly.

"Does it need protecting? From who?"

"Russia of course!" he was getting angry now.

Everyone was getting angry it seemed, first the officer from that other ship and now his friend, just what the hell was going on?

He went back home and talked to Ewan about it again.

"What's got you so worried, Peter?" were the first words out of Ewan's mouth when Peter got back, he could see that his friend was worked up about something.

"Are you not concerned about what's going on in Europe, Ewan?"

"Should I be? I have no idea what's going on, all I know is that we can't get iron from Germany anymore. So what? We'll get it from the Yanks." He was genuinely puzzled.

"Germany is being threatened by Russia!"

"By Russia? How?"

"You know about the war brewing in the Balkans?"

"Aye, I've heard about it, so what? It's in the east, too far away to worry about."

"Well, Russia could get involved if Austria gets involved."

"Again, so what? Neither I nor you are either Russian or Austrian!"

"Don't you see? If Austria gets involved, Germany will back her, and I'm a German soldier!" now he was really agitated.

"But you left Germany!" argued Ewan, genuinely confused.

"I left Germany because of circumstance. It was my plan to go back once things had settled down. I just got caught up in other events."

"Am I just 'other events' now, Peter?" now Ewan was getting angry.

"Well, yes ... I mean no ... *Gottverdammt* ... I don't know what I mean!"

"Do you regret coming tae Canada wi' me?" Ewan had never really thought about how Peter came to be with him when he left Scotland, he was just grateful that he had been there. Now he saw, for the first time, what Peter had actually sacrificed. To leave his family and friends permanently behind was a massive leap, he knew from his own experience.

"No, never!" he hastily replied, "It's just that this was not my plan, I intended to spend a couple of years in Scotland and then return home, maybe not Hamburg, but ... home. And, now when I hear that my homeland ... my Fatherland ... is threatened, I fear for her."

"What's your plan now then?" Ewan was still angry.

"I don't know ... I just don't know!" he was almost crying with frustration now, clearly this discussion had been an emotional drain on him.

Then in a moment of clarity amidst all this emotion Ewan understood. "If you have to go home I will understand. I wish you wouldn't, but I will understand."

"Thank you, Ewan, I don't think I will, but I'll think hard about what I should do. There's Elsa to consider too."

They left it alone for a while, then in late June it all, rapidly, fell apart. Apparently an Austrian prince was killed by a Serbian nationalist. Russia backed the Serbs against the Austrians and Germany backed Austria just as Peter had predicted.

In less than a month, Germany was essentially at war.

Britain and, therefore, Canada were not far behind. They weren't at war yet, but it didn't look like it would be very long. Then Ewan saw a notice in the paper stating that all German and Austrian reservists living in Canada, apparently there were quite a few, should immediately go to the local police and swear loyalty to the crown or risk being interned for the duration of the war.

That, Peter could not do. He never had felt all that comfortable in Canada or, more accurately, away from Germany, and he couldn't and wouldn't swear to what he considered a foreign country.

So he talked it over with Elsa. "Well, *mein liebling*, what are we going to do? I mean what are you going to do? I'm going back to Germany, I have to and I want you to come with me. Will you?"

"Of course I'm coming with you, I'm your wife! But you're going back to join the army aren't you?" Elsa was just as aware as the men were with what was happening.

"I'm already in the army, I'm going back to re-join my unit to defend the Fatherland." The pride was poorly concealed.

"But how?" she asked. "We might as well be at war with Britain, all German ships have been interned, how will we get home?" desperation in her voice.

"Holland hasn't declared for either side and there's a Dutch ship in the harbour. I think she's leaving soon. I'll find out."

So the next morning Peter went to the docks early and talked to the master of the Dutch ship and found that they were leaving that afternoon. He was willing to take two German refugees fleeing a country with which they were at war back across the Atlantic, for a fee of course.

The decision was made for them. It was now or never. Peter felt that he didn't have a choice. His pride at being a loyal German soldier overrode his loyalty to Ewan. But it was the most difficult decision he had ever made. All he knew was that he would regret it for the rest of his life if he didn't go.

That afternoon, he and Elsa bade a tearful good-bye to Peter's best friend and Elsa's saviour from slavery. It was not an easy moment for any of them.

*
**

Ewan and Morag waved good-bye as the ship left Halifax. Once again in his short life he was saying good-bye to people he loved for what he thought would be the last time. And Morag had grown very fond of both of them as well. Peter had made vague protestations that they would be back after the war. As if they could just take up where they had left off after a war that nobody knew how it would end or how long it would take. People were talking about it being over by Christmas, but he didn't think anybody really believed that, he certainly didn't. So, he resigned himself to continuing without Peter for a long time, probably forever.

In the event, he didn't have long to worry about it.

Germany invaded Belgium in August and so Britain declared war. As a colony, Canada was automatically at war with Germany. Peter had gotten away just in time. Things started to move very fast now. In October, the fledgling Royal Canadian Navy – it had only been formed in 1909 – quickly realised that Halifax would play a major role in supplying Britain with everything from men and horses to beans and bullets. They also realised the value of a small blacksmith's shop in helping with the war effort and made him an offer to buy his shop and have him run it as a facility that would make specialized parts for RCN ships.

He actually did think about that, but he was smart enough to realise that because he was only twenty that much of his success had come by luck and hard work rather than business brains and experience, both of which he would need to run a government-sanctioned facility. So his counteroffer was to just sell them the foundry, provided they would guarantee to keep his employees on, and he would decide what to do then.

They made him a very generous offer, three times what he had paid for it only four years before, which he accepted without too much thought at all.

He then found himself in a very unusual position. With nothing to do and only Morag to worry about he looked at helping his homeland. Scotland was his home, and he had only left because of circumstance, just as Peter had left Germany. The fact that Peter was now an "enemy" didn't even occur to him.

Morag had to be part of any decision about serving king and empire though. She too had much love for her homeland and didn't argue with Ewan for long. She wasn't all that happy about him going away to war, but everybody was saying it would all be over by Christmas. She knew she couldn't stop him anyway, so she gave in.

Things continued to move quickly. In November, an infantry battalion was raised in Halifax and within two weeks he found himself in the army. He had joined the Nova Scotia Rifles. They also had the much grander sounding title of the 25th Battalion of the Canadian Expeditionary Force, or the "MacKenzie Battalion".

He quickly found out that the army didn't do many things logically. When he informed them that he was an experienced blacksmith he was immediately assigned as a transport driver, their reasoning being that he'd worked with wagons and horses before. The fact that he'd shod the horses and made new tyres for the wagons didn't seem to register. Driving a wagon and a team of horses was a completely different skill and one that he had never mastered! The donkey cart he had at the foundry was only a small wagon with one donkey.

After he had tried driving supply wagons around for a month and after wrecking four wheels and causing a horse to break a leg and have to be put down, he convinced them that he belonged in the pioneer section where he could at least use some of his blacksmith skills.

Soldier skills such as shooting and digging and building defences he took to like a whale to water, hard work was invigorating for him. The other soldiering skills, the polishing brass, bulling boots, blancoing webbing and the marching up and down, he wasn't too excited about and spent many hours complaining about it with the other lads. It proved to be a great bonding experience though, and they found themselves enjoying it, for the most part. The purpose for all this they had pushed to the backs of their minds for now. The realities of war would come soon enough.

He was a relatively small lad, only about five foot eight and 165 pounds, soaking wet with his boots on, but he was wiry and in his element, he was young and fit, the hard work came naturally to him from his own life hardships, and he proved to be a natural leader. This was a skill that had also been honed by running a successful business. By the time they were ready to leave for Britain and France, he was a Lance Corporal (L/Cpl).

His commanding officer allowed him two days leave so he could say his farewells to Morag. They spent those two days alternating between joy and despair, holding each other and crying and making plans for what they'd do after the war. They made love with an urgency that only the desperation of imminent parting and the unspoken fear of terrible loss could bring. They found new ways to hold each other and new ways to bring pleasure to each other.

But then the dreaded, but inevitable, day came.

Kisses were exchanged, good-byes were said, promises to write often were made and more tears were shed. "Don't worry lass, I'll be home by Christmas!"

On the 20th of May 1915, to the sound of the regimental pipe band resplendent in their Seaforth tartan, the 25th Battalion CEF, embarked from the same pier that he had arrived at in 1910.

As they progressed eastwards they caught glimpses of what they supposed was either Canada or maybe Newfoundland but after a couple of days even those stopped.

The circumstances of this trip were actually more pleasant than the last, despite the fact that he was going to war, and he was able to enjoy himself.

The trip itself was boring. There were occasional U-boat scares where someone was sure he'd seen a periscope, but these were all unfounded. And a lot of the men, including Ewan, were seasick for much of the time but that was about as exciting as it got.

As they got closer to England though, the anticipation and, to some extent, the apprehension, started to grow. What had started as seasickness grew into nervous butterflies thundering around in their bellies.

Although he knew he was heading back to Britain he barely even thought about contacting his family. He wouldn't be able to visit them, and he would only worry his Ma even more than she already was, did she even know he had gone to Canada? He had no way of knowing whether they had received his letter or not. Probably not, although those detectives in Glasgow would have told them that he almost certainly got on a ship heading there. He decided that if he survived the war he would visit them before heading back to Halifax. And that was that.

By the time they landed at Folkestone they were all keyed up to the bursting point. It was a quick three-mile march to Shorncliffe Barracks where they would spend the next three months honing their skills and their bayonets before making ready to go to France.

Shorncliffe Barracks was a traditional army camp with rows of red brick buildings obviously designed by a frustrated castle designer with a reduced budget. It was in no way remarkable and didn't look nearly as warlike as the Halifax Citadel. But it was their new, albeit temporary, home.

When the Canadian army took it over a few months earlier it had been very underused. The British army had worked out of there briefly after the declaration of war but, it appeared, were happy to hand it over to the "colonials".

Ewan and his friends soon discovered why. Most of the fixtures were old or rundown or both and they had their work cut out for them getting things in order. The 1st Division had been there before them, so they added to what was already underway.

Soon though they had everything 'shipshape and Bristol fashion' as was said by the Navy.

Between working on the camp infrastructure and training for war the next three months went by in the blink of an eye. Training involved much marching and getting used to their war equipment. Their rifle was superb, the Model 10 Ross Rifle. With it you could hit a target the size of a man's head at over three hundred yards.

By September, they were ready. Honed to a fine edge and champing at the bit they were like champion greyhounds waiting for the gate to rise.

And so, they were off.

Less than a week later they found themselves in the mud of Flanders, not in France after all but Belgium, near a town they were assured was called Wipers (Ypres). There they found other Canadians, the veterans of the 1st Division who had themselves only been bloodied for the first time a few months earlier but who looked for all the world like the ancient grizzled veterans they now were. These men had faced poison gas attacks for the first time, they had stood their ground against tremendous odds when French colonial troops had fled all around them, and they had emerged bloody but unbowed.

Yet less than two thirds of the 1st Division men had actually been there, the rest were reinforcements who, like themselves, had not yet seen a German spiked helmet.

After a brief stint in a second line trench to get acclimatized to living in mud, filth, human remains, rats, lice and the other niceties of trench life they moved into the frontline trenches.

Ewan quickly found gainful employment reinforcing and adding to the trenches that had been started by the BEF a year earlier. They were good but not yet complete and much work needed to be done to the barbed wire and fortifications – perfect work for the pioneers.

Much of this work needed to be done at night, especially in front of their trenches. The problem was that this was no man's land and if this work had been done in daylight they would have been easy prey for snipers and machine guns. Therefore, midnight was the witching hour for wire reinforcement. It was on one of these forays where he saw his first spiked helmet.

The pioneer section, reinforced with a section of riflemen, was tasked with increasing the depths of the wire entanglements to the front of their trench line.

The men took off all their extra equipment, ammunition, and bombs, etc., blackened their faces with mud and soot, covered their heads with cloth or wool caps and generally made themselves as quiet as possible. They slipped out of the trench, went 'over the top' and Ewan fell straight into a huge shell hole full of mud, water and German corpses from an assault the week before they got there.

Ewan came to a stop with the spike of a German helmet pointed directly into his eyes. He flinched and rolled to the side and noticed the destroyed head of its owner below it, and nothing below that.

He had seen dead men before from the *Titanic* and a flash of Herbie's head came into his mind. But after a moment of horror he got back to the job at hand; the nightmares could wait.

The reason the Germans had got this far, barely ten yards from the front-line trench, was that the wire had not been deep enough, so they set about increasing the depth. But that meant moving closer to the German trenches which, at this point of the line, were only a hundred yards away, and it also meant crawling through the existing wire.

But they eventually got to the point where the new wire was to start. They used sledgehammers muffled with cloth to pound the stakes into the ground. The slightest noise would bring machine gun fire their way.

Fortunately, Sergeant Forbes, the pioneer section sergeant, had arranged for a few trench mortar rounds to be dropped on the German trenches and some sporadic machine gun fire to mask their sounds.

This worked fairly well, and they weren't discovered by the 'Jerries', a term the Canadians had adopted from the British, until they were almost finished. They thought they were going to get away with it but then suddenly it was bright daylight … a starshell.

They quickly threw themselves on the ground into any depression or shell hole they could find. And then the gates of Hades itself were thrown open.

Whizz bangs of all sorts started dropping around them, not accurately though, because the Jerries hadn't had long to spot their targets. But terrifying nonetheless. Canadian artillery responded in kind and an artillery duel started in earnest. Both sides already had the other ranged in and some damage was done, and men were killed. Suddenly it was very real to them all. The men stuck it out for a few minutes then one of the privates from the rifle section panicked and ran for it. By this time the starshell had burned out so it was dark again, and he didn't get five yards before the new entanglements caught his ankle and threw him headlong into the mud ten feet from Ewan.

Ewan crawled over to him. "Lie still! The shelling will stop soon if they don't have any targets," screamed Ewan through clenched teeth.

"But they're trying to kill me! I don't want to die!!" screamed the young lad very loudly. He was at most eighteen and probably less than that, the army was very generous about believing a man's age when they joined up.

"They're tryin' tae kill all of us, and they'll bloody succeed if ye dinna shut yer trap." Screaming through clenched teeth got easier with practice.

But the poor boy was beyond reason at this point and Ewan clocked him one to keep him quiet.

Eventually, the shell fire dwindled away, and they were able to extricate themselves from no man's land without any further loss.

Once they got back to their own trench, Sgt Forbes came up to Ewan and smacked him on the back. "That was a gutsy thing to do, lad. I saw the whole thing."

"Did you see that I pished mysel' wi' fear?" Ewan barely was able to reply.

"Aye, lad I did, we all did, the point was that even scared you did the right thing, you may very well have saved some lives, you definitely saved that young bugger's life. As it is, no-one else was killed and there are only three more lightly wounded. Make that four, look at your arm."

There was blood dripping off his fingers as his arm hung at his side. "Shite, I must hae caught ma arm on the wire when I crawled over tae that lad. How is he by the way?"

"Oh, he'll be fine. He's sleeping right now. It was his first time."

"It was my first time too."

"But you're not sixteen."

"Sixteen, bloody hell!"

"Yeah, I'm going to have to send him back to Shorncliffe until he's old enough. With any luck the war will be over by then."

"Do you think it might?" Ewan hoped.

"No."

*
**

Three days later, Ewan was called into Major Campbell's office, actually a dug-out in the side of a communication trench, where he stood nervously in front of the Battalion Adjutant. What had he done wrong?

"Stand at ease, lad, I'm not going to eat you!" laughed Major Campbell.

"Sir!" a nervous reply.

"I understand from Sgt Forbes that you distinguished yourself the other night during the wiring party, probably saved some lives."

"I did my job, sir."

"And bloody well too, I hear. Sgt Forbes has put you up for a gong. Can't say that you'll get one but a Mention in Dispatches at least I should think."

"Thank you, sir," an astonished Ewan stammered.

"Comes with an extra stripe too I believe."

"But sir, I'm only twenty-one!" he protested.

"Do you know how old Sgt Forbes is, lad?"

"No, sir," he was curious now.

"Twenty-three, but don't let that get around," smiled the Adjutant.

*
**

So Corporal MacBride was now the second in command of the pioneer section. He had been in Belgium less than two months, and it seemed he had found his calling.

They were now heading into the winter of 1915.

His battalion moved into the line between St Eloi and Plugstreet (Ploegsteert) which, once upon a time, had been pretty Belgian farmland but was now a desolate wasteland. There was still greenery sporadically dotted around the area but there were giant scars cut into the landscape. Every village had at least some, and usually more, buildings destroyed. The smell of death hung over everything.

The winter was spent laying wire, building fortifications, siting machine guns but mostly trying not to freeze to death. The work helped. Everything was wet and would freeze overnight. When on rotation in the rear area they would spend their time scrounging warm clothing; some men spent most of their pay on a woolly sweater!

Cold, wet weather makes boredom unbearable, and the men got creative. Ewan used his blacksmithing skills to make some amazing trench art. The raw material was everywhere in the form of shell casings and spent rifle cartridges. He and a friend he had made, L/Cpl Jimmy MacKenzie from Aberdeen, via Sydney Nova Scotia, partnered up to make custom pieces for officers and the talentless. Between Ewan's metalworking skills and Jimmy's artistic abilities, they made a small fortune … well, by Western front standards anyway, they would charge 25 cents for a small piece, two or three cartridges, or between 50 cents and a dollar for a larger piece, one or two shell casings, and a few cartridges. Or they would trade them to the local people for real food: some bread, a couple of eggs, maybe a chicken once in a while.

Back in the frontline, the war went on as best it could, the generals couldn't be seen doing nothing even though the coldest winter in Belgium in a decade prevented any large-scale operations. Instead, they resorted to raiding parties and sniper duels. Ewan had by now become an expert in anything metal and barbed. His expertise in breaching barbed wire made him a popular addition to any raiding party going into the German trenches as they would have to penetrate several layers of entanglements both quickly and quietly.

One particularly nasty night or, more accurately, early morning in February he was part of a large raiding party, a full platoon of infantry led by Sgt Franklyn and with attached experts like Ewan and Sgt Forbes, forty-two men all told. They slipped quietly over the top. It was wet and bitingly cold, but not below freezing. That would've entailed breaking through ice in the shell holes and making noise. But there was just enough wind to make it extra unbearable.

The men slithered through no man's land as silently as they could and, with Ewan's help, as quickly as possible. They found themselves on the parapet of the German trench in what felt like a week but was actually less than three hours.

The goal of the raid was to capture German officers, as many as possible. Ewan had an extra skill that would come in handy. Thanks to Peter he spoke very good German, and this skill would come in handy tonight.

By this stage of the war aerial photography was coming into its own and one photo among many showed what appeared to be a command bunker. It was about a hundred square yards, big for a frontline dugout, had two communications trenches reaching the frontline trench within a hundred feet of it and had obvious signs of telephone wires strung into it. The telltale sign, though, was that on two separate occasions carrier pigeons had been observed leaving the area. Carrier pigeons were still the most reliable communications asset that either side had in 1916.

This night they had crossed over in four groups, two groups to the right and another two to the left of this bulge, the idea being that they would flank the bunker itself as quietly as possible and then, if their surprise held they would block access to it from the main trench and then enter and kill or capture anyone they found there.

Well, in the event they got into the trench OK and their surprise held for almost a full minute. After that it was chaos.

Ewan was in the left group and after breaching the wire on the German parapet he slipped over the edge into a similar, yet different world. The German trench looked very similar to theirs but felt different somehow. More menacing.

They found three sentries shivering in the dark, trying desperately to keep warm. Being cold was one thing but being wet *and* cold was a different thing altogether.

They had the misfortune to not be officers and since that was the target of the raid they had to be silenced quickly and quite permanently.

His group was just about to enter the bunker, very quietly and were just thanking their lucky stars for getting this far undetected when all hell broke loose on the other side. It was as if all the hounds of hell had been loosed on them at once.

One of the Germans spotted them and shouted out "*Achtung, alarm …* *ALARM!*" Their surprise was shattered.

The cause of the uproar was that at almost the same moment the other two groups had the extreme bad fortune to breach the parapet of the trench at almost the precise instant that a German raiding party was getting ready to head towards the Canadian trenches. They literally landed right on top of the Germans.

The Canadians recovered first since they were expecting a reception of some sort. Plus, they were warm from slithering through mud for the previous few hours and the adrenaline was pumping through their veins.

The Jerries for their part were fresh and had almost as much adrenaline in their veins.

After a few confused minutes the Germans began to get the upper hand. Ewan heard the commotion and since he was in the front of the other group he decided to bypass the bunker for now and help his comrades who were in trouble.

His sergeant was in the other group and was well behind. Ewan couldn't wait for him.

Throwing caution into the pit of hell he charged forward shouting "*Fraoch Eilean* lads, we're coming for ye! Come on boys let's get 'em!" And with that Ewan led his band of fighting men, more than one man also giving a Highland yell, into the melee that had developed in front of them. The Germans gave ground and then broke and fled leaving three dead and four wounded.

"*Fraoch Eilean*" or "The Heathery Isle" had been a war cry of Clan Donald and Ewan put it to good use that day.

The German officers, meanwhile, had been asleep or reading when this all started but on hearing English voices quickly figured out what was happening and readied themselves. There were seven of them: three Lieutenants, two Captains, a Major and the battalion commander, a Lieutenant-Colonel. They were all combat veterans and were all ready to give their lives for the Fatherland.

One of the captains rallied the three subalterns around him and provided a bulwark around their Commanding Officer as he had figured out that they were the target of the raid.

A young Lieutenant grabbed a nearby Gewehr 98 rifle with its bayonet attached and charged the Canadians. He managed to stick the bayonet in the side of a young private from Cape Breton who screamed his last breath in anger and pain. Ewan shot him in the mouth with a Webley service revolver for his trouble.

Another German, the other captain, a tough young Prussian, screamed and charged at Ewan with his Luger, firing as he ran. He got off two rounds, both narrowly missing Ewan, before the weapon jammed, Lugers were notorious for jamming in the mud. It almost cost him his life. Ewan was about to shoot him as well but then he remembered that the reason they were there was to capture officers, not kill them. So instead he pistol whipped him with the Webley.

That left five. The other two lieutenants and their captain had backed themselves into a corner and blocked the dugout behind them where the colonel and the major had hidden.

Ewan was still the man at the front. He had support now but in the confines of the dugout no one else could come up beside him.

He saw that he had to end this quickly. The German trench raiders who had scattered would be sure to return with reinforcements soon, and they had to be long gone before that.

He was now ten yards in front of the rest of his men, but screened from view from outside the bunker. With his bayonet in one hand wielded like a dirk and his Webley in the other and another Highland battle cry on his lips he charged the three combat veterans. His battle cry must have unnerved them because their reactions were slow. He was on them before they could defend themselves fully.

He managed to stick his bayonet in the throat of one man and shoot another in the belly, but not before he himself had been stabbed in the chest with a German bayonet. The remaining captain he smashed in the face with the hilt of his bayonet.

The grenade he threw into the back of the dugout fell into a hole in the side of the trench, which shielded the men inside from the worst of the blast, but it stunned them. The momentum of his charge and his adrenaline carried him past the two wounded officers and into the dugout proper, where he confronted the colonel and his major. They were on their knees, bleeding from the muted grenade explosion and shaking their heads as if to chase the bees out of their ears. Between the shock of the grenade and the fierceness of the charge, the fight had been knocked out of them by this display of a Highlander at work.

It seems Ewan had missed one man in his estimate of the number of people in the bunker. From behind the shadows at the back of the dugout he heard a shaky but familiar voice, "Hello Ewan, I had hoped not to meet you here." A very well-known and beloved voice. Peter stepped out of the shadows. He had been stunned by the grenade as well, but was far from subdued. "I should have known you'd be in the thick of it."

Recovering quickly, the adrenaline was still pumping through his veins, he replied, "And I you, though I didn't want tae meet you like this either."

By now Peter had recovered his wits enough to say, "I don't want to be captured, even by a friend," Ewan looked down and saw the pistol in Peter's hand. "I don't want to shoot you, but I won't be captured," he said with determination in his voice.

"Then you'd better get back intae the shadows because my men will be in here in less than a minute. You may shoot me, but ye won't get past them."

Peter stepped up to him, "I would never shoot you", he thrust out his hand, they shook hands, holding the grip for what seemed like a lifetime but was only a second or two, and Peter slipped back into the shadows.

"*Auf wiedersehen,* my friend," whispered Ewan after him.

"And good luck to you also, my brother," he heard Peter reply from the darkness.

The adrenaline evaporated from his system like cold water on hot rocks, and his men found him a few seconds later staring at the dark walls of the dugout like he had been shell shocked. "Are you all right, Corp?" asked one of the privates, seeing that he was bleeding from a chest wound, truly concerned about him.

"Aye, I'm fine, just a wee bit tired is all. Let's get the hell out of here."

All in all, Ewan had taken all seven of the German officers. Two had been killed and two wounded. He had captured a company commander, the battalion adjutant and, the crème de la crème, the battalion commander. He only let one go but no-one had to know about that one.

The Canadian raiding party had suffered three men killed and half a dozen wounded, including Ewan, though none badly. They started their return to the Canadian lines.

Ewan had one more act of bravery in him before the night was over. As they were preparing the wounded and the prisoners for the return over no man's land, he heard the German reinforcements approaching and hailed them in German. "*Hallo, wir haben sie verjagt, alles ist gut*" (Hello, we chased them away, all is good).

That confused them long enough that he and his mates made good their escape. His last act before following everyone back over the parapet was to toss a Mills bomb into their midst.

*
**

The next morning Sergeant Forbes sent for him. At first he thought he was in trouble because he had lost the Webley revolver on the way back through the wire.

"MacBride, the captain wants to see you!" he said. It was the captain's Webley he had lost.

"But sarn't, I dropped that bloody gun when I was draggin' yon Hun colonel through the wire!" he protested.

"I don't think that's what he wants to see you about," he replied, "he doesn't even know about his revolver."

"Well, what then?" He was still groggy from lack of sleep, and shaken from unexpectedly meeting Peter. He had had barely two hours with his eyes closed last night. The wound in his chest turned out to be superficial but was stiffening up quite a bit.

"Go and see for yourself."

Ewan made his way over to the battalion command post. The captain was the battalion adjutant. He made his way inside and snapped to attention at the adjutant's desk as best he could in the five-foot ceiling. "Sir! Corporal MacBride reporting as ordered, sir!"

"MacBride, the colonel wants to see you, lad," Captain Baldwin told him with a twinkle in his eye and a Cheshire Cat grin on his face.

"Oh aye? What for? What have I done wrong?" he knew the colonel wouldn't bother himself about a revolver. He was too sleep deprived to think straight, or to care much either way.

"Never you mind, just go in and see him." Captain Baldwin was almost laughing outright by this point.

So Ewan stepped through the door into the colonel's office, actually a blanket hung over the entrance to a slightly bigger dugout. He was able to come fully to attention in here though his hair brushed the ceiling.

"Well lad, you had quite the night last night didn't you?" Lieutenant Colonel William (Wild Billy) Armstrong said. The men thought of him as a god. He had been a sergeant in the Royal Canadian Regiment in the Boer War and had won the Distinguished Conduct Medal (DCM) for a charge he had led against the Boers. You would always find him in the thick of any advance.

"Yes, *sir!*" he was intimidated by Wild Billy.

"Oh, relax boy, you're not in trouble, just the opposite in fact. Sgt Franklyn has recommended you for the VC!"

Stunned silence. If his eyelids had opened any wider his eyes would have fallen out.

"Now, I've endorsed it but you're more likely to receive a Military Medal or maybe the DCM as you already have an MID. At a minimum though it will be the MM."

"Thank you, sir," he managed to stammer.

"Don't thank me, you did all the work. That colonel you pinched was the plum in the pudding! He'll provide hours of fun for the bods at Div HQ, I'm sure.

"Oh, and since Sgt Forbes was one of the ones wounded last night, you also get a third stripe, that's effective as of now."

"But he's no' badly wounded, sir, he just took a bayonet in his shoulder!"

"He still needs a couple of months to recover. In any case, his mining background has him transferring to the 2nd Canadian Pioneer Battalion, where his skills will be put to better use."

Ewan's head was reeling by now.

"Oh, and one more thing, lad."

"Yes, sir," he didn't trust himself to say anything else.

"Happy birthday Sgt MacBride!"

"What?" he was taken aback.

"I'm reliably informed that it was your birthday as well yesterday."

And so it was. Sergeant Ewan MacBride, MM, MID was now a grand total of twenty-two years old.

CHAPTER 5

HAMBURG 1914

Peter and Elsa boarded the *SS Roepat* with only a small valise each and five gold sovereigns that Ewan had given them. The captain knew who they were, but the rest of the crew didn't. Peter had tried to hide his identity as a German by posing as a Swiss engineer who had been caught unawares when Canada suddenly found itself at war with Germany. Canada had no choice in the matter, as a British colony she was automatically at war as soon as Great Britain declared war. Many Europeans were caught off guard by this, so it seemed plausible enough.

His cover story started to unravel right away though. It started when he was talking to the ship's first officer, Luitenant Hans Grabner, who really was Swiss. Grabner started quizzing Peter about his work as an engineer in Zurich. Peter had been to Zurich several times while working for Joe Schulmann in his other life. He knew the city well, having spent many enjoyable days wandering through the streets of old Zurich, watching the small boats come and go under the Quaibrucke.

At first it was just friendly banter between two men who were estranged from their homeland, which they missed. Then as Grabner asked more questions about Peter's work he started to get suspicious. As Hans got more comfortable with Peter he lapsed into Schweizerdeutsch, or Swiss German, which he tried not to use outside of Switzerland because few non-Swiss could follow him. It's like a man from Glasgow going to London and trying to be understood by someone who had never even been to Scotland.

And Peter wasn't doing very well.

So, Hans accused him outright of being German, his speech had given him away. Holland was neutral, like Switzerland, and they could be interned for harbouring a man from a combatant nation. Unlikely, as the *Roepat* had an all neutral crew, including a couple of Americans she had picked up in Boston, and she was headed straight to a Dutch port in any case. But because America was friendly with Britain, the captain decided to put Peter in the brig for the duration of the trip. He was very cheerful and apologetic about it, and Peter had been treated very well, so he went along with it and allowed himself to be "imprisoned". He even had Elsa with him which made it hardly painful at all.

*
**

Thus, he spent the next three days in the comfort of a Dutch maritime jail cell where he got a lot of sleep and a few other things! He and Elsa were very well rested by the time they arrived in Rotterdam on August 21, 1914.

The captain had no trouble with them, so he let them go without any further problems, after all this war was not his war, was it? Besides, the two gold sovereigns that Peter had given him would spend just as well in Rotterdam as they did in Halifax or London.

They went to the train station and were back in Hamburg by that night. Peter went straight to uncle Joe's house with Elsa in tow.

He knocked on the familiar door, which he hadn't seen in almost five years. It seemed like a dozen lifetimes ago.

After a minute or two he heard his uncle's footsteps inside the house. Then the door opened, and Uncle Joe stopped in his tracks.

"*Mein Gott!* You're dead! Where have you been?" exclaimed Joe, who was white as a sheet, having just seen a ghost. That didn't stop him from grabbing Peter in a bear hug, however. Peter thought he was going to crush his ribcage. The last Joe had heard was that Peter had gotten himself killed in Glasgow by a couple of detectives who were on the trail of some Scottish criminal.

He had thought that a bit convenient at the time but under the circumstances decided that it was better if Peter dropped off the map for a while.

He never for one moment believed that Peter was actually dead. His friend, Ludwig Weber, had written to him from Glasgow explaining what he knew about it. Ludwig thought that Peter might have got onto a ship heading to Canada, though he wasn't sure.

Joe was ecstatic to find that he was right after all.

"And who is this pretty Fraulein, Peter?"

"Not Fraulein, uncle Joe! Frau! *Sie ist meine Frau* … Elsa!" was the proud reply.

"Your wife?! You *have* been busy, lad!" Joe exclaimed.

So, Peter and Elsa spent the rest of the night, and most of the next morning, filling in uncle Joe with his adventures over the past five years.

Joe was astounded. He had an idea that Peter might have gone to Canada and made a life for himself. But now he was back. He assumed it had something to do with the war that was not even a month old yet.

"Why have you come home now, Peter? You're still a wanted man here you know."

"I left because they were going to start interning German citizens, and I couldn't stand that. I came home to join my unit and serve the Fatherland. It will all be over by Christmas anyway. Won't it?"

*
**

The next afternoon Peter went to his unit, which was the 76th Reserve Infantry Regiment, headquartered in Hamburg where he was immediately placed under arrest. His name had been recognized by none other than Johan Becker, the policeman who had investigated the incident that had led to his being charged with murder. Becker, it turns out, was also a reservist. He was a sergeant who had been called up a couple of months earlier.

But he was still a policeman at heart, and he wanted to get Peter's side of the story before deciding what to do with him.

Peter told him the whole story right from the start, from the initial disobedience right through to the eventual "murder". His trying to stop a fight, which had gotten out of hand made much more sense than the story he had been told.

Because of this, and because Peter had been a good soldier before the war, he decided to let him go. The fact that he was also a tradesman who worked with his hands and who spoke English made up his mind. He could foresee both of these skills coming in handy soon enough. The police authorities put their trust in Sergeant Becker and because they needed good soldiers they let it pass.

Peter went home that night, kissed Elsa and told his uncle Joe what had happened.

"You were very lucky, Peter. If there had not been a war on you would not have gotten away so lightly," Joe said.

"If there had not been a war on, I would not have come home," Peter reminded him, "at least not yet."

"No, I guess not. Ah well, I suppose you'll be going off with your unit soon, won't you?"

"Not right away, they're still bringing in reservists from all over Germany. We won't fully mobilize until later, no idea when really. The regular regiment has already left for the front and once we're up to strength we will too. I was hoping to fight against the Russians but wherever the Kaiser needs me."

"You're welcome to leave Elsa here while you're away if you'd like … and if she wants to, that is." Joe turned to Elsa at that.

Elsa had been quiet up 'til then, content to absorb Peter and Joe's discussion since it answered a lot of her own questions too. "Herr Schulmann, you know that I have no family in Germany, no family that I love and trust anyway."

"Of course," he said.

"Then I would be most pleased to stay here! You are my family now … uncle Joe!" she almost burst into tears because she hadn't truly realised that this was true. Uncle Joe was her family now too! "I will earn my keep, of course!"

"You will do no such thing, I have more than enough servants as it is."

Peter started laughing. "You do remember that I said that Elsa was the office manager for MacBride & Baum, don't you? She is largely responsible for how successful the business was, or 'is' I hope! I believe she meant to help out with the cooperage!"

"Yes, of course, silly of me! My apologies Frau Baum," he bowed a little too stiffly to Elsa, "I am an old man and rather old fashioned in my ways."

"If this war goes on for very long I think you might find women doing a lot more than clean house." Elsa said with some trepidation. She was not to know just how prescient her words would be.

*
**

Over the next several weeks the regiment trained and gathered in more men and then trained and gathered in yet more men. From time to time a company would go off to reinforce the regiment at the front. Peter stayed behind since his organizational skills were more useful in planning the regimental order of battle than in fighting at the front. His talents had been recognized early, and he was made an officer almost immediately, and by the end of November 1914 he was a captain. Armies grow fast when there's a war on. He spent less and less time at home and more and more time in the field with the regimental headquarters. He was enjoying it, but he chafed to get to the front. If he couldn't fight the Russians, he'd fight the French.

Meanwhile, in France and Belgium the great Schlieffen Plan had ground to a halt without capturing Paris, and it seemed that the war would not be over by Christmas. Not Christmas 1914 anyway.

Both armies were digging in and a great network of trenches was developing. It would eventually stretch from the Belgian coast to the Swiss border.

Peter had a rather subdued Christmas at home with his uncle Joe and his beautiful young wife. They made the best of it because they knew it might be their last for a while. Or their last forever, which no-one said out loud.

Early in the new year, he got his orders, he was heading to the front. Because he spoke excellent English and had lived in Britain and Canada he was seconded to the 4th Army, 52nd Division. The 76th IR was in the 1st Army and they were probably off fighting the French. His new unit was going to be facing a BEF attack.

They arrived in the Arras area on January 5, 1915, shortly after what would be known as the first Battle of Ypres. He was initially billeted in the Belgian town of the same name. On and off he would spend more than two years in the vicinity of Arras. His knowledge of the area would eventually come in very handy. For now, he just surveyed the town from high ground to the east.

Peter was working on the staff of the Division Commander. His knowledge of the British was thought to be useful for planning to defend against them. He knew how they thought.

The next few weeks were spent preparing their defences, digging trenches, dugouts and bunkers, building fortifications and stringing barbed wire in no man's land. Much of this was done away from the frontline and was relatively safe. Work on the very front trenches and the barbed wire in no man's land had to be done at night.

As a staff officer, Peter didn't have to do much physical work but as a man experienced with building things he was giving advice to the men designing the fortifications. This meant visiting the frontlines as often as he could.

The general spent much of his time in his main headquarters which was a chateau near St Eloi, really a large farm house, but he was the kind of officer who liked to inspect the work and spent a lot of time in the trenches gathering information and chatting with the soldiers. He was very popular. It was rather dangerous though, one of the junior officers was killed by a sniper and two others were winged.

He learned about boredom, he learned about the misery of being in cold and wet trenches and about the terror of shelling and sniping and trench raids.

They were starting to build up for an assault on the Allied lines in the area of Gravenstafel Ridge where there was a large bulge, or salient, in the frontlines, the idea being to remove the bulge and straighten the line out.

Then, in the middle of April, thousands of steel cylinders were delivered to the front, each could be lifted by one man, though not easily. Nobody knew what they were for. Peter heard rumours about smoke or fog or paint or even fuel for flame throwers. Nobody suspected what it really was at first.

On April 22, he was with a frontline unit in the village of Poelcapelle where they were able to watch the attack.

Evidently the high command was waiting for the wind to be blowing across no man's land towards the British. When he heard that, he felt the small hairs on the back of his neck rising up and a peculiar feeling of dread came over him. Strange canisters and a wind blowing towards the enemy meant nothing good.

At a signal, when the wind was blowing in just the right direction, the valves on the canisters were opened and a sickly greenish-yellow coloured gas started streaming from the valves and wafted away towards the British and French lines. Nothing happened at first because it took a while for the gas to reach the opposite trenches.

The heavier than air gas poured like liquid across no man's land. Then it started to seep into the shell craters and dugouts and trenches of the French. It turns out the troops receiving the gas were French Colonial troops who were, in no way, equipped to deal with this new horror. They started screaming in pitiful French voices and almost immediately broke and ran almost before a shot had been fired.

The German soldiers who were detailed to exploit the, now empty, trenches were reluctant to follow too closely behind. Naturally enough, they didn't want to run into whatever had scared the French troops.

By the time the German troops worked up the courage to chase the French, the trenches were being filled with fresh men, this time Canadians. These men fought like lions and denied the Germans what should have been an easy victory.

Peter watched all this from the frontline German trenches. He didn't know that the men who had stopped the German advance were Canadian until some wounded prisoners were brought back through the lines. They were a miserable sight, some were blind, some could barely breathe, and all had blisters on their open skin.

He heard them crying out in pain. Crying out in English. Some with British accents and some who sounded like the men he had known and worked with in Halifax. Peter felt a heavy twinge of regret. He had gone back to Germany to fight the Russians. When that hadn't happened he was ready to fight the French, some of his relatives had suffered under the French forty years earlier. But he wasn't prepared to fight the British, much less the Canadians. They had been very good to him, they had taken him in without quibble when he had fled Germany in fear of being arrested.

Now here he was fighting against men he very possibly knew, maybe even Ewan was out there choking on chlorine gas. He felt his first doubt about what he was doing there.

*
**

Life in the trenches settled down to an endlessly brutal routine of cold and mud and blood and death. Then the spring turned to summer and the cold turned to hot and the mud turned to dust, but the blood and the death were constants. The summer was spent in trench raids at night and sniping in the day all the while digging in and improving the defences under the constant threat of instant and grizzly death.

They rotated out of the frontline fairly routinely where they could relax, after a fashion, play football and wash; where they could wear clean uniforms and eat food that wasn't infested with weevils and rats, or at least not as much. As close to bliss as you can get in the midst of war.

The other major constant for Peter was the letters he got from Elsa every week. After the war he credited those with saving his life – keeping him sane in an insane place.

Elsa talked about the flowers that were blooming around uncle Joe's house and the new kitten that she had acquired from a local girl. And about the fact that she couldn't get enough decent cloth to make a new dress, what with the blockade and all. Blissfully commonplace stuff to distract him from the reality that was Belgium in 1915.

The war continued unabated. Turkey entered the war and gave the British a major bloody nose far to the east somewhere, the French were fighting to the south of him and the Russians were being defeated everywhere on the Eastern front.

Peter couldn't stand the boredom and routine. He started asking for a posting to a unit that was more involved in the fighting and for his sins he was posted to the 117th Division in the beginning of September where he was given command of an infantry company. Their first task was to improve the defences around an area known as the Hohenzollern Redoubt, an area that was intended to be a bulwark against any attack from the west. It was a salient that jutted towards the British frontline. The high command felt that this was not only critical to the defence of that part of the frontline but also very vulnerable to attack.

They spent two weeks digging deeper and improving the fixed defences. The area was known for coal mining before the war and there was much materiel for use in the defences. Peter's men were well dug in, and they knew that an attack was imminent.

Then on September 25 all hell broke loose. The British shelling started and never ceased all that morning. It devastated the wire in no man's land and sent the frontline troops into their well-prepared dugouts. When it ended Peter knew the attack would be coming very soon.

In the brief moment of utter silence when the shelling stopped Peter actually heard the whistles blowing as the order was given by the British officers for the men to go over the top. His men came flooding out of their dugouts and quickly set up their weapons again. The machine guns and artillery destroyed the silence just as thoroughly as they destroyed the leading waves of infantry coming towards them over no man's land. The slaughter was tremendous, men were falling and being blown to bits everywhere it seemed. And yet they made it to the front trenches where they were, only very narrowly, stopped. Further south, they broke through and it took ferocious courage to retake what had been lost.

One group of Tommies made it into Peter's trench and were threatening his command dugout. They were charging his post howling like banshees and the man leading the charge very nearly skewered him with his bayonet. Only the quick actions of a brave young ensign in his HQ saved him but at the cost of his own life for the bayonet meant for Peter went in one side of the twenty-year-old Berliner's head and then came out the other side a second later accompanied by most of his brain. That sight would never leave Peter entirely and would haunt him for many years to come.

The immediate effect was to turn Peter into a Viking Berserker of old. He punched the man who had impaled his young friend and, forgetting that he still had a Luger in his fist he drove the barrel of the pistol into the man's cheek. The only way he could extract it was to fire it, doing to the man what he had just done to young Erik Bayreuth only seconds before.

An enraged Peter Baum then cleared the British from his trench, almost single-handedly repelling the British attack, personally dispatching seven more British soldiers.

He took the first with his Luger, still dripping with blood and brains, and the second also. After that the Luger jammed, already a notoriously unreliable weapon, having pieces of a man's skull in the mechanism was guaranteed to jam it. Throwing it at the third man, it glanced off his shoulder. This distracted him long enough for Peter to wrench the rifle out of his hand and shoot him in the stomach with it. He then discovered the effectiveness of an almost half metre-long steel blade when some muscle is applied to the back of it.

The fourth man he cleanly stabbed in the throat with the bayonet, wrenching it free with sheer brute force. Number five he took in the chest. The bayonet was stuck but Peter worked the bolt, chambering another round and fired, the shock of which he used to extract the weapon.

The next he took by swinging the rifle around and stoving in the skull of the man screaming at him as he charged. The last he killed by putting the bayonet through his mouth and into his brain which made him drop like a pole-axed bull.

Later, several of his men said that the sight of their half-crazed officer carrying a pistol covered in blood turned them into madmen themselves, and they regained their trench in very short order.

This action made him into a minor legend in his regiment. He was immediately awarded the *"Eisernes Kreuz 2. Klasse"* or Iron Cross 2nd Class, which his colonel later upgraded to 1st Class upon hearing the story.

Peter himself was badly shaken by the experience and couldn't sleep for weeks. He constantly relived the moment when the bayonet came out the side of young Erik Bayreuth's head, stopping only centimetres from his own.

The next two weeks were a living hell as the British tried again and again to seize the redoubt, succeeding on a number of occasions only to be pushed back again and again by Peter and his men and comrades. All the while his reputation as a Berserker grew.

The British finally gave up in the middle of October and left the Germans to lick their wounds and recover as best they could.

Peter's company had been reduced from almost 225 all ranks to less than 75 effectives in less than a month. Peter himself had been wounded four times but refused to leave his men to the mercy of some fat, incompetent sausage eater who would surely get them all killed.

This only made his image to his men all the larger. It did not go unnoticed by the colonel either and Peter was promoted to Major and became second in command of the battalion. It had suffered as badly as his company had, they were reduced to around a third of their original effective strength.

They were sent back to recover and replenish their numbers for the upcoming spring battles. Peter brought the battalion to the small Belgian town of Zonnebeke to recover their strength. At least they didn't have to spend winter and Christmas in the trenches, he even managed to get some leave and go home for the holidays.

Peter arrived in Hamburg on December 21 and fell into Elsa's arms like a drowning man, which in a lot of ways he was.

Elsa was overcome with joy to see him home, as was his uncle Joe. She couldn't believe how much he had changed in less than a year. Peter had left as an eager young man, eager to fight for his Fatherland. But also eager to prove himself to, mostly himself, but also to Elsa and his uncle Joe.

A boy had gone to war but a man had returned. As a decorated war hero with medals, promotions and scars to show for it. It was not the Peter Baum of old though. This was a different man somehow, more reserved, less gregarious, more thoughtful. She decided to give him some time to sort out his demons for himself and was determined to shower him with love and attention for the short time he'd be at home.

Over the next several days, Peter and Elsa reconnected with an intensity neither of them thought possible. They made love with a fervour that transcended the conscious mind, Peter releasing the tension of intense combat that only coming so close to death can bring and Elsa allowing the intense worry she had felt to leave her body through an equally intense passion. The unspoken possibility of Peter's violent death hung over them both, but this only intensified their reunion.

Only one shadow hung over him, he suspected that uncle Joe held a certain amount of resentment towards him because of the manner in which he had left nearly six years ago. Joe felt no such thing, however. He was proud of the way Peter had dealt with all the problems he had faced and how he had made a life for himself in a foreign country. Speaking a language that he wasn't familiar with … and finding such a beautiful young wife into the bargain.

He told Peter that the whole incident had been forgotten the moment war was declared; there were now more important things to worry about. Schmidt and Becker had both gone off to war. Schmidt, having lost a leg, was relegated to filling orders at a supply warehouse in Hamburg and even more bitter because of that and Becker was now a senior sergeant in Peter's original regiment in France – both happily out of Peter's life.

*
**

That Christmas was the most emotional Peter had ever experienced. He wasn't a religious man but the intensity of the feeling of family was something that he had missed during his time in Scotland and Canada and, of course, Belgium. He vowed that, if nothing else that feeling of family would never leave him again.

He returned to the front the day after the new year, arriving back in Belgium exactly one year after he had arrived there the first time.

His battalion was deemed fully operational again, and they moved back into the frontline near the village of Comines. The trenches here were still being rebuilt and strengthened after the battles earlier in 1915, so there was much work to be done, which was welcome because it kept them warm during the bitter cold of another Belgian winter.

Once again Peter got used to the mud and blood and fleas and rats and misery of trench life, never quite becoming comfortable with it but accepting it as simply the way things were. Frontline trenches had a unique, sickly smell all their own, a cloying stench that you could almost taste in the back of your throat.

They discovered that, once again, they were opposite Canadian troops. This made them a little nervous because the Canadians were rapidly developing a reputation as men who simply did not lose battles. They weren't there to lose it was said. But, then again, who was?

As much as Peter respected, and even loved the Canadians, he was a German soldier first, and he would make them earn every metre of mud that they took.

They were much more active in no man's land than their British cousins were. Or even their Australian brothers who were all insane. Their favourite trick was to raid the frontline trenches for prisoners. The Canadian Indians, in particular, liked to sneak in unseen and silently kill a few soldiers, take a prisoner or two and then sneak away without ever being heard or seen. It was said they even took scalps like in the movies, but he doubted that. It was very unnerving to already jumpy troops who wanted, more than anything, to survive into the next day.

One particular day in early February 1916, he was attending an orders group with his CO in a well-built bunker right in the forward trench. Peter had told his boss, Oberst Leutnant von Horst that having a bunker so close to the frontline was not a good idea, they were usually in a second or third line trench. But the arrogant old Prussian thought it was cowardly to be anywhere else but the very foremost trench. Good for morale but not very practical.

The planning session had gone on all day and into the night. Orders were being sent by carrier pigeon, but they were running out of those. Peter was running the meeting, and he decided that they should break for a meal before going back to their respective areas.

He heard some rustling outside the bunker and decided to go and investigate. Then he saw that a patrol of his own men were getting ready to go over the top to lay some extra wire in front of their frontline. Relaxing, he turned to go back inside and as he turned he saw some men slipping over the parapet from the other direction. He quickly realised that these were British or Canadian soldiers raiding his trench.

Peter didn't have time to draw his pistol, he just yelled *"Achtung, alarm … ALARM!"* and punched the first soldier he saw in the side of the head as he slid into the trench, knocking him out cold. Then his men who were getting ready to go over themselves got into the fight. Oddly enough neither the Canadians nor his men had rifles and only a few had pistols, so the fighting was like a bar brawl for the first few minutes. Peter managed to get a few good punches in before he heard a sound that froze his heart like a glacier. *"Fraoch Eilean* lads, we're coming for ye! Come on boys let's get 'em!"* He recognized that voice at once and stood frozen to the spot for a precious few seconds. Those seconds almost cost him his life because at that moment the Canadian trench raiders exploded into animated life and rushed into the area around his bunker.

Instantly realizing what was happening, as he had heard the tales of officers being stolen from under the very noses of their own men, Peter rushed back into the bunker to try and protect his colonel. The shock of hearing Ewan's voice was only barely outweighed by the need to protect his CO.

There was gunfire by now and occasional grenades as some of the sentries were recovering and those raiders who had brought, or stolen, rifles were bringing them to bear.

Then another bloodcurdling Highland yell from that most familiar voice and a grenade went off only a few metres from where he was standing. It had fallen into a hole in the side of the bunker, which masked most of the shrapnel but only some of the blast, and he fell backwards into the back of the bunker.

Young and fit, Peter recovered quickly, scrambling to his feet and cautiously looked into the main bunker where he saw his best friend, almost within touching distance. Tentatively he said, "Hello Ewan, I had hoped not to meet you here," hoping Ewan wouldn't shoot him. He then stepped out of the shadow and said, "I should have known you'd be in the thick of it."

Not missing a beat Ewan replied, "and I, you, though I didn't want to meet you like this either."

"I don't want to be captured, even by a friend," Peter looked down and realised he was holding his pistol and pointing it at Ewan, "I don't want to shoot you, but I won't be captured," his voice was recovering its strength.

"Then you'd better get back intae the shadows because my men will be in here in less than a minute. You may shoot me, but ye won't get past them." Ewan said, clearly shaken.

Peter stepped up to him, "I would never shoot you," he thrust out his hand, they shook hands, holding the grip for what seemed like a lifetime but was only a second or two, and Peter slipped back into the shadows.

"*Auf wiedersehen*, my friend", whispered Ewan after him.

"And good luck to you also, my brother."

CHAPTER 6

HALIFAX 1915

*
**

Morag was left to run the tannery with her Da, and she put her experience working with Ewan and Peter to good use and helped Sean build the business up to become one of the biggest suppliers of leather for the CEF in Nova Scotia.

The recruitment of all the cavalry and artillery and supply units, all of which needed dozens and hundreds of horses and wagons, meant that she and Sean would be very busy for as long as the war lasted. They got a tremendous amount of work from the army to make the tack and bags and seats and to supply leather for saddles, boots and everything else a rapidly expanding army needs when it's going off to war.

In addition to this she got involved in war relief charities, raising money for Belgian and French refugees. When the wounded started coming home she was instrumental in helping organize Red Cross facilities and volunteered for everything to help the war effort. All the while dreading, and at the same time hoping, that she'd find Ewan amongst them.

So, when she started getting sick in the mornings she put it down to overwork and lack of sleep. Soon though her clothing wasn't fitting quite right and when she confirmed that she had missed her monthlies not just once, which is not that unusual for hardworking young women, but *twice* she was pretty sure … there was another MacBride on the way!

"Da, I've got somethin' to tell ye," she said to Sean one day.

"Aye, what is it?" he was curious but too busy to be that interested.

"Do ye remember when you were talkin' to Grandma before we left Glasgow and how ye told her she'd have new bairns the next time we saw them?" she teased, "and how you told me ye were only joking?"

"Aye," he said.

And then the penny dropped, "Yer no … yer not … I mean … he's been gone for months!" he couldn't believe his ears.

"Only five months," she tried to sound casual about it, but failed completely. "Aye Da, I'm goin' tae have a little Ewan … or maybe a Morag!" she was getting excited now. "Or maybe one of each! Twins run in oor family don't they?"

"Aye, they do, on both sides! Well what dae ye know about that then? I'm right happy for ye lass, truly I am!" he was fairly bursting with pride and happiness for his daughter but then he realised, "I'm goin' tae be a Grandda mysel'!"

Then they were both off, holding each other and dancing in circles. It was so very nice to have a happy moment in all this sadness and misery around them.

"So, when are you due then?" he asked her, more timidly than he'd intended. He was of the generation where being pregnant fell firmly into the category of "women's things" and best left to women. He had realised though, when his wife died, that he was also Morag's mother in a lot of ways and so should, at least, take an interest in some of these things. But he still didn't feel comfortable with it.

"Well, let me see, Ewan left at the end of May, and we said our goodbyes," she started to blush a vividly bright scarlet as redheads do, "a couple of days before that so …" she did a quick calculation in her head, "sometime in late February next year I reckon."

"You'll have to write and tell Ewan right away lass, he'll be chuffed pink!"

"Aye, well I've thought about that," she hesitated "and I wonder if I should wait until I'm further along in case there are any problems."

"Why? Are ye no feelin' well lass?" he worried.

"No, no I feel fine, wonderful in fact, the morning sickness is very mild and, in any event is almost done … it's just that I don't want him to worry about me when he has so much else on his plate right now," she tried to hide her own worries, but not very well.

"Lass, don't ye' think it would be more likely to give him something positive to think about while he's in that giant mess in Flanders?" there were no illusions about the glories of war anymore.

"Aye, yer right, of course, I'll let him know right away."

With that she sat down and wrote Ewan a short but heartfelt note. Telling him the good news and all other things that had happened since she last wrote to him, one staggeringly long and lonely week ago.

Dearest Ewan,

It's been a long week without you holding me and caressing me and keeping me warm at night. A week in which I learned that the Clan MacBride is going to grow by at least one … maybe two! Yes, love of my life, you're going to be a Da! And a wonderful Da you will be I just know so in my heart … and elsewhere …!

Keep safe and know that when you come home there will be another one waiting for you. And that one will need a brother or a sister.

All my love, Morag.

CHAPTER 7

WESTERN FRONT 1916

*_**

Ewan and his unit were given some rest, far to the west of the frontline and since quite a few of the men were British ex-pats, some of them even managed to get leave in Britain to see family. Because Ewan was a minor celebrity in the battalion he was one who got to go home. He was given two weeks.

Among the letters from Morag that Ewan had waiting for him was one that was brief and to the point.

> *Dearest Ewan,*
>
> *It's been a long week without you holding me and caressing me and keeping me warm at night. A week in which I learned that the Clan MacBride is going to grow by at least one … maybe two! Yes, love of my life, you're going to be a Da!! And a wonderful Da you will be I just know so in my heart … and elsewhere …!*
>
> *Keep safe and know that when you come home there will be another one waiting for you. And that one will need a brother or a sister.*
>
> *All my love, Morag.*

There couldn't have been any better news, it put him in the best possible mood to go home and see his family.

After getting a berth on a returning troop ship, which was full of wounded, Ewan got a train from England and two days after leaving the mud in Flanders he was home in Fort William. He arrived on a Great Highland Railway train from Glasgow. He half expected to meet his Da on the train, since he was a conductor.

Hamish MacBride was indeed on the train. Ewan saw him from the far end of the car he was on. He looked over the old man quite openly since the last time he had seen him was in 1909 when he had fled to Glasgow. He had been a boy of fifteen then, now seven years later he was a man, hardened by hard work and by war, with his share of scars to prove it.

In all that time he had only written once, from Halifax to let them know he was in Canada and that he had been married. He was still afraid of being found out for the "incident" at the smithy all those years ago.

His father looked as he had in 1909, a bit leaner, a bit greyer, and his shoulders hunched some but very much his Da.

Hamish came by and punched his ticket without even really looking at him, there were dozens of soldiers on the train. The anonymity of the uniform. Ewan took the opportunity to observe his Da. In addition to the physical changes he noticed another change. The cheerful outgoing man who was always chatting with passengers that he had known had been replaced by a dour, stressed and depressed looking man who moved slower than he had and talked hardly at all.

When the train arrived in Fort William he quietly got off with a group of other soldiers, some of whom had noticed the ribbon of the MM and the MID on his uniform and gave him a respectful space on the platform.

Not wanting to go home right away in order to let his Da get home and take his boots off and relax, he went for a walk around the town to look at all his old haunts. He spent a pleasant hour visiting the old Shinty Park and some of the places that he and Rory and Sandy had spent many a pleasant afternoon.

Thinking about Sandy led him to the old foundry. It was much changed from what he remembered. Even the old building was gone, it had been replaced by a modern mechanic's garage and there were several vehicles – cars, vans, lorries, even a motorcycle or two – in front of it.

The most striking change was that the sign over the doors said. "JR McMurtry – Engines and Coachwork." Whatever had happened had been significant.

Now with the nostalgia taken care of, for the moment at least, he took the winding well-worn and well-loved path to his house.

Walking up to his old door and saw that it, like him, was a little more battered and worn than it had been. He stood there staring at it for fully five minutes. He had imagined this moment in his head thousands of times over the years, in Glasgow and Halifax and Belgium. Now that he was here he didn't know what to do.

Finally, he knocked timidly on the door and stood back. He heard a chair scrape on the floor and then the well-known tread of his Ma came to the door.

The door opened, and seven years evaporated like a puddle on a hot day.

"Ewan!" screamed his Ma, and then fainted dead away. A mother recognises her child even after all the changes of the years.

"What's going on?" came his Da's worried query, as he ran for the door.

"What have you done to my wife!?" challenged Hamish to this brash young soldier at his door.

"Hello, Da."

*
**

Three hours later his Ma was still crying, and Hamish was completely overcome. It was clear what had brought on his stress and now that Ewan was home he could visibly see the weight being lifted from his shoulders. They all had stood, just holding each other and crying when Ewan walked in the door.

Hamish hadn't recognized him until he opened his mouth and then the shock had almost sent him to his knees.

After the emotions of the moment had run their course they all sat down around the old Aga stove for warmth.

Ewan then ran through everything that had happened to him since he'd left for Glasgow all those years ago, the quick version anyway, the detailed explanation would come later.

Mary couldn't get over the fact that Ewan was married, she had received the letter but didn't really believe it until she heard it from Ewan's own lips. He didn't tell them that Morag was pregnant, he wanted to wait until the babe was born.

"What kind of girl is she?" she asked somewhat nosily Ewan thought. But then, that's a mother's right.

"Och, she's verra ugly and she only has one leg!" Ewan teased her.

"She does not, you wouldn't do that!"

"What's wrong wi' ugly, one-legged girls? Did I mention she's as daft as a brush too?"

"Aye, well she'd have to be that to take up with a young layabout like you!" Hamish interjected.

It was good to be home!

*
**

The next day Hamish took Ewan aside and explained what had happened at the foundry once he had left.

"After young Herbert … passed away, Chelmsford tried to get yer' Ma and I arrested, raised quite a fuss in fact."

"Why for heaven's sake? What did you do?" Ewan was livid, and ashamed that his parents had been caught up in his mess.

"I fathered you. Apparently, that's a crime in England." Hamish laughed. "It never went anywhere, of course, yer Ma and I hadn't done anything, and everybody knew it. Chelmsford and his whelp were never very popular here, as you know, so he was run out of town at the end of a horsewhip! Constable Stuart conveniently was in Inverness that day!"

Now Ewan laughed, "I wish I'd seen that!"

"So, the real story is well known now, and no one is looking for you anymore, you'll be quite safe in the town. They even released Angus from gaol."

Over the next week, Ewan saw the physical changes come over his folks, especially his Ma. She became the same person he had known and loved for all those years. His Da too, came out of the deep depression he had been in. Seeing their son had given them new life. Knowing he was alive was one thing but seeing him again made all the difference.

He found out that his first love, pretty little Heather MacLeod, had immigrated to Australia with her folks, and he wished her well. He filed the news of Angus' release under 'future plans'.

Ewan took some time to see Rory's family and finally tell them what really happened to their son and how brave he had been. He could see the relief in their faces.

But then, inevitably, it came time to go back to Belgium. On the one hand it was nice to bid them a proper farewell instead of just sneaking off in the wee hours. On the other hand, the tears, from all three of them, were even more genuine. It was 1916 and no one was under any illusion that the war was going to end soon or cheaply, and the unspoken possibilities hung over their heads. Ewan boarded his train, without his Da this time and headed back to Flanders.

*
**

He arrived back at the MacKenzie's bivouac area after an uneventful but thought-filled journey. Many things came and went through his head, though he thought mostly about Morag. Although he received a letter from her every week or two he still thought about her all the time.

He settled back into trench routine very quickly, apparently you can get used to anything.

And then on February 16 a telegram from Morag arrived that said only:

A boy, 5lbs 7ozs, Hamish Angus and a girl, 4lbs 12oz, Mairi Elsa, February 14, Valentine's Day! Congratulations Da! More later, love Morag.

Nothing could remove the grin from his face for two full weeks!

He thought about his home and his parents and was glad they were well. He was also glad that he had managed to allay their fears as best he could. He thought about wee Hamish and Mairi and hoped he'd get to meet them soon. He thought about Peter and what a shock it was to meet him on the battlefield and to have his best friend point a gun at him. And he wondered if he'd ever see him again. Part of him hoped he wouldn't, at least not until the war was over.

The battalion was once again fully reinforced and fully trained. Replacements from Canada, via England, had returned them to full strength. The mood was restrained yet expectant, they were champing at the bit but grimmer and more determined than they had been in 1915. Most of the men were now veterans, though not combat veterans beyond trench raids, and the others were untested. That would soon change.

On May the 25th, they moved up to the rear of the line just west of St Eloi itself. Rumour had them attacking the German lines very soon. Just how soon they did not know.

They settled into new dugouts in the second line and spent the next forty-eight hours clearing the trenches to make room for extra kit like assault ladders and extra ammunition and equipment. They also prepared the machine guns for moving into no man's land and a host of other work that kept them from getting much sleep. It prevented them from dwelling on what was coming.

The Regimental Sergeant Major visited all the companies and platoons and sections and chatted jovially with the men, especially the new ones who'd just arrived from England. He made sure everyone had all his kit, lots of ammunition and bombs and had their bayonets cleaned and honed and ready to be fixed. Everyone knew then that this was serious because the RSM was never jovial and never chatted with the men.

Then, in the early morning, the earth flew into the sky followed by a mind shattering explosion of sound and fire and mud and rocks and men only to be repeated immediately by another explosion and then another and another and then three more in almost simultaneous succession. The earth sounded like a giant piece of canvass being torn in half.

With ringing ears, the Canadians watched as the British infantry attacked across the devastated landscape into the German trenches. They were prepared to reinforce the Brits if they fell back but weren't needed right away. For the next week they watched, nervously, as the British advanced slowly over no man's land into the confused mass of churned up terrain and trenches. Trying, without much success, to evict the Jerries from their trenches.

Eventually, the exhausted British had enough and the Canadians, who had been waiting and preparing for this moment relieved them.

The Brodie Helmet was just being introduced, a soup plate shaped steel pot that was supposed to protect their heads from shrapnel, etc. But it seemed that the British were issuing them to British troops first and the colonials second.

Several men were carrying smellys, the British Short Magazine Lee-Enfield (SMLE), or "Smelly", which they said was more reliable in the mud of Flanders. Ewan liked his Ross though, so he kept it. Before the war he had never even seen a rifle like this, and he loved the accuracy and the smooth action. Two days later this decision almost ended his life.

The artillery barrage was an almost constant companion in their fear and it was only when it started to intensify that they realised they were about to go 'over the top', the officers and senior NCOs walked up and down the frontline trenches steadying the men, giving them encouragement and some advice on what to do when they got to the German trenches. Ewan found himself giving, or trying to give, inspiring talks to men older than himself and with no more, or less, experience than he.

When the time came, and the whistles sounded to go over the top, he was strangely calm. The noise of the artillery faded into the background, and it was as if he was watching himself from far away. It seemed unreal and almost dreamlike.

And, then he was up, into the wire and the mud and the blood and the bodies … Everywhere there were bodies, mostly British but also some Germans too from the many counterattacks. These men haunted him for years afterwards, but they would be joined by many more over the next two and a half years.

They were supposed to be running over no man's land to attack the German trenches but instead they were barely walking, struggling through destroyed barbed wire and over the terrain, which had been turned into a confused mass of mine craters and shell holes. Sometimes confusing the direction they were headed in, which hid the Germans from their view and then suddenly exposing them to machine gun fire from the side or the back, telling them they were headed the wrong way.

All the while they were walking on bodies and pieces of bodies. Occasionally they came across a wounded man in a shell hole who had lain there for days. They could do nothing for these poor buggers, and they had to keep going or die in the mud themselves.

The shelling punctuated this carnage and the machine gun fire underlined it. For two days they tried to get to the German frontline trenches, moving from shell hole to shell hole, crawling over dead men and seldom actually seeing Jerry closer than a hundred yards. Ewan had only fired three rounds from his Ross with no thought that he might have hit something.

Then late on the second day, April 5, Ewan found himself in a German trench. He had no idea how he had got there, but there he was anyway. Three of his men were with him, and he tried to force his way further into the trench. The Germans thought otherwise.

Once again Ewan shouted *"Fraoch Eilean …* get these bastards!"* and he and his men charged the soldiers, firing from the parapet.

He stabbed one man in the side with his bayonet and then shot another in the chest. Trying to reload, he found that his beloved Ross was completely jammed with mud and there was nothing he could do to un-jam it. His rifle was now a pike, and he used it as such.

He got one more man in the shoulder but couldn't extract his rifle because he couldn't fire a round to release it, so he left it pinned to the man's shoulder. Then he had a couple of seconds to look around and noticed that no other Canadians had followed him into the trench, so he and his men beat a hasty retreat back over the parapet and into no man's land again.

Fortunately, the broken up terrain was equally effective at spoiling Jerry's aim. One of his men was killed in the trench and another was shot in the back while they were making their way back across no man's land. Ewan grabbed a smelly from a British soldier who wouldn't be needing it any more.

He and L/Cpl Anderson made it back to the Canadian lines unscathed.

For the next fortnight the battle swung back and forth with both sides firing their artillery barrages, the incessant chatter of machine guns, the continual stream of whizz-bangs and, to add insult to injury, the constant pounding rain.

It couldn't go on forever, and it didn't, with one last push the Germans regained all of the territory they had lost in the previous three weeks.

What a bloody waste.

The remains of the 25th Battalion slid off into the night with about half of them being captured or wounded and the other half reduced to fewer than one in five of the men who had proudly left Halifax only a little over one year earlier.

Ewan was lucky to be alive.

*
**

They were pulled out of the line to lick their wounds, to regroup and to incorporate reinforcements from Canada, yet again. Ewan felt like an old man, even at twenty-two he was quite a bit older than some of these lads. Some of them were seventeen or less, he suspected that one lad was fifteen, though he said he was eighteen. He didn't even know how to shave yet. How he had fooled the recruiters was beyond him.

That lad they had sent back to Shorncliffe less than a year before, was now back in Belgium with stories of his own.

The reinforcements were not just from Halifax, or even Nova Scotia, they were from all over Canada, some even from British Columbia. There was even the odd American who had come across the border to fight. The Yanks still hadn't made up their mind whether to join in or not. Some of the more cynical types figured they were waiting to see which side was winning before they committed to anything.

During this time, they finally got their "soup plates" as the Brodie helmet was known and, by now a lot of them had smellys. All of the reinforcements did. It wasn't as pretty as the Ross, but it didn't jam as easily and if it did, one swift kick would generally clear it. Ewan grabbed a new one. The writing was on the wall for the Ross.

One member of the 25th who was extremely happy about all this was Robert the Bruce, the recently acquired regimental goat, who was enjoying himself thoroughly. When he wasn't eating the men's cigarettes he was drinking their beer ration. Still, at least he left their rum alone! He provided a much-needed distraction from the friends they had lost over the previous few months. The other happy thing was that some of the walking wounded from Plugstreet were returning and that helped to cheer everybody up.

The respite was brief, however. Less than two months later they were moved up to assist the BEF with an attack further into Belgium and back towards Ypres, at a place called Sanctuary Wood near Mont Sorrel.

Ewan's unit was spared direct involvement in that attack, which is just as well because they were still badly mauled from the earlier battle. The 1st and 3rd divisions took the brunt though, the 3rd even had their general killed. Apparently they didn't all sit in their chateaus drinking wine while their men bled on the battlefield.

After that, they were pulled out of the line properly. All of the Canadian units were coming together as a single entity, the Canadian Corps. They even acquired a fourth division in August.

Ewan felt the first stirrings of his identity as a Canadian. Before this, when he thought about it at all, he thought of himself as a Scot who happened to live in Canada. Somehow he still had at the back of his mind that this was all just temporary (except Morag of course!) and that eventually he'd go home to Fort William. But more and more he thought of Halifax as his home, and he longed to get back to it.

But in the meantime, they had a war to win and that would only happen in France. For the next three months they were able to let their collective breaths out and regain their strength. Once again, the MacKenzie Battalion was a fully equipped fighting unit. By the end of the summer they all had their tin hats and their smellys.

By September, the entire division was ready to go. The enthusiasm of two years before was still there but now it was tempered by hard won battle experience. There was now a pride gained from that experience.

In July, a big battle had started to their south, around the River Somme. They could hear the guns pounding almost continuously, and they were hearing rumours that they were to be part of this battle. They couldn't believe that it would last that long though, it had been going on for nearly two months already.

There were mixed feelings about that. There was fear that they would miss the battle and an almost equal fear that they wouldn't. Some had heard that their neighbours from across the Cabot Strait, the Blue Puttees of Newfoundland, had been wiped out on the first day of that battle, but no-one really believed that. Did they?

They moved up to a little French village called Pozières where they repaired the existing defences and helped build new ones. Ewan and his pioneers were busy re-laying wire and rebuilding trenches and building drainage systems for when the rains came back. They had no idea how long they'd be in this position.

Then the colonel came and told them that they would be joining the great battle after all. This, he said, was the battle that would break the back of the Hun and end the war by Christmas. They'd heard it all before; this would be the third Christmas that it was all supposed to be over by after all. But they cheered anyway because that's what soldiers do before they go into battle.

At 0600 on the morning of September 15, a cold but clear morning, no rain and no mud, a wondrous omen everyone thought, the whistles blew and for the second time Ewan and his friends went over the top and into hell.

CHAPTER 8

HALIFAX 1916

*
**

Before the war Morag used to rely on the twins, Anika and Agathe, when she needed any help around the shop, either Ewan's or her Da's, but now with them in an internment camp, along with her friend Rebecca, she didn't have that help anymore. And seeing that she had twins of her own now, she certainly could use the help.

She only had the one shop to worry about now but Hamish and Mairi certainly made up the difference in trouble and mischief. Only a few months old and they were already trying to outdo each other in volume and odour! Mairi was winning on the odour side but Hamish more than held his own in volume.

There were always two great pots on the old Aga stove, one with a perpetual stew and the other with boiling nappies. You certainly didn't want to get the two mixed up!

On this day, she had left her Da in charge and had gone into Dartmouth, across the bay, looking for a double perambulator that she'd heard was available over there.

She found the shop that had the pram in question, purchased it and started back home.

On her way back to the ferry she thought she saw a lad, a teenager maybe, sneak into a butcher's shop across the street. This was a quiet part of Dartmouth with very few people about at this time of day, so she went to investigate. She remembered Peter's tale of the lad at the dock when Elsa and the girls arrived who had slashed the policeman's throat. He had never been caught so she was very cautious.

She crept up to the door, which was open and stuck her head just inside the door jamb. There was an inner door, which was closed, so she stopped there for a minute. She heard sounds of chopping coming from the back of the shop and figured the butcher was back there preparing meat for sale.

At that moment the inner door burst open and this streak of pink and brown charged out of the shop and straight into Morag.

With an almighty crash she and the pink streak fell to the ground in a heap. The noise didn't travel into the back apparently because the sounds of chopping continued uninterrupted.

Morag recovered her wits first and stood up to look at what had hit her. It was a person, a boy she thought at first because it was wearing boy's clothes and was filthy. But when the hat fell off, revealing long, blonde, scruffy and tangled hair, she realised it was a girl.

A little taken aback Morag said to the girl, "What the devil were you doing in there lassy?" with a slight edge to her voice because she didn't think the girl was up to any good.

"*Je m'excuse, madame*, I am very 'ungry, I just wanted some food … anyt'ing." Pleaded the frightened young girl. A girl who looked to be in her late teens, though it was hard to tell under all the baggy clothing and grime.

"Well, ye canna be stealin' other people's things, that's just wrong!" she reasoned.

"But I 'ave no money, no way to pay, and I am starving!" she said.

"Alright, alright, let's have a look at you." Morag said with an appraising voice. What she saw once she took a closer look was a girl, a young woman really, who was about 5'9", slim judging by her face with long blonde hair and who sounded French. More detail would have to wait until she was cleaned up. When Morag thought that last thought she realised that she was going to help this girl. A girl not that different from herself, only a few years younger, who needed all the help she could get.

"Right, come back with me to the Halifax side and we'll figure out what to do with you." She had decided.

"*Oui madame, merci beaucoup!*" the girl was overjoyed.

On the way back, Morag discovered that her English was better than she had let on, she had just reverted to French because she was stressed. She was nineteen and her name was Antoinette Langlois, but she went by Toni, and she had been on what she called a "white slave ship" that arrived in Halifax a while ago, she didn't know how long. She had stolen some of the sailor's clothes and jumped ship along with a number of other girls when it docked in Halifax. She said that she had been so frightened and so stressed that she took a knife from the galley and when a policeman had tried to stop her she had reacted and lashed out at him with the knife. When she saw blood she panicked and ran for the harbour to get away.

So, she had been Peter's "young lad" at the dock, with Elsa and the girls.

"But that was five years ago, you can't have been alone all this time, surely?" Morag was incredulous.

"No, I 'ave not been alone, for the first while I stayed with the nuns at the Catholic church, but they tried to … to … 'ave dere way wid me … so I ran away. Next, I stayed with a nice German family but when the war came they were interned, so now I am on my own. I live wherever I can find shelter, and I do odd jobs for food … or … or I steal it. I am 'ungry most of the time." Her depression and shame were clear.

The rest of the trip back to the tannery was silent, Morag wondering what to do with this scared girl. Toni was just grateful that she was safe for a while.

At the tannery, Morag introduced Toni to her Da, giving him a quick explanation of what happened and why she was there.

Morag gave her some food, which she devoured like a ravenous wolf.

"Poor wee lassie, isn't there enough sadness in this world to go around? So, she's a refugee then?" he asked.

"I guess, in a manner of speaking she is, though she came here before the war," Morag replied.

"Why did you come here? What got you on that ship?" he asked frankly.

"I am from Lorraine, the French part of Germany, and I was arrested for calling the Kaiser a pig in front of a German policeman. 'e did not take too kindly to dat and arrested me for treason!" Toni lamented.

"But that's insane! You're French … the French insult the Kaiser all the time."

"Ah, but officially I am German, which is why I was on that Boche ship. The magistrate didn't go for the treason thing but convicted me as a 'trouble maker' anyway and put me on that ship. *Merde!*" she ended with feeling.

"Well, what are we going to do with her?" Morag asked her Da. "We can't just put her back on the street!"

"Can you work, lassie?" Sean asked the girl, "Are you used to hard work?"

"Since I've been in Halifax I've done everything from scrub floors and toilets to muck out stables and pigsties. Before I left Germany, I lived on a farm run by an orphanage. My parents were killed in a fire when I was only five, so I have no memory of them," was the matter of fact answer.

"Well, that certainly qualifies as hard work," he said with a certain amount of surprise. "Most of my lads have gone off to the war so I'm very short-handed right now and getting more work all the time. If you want a job … you're hired. And I dare say Morag can use some help wi' the bairns. Where are they by the way?"

"Where are they, he says … fine babysitter you are!" At that moment Morag wheeled Hamish and Mairi into the shop in their brand new double pram, all three looking proud as punch.

Morag gave Toni a bar of soap and a towel and pointed her in the direction of the bath tub. "You might want to make yourself look like a girl again, Toni! Here are some more appropriate clothes too."

Three quarters of an hour later both Morag and Sean were stunned when the door opened again and in walked this woman who lit up the room. Toni had transformed like a dirty brown caterpillar turning into the most gorgeous butterfly you can imagine. She was fully 5'9" and slim with the most incredible head of flowing blonde tresses. Her freshly scrubbed pink face was narrow with high cheeks and her complexion was so unblemished and white as to be almost translucent. Her figure was a perfect hour glass shape with wide hips. Her breasts were firm and well-rounded but not overly large, and she had an athletic build overall, from growing up on a farm no doubt.

A bit on the thin side, but that came from being hungry all the time.

It was clear that she would be popular with what boys were left in Halifax.

*
**

Soon Toni was such a fixture around there that she and Morag had become best of friends. They were only three years apart. She began to assume more and more responsibility for looking after the workings in the tannery, while Morag ran the business side and looked after the books. Sean was finally able to slow down and catch his breath a little, after many years of struggle.

Toni looked after the twins when Morag had errands to run, and she turned out to be an amazing cook. She was able to do much with the smaller quantities of food that they had.

All in all, it had been a very happy accident to have, literally, run into this stunning young woman. Somehow Morag had a feeling that Toni would turn out to be a very valuable asset indeed. Second sight? Maybe. The feeling persisted at any rate.

CHAPTER 9

VERDUN 1916

*
**

After that unnerving meeting with Ewan in his dugout in February, Peter thought long and hard about what he was doing. He had come back to Germany to fight the Russians, to keep them away from the Fatherland and from his people and his family, and now, two years later he found himself not only fighting with his friends but also against them. It didn't make any sense at all.

He tried to rationalize it all but was too tired and fatigued to put much thought into it right then.

His unit was pulled back for a well-deserved rest, to a quiet area where they could, once again, regain their strength before inevitably moving back into the trenches to fight whoever was next.

The German army had been receiving a severe mauling from the French in the Verdun sector. They had given as good as they got but they had still haemorrhaged blood in the form of many fine and brave soldiers. They were particularly short of experienced combat officers, so Peter was transferred to a unit which had been decimated by the French Artillery at a place ominously called Le Mort Homme, meaning 'Dead Man's Hill'.

What Peter took charge of was a unit that had been a full strength infantry company of 250 men only two months before but was now reduced to barely seventy-five effectives with only two being officers, both ensigns still in their teens who shouldn't even have been at the front.

But, as he knew, the heart of a fighting unit was its NCOs. He had half a dozen good sergeants and nearly a dozen good corporals. With that he could build an army.

So, he set to with a will and within another two months he had rebuilt his new company to its former strength. Only half of the reinforcements were raw recruits and the other half were veterans of other units that had been reconstituted from those bloodied by the Russians on the Eastern front.

They finally turned in their Pickelhaube and received their new Stahlhelm, which they all thought was too heavy and got in the way of everything. That would soon change.

By the 30th of June there was a lull in the battle, the German assaults had worn themselves out with casualties into the hundreds of thousands.

On July 5, Peter's company, part of the 140th Infantry Regiment moved into the area northeast of Fleury where they could see Fort Souville. He guessed, correctly as it turned out, that this would be their objective.

They took over an existing trench and set to work repairing and improving the defences, adding machine guns and wire and more modern communications not knowing how long they'd be in this position. Doing what infantry always did when they move into a new location … they dug in.

They were not there very long, as it turned out, because on July 9, the German artillery tried to obliterate the fort. They blasted the surrounding defences with everything they had, including gas.

Peter figured that this was the preliminary bombardment before the assault, and the next day he was proved right once again.

A runner came to his dugout, "Major Baum, sir! Major Baum!" stammered the over excited corporal. "The Oberst wants to see you immediately, sir." If he had snapped any more rigidly to attention he would have broken his back.

"Tell him I'll be right there." He turned to his sergeant-major, "This is it Kurt, this'll be the orders for the assault tomorrow, get the men ready, they know what to do by now."

"Yes, sir" said Feldwebel Kurt Langer. "Don't worry, sir, they'll be ready," giving him a smart salute.

"I know they will, Kurt, I'll be back soon." And with that he went to the CO's bunker.

"Peter!" said Oberst ter Horst in a jovial mood, "How are you my boy?" Oberst Johann ter Horst was a friendly giant of a man from Lower Saxony who was in temporary command of the 140th. He was happy because he was going to lead troops into battle for the very first time. You could tell it was his first time because he was happy. Veterans were never this happy going into an area that some called 'the two-way rifle range'. It wasn't that he was incompetent or too sure of himself it was just that he was inexperienced and that could get people killed easier than accurate machine gun fire.

"Good morning Herr Oberst, why so happy this morning?" Though Peter knew full well why.

"Because my boy, I will be leading you fine men right into Fort Souville through the front gate!" he was fairly gushing with excitement.

Peter knew that as the senior company commander it would fall on him to get the boys out of trouble faster than the well-meaning but over confident Oberst could get them into it.

"I'll be right behind you all the way, sir," Peter replied. 'In order to keep an eye on you' he didn't say.

Early the next morning the barrage stopped, and they knew it would be time to go. Whistles blew, and sergeants yelled, and soldiers walked, calmly at first, towards Fort Souville.

What Peter didn't know was that three German divisions were converging on the only route into the fort, a route which had been zeroed in by the French artillery just waiting for such an opportunity.

His company was one of the leading elements of the attack, facing directly at the fort, but so was everyone else, and it was this conversion that led to the slaughter that ensued when the French artillery opened fire and effectively destroyed all three divisions in a matter of minutes.

Those in the lead were spared the worst of the destruction but there were still explosions and flame and smoke and all manner of steel fragments … and pieces of human flesh turning the very air into a vast pink cloud of insanity and death.

One of the first to die was Oberst ter Horst who, true to his word, was leading his men from the very front. But then a French shell landed about ten metres in front of him, and he ran right into the blast and … ceased to exist. No part of him was ever found.

And true to his word, Peter was about thirty metres behind and to the right of him and saw the flash that left him in command of the whole battalion. A piece of shrapnel from the same round, or maybe a piece of Oberst ter Horst, smashed into the front of his new Stahlhelm and left a large dent. Peter would later reflect that that piece would have gone straight through a leather Pickelhaube and counted himself lucky.

They couldn't retreat because he now saw that French machine gunners were manning the parapets of the fort, the approaches to which they had covered with their guns and were reducing the survivors of the artillery barrage into an almost liquid mass of humanity trying to go in every direction at once.

So, the only way was forward. Only a small group of about forty or fifty men could hear him scream, "*Forward men, the fort is ours for the taking, on me!*" and with that the Viking berserker of other battles was back again.

Peter drew his Mauser C96 and screamed a Viking battle cry as he charged the parapet of the fort. He was completely possessed by the bloodlust of battle, gone were his doubts about why they were here, this was now, this was just him and his berserkers charging into Valhalla!

The French were only just realising that some Germans had made it into the fort and were slow to react. Peter rushed at three of them, shot two and then shoved his C96 into the mouth of the third and shot him. His pistol was empty at that point and he grabbed the Lebel rifle that the man had. He noticed that it had a sword bayonet on it but still managed to shoot three more French soldiers before he was too close to reload and used the bayonet. The next man he stabbed in the side and fired the rifle to extract the bayonet. The last he took in the eye, and the bayonet stuck in the back of his skull.

But then he was through, he had made it to the peak of the hill that the fort was on and he stopped. All around him his men were also in a berserker blood rage and were reaching the top with him. About thirty men all told made it to the top from which they could clearly see the spires of the cathedral in Verdun … they had made it, they were there.

Peter quickly realised, though, that their position was untenable, and he came to the reluctant conclusion that they must retreat or be overwhelmed by a French counter-attack that he knew must be coming.

So they hastily withdrew back to where they had started from only a very few minutes before.

Peter was at the rear of his battalion conducting an organized rear-guard as they made a tactical retreat through the growing French resistance. He was everywhere, orchestrating the shoring up of gaps in the battalion's flanks as it moved back to its start line, still managing to kill four more French soldiers on the way back through their frontline.

He was shocked to find that so very few of his friends and comrades had made it back with him. And even more shocked to find himself virtually unscathed, only a couple of light wounds.

Recognising that only Peter and his small band of berserkers had made it to the top of the fort in a spectacular fashion, the real commander of the 140th, who had been in Berlin at that time, Oberst Karl-Heinz Richter recommended Peter for the Pour le Mérite, the coveted Blue Max. Once the Kaiser read the citation it was confirmed.

Thus, Peter Baum, onetime Jewish cooper from Hamburg via Glasgow and Halifax was now a member of the order of the Pour le Mérite … The Blue Max.

CHAPTER 10

THE SOMME 1916

*
**

There was rain all right … steel rain … and smoke and noise and blood and all the, almost normalised, horror of battle.

The MacKenzie Battalion's immediate goal was to capture a German trench about 150 yards to their front, just like every battalion's goal in every battle of the Great War.

By 1916, very few men still held the illusion that this would be easy, or even likely. They would be happy just to survive the day.

Ewan almost didn't survive that day, again, just like every soldier in every battle of the War to end all Wars.

His company of the 25th advanced through no man's land quicker than their friends on the flanks because someone had to be faster, and this time it was them.

Ewan found himself in the lead of his platoon, as was normal for him and as a good leader should be. This is what almost got him killed. True enough, he had almost been killed every time he left the relative safety of their own trenches, but this time was different. This time it was one of his own that almost killed him. Not on purpose mind, this lad had simply had enough; he was going home and that was all there was to it.

Pte Albert Jones wasn't a coward, he wasn't weak, he wasn't even sick, he was simply done. Artillery fire can do that to a person. It can deafen you, it can shake you, it can rattle you, it can burn you, it can bury you. It can violently remove parts of your body, and it can even make you cease to exist by tearing the component molecules of your entire body apart so that nothing is left.

But it can also shatter the mind in such a way that even though there is no blood and no obvious wound the mind is just as destroyed as if a whizz-bang had exploded the moment it penetrated the skull.

This was the fate of twenty-two-year-old Albert Jones of Winnipeg, Manitoba who had joined the army, partly for a lark, partly because he *thought* it was his duty, partly because he was *told* it was his duty but mostly to impress Eliza Miller also from Winnipeg, from the same community, the same school and even worked in the same factory as Albert. He was completely smitten by her, although her only remarkable feature, other than large breasts, was her explosion of red hair, which made her face glow like an early morning sunrise. That and the fact that she had told him she would only sleep with him if he won a medal in France, had sealed his fate.

Albert had been one of the first out of their trench, once again there has to be a first. He was the first into no man's land, and he was the first to reach the German trench. He had moved so fast in fact that he had run into their own barrage before it had lifted.

He arrived at the parapet of the trench less than a second after the Canadian shell landed on the rear edge. It went so deep into the ground that when it detonated it lifted that entire section of trench and everything in it, including Albert Jones, twenty feet in the air. What saved young Albert's life was the German soldier who was standing in the trench at that moment trying to un-jam his Spandau machine gun. He took the brunt of the explosion and ceased to exist. What destroyed Albert's mind was seeing this happen in combination with the explosion itself. In about a quarter of a second this exploded his mind and sent him into an insane wide-eyed screaming charge back towards the Canadian trench still clutching his rifle with its foot and a half long sword bayonet on the end.

This is when Ewan came through a shell hole only to see the business end of Albert's bayonet entering his chest. He was so stunned by this that he didn't even notice that the man was wearing the same uniform and he reacted as any soldier would, he smashed him across the face with his rifle knocking him cold. The bayonet with the rifle still attached was sticking right through his upper left chest, just below the shoulder, effectively pinning him to the shell hole, like an insect in a museum collection.

The attack went on around him for what seemed like hours but was only a few minutes. The trench was taken pending any counter attacks and reinforcements with stretcher bearers came forward picking up any wounded along the way. Ewan and Albert were both picked up and moved back to a Regimental Aid Station in the rear Canadian trench.

Ewan was not that badly hurt, the blade had missed any major arteries and had done minimal damage to the muscle. A good rest behind the lines would do him good anyway. What kept going through his mind though was, why had he been stabbed by a man wearing his own uniform? What had made him do that? Had he gone over to the enemy? That seemed unlikely. Had he just been going the wrong way? It's easy enough to get turned around in the heat of battle. Was he a coward and running away? That seemed the easy explanation but anyone who has been on the receiving end of artillery fire and seen this much blood and death doesn't believe that. More likely he had just snapped, and the shell shock had turned him into a man possessed.

The higher ups didn't think that way though. What they knew was that a coward had stabbed one of their best soldiers with a bayonet, almost killing him and that an example must be made.

Three days later, after he had recovered most of his wits, Private Albert Jones of Winnipeg Manitoba was stood up against a wall with a small slip of paper pinned over his heart, and he too ceased to exist.

*
**

Ewan couldn't put Albert out of his mind. He went through the events of that day over and over again. Could he have done anything different … *would* he have done anything different? Would it have mattered? What if that had been him? What if that had been one of his own men? Would he have stood up for him? Would that have mattered?

He understood that discipline had to be maintained especially in the face of what these men were expected to do for their king and empire. But could normal, patriotic, young men who had a lapse of their senses be held to task for that and then be shot as an example?

Ewan knew that everyone had their limit, that eventually he too would snap. There had been times where he had found himself cowering in the corner of a dugout during one of Jerries bombardments. Everyone did, was that cowardice?

If so, then they were an army of cowards, everyone just a whizz-bang away from a firing squad.

And with those thoughts fresh in his head Ewan went to the rear to heal his body and, eventually, his mind.

The rent in his shoulder healed quickly and cleanly, he was still young and fit, and his mind healed too, though more slowly because it is a complicated organ made of more than just flesh and blood.

He re-joined the 25th three months later, a little wiser and a little more aware of things and people around him. Just in time to miss the battle for Regina Trench, which saw more good men die for little gain.

But just in time for Christmas. Once again spent in a barn in a field in northern France. Little different from the barn in Belgium that they'd spent Christmas 1915 in.

Still a barn is better than a trench any day of the week. He wondered which poor buggers got that joy to look forward to. There were no more football matches or Christmas carols with Jerry in no man's land, the Brass gave him a present instead, several tons of high explosive and steel just to prove that we are, in fact, fighting a war and you jolly well shan't enjoy yourselves, hang it all.

The men, on the other hand, *were* enjoying themselves as best they could. They were playing football, both kinds, and baseball, and singing carols, though not with Jerry, and doing the best they could to forget where they were and why they were there. The Dumbbells came by and gave everyone a good cheering up.

God knows they needed it.

For the most part it worked. Ewan was learning about how fast the twins were growing and how much they loved their Auntie Toni. He had thought that Toni was a lad's name, but times were changing so who knew?

Sean was growing the tannery by leaps and bounds. People were accusing him of being a war profiteer, but he had a skill, was too old to fight and the army needed the leather so what was the harm in making some money too? Apparently 'Toni' was being endless help … there was that name again.

Some men, of course, got bad news: their mother had died, or their brother was killed at the battle of Jutland or the Somme, or their sister had died of the flu. But even these reminders of home helped to restore some level of normalcy to the hellish nightmare that was France and Belgium in the second decade of the twentieth century.

Christmas became New Year … 1917 … surely this would be the last year of this madness, of this nightmarish slaughter, though no-one was saying it out loud. Surely the powers that be, on both sides would realise that they were bleeding a whole generation white. If it lasted too much longer there would be no men left.

One other nice thing about the winter was that the fighting was generally limited to a few trench raids, some desultory shelling, and the inevitable snipers. But this far back from the frontline you could barely hear the shelling, and if you were lucky enough you could pretend it was thunder and forget that with every thunderclap some poor bastard was getting torn limb from limb.

CHAPTER 11

ARRAS 1917 – I

*
* *

The downside to being awarded the Blue Max was the fame or, more accurately the notoriety that went with it.

After the award, things changed for Peter and he was not sure it was for the better. He was promoted to Oberst Leutnant and given command of his own battalion, but it was some months before he got to see it, he hadn't even been told which one it was yet. So he spent much of the rest of 1916 touring the cities of Germany giving speeches about the inevitable victory of the Fatherland and of the German Volk. He did his duty, he lied to the people with all the eloquence he had acquired over the years in the cooperage in Hamburg and the manufacturing shop in Halifax. For the thousandth time he wondered if he would ever see Halifax or Ewan or the others again.

He was very young for this honour, he was still only twenty-six and there were many older officers who were still not even Majors yet, let alone battalion commanders with a Blue Max. There was certainly some jealousy and envy but there was far more adulation and respect from all quarters, not least from the feminine quarter. He had more than one 'invitation' from a fraulein or two to keep them warm in the long winter nights ahead. It didn't hurt that he was also a fine looking young lad. At this point, he insisted that Elsa accompany him on his tour because, he hoped, having a wife who was much prettier than most of these girls would deter some of them. Also, she was just as eloquent as he was, having run the shop in Halifax almost single handed, and that in a foreign language to boot!

They were a big success. Who could resist a handsome, highly decorated war hero and his beautiful bride?

He also got to spend Christmas at home with Elsa and his uncle Joe again, which was a bigger reward than the, "damned spiky medal, always sticking me in the throat whenever I bend my head." He groused about it all the time, but always with a twinkle in his eye.

Peter and Elsa spent the entire month he was home joined at the hip. During the days he would put on civilian clothes and they would explore the markets and the shops and the hills around Hamburg as he hadn't done since he was a boy, showing Elsa all his favourite places and all his secret hiding spots.

At night they would reunite in the most blissful ways imaginable.

*
**

They spent as happy a Christmas as was possible under the circumstances, laughing and loving and living with a fierce intensity as if their very lives depended on it.

But with an inevitability, like night following day, their time together came to an end with an emotional intensity that neither of them had ever experienced before. The unspoken dread almost overwhelmed them. He had to return to France. It was a sombre parting, as they always were because they didn't know if they'd see each other again. Neither said it but the looks on their faces spoke volumes.

Peter returned to France at the end of January 1917, he had been given command of a rebuilt battalion in the 263rd Reserve Infantry Regiment of the 79th Reserve Division. They had been badly cut up in Russia over the past two years and had come to France to rebuild. In a sense he was coming home. This was a Bavarian Division, and he had served with many good men from Bavaria. His own uncle Joe had been born in Munich.

He was introduced to his staff, his adjutant was a Prussian career officer, Major Fritz Weber, thirty-nine, who fit the stereotype perfectly, all he lacked was the duelling scar on his cheek. He was a supremely competent man, the only reason he wasn't a battalion commander somewhere else was his complete lack of imagination, but he thrived on paperwork, which was a godsend to a combat commander. His four company commanders were, like him, very young but all hardened combat veterans who had been in the thick of it right from 1914. Major Otto Langmann, twenty-nine, was from Munich and had been a school teacher before the war, he had been lightly wounded at Ypres in a gas attack early in 1915 but had fully recovered. Major Hans Lechter, thirty, was from Ragensburg and had commanded a company against the Russians before having his command decimated by Russian shell fire. He was out to prove to himself that this decimation hadn't been his fault. Major Rolph Schmidt was the youngest at just twenty-six, he was from Augsburg and had been second in command of a company at Verdun and had received the Iron Cross 1st Class for an assault on a bunker complex at Fort Douaumont. And Hauptmann Jan Frieden was the oldest of the group at an ancient thirty-one years old, he was the Machine Gun Company commander. He was built like a bull, not very agile but had a quick tactical mind so he was perfect for designing defences and siting machine guns, etc.

These gentlemen had all been facing him in a semi-circle when he walked into the room, trying desperately not to stare at the Blue Max and the Iron Cross around his neck. There had been another man standing to the side, which he had assumed to be the Regimental Sergeant Major. When he turned to face him, the blood drained from his face and his eyes popped wide open, metaphorically speaking at least. Standing before him was Senior Sergeant Johan Becker late of the Hamburg Police Force.

Keeping it together was a supreme act of will. He would tackle any hill while in a Viking berserker fog but to stand in front of this man while completely calm and not show any emotion took a massive effort.

"Ah, Sergeant Becker, we meet again!" he said, cautiously, not knowing how Becker would react.

"Yes sir, it has been a while," came the blank reply.

Taking the bull by the horns, Peter turned to the assembled officers who were looking at each other quizzically, he said "Sergeant Becker and I first met in Hamburg before the war when he was a policeman and I was a criminal!" Peter laughed.

The quizzical looks only intensified. Fortunately, Becker took his cue and said, "Yes, I was supposed to arrest Herr Baum for murder!" He, too, laughed, "but the charges were trumped up." The concept of murder was almost a joke among men who had, themselves, killed many men.

And with that the ice was broken, and they could get down to business.

That business was forming a fully functional combat ready battalion of about a thousand men from a group of what were, essentially, children.

As before, he knew the key to a successful battalion was the NCO cadre and its relationship with the junior officers in the companies. If this meshed then they would be effective, if it didn't then they were doomed.

Discipline in the German army had drifted since the early days of 1914 when it had been a largely experienced army of highly motivated volunteers to, only three years later, a group of civilians in uniform who mostly were called-up reservists or conscripts. But somehow this worked, much like a purebred dog is prone to many illnesses and genetic defects whereas a multi breed mutt is generally more healthy and happy, so too the new German army had moulded itself into a supremely effective fighting machine by merging all the skills of the civilian world with the raw talent and energy of youth.

Holding the whole group together were enough veterans and professional soldiers who acted like the cement in concrete, binding the stones and sand together in a solid matrix that is stronger than the sum of its parts.

Years later, Peter would reflect on this time as the most fulfilling in his entire time in the army. He was surrounded by highly motivated and supremely focussed individuals who were not so much like the links in a chain but more like the links in mail armour. In a chain if one link broke the whole failed but in chain mail the strength was maintained even if a few links were broken. This is how combat units fight.

Peter was in his element, bringing in soldiers from across the army, from recruit depots, to convalescent hospitals and from battle schools to reconstituted units. He ordered stores for a battalion, including uniforms and equipment and weapons and horses and ammunition and pay and rations and bedding and transport and the list went on and on. Fritz Weber came into his own now, organizing all the paperwork in triplicate and quadruplicate for all this was what he lived for.

Planning and organizing training became more and more intricate as weapons and tactics evolved. The British had designed a new type of weapon that could breech trenches. It was called the "tank" and was basically a steel pillbox mounted on a tractor chassis, which could simply cross over a trench while protecting the crew inside with armour plate. A brilliant invention for which tactics had to be developed and practised to counter it and many hours were spent in this endeavour.

If only Germany could master the concept of the tank, they would rule the world …

*
**

It was while he was building up his battalion that he got a letter from Elsa telling him that he was going to be a father. His happiness was complete. Professionally and personally this was bliss.

Of course, all good things must come to an end and at the beginning of March they were told they were moving back to the frontline. Peter felt his men were as ready as they would ever be and so he was happy to go.

They were going to take up a position on a small hill in the Douai area near a small village close to Lens called Vimy.

CHAPTER 12
HALIFAX SPRING 1917

*
**

"Toni! Can you come here for a moment please, lass?" Sean called.

"Oui, Monsieur Sean," replied the young French girl happily.

"Oh, for heaven's sake girl, it's just Sean," he said for the umpteenth time.

"Oui, mister Sean … err … I mean … Sean," she was getting flustered again. Toni still hadn't fully come to terms with her newfound happiness. It had now been a full year since she had been found by Morag and she was, by now, a full-fledged member of the MacBride clan. And a fulltime nanny, cook and floor manager in the tannery. She had indeed come a long way.

Sean needed her to review an order for material for halters. It was for an order of large wagons that were being made ready to ship to France. Each wagon needed eight cart horses and there were sixteen wagons being readied and that was a considerable amount of leather. He wanted Toni to confirm his figures before he finished his estimate. She had proved to be an invaluable asset to the business both in the tannery and in the office. Morag still ran the business as a whole, and she still ran the household with an iron fist (and a wink), as she always had done but Toni was her much valued right hand … man … as it were.

Morag came in then and announced that they were all going to a ceilidh at a local Scottish pub where there were lots of boys about to ship off to France and who deserved a good sendoff. Plus, she hoped that Toni would meet someone like her Ewan though she kept that part to herself. It was that Saturday at seven o'clock sharp, best bib and tucker and don't be late.

In the event Sean begged off because he was feeling tired. He was 'feeling tired' a lot lately and Morag was vaguely worried about that. But for the moment she left him with the twins, who were almost walking. They were sure to cheer him up. The two girls were able to go out dancing like they seldom could.

Morag was meeting some friends there, so she and Toni joined them. The two other girls were from the fair grounds and had been friends of Anika and Agathe in happier times. Sheila was one year older than Morag, so twenty-four, her husband had been lost at sea in one of the early convoys to England. Elizabeth was one year younger and her beau was in France fighting in an artillery unit.

Sheila and Liz were just about as good looking as Morag and Toni, well maybe not as pretty as Toni. They didn't have incredible blonde hair, but the four of them were a prime attraction at the ceilidh. Morag showed the others how to do some Scottish dancing.

They danced with the lads in uniform, trying to make them feel appreciated before going off to war. They ate the food provided by the Red Cross, they sampled the wine and whisky provided by the pub. They danced with the lads, and they danced with each other, and they danced with some of the other girls.

And they generally had a good time. It was a moment away from the war for them too.

Until, that is, some of the lads heading to France decided they wanted more attention from the girls. Attention of the horizontal kind. They had singled out Toni as their particular target and were making a real nuisance of themselves.

"Bugger off, ye bloody eejits," Morag said with some venom in it, she had just about enough of their lewd suggestions and gestures. "Can ye no behave better than that when ye're about to go and defend yer country?"

"And how should we behave, missus?" asked one of the louder and bolder ones.

"Like gentlemen and soldiers! Not like uncouth hooligans that's for bloody sure," she was getting heated now and that isn't a good combination for a fiery-haired lass from the lowlands.

"Is that right then? And just who the bloody hell do you think you are then?" This lad wasn't getting the hint.

"I'm the one that's telling you to bugger off." She held her ground like a regiment making a heroic last stand.

"*Oui, tu petit cochon!*" came the surprising reinforcement from Toni, who was coming out of her shell more and more these days.

"Oh, a frog eh? A pretty little froggy too, look at the talking frog, lads!"

"*Sale porc. Va te faire foutre!*" Toni was getting heated too.

"Listen to them pretty words boys, I wonder if she can speak through her cunny just like all them other French sluts?"

"Right, that's enough of that you stupid arses, get away from us!" Morag had had enough. "Either you bugger off right now or I'll call the police!"

"Fine, you little sluts couldn't handle us real lads anyways, yer too stuck up. Right lads, let's get out of here" and with that the ringleader led them away.

Morag turned to Toni and said. "Well, that was quite the display from our country's finest, I hope they straighten themselves up before they meet the Boche, in France, or they'll be in for a short war!" Morag was indignant now. "I must say you stood up for yourself pretty well Toni, I haven't seen that side of you before! I'm a little impressed, I must say!"

Sheila and Liz piped up at this point, they had stayed well out of it up 'til then, "Yeah, that was bloody brilliant Toni, I don't want to know what you said to them but whatever it was it seemed to work, bravo!" said Sheila.

"Too true, luv," chimed in Liz, "I couldn't have put it better myself!"

"Oh, I 'ave dealt with little pipsqueaks like zat in France … and Germany before, why should not the British 'ave such gentlemen too?" Toni was calming down now but still agitated.

"You're right there, more's the pity, every land has such 'gentlemen' I expect," said Sheila.

"They were all bloody drunk too," Morag added. "Well, I don't know about you but that's killed the mood for me, besides it's one o'clock in the morning! It's time we left, ladies."

The others all agreed and so they said their goodbyes and wished the departing lads well and then left by the front door of the pub.

Their good moods returned quickly because they were young and generally happy and full of the joy of life that couldn't be destroyed by the news of war that was ever present. Or even by a bunch of drunken louts who just didn't know any better.

The night was a beautiful spring night without a breath of wind and warm for late February. And the stars were out in force. Because of the blackout they were able to see the Milky Way in all its glory, it fairly lit up the night sky for their walk home.

They hadn't gone two blocks from the pub when someone rushed out of an alley, grabbed Toni by those beautiful flowing blonde locks and dragged her into the alley. Morag was quick to respond and went after her. The other girls were a little slower but were only a few yards behind.

The attacker had gotten Toni onto the ground and had almost ripped her dress right off her body and was trying to get into her brassiere and knickers. The three other men joined in and one of them helped to hold Toni down while the first continued to try and molest her and beat her. The other two held the other girls at bay while the attacker carried on with his assault.

It was at this point that Morag recognized the ringleader from the pub from just a few minutes previously and screamed, "*Help, help, rape! Police! Police!*" Within seconds, or so it seemed, help arrived in the form of two burly Halifax policemen. They had been making sure the ceilidh didn't get out of hand and were on the lookout for just such an incident.

They waded in with their truncheons and billy clubs and in short order had cold cocked the two blockers and had laid out the one helping the ringleader assault poor Toni.

The ringleader had succeeded in prying one of Toni's breasts out of her bra and was fondling it, all the while reaching under what was left of her dress to get his hand into her knickers to try to rip them off. One of the young policemen punched the would-be rapist in the side of the head, which just had the effect of shifting his focus from the loudly hysterical Toni to the thing that had hurt him. At least Toni was free though and Morag was instantly at her side helping her to get her clothes together, with Sheila and Liz in close support.

The cop and the soldier were fighting it out, while the other cop was busy restraining the remaining thugs before they woke up and caused more havoc. The policeman, being younger and fitter … and sober, quickly got the better of the thug, however. Once the second cop was free he distracted the man and the first was able to wrestle him to the ground and pin him. Sheila and Liz waded in like pros and helped make short work of the bastard.

The whole incident had taken less than five minutes from start to finish. It left all the girls a crying mess, especially poor Toni who was still traumatized and shaking with emotion.

Morag recovered first and surveyed the scene around her. What she saw made her blood boil. She saw four thugs, she no longer thought of them as soldiers, laid out like fish on the cobbles of the alley, all bleeding from superficial wounds, and in the process of being trussed up like the Christmas goose by the larger of the two cops. He was a well-built lad, about fifteen or sixteen stone, and tall, close to six feet. No wonder he had dealt with these louts as quickly as he had.

She then saw her three friends, all now huddled in a group trying to bring some sense of life back to Toni.

The cop who had dealt with the attempted rapist was a small, slender lad, about five foot eight or nine, and about twelve stone or so but obviously very fit and wiry. She saw that he was a good-looking lad with classical English features, dark brown, short cropped hair and blue eyes. In fact, he made Morag blush with guilt for sparking something in her, which she quickly extinguished.

The only thing that marred his good looks was a scar right across his throat. There was probably a good story there. Morag didn't yet put two and two together.

*
**

Alan Fairford for his part had been patrolling with his partner, Jack Simpson, around MacTavish's pub during and after the ceilidh. They were always on the lookout for troublemakers at these kinds of events.

When you mix soldiers, alcohol, and pretty girls together the results weren't always what was hoped. They saw a group of four such girls leave the pub at around one thirty or so. They were obviously a little worse for wear with the alcohol themselves, and they decided to follow them, discretely, to make sure they got home all right. They were exactly the kind of target some unscrupulous bastards might prey on if they were in their cups and needing some home comfort before going off to France. He particularly noticed one very beautiful girl among them who had gorgeous blonde hair.

Just as he was admiring her hair and her shape and was wondering how he could get to meet her without looking inappropriate as a policeman, something, or someone, rushed out of an alley and grabbed the girl and started dragging her behind the building. Then three more somethings rushed out and tried to grab the other three girls.

He and Jack reacted immediately, their training kicking in instinctively. They ran towards the alley and turned into it. On rounding the corner, the scene they were faced with was hard to take. One of the somethings, they turned out to be drunken soldiers, was on top of the pretty blonde girl and obviously trying to rape her, he had her dress torn half off and her brassiere undone with one hand inside it and the other up her dress trying to get her knickers off. A second man was holding her down and the other two were holding off the other three girls while their 'friends' had their fun.

Wasting no time at all, he and Jack drew their truncheons and waded right in. First, they went for the two thugs guarding the alley, Alan took one and Jack the other and with speed and surprise on their side they had them flat on the ground in just a few seconds. Turning their attention to the rape scene Alan noticed that the blonde girl was partly naked with one thug on top of her beating her and trying to tear her clothing away. The other was holding her down so his friend could get better purchase on the cloth. Jack took care of the helper while Alan went after the would-be rapist.

He smashed him in the side of the head with his fist which stunned him enough to make him let go of the girl. They then started brawling like street fighters in the middle of the alley, neither really getting the upper hand until Jack came to his aid after having dealt with the other man. Between the two of them they got the best of the man. Fortunately, he was too drunk to offer much real resistance.

The only thing he said was, "Bloody frog bitch, I sure showed her." Then Alan punched him in the solar plexus, which made him puke up all the beer he'd been drinking. One last blow to the temple with his truncheon and he was out for the count.

Alan rushed to the victim to see if she was all right. He noticed that by this time her friends had covered up her nakedness and he could also see that, apart from a number of obvious bruises and scratches where the man had grabbed her, she appeared relatively unhurt, physically at least. He also noticed that despite the bruises and blood and smeared makeup she was an extraordinarily beautiful young girl. He wondered just how beautiful she must actually be when she hadn't just been attacked by four bullies. Then his duty as a policeman took over, and he went to her and said, "Hello miss, how are you feeling? Are you hurt badly anywhere?"

This roused Toni a little from her torpor to the point she could answer him, "*Oui monsieur,* I am OK … ze shock … you know?" still sobbing but more gently now. Morag had her arms around her and was holding on for dear life.

At this point their eyes met for the first time and they were instantly, head over heels in love. They stared at each other for what seemed like hours but was only a second or two. It took a physical effort for Alan to tear his eyes away from hers. He had never seen a creature lovelier and more alive than this girl. The mud and blood and bruises did nothing to detract from her aura of femininity and only enhanced his desire to protect her forever.

But he still had his duty to perform. "I … I …I'm sorry, miss," he stammered, "can you tell me exactly what happened?"

So, Toni told him everything that had happened at the ceilidh and afterwards and all the while her eyes never left his. She completely forgot that she had almost been raped only a few short minutes ago and fell into his deep blue eyes. Irrevocably and for ever.

*
**

Morag told the policemen where to find them all. She and Toni at the tannery and Sheila and Liz at the fairgrounds. They would come by the next day to get formal statements.

After commiserating with Toni with hugs and kisses all round, the other two girls went back to their lodgings by the fairground.

This left Morag and Toni alone. "Are you really all right? Ye're no hurt bad anywhere?" Morag was very concerned. Toni seemed to be in denial of the whole incident, instead of crying and withdrawing she seemed to be in the happiest mood she had ever seen her in.

"But Morag, *ma chère*, can you not see that I am in love?"

"What? Ye've just been beaten and nearly violated you mad girl!" Morag was incredulous. Toni must have hit her head after all!

"Did you not see that beautiful gendarme that rescued me from that beast? 'E was so 'andsome and brave. I fell into his eyes as if they would support me always." Toni, clearly was in love. She was also clearly in shock as the realisation of what had just happened sank in and was shivering and vibrating as the shock was taking hold. She and Morag slept together that night holding each other and quietly crying until the middle of the next morning.

They came out of Morag's room still desperately clutching each other. Morag had done her best to clean Toni up, but she still bore the scars of the previous night.

As soon as Sean saw her he knew something was up.

"What the bloody hell happened to you, lassie?" You knew Sean was upset when he used words like 'bloody' or 'hell'. Toni was family.

Morag then explained what had happened and, after Sean calmed down a little, his daughter told him that the upshot of the whole incident was that Toni was in love.

Seeing the confused look on his face, Morag took pity on him. "One of the policemen that saw to us last night was fairly handsome I gather, of course I didn't notice," she said primly but with a wink.

"'Andsome? 'E was beautiful!" Toni defended her man.

"Beautiful eh? What was his name then?" teased Morag.

"I don't know 'is name but isn't 'e coming 'ere to talk to us today?" Toni was almost pleading.

"Yes, they both said they'd be by today … the less beautiful one too!"

"Oh, don't make fun, I am still 'urting from last night, this beautiful man saved me from much worse."

"You're right, I'm sorry, beautiful men don't need names!" grinned Morag.

*
**

Alan Fairford went up to the tannery by himself. He had managed to convince Jack that he didn't need to be there too. He had scrubbed himself to within an inch of flaying the skin off his body, so he was a nice bright pink. He wore his 'Sunday Best' uniform, well it was Sunday wasn't it? And he kept telling himself that he was just going there to interview the victim and one of the witnesses.

Not wanting to intrude too much, he got there after lunch. For some reason he was nervous. Usually, he was the calm and confident policeman who always knew how to put people at ease. Today he felt like a sixteen-year-old boy asking his first crush for a date.

Morag answered the somewhat timid knock. "Hello Constable, you must be the one who saved Toni from a horrible fate? We can't thank you enough."

"Yes, mum, I would like to see the … err that is … to interview the victim if I could, mum? … Please?" If he'd had a cloth cap he would have been wringing it in his hands.

Morag couldn't help but smile. Toni had said she thought the spark between them had gone both ways, and it seemed she was right. "Right this way … mister …?"

"Oh, I'm sorry, mum, Police Constable Alan Fairford, mum." He murmured, still nervous.

They went through into the parlour where Toni and Sean were waiting. "And this is Miss Antoinette Marie Langlois, originally from France." Morag announced, rather too formally she realised. It felt like she was a mother introducing a potential suitor to her daughter, who had just come of age.

Toni and Morag had time to cover all the damage done the previous night and what little remained visible Morag had expertly covered with makeup.

So what Allan saw was a stunning, petite, young French beauty done up to the nines. How he made it through the interview he didn't know. It was a good job he was keeping notes, though, because the only thing he could remember afterwards were her glistening blue green eyes. He had memorized every vein and colour variation and eyelash in them.

CHAPTER 13

ARRAS 1917 – II

*
**

It was the coldest winter in decades in that part of France so most of January and February was spent trying to keep warm. Generals interpreted this as opportunities to plan ahead while keeping warm in their chateaus and cafés, or so the troops thought, the constant visits by senior officers notwithstanding. Junior officers interpreted this as the need for training and other forms of physical exercise, the good ones even joining in. Sergeants interpreted this as work parties and physical training and marching and drill.

The overall result of all this was that the troops didn't freeze to death but almost died of overwork instead.

True, it was nice to be away from the trenches for a while but at least up there, the work had an immediate effect, a purpose, and danger to keep you motivated.

"Ye know we're having too easy a time when we start missing the bloody trenches," Ewan said to Archie McGrath, another sergeant from his battalion. Archie had recently come in as a replacement from a battalion in another division which had been badly cut up at the Somme the previous year.

"Aye, ye've got that bloody right," Archie replied. Like Ewan, Archie was an ex-patriot Scot who had come to Canada from necessity, following the new Scottish habit of escaping the growing poverty in small town Scotland, in his case a village near Dundee.

"Do ye think another game of footba' or another bloody parade or another bloody frontal assault practise is going tae help?" Ewan said with a surprising amount of frustration in his voice. The truth was he was missing the twins, even though he had never met them, and he was missing Morag more and more each day. He just wanted to get this whole damned war over with.

"Probably not, but unless you've got any other brilliant ideas we don't have much choice."

"Right then, let's get to it," and with that Ewan got to his feet. He and Archie then launched into another round of calisthenics and football and marching up and down and advancing into simulated machine gun fire before collapsing once more into their beds (mostly hay-filled palliasses) exhausted, but warm.

In the event, they didn't have much more of this to endure. In late February, they started to hear rumours of something brewing around Arras and by early March they were digging in on the approaches to a hill just north of Arras.

This hill had a ridge at the north end of it that overlooked the whole of northern France, or so they were told.

Immediately on the other side of that ridge was the small French village of Vimy.

*
**

Moving into the nearly abandoned French trenches was a sobering experience. Since 1914 the Poileaus had tried to take this ridge on numerous occasions. And failed every time. This had resulted in the trenches being mostly destroyed and filled with rotting French corpses. This was nothing new to the Mackenzies, but you never really got used to it.

Over the next month, when they weren't training they were doing as best they could to clean up and repair the trenches and defences. Also removing as many of the poor bloody French soldiers as they could and treating them with as much respect as was practical. Ewan and Archie were regretting their comments about "always having work to do".

Behind them they heard rumours of mining companies and specialist engineers digging tunnels towards the ridge. He ran into his old sergeant, Colin Forbes, now the RSM of an Engineer Battalion, who told him that there was more work going on underground than above it. And there was plenty enough of that, with other engineers working on fortifications and gun positions and machine gun bunkers.

Tunnels and more tunnels and yet more tunnels. Some reinforcing or redirecting of ones that had been there for centuries and some that went under the German positions, clearly for mines. Something was definitely afoot.

Their Vickers guns had all been withdrawn and given to newly dedicated Machine Gun Regiments and they had to rely more on their Lewis guns. This suited everyone though, because they were lighter, and they had more of them. The organization of the battalions was changed, the platoons were no longer just administrative groupings they were actual tactical organizations. Ewan was now not just the Pioneer section commander but the platoon second in command, right behind the lieutenant.

Harold Dundas was a very good and experienced young officer. He had joined the army in Toronto after deciding that sitting out the war in his lawyer's office on Bloor Street was not very appealing and wouldn't be very likely to attract the young ladies of his acquaintance.

He was twenty-six and had joined the CEF right before Christmas 1914 – the first one that it was all supposed to be over by. Because of his education, he was made an officer and spent the next six months training at Petawawa and Valcartier, learning *'how to blow a whistle in an offensive manner,'* as he often said.

That comment always got respect from the soldiers who had to react to that whistle. It was one of the reasons the men liked and followed him.

The other reason was the fact that he wore the ribbons of a DSO and bar and an MC on his tunic. Those little splashes of cloth spoke volumes to fighting soldiers. The first DSO he had won at Ypres in 1915 during the first gas attack, the second at Mont Sorel in 1916 and his MC earlier in the Somme. That battalion had been cut up very badly and Harold had been wounded.

The 25th needed experienced officers before the Battle of Thiepval Ridge in the Somme just six months earlier, so Harold was transferred to them.

All of that and the fact that he was a whizz on the Harmonica, or "Mouse Organ" as it was called, made him the most popular officer in the battalion. Robert the Bruce idolized him.

As for the training, that too had changed dramatically.

Wonder of all wonders, the generals had finally figured out that simply going over the top into devastating machine gun fire in the hopes of the Jerries running out of bullets before you got to their trenches wasn't a very sound strategy. It had only taken them two and a half years to figure this out. That was certainly the impression that most soldiers had anyway.

They were finally learning from all this carnage. The French had learned some valuable tactical lessons at Verdun and had passed them on to their allies, with the result that they launched into a whole different style of training. The senior officers were spelling out the reasons for the upcoming assault. The ones that applied to the 25th anyway. They were explaining the routes the battalion would take and the objectives they were after along the way. The junior officers had received even more detailed information and, for the first time ever, they were letting the NCOs in on it. And the NCOs, Ewan included, were then explaining all this to the soldiers.

You could see the optimism lighting the faces of the men. No longer would they be charging into the machine guns without any idea of how to deal with that. Or why or where they were going. Even the "how" was changing. The platoons, broken into tactical groupings, which were still called sections, but now with a deliberate purpose in mind. They were encouraged to advance more cautiously through no man's land rather than just blindly moving across it.

They were told of something called a "Creeping Barrage," which was supposed to keep them as safe as possible while moving through no man's land, the idea being that the artillery would fall on the enemy on a certain line and then it would move back in coordinated leaps in time with the infantry advance in order to prevent the Jerries from manning their positions before the Canadians were on them. Though sceptical at first, they rehearsed it and rehearsed it until they began to believe in it.

Most unbelievable of all they were told that they wouldn't even be in no man's land for very long because they would be moving to the frontline through tunnels, called subways, built by those engineers they had been watching for weeks.

It all sounded too good to be true. Ewan and his mates had grown ever more sceptical as the bloody and vicious years went by and time after bloody time promises of victory were either phenomenally exaggerated or just plain and bloodily wrong.

That being said, there was no denying the palpable feeling of optimism that everyone had.

Ewan's growing patriotism as a Canadian was infectious, and he could see it all around him. He heard that all four Canadian divisions would be fighting together for the first time, albeit led by a British officer and heavily reinforced by further British divisions and artillery and so on. The simple fact that he even knew this was astounding. Never before had they even known who they'd be fighting beside, if anyone. Let alone details like that.

He'd even seen a "tank" rolling ponderously by the other day! They'd heard very little about these noisy, smelly contraptions beyond the fact that they could bridge a trench ... well, we'd see about that. Bridging it was one thing but the PBI would still have to capture and occupy the bloody things.

*
**

Some things never changed though.

By this time it was late March, and they knew the battle was approaching fast. There were still trench raids to be conducted. The brass hats needed information about which units they'd be facing, the strength they were in and their morale, etc.

That meant prisoners and that meant men would likely die getting those prisoners. But, so the theory went, information gained from captured German officers could save Canadian lives, so it was worth the risk.

And Ewan being Ewan, he volunteered to lead one of the bigger ones. It would involve two complete sections from his platoon, almost half its fighting strength, in an effort to grab some Jerry brass hats from a forward trench.

He had a flashback to when he had almost killed his friend Peter in just such a raid and put that out of his mind ... what would be ... would be.

"Sir," he addressed Lieutenant Dundas as he walked into his command post (really just an enlarged shell hole covered by a piece of corrugated iron). "We need to capture some Jerry officers tae get information about who's who and what's what don't we?"

"By '*we*' you mean '*you*' don't you?" he replied knowing full well what the answer would be.

Ewan's answering grin was all he needed to know.

"I presume you have a plan?"

"Aye sir, I do."

And the two of them spent the next hour or so going over Ewan's plan with Lt Dundas offering advice and suggestions rather than giving direct orders. One advantage of an army made up of gifted amateurs rather than stuffy Sandhurst graduates (most of whom were long dead by this stage of the war anyway) was that you could discuss things as equals rather than just give orders and expect them to be blindly obeyed.

The next night was a cloudy, but dry, night. It was cold but not so cold that the puddles froze over and created noise as they moved over them. In any case, they timed the raid to coincide with one of the, by this time almost continuous, artillery bombardments that were happening all up and down the front.

He had picked an area where the barbed wire entanglements had not yet been repaired from when they had been destroyed by German artillery the previous year. Ewan had borrowed some tools from his former pioneer mates for those areas where the wire was still intact.

His twenty plus handpicked men, all veterans of numerous trench raids, slithered quietly over the parapet without either helmets or webbing or rifles in order to keep the noise down, though most brought pistols or revolvers. They all had their bayonets however, because, they reasoned, you were more likely to capture a Jerry officer willingly with eighteen inches of cold steel up his nose than with stern words whispered in the dark.

There were two hundred yards of muddy, wet, rat and rotting French corpse infested shell holes to cross before they reached the targeted Jerry trench. You can get used to anything though and most of these men had been doing this for two or more years.

Ewan had been observing this point in the German trench for days, which was why he'd planned the raid in the first place. He had noticed that though there were machine gun bunkers on either side of this approach, their fire didn't cross until the middle of no man's land and there was a dip right in front of the Jerry trench that wasn't covered by either gun. He would have to trust to luck about finding a German officer there but even a sergeant would have valuable information.

The trick was finding one.

Making it into that dead ground unseen would be the first hurdle.

They made it across no man's land without disturbing a soul. There was just enough room for all of them to take cover in the dip in front of the trench.

It had taken them three full hours, with much snipping and under-the-breath cursing but make it they did.

Ewan signalled for everyone to stop and recover their breath and listen for any movement on the German side of the parapet but all they could hear was the sounds of the barrage which was still going on about five hundred yards to their left.

He sent two men over the parapet to have a look see. One of them was a Blackfoot Indian from Calgary who was a magician when it came to silently approaching someone. L/Cpl Doug Crowfoot had almost been stabbed a number of times sneaking up on people while they had been resting behind the lines. To him it was great fun.

This was altogether more serious though, and he took it as such. They returned five minutes later as silently as they had left.

"Sarn't MacBride," Crowfoot reported.

"Aye Doug, what did ye see?"

"Well, there's a sentry about twenty-five yards down the trench to the right but he's more interested in keeping warm than anything else" he said. "The entrance to one of the Spandau bunkers was about the same distance to the left but I couldn't see the other one. It's past that sentry I guess."

"No matter as long as it's pointed outside the trench, not inside it." Ewan replied with his usual wolfish grin. "Any sign of a command bunker or anything like that?"

Crowfoot said with an answering grin. "Well, there was a small depression in the back of the trench which did look like a large sleeping area, in fact a bit too large for just that."

"That sounds like our target then, at least we'll be able to kill some of the bastards, even if we can't make them our prisoners."

Ewan split his men into roughly equal thirds, one group to guard the trench to the left, one to guard it to the right and the remainder, with Ewan leading, to take the bunker, or whatever it was. L/Cpl Crowfoot had a special task, to silence the cold and drowsy sentry. He felt little guilt as he realised that the man would be dead before he even knew he was being attacked.

Things started smoothly enough with all three groups moving over the parapet without making a sound.

Each group moved to their respective spots. The right-hand group moved first and secured the right flank where Doug Crowfoot joined them, his gruesome task now complete.

The left-hand group advanced with Ewan immediately behind so they could take up the left flank guard at the same time as Ewan's group entered the "bunker" and to act as backup in case anything went wrong.

In the event, the left-hand group both caused the alarm and saved the day.

Ewan moved quickly but silently into the bunker, there was no *"Fraoch Eilean, lads!"* this time. What they encountered there was a sort of Sergeants' mess. There were four sleeping forms and judging by their great coats, which they were using as blankets, they were all senior sergeants. The same rank as Ewan or higher. He detailed eight men, two to a Jerry sergeant, to put handkerchiefs in their mouths at the same time as they trussed up their hands from behind. There was a bit of a scuffle, but things went pretty smoothly, the four senior NCOs were subdued without waking anyone else or having to kill any of them, though one or two had their throats nicked with a bayonet to convince them to come along.

So, they had just crossed no man's land without a sound, slipped into a Jerry trench also without a sound and trussed up four Jerry sergeants with barely a whimper.

The gods of fortune and war are never this kind though, and Ewan had just started wondering what could go wrong.

From a nearby communications trench, another Jerry sentry arrived, probably come to replace the first, now dead, man. This one blundered full tilt into the group guarding the left approach.

He was probably late, so he was hurrying, and he ran straight into Pte Ian Robertson's bayonet, which was being held fairly loosely as Robertson wasn't expecting anyone quite that quickly. The blade did little damage initially, so the man had time to scream, *"Alarm, alarm, Englander!"*

Robertson didn't feel the need to correct him, he simply rammed his bayonet with full force into the man's throat, cutting him off midway through the second, "*Engla—*"

The damage was done however. They were right outside the left-hand Spandau bunker, and they had heard the commotion outside.

"*Was ist los? Was geht hier vor sich?* cried out German voices from inside the bunker, followed immediately by five large soldiers carrying rifles and shovels. The first one was wielding a shovel with which he took off the right hand of Pte Robertson with one blow. He now started screaming as well and the German was put down by Cpl Rathbone with one round in the left eye from a Webley service revolver. This weapon was quite useless beyond fifty yards but was very effective at less than one yard. The man's head disintegrated like an overripe melon.

The whole Jerry trench was now fully awake. The better part of a platoon was sleeping nearby, and the four sergeants were evidence that there may be as much as a company in the vicinity.

It was time to scarper.

Ewan sent the group with the four sergeants back over the parapet first, they had the valuable cargo after all. One of the NCOs made a break for it. He ran right past Ewan, elbowing him in the side on the way so Ewan shot him in the back for his troubles. If he couldn't have him, then neither could the Germans.

Ewan then took three men and sorted out the remaining crew of the Spandau. He then destroyed the gun with a Mills bomb tossed into the bunker.

By this time, both the left and right groups were fighting for their lives, the men on the left had the presence of mind to grab the rifles from the machine gun crew, now deceased, and formed a rear guard at a corner in the trench. The right-hand crew moved to the left side where the gun had been silenced and followed the prisoner group over, only suffering a couple of wounded.

After seeing the last of the right-hand crew over the parapet Ewan went to join the rear guard. They made a fighting retreat but were cut off, so they went over the parapet where they were. This spot was not in the dead zone that they entered from and was fully in view of the remaining Spandau. The one on the left was kaput but the one on the right now opened up on them and cut into the ten remaining men with gusto.

Rathbone led the charge across the parapet and he and Robertson, now with only one hand, along with Ewan and two others fought a valiant rearguard action right into no man's land.

The six other men linked up with the other groups and under cover of Canadian Vickers and Lewis machine gun fire, aided by enthusiastic rifle fire, made it to the MacKenzie's front trenches with the remaining three sergeants. They had two men killed but everyone else was alive and with only a few superficial wounds.

The remaining five men, including Ewan, were cut down by Spandau fire as they crossed into a large shell hole. Only Crowfoot made it back, and he was wounded.

*
**

Ewan came to several hours later, or was it days? It was night, but he wasn't sure which night.

He had a splitting headache and when he put his hand to his head it came away sticky and wet and in the withering light of a dying star shell he saw blood. That would explain the headache then.

What worried him more was that he couldn't move his legs. A hole in his skull he could deal with but no legs?

Another star shell went up and he could see a shape, maybe a body, lying over his legs. Hopefully that explained his immobile limbs. He felt around to see what kind of body it was and heard a faint moaning. Well, the body appeared to be alive, that was a start anyway.

He decided the body was lying with the torso right over his thighs effectively pinning him to the ground, so he tried to roll the man off him and discovered that he was surprisingly light. Once he wriggled out from underneath he felt around the body some more, found the head and then the arms but when he came to the waist and felt below it he discovered there was nothing below mid-thigh. The poor bastard had caught the full force of that Spandau burst right across his legs and it had removed them cleaner than a surgeon.

At least he knew he hadn't been out of commission too long because there's no way this man would be alive for very long with wounds like that. Using the man's belt he tied a tourniquet around one leg and then he tied another one around the other leg with his own belt.

Discovering that his own legs were miraculously intact, he quickly took stock of his own injuries and decided that, apart from a giant headache and a bullet wound in his left calf, he was pretty much intact.

Then looking around he remembered what had happened and decided that they were about 150 yards from their own lines and that he would have to crawl that distance with the wounded man on his back. Perversely, the thought came to him that at least the man was lighter because he had no legs. After a short while, Ewan discovered that it was easier to crawl on his back with the wounded man on his stomach. He had discovered that the man was Cpl Rathbone by now. It was still by no means a simple task though. Because although he knew roughly where they were, he was by no means certain of anything else. Was it really just three or four hours ago? It seemed like several lifetimes. Having no tools anymore he would have to find one of the routes that they cut on the way across the first time.

He decided to put Rathbone down for a minute and find the entry to the route back. This took him almost an hour and by the time he got back to the corporal he was surprised to find him still breathing. Grabbing the man by the collar of his tunic and hauling him back onto his stomach, Ewan set off for the forward trenches again. After a nightmarish night of crawling backwards through shell holes and mud and blood and bodies and wire he finally reached what he thought were their own frontlines. He put Rathbone down again and risked a peek over the edge of a shell hole and discovered that they were indeed only about twenty yards away, but it was starting to get light out and he would be losing any cover he had left, very soon. Reasoning that he had little left to lose at this point, and never for one second considering abandoning Frank Rathbone, he called out, quietly at first.

"Hey, the Canadians! Oi!"

Nothing.

He tried that another couple of times with no result.

Then louder, "Up the MacKenzies!" – still nothing.

Finally, since he knew Rathbone couldn't last much longer … *"Fraoch Eilean!"* … and then passed out.

*
**

Ewan awoke a couple of days later aching all over and more tired than he had ever been. His first thought was for Frank Rathbone. He was feeling guilty for being glad that he had no legs thus making him easier to carry. He really hoped that he'd made it so that he could apologize to him for thinking that.

The first person he saw was a pretty French nurse who, it turned out, was from Montreal rather than Paris. He asked her what happened to Cpl Rathbone. She pointed to a bed three down from his own and said, "'E is right there, Sergeant. You saved 'is life, you are an 'ero!"

"Not me, Cpl Rathbone is the hero, I'm going to put him in for a VC, he saved all our lives, him and a young one-handed private by the name of Ian Robertson, they both deserve medals."

In the event, he did get to apologize to Cpl Rathbone, moments before he died. And he did put him in for a VC but since he was only a Corporal and Ewan wasn't an officer his testimony wasn't good enough and the lad wound up getting a posthumous MM which is less than he deserved. Pte Robertson got a MID, also posthumous and also less than he deserved.

What they really deserved was to go home and that too was permanently denied to them.

Ewan got back to his battalion a few days later, the wounds to his head and leg were superficial. The physical one anyway, and the headaches gradually faded away.

He was told that the information gained from the three sergeants was invaluable, and it helped them pinpoint several other machine gun positions hopefully saving lives.

And Ewan could add a DCM to his growing collection. He couldn't have cared less.

CHAPTER 14

VIMY 1917 – I

*
**

Peter's battalion moved into its position in early February 1917. This position had been occupied since early in the war in 1914. Consequently, it had been built up with bunkers and trenches and wire and had a very strong façade. But it was just that, a façade, it had no depth. The German army had learned from some of their defeats over the last few years, particularly against the French. A rigid defence was well and good, if it held, but if it was breached there was no room to fall back and regroup to counterattack.

The hill before Vimy would be hard to defend for long because there was nothing behind the ridge except the slope into the surrounding plains. Impossible to counterattack from and very difficult to build deeper defences. Still, they would try so Peter set his men to deepening the lines of trenches and fields of barbed wire as best he could. They had no idea when the British (he didn't yet know he was facing Canadians) would attack, if ever, but it was spring and that was the traditional time for a battle, so he needed to be prepared.

There were also a growing number of aircraft over their heads, both theirs and the British. Mostly RFC reconnaissance aircraft from what he could tell. That only gave more credence to the thought that they would be the target of any coming attack.

On one particular day, Peter and Sgt Becker were on their way to a meeting for Battalion Commanders at 79th Reserve Brigade HQ. It was a clear but cold midwinter afternoon and apart from some desultory shelling in the background and the occasional burst of machine gun fire it was relatively quiet. As they were walking past a number of their men they were chatting with them and exchanging friendly banter back and forth. Peter was a popular CO since he was the same age as most of them.

"That sounds like an aircraft, sir," Sgt Becker, hearing engine sounds, said to Peter.

"Yes, I believe you're right but what of it? They come over us all the time." Peter was a little perplexed.

"No, no, listen carefully sir, it's not one engine but two … there are two planes coming towards us … it's getting louder."

Sure enough Peter looked up and within a few seconds he saw a small double-winged aircraft coming straight for them. He still thought nothing of it until he saw some sparkling lights at the front of the machine and quickly realised that this must be a British fighter strafing their trenches. The distinctive sound of a British Lewis gun firing was confirmation enough. He grabbed Sgt Becker and yelled, "Get down, Becker, you'll get your head blown off!" throwing both himself and the sergeant to the floor of the communication trench.

Nearby, he saw three of his men struck squarely by the heavy British .303 bullets. Two men were luckily just hit in the legs, but the third man was less fortunate. The bullet hit him right in the centre of his back exiting through his sternum and taking most of the contents of his rib cage with it. He fell forward onto his face, mercifully dead before he even started to fall, hiding most of the damage from the other men.

This just emphasised the random horror of this war to Peter and how much he was starting to hate the whole endeavour.

Some of the men started firing back with their rifles and from further down the line a Spandau tried its best to swat him out of the sky.

Then the second machine came into view. It was very different from the first, this one was painted a bright red. The Maltese Cross emblazoned on its side marked it as German, but the red paint identified who was flying it. It could only be his fellow Blue Max recipient, Manfred von Richthofen. Peter had met him in Berlin when he was on his morale tour and had liked him.

It was immediately evident why he had made the reputation for himself that he had. He went after the British craft with a tenacity that Peter had rarely seen before.

The two men were soon weaving and contorting in the sky like two swallows chasing the same mosquito. Soon enough though the red plane got the better of the plain green and brown one and one solid burst from his machine guns into the engine of the Tommy put an end to the fight.

Being quite low though, the Britisher had time to crash land his machine and thus survive the landing. It was less than a hundred metres from where Peter and Sgt Becker stood. By the time they got there several other soldiers were already there and had found the pilot dazed but very much alive.

He was waking up when Peter arrived so the first thing he saw when he opened his eyes was a German officer standing in front of him.

"Bloody hell, a Jerry! I guess that means I lost then, wot?" he grinned.

"Yes, you did but you killed one of my men first."

"Terribly sorry about that, old boy, but this *is* a war after all," came the somewhat laconic reply, said with the same tone as if he had just lost a game of chess, or, more likely, cricket.

Peter was really starting to not understand this war at all.

"I say, did I really just get shot down by that Red Baron chap? Top hole, I really must say! Top hole indeed!"

*
**

Captain, the honourable, Percival Aloysius Pendragon didn't like being dirty and war, he had discovered, involved being dirty ... a lot. Therefore, he had transferred to the RFC from the 2nd Dragoon Guards, which he had joined as a Cornet straight from Eton in 1912 when he was eighteen. Sandhurst had taught him how to ride a horse in a military manner but little else that was useful.

Percy Pendragon was the stereotypical, stiff upper lip, mad dogs and Englishmen, British army officer. The only thing he lacked was a monocle and that only because he was twenty-three years old and it didn't fit the image of a young cavalry officer. But he was no fool, it was largely an act, designed to keep people off their guard, he wanted them to be unsure of what to make of him. He was fearless to the point of recklessness and had excelled at rugby football at Eton, causing many a sore head both on the pitch and off.

France had been to him, as well as hundreds of thousands of other young men, a great shock. It had been a shock for multiple reasons. Firstly, he had just taken command of a troop within the regiment and had very little time to train with them before going to France. Secondly, the main thing that happened in France was that they were involved in one retreat after another from Mons to the Marne where the much vaunted cavalry skills that he had excelled at were about as useful as a carousel ride at a country fair. Third, he didn't like mud and there seemed to be an awful lot of that in France.

So, it was inevitable that when the opportunity came to transfer to the Royal Flying Corps he jumped at the chance. He had often looked at the rickety canvas covered frames of sticks and wire that appeared to be held together by luck rather than judgement and said to himself, *right, I bloody want one of those, I bet those buggers are clean.*

He spent several weeks badgering his commanding officer with request after request upon request to transfer to the RFC. So much so that eventually his CO gave in, if only to shut him up.

So, he got his wish and Beaulieu Aerodrome was to be his home for the next few months while he learned the differences between the operation of one horse and a hundred of them!

Percy went back to France in early 1916 and was in his new element. He quickly realised that his reckless streak could be turned to good advantage in the skies over the trenches. Within a year, he had built up the reputation of a tenacious flyer, always pushing the envelope on both his reconnaissance and ground attack missions. By 1917, he had racked up twenty-two kills: mostly slower reconnaissance machines but a couple of superior fighters as well. His favourite sport though was downing Jerry observation balloons. It wasn't very sporting, but it did save British lives and that was the point after all, wasn't it?

The Nieuport 17 was to be his chariot for the Vimy Battle, and he was a magician with it, sneaking low over enemy wire where he could strafe Jerry trenches and supply depots and wagon trains.

It was on just such a mission that he ran into the red Albatros D.III belonging to Manfred Albrecht Freiherr von Richthofen, the famous, or more accurately infamous, Red Baron.

His mission was to disrupt troop movements immediately behind the Jerry frontline trenches where fresh troops were sure to be strengthening the leading edge of their defences. At first all went well, he beat up an artillery position and a wagon train that must have had ammunition on it because one or two of the wagons blew up like Guy Bloody Fawkes night! He then saw some activity in a communication trench where there hadn't been any on the way over, so he went to investigate. He saw what he thought was a knot of officers or senior NCO types, too clean to be frontline bods at any rate. A quick strafing was all he could manage though, and he wasn't sure if he'd hit anything before feeling the impact of several rounds on his machine. Percy looked over his shoulder only to see the one thing he didn't want to see.

"Bloody hell, I know that bloody red plane, that's the bloody Red Bloody Baron that is," he cursed, not quite under his breath, "I'll be lucky to get away from that bastard."

Still, he would try, he knew the Nieuport was a match for the Albatros, and he was pretty confident in his own skills even giving the Red Baron his due.

The bloody trenches were too bloody close, he'd have to gain some altitude where he could manoeuvre. So he opened up his nimble little Nieuport and flew as if his life depended on it, which it did. At one point he got behind the red aircraft and he fired his guns … nothing. He must be out of ammunition, or jammed, either way he was done for. All he could hope for now was that the Baron was low on petrol, but he had no way of determining that. Fly on was all he could do.

Inevitably, the bright red Albatros got behind Percy and let loose a short two second burst from his twin LMG 08/15 machine guns. That was more than enough to kill his engine and make his little Nieuport into a brick rather than the beautiful flying machine that it had been.

Percy got lucky though. He couldn't steer very well but he was low to the ground and there was an open field more or less in his glide path. He had moments to react, but his youth and a year of combat flying had given him the reactions he needed to bring her down in one piece, again … more or less. Coming down slowly he glided onto the heavily pockmarked field behind the front trench, on the German side he figured. His luck continued though as his wheels clipped the rear edge of a trench and were torn off.

This allowed his aircraft to slide over the ground and come to a smoothish landing. Not so smooth that he didn't stun himself on the edge of the cockpit as it flipped upside down at the end.

He decided to play dead until he found out what their intentions were and pretended to be out cold when they got to him. The blood flowing down the middle of his face was a nice touch, he was glad he'd thought of it!

Once he realised that the Jerries weren't going to lynch him … not immediately anyway, he decided to play the upper-class fool in order to give himself some thinking room.

"Bloody hell, a Jerry! I guess that means I lost then, wot?" he grinned.

"Yes, you did but you killed one of my men first." The jerry officer said, in extremely good English he'd thought.

"Terribly sorry about that, old boy, but this *is* a war after all," he said as nonchalantly as he could. "I say, did I really just get shot down by that Red Baron chap? Top hole, I really must say! Top hole indeed!!"

Apparently, his upper-class idiot act had worked since they weren't paying much attention to him at all. His school boy German wasn't very good, but it was good enough to get a fair idea of what the Jerries were up to. It was obvious that they were preparing to be attacked but they had no idea what was coming. Percy knew the Canadians were training hard and practicing their assaults endlessly day after day. He knew the Germans were in for a rough go of it.

*
**

On another night in early March, Peter was touring his frontline positions inspecting the extreme frontline when he heard a commotion in one of the forward bunkers. He went forward to investigate. What he saw made him look around himself very cautiously. Two of his sentries were holding what appeared to be a British soldier at bayonet point and he, in turn, had his hands up. Apparently, they had captured an infiltrator. Peter was always worried about trench raids, having almost fallen victim to one himself, and he couldn't rely on all British raids being led by his best friend.

On closer inspection the man was wearing a Canadian uniform rather than a British one. The word "CANADA" on his shoulder being the most obvious difference.

There had been no sounds other than the brief scuffle that led to the man being held at bayonet point, so he was intrigued. The man wasn't even carrying a rifle.

"What are you doing in my trench, soldier?" he asked in colloquial English.

It was hard to tell who was the more shocked, the Canadian or his own men because none of them had seen him approach. Peter liked to do these inspections alone because he could get a more accurate picture of what was being done, consequently there was no-one with him.

"W-what?" stammered the man. Taken aback by being asked this question in English by a man of obviously high rank.

"I asked you what you were doing in my trench," Peter repeated, still in English.

It was then Peter's turn to be taken aback as the man answered in flawless German, "I wish to join the Kaiser's army, sir!" He snapped to attention.

"What did you say?" Peter had switched to German but was no less confused.

The man went on to explain how he had moved to Canada some years before the war in the hope for a new life just like thousands of others before him. When war broke out he found himself stranded inland, away from any port and with no means to return home to fight for his Fatherland. He conceived the plan of joining the Canadian Army as his English was nearly perfect. He would then desert while in France. So, here he was.

It struck Peter just how similar their stories were and how, if he hadn't been living in Halifax, he could have been in a very similar predicament.

Meeting this man didn't so much arouse conflicting loyalties as it reminded Peter of who he was and who he had met and become friends with while he was away from Germany. Not Just Ewan and Morag but all of their friends and the clients at MacBride & Baum. They were all perfectly ordinary people who were just like the clients at his uncle Joe's cooperage in Hamburg. All normal people who were just trying to live their lives as best they could, to raise their children in the correct manner, to build businesses and careers and families. Germans and British and Canadians alike.

What had driven this man to leave the relatively comfortable life he had built for himself in Canada after making the deliberate decision to leave Germany in the first place? Why give all that up just because the country you were born in "needed" you? Germany had never needed him before, why now?

Peter realised he was no longer thinking about the German-Canadian soldier, he was thinking about himself because those very same things applied, just as much to him as they did to the conflicted young man.

He remembered his chance meeting with Ewan in that trench in Flanders only two years ago … it seemed like a lifetime of eternities. What if it had been someone other than Ewan? He would likely be dead or captured instead of commanding a German army infantry battalion on the brink of being attacked by Canadians again. It wasn't so much the irony as it was the insanity of the whole thing that was confusing him.

Returning to Germany, he had planned to fight the Russians but even that had him wondering if the Russians were any different really. They were also people who wanted to live their lives and raise their children just like all the others did.

Now, here he was preparing to kill people from the country he had grown to love just as much as Germany … the Fatherland … it seemed such an odd concept now.

These were all things that he could no longer ignore, but he could also not ignore the upcoming battle and the lives of the men entrusted to him. It was his duty as a German soldier to do his utmost to stop the Canadian attack, but it was also his duty as a human being to keep as many of these men alive as possible, so that they could live their lives and raise their children just like everyone else.

*
**

As it turned out, the information the soldier gave confirmed many rumours and theories the German High Command had about what was brewing.

They now knew for certain that Vimy Ridge would be the focus of the coming attack. They had a much better idea of the size of the force that would be arrayed against them and its composition. It was not an encouraging picture.

What they didn't know was the range of new tactics and techniques that were to be employed in that attack.

They spent the best part of the next month intensifying the work on their defences and when the shelling started in late March they knew something was coming, and soon. They redoubled their efforts and were able to add another few hundred metres to their trenches and wire entanglements by the start of April.

Peter spent the night of April 8 writing to Elsa and pouring out his love for her and his uncle Joe and his new baby whom he couldn't wait to meet.

Sergeant Becker stopped by later to check in with his CO.

"Sir, all is well, it's bloody cold but the men are well huddled into their dugouts like a bunch of steaming sausages before dinner!" he laughed.

"Well, let's hope no-one eats them before the morning, or you and I will be defending this place on our own Sergeant Becker!"

"We could take them, sir," was the grinned reply.

"I dare say we could, but I'd rather not try," returned Peter with an equally bright grin.

"Yes, sir, the sentries are out, all good men, there should be no surprises before dawn."

"Thank you, good night, Sergeant Becker."

"Good night, sir."

And with that Peter drifted off to catch what sleep he could, dreaming about his new family.

At exactly 5:30 am on April 9, all hell broke loose.

CHAPTER 15

VIMY 1917 – II

*
**

Three weeks after returning to his home away from home, Ewan and his platoon were gearing up for the assault that was only hours away. It was 2300 hours on April 8, 1917. The attack had already been put back a day because of the bloody French. No one was sleeping that night.

They were shaking out their kit, making sure that their rifles were clean, that they had plenty of ammunition and that their bayonets were gleaming and rust free. Making sure that all the rest of their kit was complete and stowed away where they could get at it.

Ewan made every one of his soldiers show him their feet, and he made them change their socks. Not only was this a very practical thing since trench foot was endemic and they didn't know when they'd be able to do it again, but such a mundane task helped relieve the tension at least a little bit.

By now everyone had a brand new Short Magazine Lee Enfield Mark III*, the famous "Smelly" with an eighteen-inch sword bayonet and a Brodie helmet or "soup plate". Some men had Lewis Guns and most had No.23 Mills Bombs.

They were armed to the teeth not just with weapons but with a new sense of optimism that they hadn't had in three long years. Everyone was keyed up and ready to go. Scared to death but also with adrenaline coursing through their veins to keep them going straight and fighting through the German steel.

In the wee hours of the morning of April 9, the MacKenzie Battalion was just one of almost fifty Canadian infantry battalions that were getting themselves ready for the off.

Most moved through the so-called "subways" to their jumping off point where they arrayed themselves in assault formation.

The artillery bombardment had been such a constant over the past weeks that it was barely noticed until it stopped just before 5:30 a.m. Ewan looked at his new wristwatch, all the rage by 1917, and noticed the time. "Right lads, this is it, we'll be moving any minute now."

Three minutes of eerie silence and then the gates of hell were opened.

Every gun along the entire front began blasting the German lines with every type of shell in the inventory. Seconds later, several even larger explosions signified mines going off under the German trenches.

Whistles blew, and it was time to be off.

"*Fraoch Eilean,* lads, next stop Berlin!" Ewan cried as he and an entire platoon of angry Highlanders, buzzing like angry bees, charged forward into whatever future lay ahead. This was repeated a hundredfold, up and down the line.

They flew through no man's land and into the Jerry trenches so fast that it was a toss-up who was more surprised, them or the Germans. For their part, the Jerries were used to hunkering down in their bunkers to wait for the shelling to stop and then having time to set up their machine guns before the assaulting soldiers arrived. This time, however, the shelling didn't stop, it just moved back a little and the assaulting Canadians were on them while their ears were still ringing.

In fact, the assault was so swift and so successful that at first the MacKenzies were unsure of what to do next. They'd never been that far into a German trench before. Ewan quickly regrouped the men though, and they carried on into the communication trenches leading to the second line of defences.

Lieutenant Dundas was about fifty yards to his right with half the platoon, and they were keeping apace with him. They naturally divided the men into two equal halves and were almost leapfrogging each other as they took dugouts and occupied shell holes. Once they moved into the trenches themselves they were no longer able to see each other but they had enough experience to know where the other was. In this manner, they had taken their first objective within a few short hours and were able to have a short rest before moving on to the next.

"My God! I can't believe we're in their forward trenches already!" Harold Dundas exclaimed.

"And wi' so few men hurt," Ewan added. "We've only lost a few."

"It's early days yet, we've still got a long way to go."

"Aye," said Ewan, "and I dinna think they were running away when they retreated either, it looked like far too organized a withdrawal."

"Yeah, I think we should expect pockets of Jerries and probably a counterattack at some point, Ewan." Harold had a hard won and well developed sixth sense about situations like this, and Ewan took it to heart.

Sure enough, as they were entering the next, incomplete, trench they were met by a stream of bullets from a Spandau, which had been hurriedly set up around the next corner. One man was caught full on by the stream of hot bees coming from the gun and fell onto his face, dead. Ewan sent three men around the left flank to draw its fire while he and two men went up the middle. Waiting for the gunner to change belts he finely judged the moment before they charged the gun. "At 'em boys, *Fraoch Eilean!*" he screamed. The answering yells from the men with him carried them right into the midst of the gun crew. The gunners had just finished loading the new belt when Ewan and his boys were on them. They managed to get one quick burst off before they died at the hands of some very angry Canadians.

One round, though, went straight through the nasal cavity of Private James Robinson of Guelph, Ontario who would never see his mother or his father or his sister Janet again. James Robinson's war, like many other young lads', had ended.

Ewan collected the surviving men and went on to the next obstacle in their path.

Round the next bend they came across four Jerries well dug in behind the rear of the trench they had just taken. They were able to fire down into the communication trench and keep their attackers pinned down.

Ewan grabbed a Lewis gun from one of the men. Leaving the rest of them with orders to keep the Jerries' heads down he slithered through the mud around behind them. Once in place he stood up and screamed "*Fraoch Eilean!*" at the top of his lungs causing all four of them to turn towards him to see what nature of Banshee was upon them. Ewan opened up and put a full 47-round drum into them.

The effect that a heavy .303 bullet has when entering a human body at 2440 feet per second and at point blank range is not pretty. The effect that forty-seven of them have when entering four young German boys was spectacularly ghastly. Ewan was looking into the frightened eyes of an eighteen-year-old conscript from Dortmund by the name of Albert Zimmermann just as he squeezed the trigger and watched his face disintegrate in front of him. That face would never completely leave his thoughts.

*
**

Peter was thrown out of his bunker by a massive explosion, which simultaneously vaporised two of his men and mangled three more while collapsing the roof on top of them. He and Sgt Becker were lucky, they were standing near the entrance when it happened and were blown outside into the trench itself.

They and three more of their sergeants were able to extricate themselves from the now non-existent bunker. Peter and his sergeant major went in different directions to make sure the men were all under cover waiting for the barrage to lift. Moving through the front trench he came across the crew of a machine gun who had been too slow removing their weapon and had been destroyed so thoroughly by an artillery shell that it was hard to tell where metal ended, and flesh began.

At least it had been quick.

Moving through the trench Peter was gratified that he saw no more men, alive or dead, which meant they were all under cover, waiting for the barrage to lift before rushing back into position.

The barrage didn't lift though, it simply moved back a hundred metres or so. Momentarily, Peter thought it might be a lull in this area. He didn't have time to put too much thought into it however, when he heard the distinct shrilling of whistles and the shouting of men far too close to the lines than they ought to have been.

Quickly he realised the assaulting Canadians were far closer than expected and that he had better get his men moving before they were overrun.

He ran to the nearest dugout and yelled down into it. "*Achtung,* the Canadians are already here! Man your positions!" He ran to three other dugouts with the same message, "*Achtung,* the shelling has moved on, and the Canadians are already here!"

Peter knew it wouldn't be enough though and already he could see mud-covered khaki uniforms pouring over the parapet into the trench he had been in only seconds before. He stood there in wonderment, watching the almost balletic flow of death as it moved swiftly towards him. Sgt Becker grabbed him by the arm and shouted, "*Sir,* we've got to get out of here! Peter, come on man, we've got to organize a retreat while we still can!"

That snapped him out of his trance, and he instantly recovered his wits. "Right, get the men moving, we have to fall back to the second line."

They spent the next few minutes getting as many men and machine guns as they could, moving back to the next line. He felt a stab of pride when he saw his men galvanized and moving purposefully, in an organized, unpanicked manner back to the next trench just as they'd rehearsed time and time again over the past few weeks.

The next thing he felt was a supersonic crack right beside his head and realised he was being shot at. He looked behind him and saw khaki figures darting through the trenches and dugouts and coming towards him far too fast.

It was time to leave.

"Sgt Becker! Let's go, we've got to get to the second line! Where we planned will work nicely!" Peter and his staff had anticipated much of what was now happening and had planned fall-back positions they could move into very quickly. The problem now was that the Canadian advance was happening much faster than experience told them it should. The fact that the barrage had only moved back a little and was preventing them moving into their planned positions had not been anticipated and was throwing a big wrench into their works.

Fortunately, at that moment the barrage moved further back, past the trench they were moving into, so they were able to continue their orderly retreat. It was at that moment that Peter realised what was happening. Every time the barrage moved back the Canadians moved ahead … it was planned that way! Brilliant! If only his own high command had thought of it.

They moved into their new positions just in time to see Canadian bayonets poking around the corners of the communication trenches. Peter heard a Spandau barking nearby and when it was suddenly cut off by two small explosions he knew they were getting nearer.

It was time to take cover for the next assault, "Get ready men, they're coming!" he said quietly and calmly, mostly to himself, though he felt anything but calm.

His men had set up another Spandau to cover the exit from the communication trench, so it could catch anyone exiting the trench on their end. The first gun had made the Canadians think twice about rushing down the trenches blindly. Peter was watching from a dugout just to the side of the trench next to the machine gun when he saw three khaki clad figures tentatively make their way around the corner of the trench and move into full view.

He was about to give the order to fire when he recognized the man leading the trio. It was Ewan! He was faced with a most horrible choice. Let his friend live and face possible defeat and the deaths of more of his men or kill his best friend and live with that the rest of his life.

In the end it was no choice at all.

"Ewan, get down!" he screamed as he shot out of his dugout to protect his friend, just as the Spandau opened fire.

*
**

"If ye're wounded go see the Doc … and if ye're dead, go see the Padre!" Ewan told his men when they finally regrouped and got a chance for a few minutes rest before moving on to the next objective. The black humour was greeted by some genuine laughter. He was glad to see the men's spirits were still up and that they were in a good mood.

How could they not be? he thought. They had just moved through the Jerry frontlines like a hot knife through butter. Far from being reaped like wheat by millions of impersonal scythes as in previous battles they had suffered relatively few casualties. The rolling barrage had worked; it had not allowed the Germans to move their machine guns back into position before they left their start line. *The bloody brass hats do know what they're doing after all … will wonders never cease?*

Hal Dundas found him in a shell hole, replenishing his ammo pouches from bandoliers, reloading his rifle and wiping the blood off his bayonet. "Sgt MacBride! That was bloody marvellous! We swept them away like so much dust!"

"Aye, we did that sir, and no mistake, but as you pointed out yersel' they retreated in good order and no like scared wee bunnies, they're no done yet." Ewan demurred.

"Yeah, and we didn't capture nearly as many machine guns as we ought and that means they took them with them."

"Well, sir, why are we sitting here chatting about it then? Let's go get 'em!"

"Right you are Sarn't!" then louder "Come on lads, we've got them on the run! Let's push 'em to Berlin!" And with that the platoon moved off again. They had to keep the momentum going, or they would be stopped.

Ewan and six men moved down a communication trench, which only had a few zigzags in it. All went well for the first two or three corners but that all changed at the next one. Two young privates were leading when they went round the next corner and the unmistakable bark of a Spandau met them. The poor young buggers were nearly cut in half instantaneously as they came into the Spandau's field of fire. Only years of battle-tested reflexes saved Ewan and the others.

That avenue was cut off to them.

Over the top it was then. Dozens of trench raids had honed their skills at slithering over muddy pockmarked terrain so moving up to the next trench, where the Spandau was, was fairly routine. The problem came when they were at the edge of the trench parapet and didn't know what was on the other side. He didn't think any other MacKenzies had got that far yet, so he took a risk.

Ewan solved the dilemma by throwing first one then a second Mills bomb over the edge where he thought the machine gun was.

The sound of a life ending scream is, oddly enough, the same in either English or German so it was fortunate when the screams were preceded by a terrified *"Verdammt!"* With that, Ewan and his group rushed over the parapet and finished off the remaining Jerries, all four of whom were wounded and dazed. Prisoners were not an option in the heat of battle … or so he thought at that moment.

Ewan quickly gathered his men and pushed on. He was dimly aware that the rest of his platoon were also moving forward, so his confidence was high. They shook themselves out and reloaded before moving forward again. Ewan took the lead this time and peeked cautiously round the corner. Seeing nothing, he started to move again. Around the next corner he was moving cautiously forward when he heard, "Ewan, get down!" and then a field grey streak shot out of the neighbouring trench and flattened him to the floor of the communication trench just as a stream of Spandau fire went over the top of his prostrate form.

He recognized Peter's voice at once but didn't understand the context until he rolled over and saw his friends face inches from his own. Peter had saved his life.

Seconds later, he returned the favour as two of his men were about to thrust bayonets into the field grey clad form lying on top of him. "*Stop* you bastards, this man's my friend!" He stopped one in time but the other had enough residual momentum to stick his bayonet through Peter's right upper thigh. He'd been aiming for his back but was distracted by Ewan's yell.

The Spandau was silent, but Ewan didn't understand why until later.

The thing that ultimately saved Peter's life was not Ewan's cries or the strangely quiet machine gun. It was Lt Dundas who was coming up behind and recognized first the Blue Max at Peter's throat but also the insignia of a German Oberst Leutnant. "Don't shoot! Don't shoot! This man is a senior officer … he's valuable!"

He was more than valuable to Ewan. Seeing that Peter was safe after all this time was everything to him. So much so that he and Peter hugged each other like the long-lost brothers which, in the ways that matter, they were. Ewan now knew why the Spandau had held its fire, they didn't want to kill their own Commanding Officer.

"You know this man Sgt MacBride?" said a somewhat dumbfounded Lt Dundas.

"Aye sir, he's my partner!" Ewan started. "You remember when I told ye how I came tae speak such good German? That my partner at my business before the war was German and had taught me? Well this is the man!"

"Well, I'll be damned," Harold said, "I never would have believed it if I hadn't seen it for myself."

The war went whirling off into the distance now as this odd reunion continued. The now silent Spandau had slipped away and the MacKenzie Battalion, in pursuit of it, were pushing on to the next objective.

It turns out that the bayonet that had skewered Peter's thigh had also gone about three inches into Ewan's arse! He wasn't going anywhere anytime soon. Neither man was badly hurt but they couldn't walk so they had time to catch their breath and figure out what the hell had just happened.

Ewan went first, "Bloody hell mon, ye saved my life but ye got yersel' captured! What were ye thinking?" he was still full of emotion from the adrenaline.

"And I'd do it again a hundred times my friend," vowed an equally emotional Peter, "I owed you from that time in Belgium," he said.

"Ye owe me nothing. Ye're my friend, and ye always will be." Ewan told him, "I could no more kill you then than I could kill Morag! I'm just happy ye're safe now."

"I'm glad too. The truth is I am sick of this *verdammt* war and I'm glad I'm out of it now," he said with feeling, "I may even see my child one day!"

"Ye have a child? That's wonderful! I ha'e two, one of each! I promise you that I will do everything in my power to make sure that your child and mine will be the best of friends one day." Ewan said with a prophetic certainty that both surprised and strengthened the two friends.

Ewan and Peter lapsed into their old banter as if they'd just been away on separate holidays, Peter talking about Elsa and his uncle Joe and how his new child, a son he was sure, would be born in late summer and how he knew they'd be together soon. Ewan talked about Morag and Hamish and Mairi like any proud parent would even though he had never met the latter two.

They were still chatting away like the two old friends they were when the stretcher bearers came much later in the day to pick them up and take them to the aid post. There were more urgently wounded men though, so they still had a wait and continued their reunion to the amazement of everyone who walked by them.

Both men felt happier than they had since they had parted in 1914. They hadn't realised just how important they were to each other until this bloody war had forced them apart. They hadn't had the time in Belgium two years before but now they made up for it.

Eventually, the stretcher bearers took them to the same aid post, Peter was pleasantly surprised that he was treated just the same as any Canadian soldier was, in fact they even showed deference to his rank. Apparently, a colonel was a colonel in any army.

The shiny Blue Star at his throat didn't hurt either. No one tried to steal it or mock it and even if they had Ewan would have prevented it, in no uncertain terms!

Three days later, Ewan learned that the battle for Vimy Ridge was won and that the MacKenzie Battalion had distinguished itself once again and that he could add a bar to his MM, but he cared only that his best friend was out of the war and safe. The truth was that Ewan was heartily sick of this war too and could not wait for it to be over so that he could go back to Halifax, to Morag and his bairns.

He realised too, though, that he had a duty to the men of his platoon … his army family was every bit as important to him as his real family, and he couldn't just abandon them. They had shared blood and tears and hardship and terror for two long years, and they would see it through together to the end. He would finish the war. He would finish it to the best of his ability. He would finish it, and he would go home and he would never touch another rifle as long as he lived.

But first there was Passchendaele.

*
**

Peter now had nothing but time on his hands. Time to relax, time to heal, time to reflect, time to rest and, above all, time to think.

What had he just done? He had thrown away a distinguished career as a battalion commander in the Imperial German Army. Attaining that level had been no small feat and something that he had dreamed of as a boy in Hamburg all those years ago. He had thrown away his chance of seeing Elsa and his yet to be born son … it *must* be a son …anytime soon, possibly at all. He had spurned the trust that his men had given him, unconditionally. And for what?

For the life of his best friend in all the world, for the man that had taken in an accused murderer based solely on the faith he had in his strength of character, for the man who had trusted him with the legacy of another falsely accused murderer, a man that he had built a business with, built families with. One that he trusted his life to implicitly.

He was no longer proud of being in the German army. The things he had seen, the things he had been obliged to do, the men he had sent to their deaths and the men he had put to death. This all now sickened him.

He knew in his heart of hearts that he would one day see Elsa again, and he would meet his son, of this he had no doubt.

His men knew only that he had been captured. They must be trusted to realise that duty comes in many forms, but the love of a brother trumps them all.

The immediate future, though, was less certain. His wounded leg, though not serious enough to get him hospitalized in England in a VIP PoW camp was serious enough to keep him in France at a hospital for captured senior officers, of which there were quite a few. The Blue Max made him a celebrity of sorts. Though, oddly enough, more so with the British than with his fellow Germans. His colloquial, though accented, command of the English language made him a much sought after dinner companion for senior Allied officers who were touring the hospital.

One day, he was introduced to Major General Arthur Currie who had led a division at Vimy Ridge and who was fascinated by Peter's tale of having lived in Canada before the war and how he had been captured at Vimy by his former business partner.

Over the next three days Peter spent several hours talking with General Currie about everything except the war. About family and friends and about Canada and how Peter hoped to return there after the war with his wife and child, hopefully to take up where they left off.

Currie recognized that this was a tall order, but he also recognized that the war was turning in their favour. The Americans had declared war on Germany just a week before and were sure to start sending troops to France any day now and when that happened it would be all but over. When the war ended there would have to be a rebuilding of relations between the British and German empires. The world would have to go through a major shift in outlook to accomplish that. The bloodletting of an entire generation must not be in vain.

There must never be another war like this one. Of that he was sure.

To that end, Currie decided that Peter had some small part to play in rebuilding the relationship between Germany and Canada after the war. He further decided that Peter would go to Canada as a celebrated prisoner. Not so the people could gloat over a conquered foe but so that there could be a focus for a rebuilding of trust after the war.

Having made that decision he set in motion the wheels that would bring Peter back to Halifax and to the next chapter in his life.

CHAPTER 16

HALIFAX APRIL 1917

*
**

By the end of March, Alan Fairford and Toni Langlois were joined at the hip as if they had always been that way. Though both were very busy they spent every spare moment together. It was quite obvious that they were in love and yet they were still very shy about intimate contact. The incident at the pub had affected Toni more than she let on and, for more than one reason, she was still reluctant to have a physical relationship with Alan.

For his part Alan realised this. Both his training as a policeman and his natural kind heartedness made him sensitive to her reluctance, and he didn't push the issue. He was just happy to be with such a beautiful, intelligent, and talented girl.

Another reason was that once Toni had recovered from the trauma of nearly being raped and she had settled back to normal life, she was able to examine Alan a little more objectively. What she saw made her fall in love with him all over again. He was perfect in every detail.

Every detail, that was, except one.

He had a very noticeable scar on his neck.

When Toni saw this for the first time the memory of her entry into Canada came flooding back. She relived the fright of leaving the ship, of stealing the knife, of being spotted by the crew of the ship, of tangling with the policemen on the shore. And the all too vivid memory of dragging a knife across the throat of the most beautiful man she would ever meet.

The first time she noticed this she panicked and ran, crying, from the room. Alan rushed after her and tried to comfort her, but she shrugged off his embrace and ran away again.

Alan, wisely, though wrongly, put it down to her still recovering from the trauma of the assault and left her alone to sort out her demons for herself.

Toni couldn't face Alan with this knowledge, and she didn't know where else to turn. Morag was as much a big sister as a friend. She needed to confide in someone and it seemed natural to confide in her. She didn't know if she would be sympathetic with her or not, but she had no-one else to turn to.

She tracked Morag down at the tannery where she was making arrangements for a large shipment of leather to leave for the factory that made soldiers' boots. The wagons were just moving off, and Morag was wrapping up for the night.

Toni approached her timidly and said, "Morag I need to tell you something, something very 'orrible." She was crying. "But also very important."

Morag realised that something was very wrong, and that Toni was terribly distressed by whatever it was she needed to say.

"Of course you can lass, anything for you." She was very concerned by Toni's tone of voice. "Sit down and relax." Morag led her by the hand into the office where they sat at the desk. Sean had left early, so they had the place to themselves.

They sat next to each other and Morag, realizing the level of distress that Toni was feeling, put her arm around her and took her hand to comfort her.

Toni was silent for several minutes before finally saying, "Do you remember when I told you 'ow I escaped from that dreadful ship at the 'arbour that 'orrible day all doze years ago?"

"Yes, of course," she said. That had been another traumatizing incident in her young life, "but that's all behind you now." She misinterpreted where Toni was going.

"No ... no it's not, it has come back fully to meet me again," she was clearly very flustered.

"But how? You've become a valued member of our family as well as a useful citizen, what could possibly be wrong with that?" Morag was trying to understand.

Toni was silent again for several minutes, clearly working up the courage to go on. Eventually she just blurted it out. "I nearly killed 'im! My most beautiful man … I nearly killed 'im!" She was in tears at this point. Morag pulled her to her knees on the ground where they hugged each other as if life depended on it. Morag was crying now too, though she didn't know why.

"But how? What happened?" Morag managed to get out around her own tears.

"Do you remember when I told you I stole a knife from the ship before I left?"

"Yes, I do." Morag was starting to have an uncomfortable feeling in her stomach.

"Do you remember when I said that I lashed out with the knife in a panic?"

"And slashed a policeman's throat!" Morag suddenly saw the scar on Alan's throat clearly in her mind. "Oh my God! It was Alan!" She gasped because it was very clear now. The policeman's scar with the "interesting story" and the scared young French girl disguised as a boy who had, in a panic, slashed the throat of that policeman. Morag hugged Toni all the tighter now. She understood Toni's panic and her almost tangible hysteria.

"But he loves you, he'll understand," she tried.

"No 'e won't! 'e'll 'ate me forever!" Toni sobbed into Morag's shoulder. "I almost killed 'im!!" Toni's panic was almost out of control.

"Do you want me to tell him?" she offered.

"No … no … I 'ave to do it myself … but I don't know 'ow!" her reply was almost pleading.

She agonized about it for weeks. To the point where their relationship was becoming strained.

In the end, Alan came to Morag to ask her what was wrong. "Morag, I thought Toni was getting better, but she seems to be withdrawing into herself again, like right after the attack." He was clearly concerned.

"She still has demons from her past life that she needs to work out," she hedged. She had promised Toni she wouldn't tell Alan.

"She's not worried about this is she?" he said pointing to his throat.

Morag panicked, "What about that? It's just a little scar, it hardly shows at all!" she blustered.

Alan said, "Morag, I know she's the one who gave me this. I've known almost from the start, and I couldn't care less!"

"But how could you know? She was disguised as a boy!" Morag was dumbfounded.

"Well I am a policeman after all!" he said with a cheeky grin. "I put two and two together when I overheard you and Sean talking about Toni's history. It's the only thing that makes any sense. And, as I said, I couldn't care less, she was obviously under great duress. I'm under no illusions about what that ship was up to."

Unbeknownst to either of them, Toni had been listening in from the next room and could no longer restrain herself. She rushed into the room and ran straight to Alan and leapt into his arms crying happy tears for a change. Alan met her with open arms and crushed her to him with a fierce yet gentle embrace.

Morag discretely left the room.

*
**

Then on April 13, Morag casually picked up a newspaper and read about the great victory at some place called Vimy Ridge. Sean had always accused her of having the second sight and right now she felt a strong tug at her heart. But not a bad one. She had the feeling that something important had happened, but something good not something bad. She knew that Ewan had been involved but not how. She would have to trust that he was well and had everything under control.

*
**

A month later, Morag got a letter from Ewan, which told her about how he and Peter had saved each other's lives. And that Peter was now safe, and on his way back to Halifax as a guest of His Majesty the King! It was a lightly-veiled euphemism for '*Prisoner of War*'. She was doubly happy that Ewan was safe and that Peter was out of danger for good.

Sure enough, two weeks later she was contacted by the army and asked to meet a certain ship when it docked at the pier in Halifax the following week.

On the appointed day and time she arrived at the pier just as the ship was docking. She wondered how they could possibly know so precisely when the ship would arrive. She later learned that it had been waiting outside the harbour since the previous day for the appointed hour to come. She immediately saw why. A large body of soldiers were waiting at the pier with a string of ambulances, as well as a small knot of dignitaries and military officers. There were also policemen around the periphery and she saw that Alan was one of them, so she went to him to find out what was happening.

"Hello, Alan! What's all this about then? I was contacted by the army and told to be here today. *Told* mind you, not asked!" Morag queried him.

"Ah, hello, Morag! Yes, I've been told to direct everybody to that little knot of people down there by the pier." He said, pointing at the obvious group of people in suits and uniforms. "Beyond that I have as much idea as you do as to what's going on. Good luck!"

"Thanks, hopefully I won't need it!" she replied with a grin. She was suddenly in a very buoyant mood but didn't quite know why.

She made her way to the pier where she saw someone she knew, a client of the tannery who purchased a lot of leather for his carriage manufacturing firm.

"Good morning, Mr Arbuthnot, how are you?" she enquired politely.

"Ah! Mrs MacBride! Glad you could join us; your husband sends his love and greetings I understand!" He was very jolly!

That took her aback, "You've seen Ewan? How? Where is he?" hope bloomed in her. Only to be quickly dashed again when Mr Arbuthnot said, "I assure you he is well! He cannot be here in person as he is still valiantly defending King and Empire in France, but he sends his greetings!" It was a very cryptic explanation to be sure. "Don't worry, all will be clear soon!"

The ship finally docked, and ramps were brought up, so the cargo could be unloaded. The first "cargo" that Morag saw was dozens of stretchers carrying the wounded from France and Belgium – those that were too badly wounded to be returned to duty. Morag could see that most of them were heavily bandaged and that many were missing one or more limbs and yet those that could manage it let out a cheer because they were back home, and the war was finally over for them. Next were the walking wounded, similarly missing limbs or blinded by gas.

All the wounded were loaded into the ambulances and driven off to the hospital where the next phase of their rehabilitation would start.

The next group off were prisoners of war. Not very many, about a hundred or so. They looked like they were all officers and carried themselves accordingly. About half of the soldiers took them in hand and marched them off to the Citadel where their fate would be decided.

The last group was why they were all there. It was more prisoners of war, but these ones were of obviously higher status. Some were also wounded but were nonetheless able to hold themselves correctly. They were all very smartly dressed, and they all had many decorations on their uniforms. She noticed a small number of them had a sparkling blue cross at their throats. This must be the fabled Blue Max that was so well known.

Her eyes were drawn to one man in particular. He had a very familiar stance. Where had she seen him before?

Peter! That was Peter! As soon as she realised who it was she was off, sprinting for the group of senior German officers like a greyhound chasing a rabbit.

The assembled dignitaries did nothing as they had hoped something like this would happen.

The Germans meanwhile had no idea what was happening but seeing a beautiful woman sprinting for them caused an awkward stirring amongst them.

Except for Peter who, recognizing Morag immediately, set off to meet her half way. He was still feeling his injury though, so he was only able to hobble painfully towards her. They met closer to the ship than the dignitaries but that didn't lessen the greeting. She leapt into his arms and hugged him half to death, crying and vibrating with happiness.

"Peter! Peter! You're alive! You're in one piece! Have you heard from Ewan?" She hadn't seen Peter since he and Elsa had left for Germany back in 1914. Was that only three years ago? It seemed like centuries! She was happy and grateful that he was back alive and well but desperately wanted to ask him about Ewan. She felt sure that he had seen him recently.

Morag didn't see an enemy that had killed Canadian soldiers. All she saw was a very dear friend who she had feared she would never see again.

She was just realising that the little knot of dignitaries was making their way towards them.

Peter knew immediately what was happening. For one thing, he had been briefed that it would and for another he welcomed it.

General Currie had explained it to him before he boarded the ship in France. He had told him that his primary task was to be prepared to help mend fences between Canada and Germany when the war inevitably ended. He would not be asked to betray his country. His reward would be the return of Elsa and his child to Canada as soon as that could be arranged. For that he would do much.

The immediate manifestation of this though was this meeting between selected Canadian politicians and senior officers. A small number of like-minded captured German officers, some of whom were in similar circumstances, were willing to help.

The meeting was cordial enough, and he was more than happy to play his part. He was determined that he would do what he could to prevent this mindless slaughter from happening again.

His only regret was that he had not been able to warn Morag about what was happening. He was sure though that she would understand and do her part as well.

"Morag! I am so happy to see you well! Ewan told me about Hamish and Mairi. That made me happy to hear. Elsa is pregnant as well and is due in September." He blurted all this out with one breath.

Morag was ecstatic that Peter had talked to Ewan so recently and at the same time shocked that she should see Peter before she saw Ewan. "How is he, Peter? When did you last see him? Is he well?" she realised that they were both just blurting their emotions out.

Before Peter could answer, the knot of dignitaries had reached them.

"Mrs MacBride! I see you recognize one of our celebrity guests?" said a well-dressed older gentleman who turned out to be a senior member of the External Affairs Office. "We hope to show that Canadians and Germans can still get along and now that the Americans have entered the fray we are clearly winning the war … my apologies Colonel Baum …." who nodded noncommittally, "We need to start fostering friendship or at least tempering animosity, in order to forge a new world." The speeches were already starting it seemed. It was then that Morag noticed the small group of reporters that were present, furiously scribbling in their notebooks. Peter had been assured that none of this would be publicized until after the war.

After about an hour of speechifying and glad handing all round Morag was given an opportunity to talk to Peter alone.

They found a bench by the waterfront (with the MacBride & Baum stamp on it!).

Peter's leg was hurting him, so he needed to sit down. There were a number of soldiers circumspectly guarding him. "Who are they kidding? ... I'm obviously not going to run away!" he laughed, unexpectedly in a good mood. It was good to be home, he realised that he was thinking of Halifax as his "home" now, and with good friends again.

"How are you, Peter? How are you really? We've all missed you and Elsa terribly, it was like a piece of our heart was torn out when you left. No one thought badly of you, no one who matters anyway, and no one important will hold it against you." She felt like she was also making a speech.

"I never regretted leaving when I did," he started, "even when I knew I might be facing Ewan in battle, which I eventually did ... twice! I left to do my duty to my Fatherland. And I have some pretty baubles to show for it," he continued, fingering his Blue Max at his throat, "but precious little else."

Morag was astounded that Peter had met Ewan not once but twice on the battlefield, "Twice! Bloody hell! ... That story can wait though, how is he?" she pressed.

"Ewan is well, a little banged up but nothing important is missing," he said with a wink, "he sends his love, of course, and he asked me to give you this." He handed her a small package which she longed to open but would only do so in the privacy of her own bedroom.

"Elsa is also well, I saw her at Christmas time ... that's why she's now pregnant!" he joked with a wink. It was a little strained, but it was a shade of the old Peter, maybe there was hope after all. "I'm sure she would send her love too. We talked of you often when I was last in Hamburg."

Morag realised that Peter was not the same man who had left so full of pride and purpose only three short years ago. He had changed, hopefully for the better but only time would tell. Mostly he had matured but there were darker shades hidden below the surface. He had experienced horrors that she was glad she had never seen and hoped she never would.

CHAPTER 17

PASSCHENDAELE NOVEMBER 1917

*
**

Ewan was back with his battalion after a brief respite to heal and reflect. The mood was still positive. Relatively few men had been killed, and a great victory had been won. The British, of course, barely acknowledged Canada's part in, what was to them the greater Battle of Arras, but the Canadians knew better, they were now a force to be reckoned with. Never again would they fight as just some random "British" force, from now on they were the Canadian Corps and would fight as such. And General Currie, a Canadian, was now in command of that corps.

He was happier than he had been in quite a while. His best friend was now safe and back in Canada, bizarrely, and he had carried his precious present with him for Morag. A piece of the hard chalk that underlay much of northern France and Flanders on which he had carved his and Morag's likenesses. Copied lovingly from a photo that he carried with him at all times.

His ebullient mood was tempered by his renewed purpose. To see this war through and then to be done with horrifying death and destruction forever more.

They had a brief respite while they integrated new reinforcements into their battle hardened ranks. Less were needed this time, thankfully, but it was still a sombre process replacing men that had been with the battalion since the beginning of the war.

Once again, they licked their wounds, put on their metaphoric war paint and headed east, back into Belgium once more.

In mid-October they moved into a farm somewhat west of the village of Passchendaele, just inside France, which had last been occupied by an Australian battalion. Queer birds, the Aussies, they wore these great big hats with one side pinned up which kind of made them look like they were for show rather than for any particular purpose. Bloody good fighters though … second only to the Canadians they reckoned!

Ewan would have been glad of one of those floppy hats when the rains started in August. They never let up for more than a day here and a day there. Everything was cold, wet and miserable.

Welcome to western Belgium!

*
**

Once they had settled in they found they were billeted near a British Royal Engineer unit. As a pioneer and blacksmith Ewan was interested in talking shop with fellow tradesmen so he wandered over for a chat. Maybe some of them were Scots?

No sooner had he started talking to them when he noticed one man in particular. A giant of a man who he could hardly fail to notice because he stood head and shoulders above anyone else. A man who Ewan owed his life to, both metaphorically and literally since this man had passed his own legacy to Ewan and his friends without any hesitation.

Angus Watt. Or Angus Og or Wee Angus. The man who had been falsely accused of deliberately breaking that nasty English bastard's jaw and murdering Ewan's friend in a fit of rage. Ewan had thought of him often over the years but had never expected to see him again. Yet here he was, in France, large as life and a sergeant in a Royal Engineer unit.

Angus was looking the other way, so Ewan walked boldly up to him and said, with an enormous smile on his face, "Who let this big ugly bugger in here?"

Angus swung around, prepared for battle, "Who said that? I'll wipe the floor with the bastard!" He then noticed a small soldier with an ear to ear grin on his face staring up at him like an eejit. He didn't look familiar, but something was familiar about the voice.

"Angus, it's me … Ewan MacBride! Frae Fort William, dae ye no mind me?"

Then the penny dropped with an enormous clatter, "Ewan MacBride! I never thought I'd see your scrawny wee face again. I heard you'd disappeared to Canada or Australia or some other bloody place!" then he noticed Ewan's shoulder flashes and grabbed one in his paw, "I see the rumours were true, a bloody colonial now, are ye?" but he had an equally large grin on his face.

Angus grabbed Ewan by the shoulders and enveloped him in an immense bear hug, nearly crushing the life out of him. He was in real fear for his life! Angus's friends were all in awe of this colonial who had the balls to address Wee Angus in such a way! There was much laughter and back slapping to go around.

Ewan then turned serious. "Angus, I have thought about you and yer Da constantly these past years and always worried what had become of you. My Da told me you'd been released but I never thought I'd see ye again."

Angus was now equally serious. "My Da went into a deep depression. He was already ill when that whole thing with Chelmsford happened. If you hadn't killed that bastard I probably would have. He lasted another two years but died while I was in prison," he said with feeling.

"Actually, 'twas Rory that killed him, because of what he had done tae Sandy, but if he hadn't, I would have," Ewan explained.

"Ah, I never did hear the truth of it," Angus replied.

"I'm glad to see yer no in jail anymore. And I'm right sorry to hear about yer Da, he was a giant of a man in every way."

"Aye, well, as soon as the whole story came out they realised I was innocent and let me go. 'Course that was only after I'd spent three years breaking rocks at His Majesty's pleasure!" he said it with a grin though.

The two old friends spent several hours getting caught up with each other's stories, neither saying anything about Angus's gift to the boys those many years ago. Ewan finally brought it up.

"Angus, I can't thank you enough for your gift back then, without it I would be just another unemployed Scottish immigrant."

"Och, I was happy to do it, you and yer Da looked after my Da in royal style and they kept most of what you left in trust for me so I'm no doing too badly. I was running a farriers shop in Edinburgh when Uncle Willy made a dash for Belgium ... and here I am!"

At that point Ewan became very serious and was fighting back tears, "Well, I can never repay you and I will always owe you a great debt, of gratitude at least. You'll have tae come tae Canada tae visit Morag and the bairns after the war."

"Aye, I'll dae that for sure, lad!"

And with a bone crushing handshake they parted as friends once more and as equals and another of Ewan's worries was finally cleared up.

*
**

But then the war intervened again. There was a brief little fracas at a hill called "70". Not as big as some previous skirmishes but there was a new nastiness for most of the Canadians ... gas. They were well trained to deal with it by this point in the war, but it added an unnecessary evil to an already evil situation. And the battle of Hill 70 only resulted in more people being displaced and more houses being destroyed and more men being dead and there was still no end in sight.

By this time, Ewan and Lt Dundas had made a name for themselves as a team that could get almost anything done.

Harold was promoted to captain and was given command of the company and he brought Ewan with him as Company Sergeant Major. They immediately set about turning their company into a unit filled with the finest "shock" troops in the CEF. It was always "their" company not "his" company to Harold Dundas. They weren't above stealing men or materiel from other, "lesser", companies when those company commanders or CSMs weren't looking.

All was fair in love and war, after all. He had even traded one of his "liberated" Lugers, a war trophy, with a Belgian officer for his FN M1903 pistol, which he figured would be more useful in the trenches.

By the time September rolled around, "their" Company was at full strength with more than ninety per cent of them being battle tested veterans. They had none of the rumoured conscripts that Canada had finally had to resort to now that the flood of volunteers was dwindling. They were the lead company of the MacKenzie Battalion and everyone knew it.

So, when they moved east, back into Belgium, to prepare for the coming battle they were champing at the bit and ready for anything. Anything, that is, except the bloody rain.

While on their way to their start lines it all started to seem too familiar. They moved past Ypres and Zonnebeke and other places they knew all too well from other centuries, decades in the past. Once again, Ewan wondered what the hell they were doing there and quickly moved his mind on to worrying about his soldiers and how to keep them alive for another day.

Earlier shelling had destroyed the carefully husbanded field drainage systems and had, with the enthusiastic help of the rain, turned the entire country of Belgium into one giant quagmire.

The tactics introduced at Vimy Ridge had been refined to the nth degree. Every man knew every other man's job so there would be no interruption in the command structure should one key man be killed.

The MacKenzie Battalion learned that their objective would be the village itself, or, more accurately, the piles of mud and bricks that were once the pretty Belgian village of Passchendaele. They also learned that they would be in the third of three stages of the battle, only going over the top when the outcome of the battle was assured or so their CO, Colonel Blois, told them.

They, of course, believed that. Just like they'd believed they'd be home by Christmas. But, thanks to the success of the tactics and training practiced before, at Vimy, they felt some real confidence and at least had some hope of bringing the war that much closer to an end.

Just after 05:30 on October 26, they heard the guns begin their slow death beat on the ground to their north and east.

It had started.

Between then and Guy Fawkes night, November 5, they heard the guns and the machine guns and the yelling of excited men and the screams of dying men and the smell of cordite and saw it all moving slowly east and north, ever so slowly, like honey flowing over broken glass.

Ten days and ten nights they listened to that cacophony of death, realising that they were losing friends with every crash of a whizz-bang or with every stream of Spandau bullets that came across no man's land, and all the while trying not to dwell on the fact that it would be their turn next.

Then on the morning of November 6 their turn came.

Harold and Ewan had the company lined up by platoons in the forward positions, which were now, like the men they contained, battered and well worn. Then, at precisely 06:00 hours the whistles blew, and they were off, like the finely tuned greyhounds that they were, albeit slow and heavily weighed down greyhounds, with weapons, kit, and ammunition.

The Germans had miscalculated their counter barrage, due to the speed of the advance, and it fell well behind Ewan and his mates. Thus they had relatively light opposition as they approached Passchendaele proper.

By 07:00, Harold and most of a platoon were well on their way to the village but they were being held up by a pillbox about two hundred yards south of what was left of the church.

Ewan spotted this and realized that one pillbox was holding up the whole company advance. So, he decided to go and see what he could do about it. He left the rest of the company in place under a trusted sergeant with instructions to hold until instructed otherwise and moved towards Harold's position, taking half a dozen well-seasoned men with him. By the time he got there, three of Harold's men had been shredded by one of the Spandaus in the pillbox and six more had been wounded. They were effectively stalled because the pillbox had fields of fire, which encompassed at least three hundred yards of the line. They needed to cross this killing zone before they could secure Passchendaele proper. And what light there was was getting stronger.

Ewan slithered over to where Harold was conferring with some junior officers and NCOs from the company.

"Sir, we've got tae take those buggers from behind. We can no get around them in force from the front or from either side. Ye've proved that right enough," said Ewan as soon as he slid into the shell hole that served as a company HQ.

"We've nothing bigger than Mills bombs, and those aren't even marking that bloody pillbox let alone killing it. Plus, if you can't get around them how the devil are you going to get behind them?" Harold responded. "What's your plan for that, Ewan?"

"There's a route past them on the right, sir, I'm sure of it," Ewan said, "Cpl Crowfoot, find it if you please."

"Right, Sarn't," Doug Crowfoot replied before heading off into the clearing fog to the north.

"If he can't find a route, then there isn't one." Ewan told no-one in particular.

Harold said, "You think highly of him don't you?"

"Aye, sir, for this task, none better. He's the best sneak we have, he thinks it's awfy funny tae creep up on one of the young sentries and draw a line with red lipstick across his throat. If he's no payin' attention or dozing the wee lad'll usually crap himself. And he can wind his way through barbed wire faster than any man I've known."

Sure enough, Crowfoot was back twenty minutes later with good news … and gifts. He walked up to Harold and presented him with a shiny new Luger, complete with leather holster and ammunition pouch. After putting it in Harold's dumbfounded hands he said, "The owner won't be needing it anymore, sir!" grinning from ear to ear like an idiot but with a cheeky twinkle in his eye.

Then, more seriously, he turned to Ewan and reported, "Sarn't Major, that pillbox is well defended. There are two Spandaus inside, and they have clear fields of fire for at least ninety degrees on either side of them, probably more on their right, and there's about twenty yards of trench leading north from one side of the box and another section of about forty yards leading south. There are about twenty men, including six crew for each of the guns and a sergeant. There was an officer but …. well, that's his Luger, sir!" and the grin returned.

"Best approach from the north then?" he asked Crowfoot.

"Yeah, I reckon there's four Jerries in the north trench plus the access door to the pillbox is on the northeast corner. The good news is that they're isolated, there's nothing covering them for at least thirty yards"

Ewan detailed the assault. "Right, that's our plan then, ten men. All ten circle around behind them following Crowfoot. Three of you take the north trench, four take the south and myself and two others take the bunker with grenades. Three Lewis guns, one for each group," one of which Ewan acquired, "and every man with as many Mills bombs as he can carry. Questions?"

Harold piped up. "Sounds good but you'll need a signal for the attack, a diversion would be best. I'll take ten men and try and flank them on their left flank. Nothing too obvious but enough to catch their eye. And when they open fire … you go."

"Aye, that should work. Right, you men that came o'er wi' me, that's seven, and you three likely lads o'er there. Bomb up and we're off."

And with that they were gone. Less than five minutes after Doug Crowfoot returned from his recce they were away. After two and a half years of hard fighting these men didn't need to be told how to do anything. This was a routine obstacle clearance, one that they'd all done a hundred or more times, and, for a change, the rain had stopped.

Harold and Ewan had synchronized watches before they left, and Harold decided that at precisely seven minutes after eight he would start his distracting move. It wasn't full light yet, but fog still lingered in the trenches, so it should hide their exact positions well enough. They'd have to move across the front of the pillbox to make sure the Jerries spotted them.

Ewan and his group had moved round back without being spotted, once again the slippery fog helped. The three groups got in place with about a minute to spare with Ewan in the middle.

There was a cacophony of noise all around them, yet they could hear their own hearts beating and could feel the breathing of the men next to them. Though they had done this sort of thing dozens of times the anticipation was still felt as keenly as a finely stropped razor blade.

Right at 08:07 he heard *"Achtung, Englander!!"* and then the firing of the two Spandaus, as Harold's group moved from right to left across their front.

Ewan screamed *"Fraoch Eilean, get em!!"* Two of his companions threw their Mills bombs into the pillbox. Waiting until they went off, Ewan sprung into the entrance with his Lewis gun in front of him and fired a five second burst into the interior. It proved unnecessary since the two Mills bombs had taken care of the poor buggers inside. Their war was now over.

The other two groups had dealt with the remaining Jerries around the pillbox and that part of the trench was now theirs.

What Doug Crowfoot had not seen, through no fault of his own, was the twenty or so German soldiers rapidly approaching them from the empty area behind them. Crowfoot was not the only one who had observed the thirty-yard open space behind the pillbox. So had the Jerry commander.

Harold and his men ran straight into the Jerry reinforcements at full tilt and only saw them coming at the last possible fraction of a second. Too late for six of Harold's men who fell to the concentrated fire of twenty angry

German soldiers. The rest rallied quickly and were joined by the remainder of the platoon.

Ewan and his group were, by now, sheltered by the pillbox. That now became their rallying point.

What started as a simple obstacle clearance now became a general melee with fifty or so angry soldiers fighting furiously hand to hand, and to the death, for control of what was now, essentially, a hollow cube of concrete roughly three yards on a side and full of nothing but mangled German corpses.

Ewan and Harold met at the back of the pillbox and Ewan had time to say, "OK, one down, on to the next one," before the business end of a German bayonet appeared in the centre of Harold's chest having entered from the back under the impetus of a large, and very angry, German soldier.

Harold said, quite calmly Ewan thought later, under the circumstances, "Bugger," and collapsed at Ewan's feet with the German's bayonet, with rifle and German soldier still attached, still sticking in his back.

Ewan reacted instantly and raised his Lewis gun, which he still had at the ready, and fired another short burst into the upper chest of the German, which disintegrated under the impact of a dozen .303 bullets entering it in a matter of seconds. He then dropped the now empty Lewis gun and drew his FN M1903 pistol, which he then put to good use dispatching four more German soldiers.

Quickly checking to make sure Harold was still alive he then rallied the men and plunged off to take another pillbox behind the first. This time he let momentum carry him right into the entry way just as the loader was changing belts. He pistol-whipped the gunner, shot the loader in the face and tossed a Mills bomb into the communication trench leading up to the pillbox, killing three more men.

He ran into that trench far too fast and caught a piece of his own grenade in his cheek where it tore a hole right through it and took a couple of teeth with it.

Recovering his breath and reloading his pistol he then led another charge into the next trench where he ran into a Command Post bunker, shooting three junior officers in the legs and rounding up the remainder of the occupants, two majors and a colonel, and making them all his prisoners.

After placing a guard on the prisoners and reloading once more he took six men and captured another bunker with wounded and medical staff in it. He left one soldier to guard them with instructions to protect the two German medics from any interference whatsoever.

Then going round another corner he came face to face with three German soldiers in the process of setting up a Spandau to cover their retreat. He shot one in the stomach and a second one in the neck but the third one had drawn his bayonet and rushed him before he could shift his aim. The bayonet stuck him on his right side but didn't hit anything critical, it just made him even madder than before. He slammed the Jerry on the side of his head with a bunched left fist. Stunned for a second, the German, who was a foot taller and a couple of dozen pounds heavier, recovered and smashed Ewan in the face with his bayonet hilt, which doubled as a pretty effective cudgel. Still smarting from the grenade fragment he was barely able to respond. But respond he did by drawing his own bayonet and shoving it under the man's ribcage up into his lungs and silencing that bunker too.

Regrouping the platoon he then went to re-join the main company assault, which was now centred on the recently acquired pillbox. But first he checked on Harold.

Harold was now resting behind the pillbox with the bayonet still protruding from his chest. It had missed his heart, but only by a whisker. Even with the Gewehr 98 removed there was still five inches of the bayonet sticking out of his back preventing him from lying flat. He was awake, more or less, and lucid when he called Ewan over, "Ewan, I don't think I'll be leading the men anywhere anytime soon," his breath was halting and laboured, there was bloody froth in his mouth, a lung wound, and he was obviously in great pain. "You're in charge now."

"Sir … Harry … what about Lieutenant Graves? He's your number two."

"Graves? He's twenty-two and he joined us after Vimy, he's never seen a big fight before. No, you're it I'm afraid," he reasoned.

"But I'm only a sergeant!" Ewan said.

Harold thought for a minute. "Get Graves for me," he said, bloody froth emerging from his mouth. Harold was fading … fast.

"Lieutenant Graves!" Ewan yelled, "Come here if you please sir, Captain Dundas wants a word."

Young Graves scrambled over as quick as he could, slithering through the mud.

"Tom, I'm giving the company to Ewan, you'll learn quickly from him."

"No argument from me, sir, I know well enough I'm not ready for this kind of thing." Graves was young, but he was smart, he knew his limitations. "But the men, sir, what do we tell them?"

"Ewan, I'm giving you a battlefield commission, you're now Acting Lieutenant MacBride. You're a witness, Graves." Graves nodded.

"Aye sir!" Ewan said matter-of-factly.

And with that Harold Dundas joined the lists of the fallen.

Ewan quickly got the platoon commanders around him. He would grieve for his friend ... for all his friends ... later.

"Right lads, Captain Dundas is gone. I'm in command now, any questions?" it wasn't a dare, it was said with determination but without any condescension because he knew and respected these men as they did him. There were no questions.

A bare ten minutes had elapsed since they took the last pillbox and battles are won and lost in less time than that, so no further time was wasted.

He looked to their left and to their right and saw that the neighbouring companies had caught up with theirs ... his ... now ... and he needed to get moving to stay on pace.

At this point, the church at the centre of Passchendaele was nearly in their grasp, and they could see another attack from the west was heading towards it, so they moved to the east of it and helped secure the remains of the village on that side.

One last obstacle remained in their way. It was the remains of a building. Farmhouse, factory or school, there was not enough left of it to tell, but take it they must because there were a number of Spandaus in it, or around it. At least three judging by the amount of fire coming from the interior. And there also appeared to be some mortars inside as well. Again, he couldn't tell how many, but they were affecting the advance to his west, so they must be destroyed.

Once again Doug Crowfoot was going to earn his pay. Ewan sent him with three men to scout the area leading up to the building and see if there was a way around it and into it from the back.

This one would be a tougher nut to crack.

Crowfoot came back five minutes later but without much in the way of good news.

"Sure enough there are three Spandaus in that building Sarn't … err … I mean … sir, that is …" Nobody was used to Ewan being an officer yet, least of all Ewan.

"What else?" he asked.

"There's two on the sides, one covering each flank, and the third doesn't have much of a field of fire to the sides because its back is into the doorway," Crowfoot reported.

Ewan had the platoon commanders and their sergeants around him. "Cy, you tak' yer platoon and draw the fire of one Spandau from the left, Ed, you tak' yours and do the same on the right, and I'll tak' a platoon up the middle and try and catch that centre gun in one o' his blind spots," he said with a bit more confidence than he felt.

Cyrus Gibson was a young subaltern from Winnipeg who was only twenty-three but already had two years of experience doing this sort of thing and could be trusted to do what was necessary. Likewise, Ed Belanger would do a good job. He was an old man of thirty-one but had been a history teacher in Montreal before the war and soldiering came quite naturally to him as well. He would leave one platoon under young Alec Graves and all others except the grenadiers in reserve.

Ewan gave the others twenty minutes to get in place and start their diversions. They were to draw fire from the two flanking machine guns while he tried to find a blind spot for the gun in the middle. Right on cue the diversionary attacks started, and he started his group moving towards the badly broken doorway to the building. He knew there was a metal spitting monster in the shadows behind the threshold, so he moved cautiously at first.

What he didn't know was how many German rifles were supporting their gunners, so he started poking his head up to draw their fire and try and spot them. This was a dangerous game and he felt a bullet spang off his helmet as a warning. This gave him a pain in the neck, in more ways than one, and got his Celtic blood boiling again.

"Fraoch Eilean!" came the call as Ewan noted a lull in the machine gun fire in the centre and assumed, incorrectly as it turned out, they were changing belts again. This time the gun had jammed. That took longer to fix.

He led the charge into the entryway. The German gunner cleared his weapon and got one short burst away before Ewan ran into him with his pistol leading the way. The loader met him with a bayonet, and he smashed the weapon aside with the FN before firing two rounds into his head and clubbing the gunner in the face on the backswing.

The short burst that got away was aimed dead at a dozen of his men who were charging with him, two were wounded by it. His quick action prevented any further injuries or deaths and earned him the further respect of his men.

With this last action the village of Passchendaele was secure, and the Third Battle of Ypres was won. There was some intense mopping up in the next few days and weeks, but the major actions were done.

For his endeavours over the previous days, Ewan's battlefield commission was confirmed, and he was awarded the Victoria Cross for his selfless acts. Almost singlehandedly taking or destroying several Spandau machine guns in the run-up to Passchendaele village.

Once again, he cared only that he had made sure that more of his men would get home in one piece … or, at least, alive.

But Harold Dundas wouldn't be coming home …

CHAPTER 18
HALIFAX DECEMBER 1917

*
**

"Where are those bloody wee scoundrels?" Morag was beside herself looking for the twins.

"They're with Sean in the drawing room, Morag," said Toni with a certain twinkle in her eye.

"Da, what are ye' doin' to my bairns?" she scolded him gently.

"*To* them?" he said innocently, "why nothing lass … *with* them on the other hand …!" though speaking through a grin so large was very difficult. He was in the middle of playing 'horsey' with them, and they were taking turns riding on his back like he was a prize stallion. They were just the tonic he needed, and they brought him right out of the doldrums that he'd sailed into with all sails set.

He wasn't quite the same man he had been, but his depression had been caused mostly by overwork and with Toni taking a huge load off and the twins to keep him happy he had regained much of his old energy and sense of fun.

Morag in her turn was heartened by her father's recovery and by the help Toni was giving both of them. And she was so happy to see her living her new life with Alan and pleased that they had announced a date for their wedding. It would be on Sunday December 9, at the same kirk that she and Ewan had been married at, down by the Fair Grounds.

That morning, December 6, was a beautiful, if cold morning with not a breath of wind in the air. Morag and Toni were heading down to meet Alan and Peter at the Fair. From there they would all go down to the kirk, so they could have a closer look at the layout. Then they could finish making plans for the wedding.

Morag was to be Toni's Matron of Honour and Peter would be her escort. She had secured parole for him through the Mayor of Halifax. It was granted because he had been a well-known and liked businessman before the war and because the army wanted it. He had agreed on condition that Peter was escorted at all times. Alan was escorting him in case there was any ill will displayed. One of the conditions of the parole was that Peter could not wear his uniform in public, for obvious reasons. Therefore, he was in mufti.

As they headed down the hill, they noticed that there was a commotion down at the docks, and they saw that there was a fire on one of the ships. There were quite a few people milling around down there. But they were all too happy to pay it any mind.

Peter looked quite his old self since he wasn't in German uniform, like he had been the last time Morag had seen him. She had to admit that he had looked quite dashing in his dress uniform particularly with that pretty blue medal at his throat, if you could forget what it represented. But, again, for obvious reasons he couldn't wear it when out in public. She also noticed that he was still quite reserved and not as open and friendly as he had been. She correctly assumed that he had suffered in the trenches. He would take months to come to terms with his experiences, so she would leave him to talk about that in his own time.

For his part, Peter was just happy to be in Halifax again. He was sad that he couldn't be with Elsa and his son or his uncle Joe, but he was sure they were safe. For now, that would have to do.

They got to the church and had a look around. It was perfect. They weren't going to have a big wedding, only a dozen or so friends, mostly Alan's, so its small size suited them well. Toni and Alan even practiced the walk down the aisle, perhaps spending a little too much time practising the kiss at the alter! Then they all went outside to enjoy the crisp morning air.

"Oh Alan, mon cher, it's perfect!" Toni enthused, "We will be so 'appy living 'ere!"

"You can't believe how much I love you, Toni, you are the light of my life."

"OK, break it up you two, or we'll have to have the wedding right now!" Morag said through gales of laughter, even Peter was smiling. Their joy was palpable.

Meanwhile, down at the docks the commotion was getting more pronounced and the fire was growing by leaps and bounds. It appeared to be out of control. Morag assumed the dock workers and firemen would be able to deal with it so they all turned to go back into the church to have a closer look around.

She couldn't have been more wrong.

At 9:04 a.m. there was an almighty explosion, which rocked the ground and instantly turned everything around them into a flaming, roiling shambles. They, and everyone around them, were blown to the ground along with every building and every wagon and horse and every truck and car. Even the roads themselves seemed to vanish all around them.

The shock wave was accompanied by a wave of searing heat, which washed over them with an intensity that seemed to turn everything into molten light.

Halifax had been turned into the very entryway to hell itself. Flame and smoke and screams and blood seemed to be everywhere. A cacophony of rending metal and shattering glass accompanied by the screaming of people and animals. Metal and bricks and glass ... so much glass ... had flown from the harbour. It was daytime but there was no sun, only an ethereal blood red cloud of destruction boiling the air. Secondary explosions were punctuating the atmosphere with staccato bursts of death. The ground shuddered like a dying animal.

It seemed like hours, but it was only a few seconds before Morag opened her eyes to find that her world had changed forever. Peter was alive and lucid, though bleeding from a hundred cuts caused by flying glass. Only he had ever experienced anything like this before and even he was stunned by the sheer magnitude of the violence that had just happened. It reminded him of the mines at Vimy but even they didn't come close to this level of destruction. The only saving grace was that they had all had their backs to the harbour when it happened so their eyes were spared the worst of the flying glass assault.

Recovering her wits enough to function took a few horrifying minutes and then she and Peter went to look for Alan and Toni, trying not to assume the worst. They were not where she had seen them just moments before. They had been standing in the doorway of the kirk, next to a carriage, which was to be their conveyance to and from their wedding.

Peter found the carriage itself, or what was left of it, hanging from a shredded maple tree next to what had to have been the church, though all they could see was a jumble of wood and bricks and glass.

They found the two horses fifty yards away lying on their sides. On looking closer they noticed that the horses' heads were missing. Morag started frantically searching for her friends.

Peter found them in the ruins of the church. They were both alive, though unconscious. Most of Toni's dress and Alan's suit had been blown off and they had sustained dozens of cuts over their whole body though none looked serious. It was then that Morag realised that she herself was also cut and bleeding all over and wearing only rags.

Morag had found Toni under what was left of a pew near the front of the building, also unconscious but relatively uninjured. She had a large gash on the side of her head, though, which was swelling already. That didn't look good.

When Peter found Alan, he was trapped under several feet of rubble from the collapsed church. He was pinned by the heavy doorframe from the entrance way. The door itself had shielded him from the worst of the blast but had slammed him into the frame, which was now squeezing the life out of him.

"Morag, help me with this door, he won't live much longer if we don't get it off of him." Peter said with the authority of three years of commanding soldiers in battle. And like a soldier, Morag reacted. She moved beside Peter and grabbed the other side of the frame. They pulled, and they heaved with all their might, but it wouldn't budge more than a few inches.

That little bit of movement had roused Alan though and with his help and one more mighty heave they lifted the frame enough that Alan could wriggle out from under it. He had not been too badly hurt. A few bruised ribs, a broken nose and two black eyes but the door had shielded him from most of the flying glass.

The three of them took a moment to shake themselves off and then went to Toni who was still unconscious. The swelling at the back of her head was getting worse and Morag knew they'd have to get her some medical attention very soon or things would get very bad indeed.

Taking stock of the situation around them they stared, unbelieving, at the extreme devastation of the once beautiful Halifax harbour. Fires were burning out of control everywhere. Dead and horribly mutilated bodies of people and animals hung from roofs and windows and shredded trees everywhere they looked. Looking towards the harbour they could see nothing still standing. It seemed that all life and buildings had been blotted from the earth like an evil giant swatting an immense fly.

Peter was reminded of the remains of dozens of formerly pretty towns and villages in France and Belgium, which had been likewise destroyed by this insanity of war.

Behind them was little better but there were buildings still standing, though heavily damaged. They knew they had to get Toni to a hospital as soon as possible. Alan, now recovered enough to carry the woman he loved, picked her up, and they moved off to find help.

By now other dazed survivors were moving in the rubble. They were pulling themselves, and others, out of the devastation and were, likewise, searching for medical treatment.

Alan kept a death grip on Toni, afraid to let go of her for even a second because he thought he would lose her forever if he did. Morag led the way, finding the best route through the devastation and Peter kept right with them to lend a hand whenever needed. There was debris everywhere, and they had to traverse the rubble many times before getting to a hospital on a hill to the west of the harbour.

The hospital itself was little more than rubble. It had survived the main blast, but shock waves and shrapnel had shaken the building to its core. The staff were already overwhelmed even though the explosion had only been an hour before and many of them were casualties themselves. Still, they did the best they could. After stopping the immediate bleeding for Toni and the others they had a closer look at her. After a doctor quickly assessed that she was in no immediate danger they left her there, though he was worried about that lump he said. Peter and Alan went to help with the rescue of as many people as possible. Morag stayed at the hospital partly to keep an eye on Toni but also to help there. They were horribly understaffed.

*
**

The day after the explosion a heavy blizzard hit Halifax as if the gods of fate were cruelly laughing at them. This added another level of suffering to the victims.

The two new friends spent the following week rescuing trapped survivors, injured women and children, and animals. The days after that merged into one horrifying blur of death and destruction and were mostly spent recovering bodies. Peter was reminded of the *Titanic* and the floating horrors from that, and he was also struck by how much worse this disaster was than anything he had seen in the trenches. As horrific and devastating as that had been, there were no small children or pregnant women or old men and women amongst the dead on the western front.

Seeing dozens of children blinded by flying glass or torn apart by blast or shrapnel was infinitely more traumatic than seeing men, little older than some of these children, torn apart by artillery or machine guns.

He saw a line of a dozen small children, none more than six or seven years old winding their way to a hospital, each one with a completely bandaged head and with one hand on the shoulder of the child in front because they were all blind. Less than a year before he had seen an identical line of boys, not much older in grey uniforms likewise bandaged and leading each other because they had been blinded by gas. This barbarity had to stop.

Although they had quickly squashed rumours of German bombs causing this it was still caused by the war and Peter was more determined than ever to prevent this madness from happening again.

*
**

Alan checked in with Morag a dozen times a day. The swelling had not become any worse but neither had it lessened. Toni was in a coma but that allowed her body to concentrate its efforts on healing her superficial wounds. By the time she came out of the coma, six days later, her physical scars were well on the way to healing but when they took the bandages off her head her beautiful eyes were unable to see anything at all.

She was blind.

The doctor wasn't sure what had caused the blindness because there was no obvious trauma to her eyes. He would have to just keep monitoring her condition when he could. They were still overwhelmed.

Morag was also worried about her Da and the bairns. It wasn't until two days after the explosion she was finally able to go home to find the tannery shaken but standing. Sean was helping to shelter survivors in the many out-buildings, plus contending with the heavy snowfall that had added insult to injury. The bairns were as safe as they could be and staying out of the way was the only thing expected of them. Reassured, she went back to the hospital where she was still needed.

She saw many horrors over the next few days and the blizzard made things far worse. There were casualties caused by hypothermia after that. People were being brought in with limbs missing having been wrenched from their bodies by blast or cleanly severed by flying metal or glass.

The worst were the children, many were blinded by flying glass, others were horribly burned in their destroyed schools. School had been in session at the time and many students were crushed by collapsing walls and roofs. Many were killed outright … they were the lucky ones.

Days later, how many she didn't know, Morag found the time to send Ewan a telegram. The army provided the means to send brief notes to loved ones in France. The sick irony of soldiers losing loved ones who were supposed to be safe at home in Canada was not lost on them, and they made every effort to allow for communication between families.

Ewan's old foundry had been utterly destroyed.

Several children had now lost both fathers and mothers due to the war.

*
**

By the spring, things were returning to normal, heartbreakingly slowly but the human spirit is a remarkable beast. Millions of years before it had evolved to keep our ancestors alive on the plains of Africa, and now it kept people from despairing when all seemed lost. Gradually the city was rebuilding, the homeless were being housed, and children went back to school as the schools were rebuilt.

Morag was still helping at that same hospital as she had in December, primarily because she wanted to be a part of Toni's recovery.

"Morning, Toni! How are you, lass?" she said as cheerfully as she could but got no reply. Toni had lapsed into a deep depression after discovering her fate. The doctors were optimistic that things would improve once the swelling went down on her head. But three months later all her physical injuries had healed, and she was, once again, the extraordinarily beautiful young woman that she had been. But she was still blind.

Alan seldom left her side. When he wasn't working he was there. There was still much to be done in the critically injured city, but recovery was now on the horizon. He held her hand to let her know he was there and she stared, blankly, into his face, breaking his heart.

Morag watched this with sorrow because she knew the potential that had been lost. But thousands of people had been killed or injured or made homeless by this disaster, so this story was just one of many played out throughout the city. She now fully realised just what was happening all through Belgium and France and other places that the war had touched and that Halifax was just a snapshot of the horrors that were occurring all around the world. But this was her family, her friends. Her husband was enduring far worse in France. One of her best friends, Peter, had fought for the other side and yet he was a wonderful, decent man who had saved many lives in the destroyed city. It made no sense.

It was hard to keep her own morale up.

One day Dr Morrison found her and pulled her aside. He had tried telling Toni, but she was still unresponsive. "Morag, I don't want to get your hopes up just yet, but I've taken a closer look at Toni's head now that the swelling has gone down, and I've noticed a little cut just below and behind her left ear, exactly in the centre of where the swelling was. It hasn't healed like the rest of her has. I think it's infected."

"Isn't that bad?" she hedged.

"Well, yes, normally it would be, but in this case maybe not." He continued, "I'm positive there is something in there. There is an X-ray machine at the naval hospital. I want to take her there and see what's causing the infection. Maybe it's something that can be dealt with. As I said, though, don't get your hopes up just yet, it could just as easily be nothing."

Two days later Dr Morrison was back with the X-Rays. He called Morag into his office again. "See, right here. There is a small but sharp-edged and distinct shadow right where that inflammation is, and deep in her skull. There is a possibility, slim mind, that it can be removed. We'll see after that."

"Will it hurt her?" she was worried.

"No, the worst that will happen is that I confirm that she will stay blind." His confidence, she knew, was well practiced, but genuine.

"Well, what are you waiting for then?" she exhaled.

Three days later he was back. "The operation was, as I had hoped, relatively simple, and I'm cautiously optimistic. A small piece of metal was pinching off the optic nerves, right where they cross," he put a piece of jagged iron less than a quarter of an inch in diameter in her hand, "and once I removed it the nerves regained a uniform colour. Toni is young and otherwise healthy, so we shall see."

"When will you know?"

"When the swelling from the operation goes down we will be able to see if there's any change."

Another, interminable, five days went by before he removed the bandages once again. Both Morag and Alan were there. They were greeted by a scream. Not one of horror but one of joy. "I can see! I can see!" was Toni's joyous cry.

Cautiously the doctor said, "Exactly what can you see?"

"Just shadows but enough to know where each of you are! Alan, *mon coeur,* I see your wonderful shape!" She was, in fact, looking at the doctor but it was still a great victory.

Over the next few months her sight improved to almost its original strength. She would always wear strong spectacles, but it was a small price to pay to see her friends again.

By the summer of 1918, she and Alan had their wedding, and she confidently walked down the aisle with the help only of the man giving her away, Sean MacInnes.

CHAPTER 19

BELGIUM AND FRANCE – WINTER 1917/18

*
**

Ewan had spent Christmas 1917 worried about Morag and the bairns. He'd heard about the explosion in Halifax and feared the worst. He received a telegram from her a fortnight later saying that everyone was fine, and the city was recovering. That only made him worry more because after three years of war he was good at reading between the lines. Morag would never have been that cheery if everything was fine because then she would have mentioned the explosion or talked about the goings on in the city. He hoped he was just being paranoid but until he got a more detailed letter he would continue to worry.

Of more immediate concern was the interminable war.

Mercifully they were spared further fighting for the time being. Long cold winters were welcomed because it meant little or no death and devastation. They still rotated in and out of the trenches, they still patrolled and repaired and built and dug and ate bad army food, but relatively few died horribly.

They were able to bring their numbers up to strength again, or nearly so, volunteers were getting fewer and fewer back in Canada, so conscripts were finding their way to France. Very few in the frontline units like Ewan's but enough that they could sense the rot starting within the proud and keenly honed Canadian battalions long tempered by the forge of battle and quenched in the blood of heroes. Legends had been built, stories had been written and names like Ypres, Vimy and Passchendaele would be carved in the headstones of the fallen and the memory of a young and proud nation.

A sense of nationhood amongst the Canadians was growing ever stronger. Before the war, Ewan would have considered himself to be a displaced Scot, now he was a proud Canadian.

Ewan himself was not the wee blacksmith laddy that had joined a local battalion in Halifax because it was the thing to do. He was now the newly confirmed and promoted, Captain Ewan Duncan MacBride, VC, DCM, MM and bar, MID, hero of Ypres, Vimy Ridge and Passchendaele.

And yet he was still just Ewan MacBride from Fort William who was not yet twenty-four years of age.

For his sins, the Canadian army sent him on a public relations tour of the UK. Not many VC winners survived in good enough shape to be paraded about for the population to goggle over and to cheer. He had just enough wounds to make him look dashing. The scar on his mouth from the Jerry grenade gave him just the right air of the swashbuckling hero (he told them it was his own grenade, but they thought saying it was a Jerry grenade would make a better story). He agreed to do the tour on condition that he be allowed to go home to Scotland for an extended period.

So, much to his Ma's surprise, she got to have her wee bairn home for his twenty-fourth birthday.

The last time Ewan had made the journey by train to Fort William was only two years before but so much had happened since then. At that time, he had been just another anonymous soldier on a train full of soldiers. But this time he was a decorated war hero who rated a cabin to himself. He preferred the first trip and not because he was anticipating seeing his family again after so many years but because he hated being famous for something so horrible as killing fellow human beings – of almost killing his best friend … twice.

Still, this was the hand he had drawn, and he realised that he had done everything in his power to keep as many of his own men alive as possible.

"Hello, Ma … Pa," he said as he knocked on that beloved front door, less timidly this time.

He had wired ahead so they were expecting him, but his Ma still enveloped him in her motherly embrace, crying like she always did whenever something good happened.

"Son! It's good tae see ye, lad!" His Da was trying hard not to cry as well. Taking in the ribbons on his chest, the Sam Browne belt and the pips on his sleeves he realised that his son had been through a lot in his young life. He knew full well what those small badges meant and what had to be done to earn them. His fatherly love had grown into respect for the man his son had become.

Ewan had received a letter from Morag just before he came north and in it she had described how the bairns were growing like weeds, walking and talking now though not yet running the shop, their grandfather yes, but the shop, no! She went on about how Alan and Toni were doing, he couldn't wait to meet them and thank them for all they had done for her. He couldn't believe he knew so much about them but hadn't actually met them yet! He was truly amazed that Toni's sight had returned after the swelling on her head was discovered to be caused by a small piece of shrapnel. The surgeon in the hospital had been an army surgeon who was wounded in Flanders and had seen that happen in the trenches. It was good to know that at least some good was coming out of all this destruction and pain.

Most of all he was overjoyed to hear that Peter had been allowed day parole almost every day after all the good work he had done rescuing survivors of the explosion. He was a little jealous of the fact that Peter got to see Morag and the bairns almost every day. He understood why though.

Hamish tried desperately to talk to Ewan about what he had been through, but Ewan wanted only to talk about Morag and the bairns, and his life in Canada, and his friend Peter. The darker things would wait until after the war. His Ma was overjoyed that she was a granny and couldn't wait to meet wee Hamish Junior and Mairi. That led to promises that his folks would emigrate to Canada after the war.

The next two weeks went by in the blink of an eye. Ewan spent most of the first week sleeping in his old bed, too small for him though it was, listening to all the wonderful silence that seeped through the Highlands like a comfortable blanket.

For the second week, he spent the days walking around the town, healing both physically and mentally. He was in mufti, so he wouldn't cause a stir. He had been away so long, and he had changed so much that no-one recognized him. It was for the best though because as comfortable as this was, it wasn't home anymore, and he couldn't wait to get back to Halifax and to his new family.

He left his folks with promises that he would arrange for them to come to Canada as soon as possible after the war.

The next three weeks were spent fulfilling his obligation to the army for getting such a generous leave. An endless string of morale speeches and hospital visits and school visits and talks at church halls and on and on and on. He grew to hate it with every fibre of his being just as Peter had after winning his Blue Max. By the middle of March he'd had enough and wanted to return to his men … his brothers. It was where he belonged. If he couldn't be in Halifax with his real family then he'd be with his other family: the MacKenzie Battalion.

*
**

By the end of March, Ewan's company had returned to fighting strength. The walking wounded (including himself) had healed and returned to the lines. The half dozen conscripts they had been forced to take were now fully integrated, and you couldn't tell them from the veterans.

Cy Gibson and Ed Tremblay were now full lieutenants, Ed was his second in command and Cy commanded the lead platoon. The only dark spot was that Alec Graves had been killed by a sniper while he was away. Another good man gone. He had been replaced by an even younger Mike Anderson who was straight from Canada and barely nineteen years old.

Doug Crowfoot was now the CSM with a collection of his own medals.

Ewan was gratified to see many of the men that he'd come with from Halifax not only still there but leading the company. They were symbols of his vow to bring as many of them home as possible.

There was a definite feeling of optimism in the air. The deadlock of the trenches had been broken at last. Tanks had smashed that forever, and they were now efficient and plentiful. Aircraft had evolved from flimsy powered kites to powerful flying pillboxes. Used together they were an unbeatable combination. Artillery was now a surgical instrument rather than a bludgeon and the infantry were now a well-trained and highly experienced and professional force. Surely to God this Christmas would be the one they would all be home by?

From March to August they spent the time training and relaxing with brief spells in the line defending against an almost unthinkable attack … the Jerries were all but broken.

In late March, the Germans launched that unthinkable attack. One last series of desperate attempts to break through the British lines, which very nearly succeeded. This was well to the north of the Canadians though, so they weren't too worried. The Brits were bowed but unbroken and after July it was apparent that the German army was all but finished. They had spent their last experienced and well-trained soldiers in a futile attempt to win the war before the Americans were present in significant numbers.

So, Ewan and his lads took the opportunity to heal and rebuild their strength. They knew the war wasn't over yet, but they felt that the worst *was* over and that they could afford to relax a little.

One day in late March, Ewan received a letter from Morag. Not an unusual thing, she wrote every week. This time though it was odd because he would swear that she didn't actually write it. When he read the sentence, "Please write to your good friend, Peter Martin, the Mayor of Halifax. He has a request of you." he was suspicious. Very odd indeed he thought, the wording didn't sit quite right. It was written in her hand but the words were someone else's. The rest of the letter was obviously Morag because she was more cheerful, the twins were running around chasing their grandfather, Toni and Alan were so happy and planning a family after the war which must be any day now. The usual wonderfully banal stuff.

She didn't say anything about the rebuilding of Halifax, but he supposed she wasn't supposed to write about that. So, what was that stuff with the Mayor of Halifax about then? A request for him?

Ewan didn't think anything of it for a while. He was too busy rebuilding the 25th. But then on re-reading the letter a week or so later he realised that the part about Peter Martin, who had been a client of his, was written by Peter Baum, his writing style was distinctive enough for him to recognize it. What was he up to?

The only way to find out was to write to Peter Martin and hope he could shed some light on the subject. So he did just that.

Then in late May he received a small envelope from the City of Halifax addressed to him and ostensibly on government business. This was also not that unusual, he got official correspondence in his capacity as a company commander all the time, but from Halifax? His interest was piqued, what was going on?

He opened the letter not knowing what to expect and this is what he read.

Hello Ewan,

I hope all is well with you and that you are getting Morag's letters OK.

You must be wondering what this is all about. (That was an understatement!) *Well, what I can tell you comes straight from the office of General Currie himself. He knows that the war is all but won and that we will have to start the process of re-establishing relations with whatever is left of Germany afterwards. To that end, when he met Lieutenant Colonel Baum in France he was impressed by his candour and his determination to stop wars like this from ever happening again. Therefore, he arranged for him to be sent back to Canada after finding him agreeable to helping.* (Ah, that explains it!)

In return, General Currie promised to find Colonel Baum's wife Elsa in Hamburg and bring her, his son and his uncle to Canada.

General Currie has authorised me to tell you that whenever the war is won, you will be promoted to the rank of Brevet Major and given the task of liaising between the occupying forces and the German government, if they still have one by then.

This is entirely voluntary, of course, but let's face it, your fluent German would have led you to that, or a similar, position anyway.

If you are agreeable, when the time comes you will be sent her address in Hamburg and instructions on how to arrange the passage.

Please keep well Ewan,

Yours,

Peter Martin

He couldn't have been more stunned. Of course, he would help Peter. Of course, he would help find Elsa, he loved her like a sister. He had to meet Peter's son and uncle Joe, whom Peter had talked of endlessly.

However, staying behind after the war was something that he hadn't even considered. And going to Germany! He never would have imagined that four years ago … or last week, for that matter.

The thought of delaying his reunion with Morag and his meeting with the bairns made him pause. But, he owed Peter much, including his life so it was a small price to pay in the end.

But first there was the small matter of finishing the war.

*
**

By August, the twins were a going concern. They were running their grandpa ragged and he was enjoying every minute of it. Morag was still helping at the same hospital.

War work was on hold because the devastation in Halifax had been so great, it would be years before the city was back to its former glory. Thousands of people were homeless or injured or both. Sean kept some of the refugees in his sheds and other out buildings well into the late summer. He himself was helping with organizing the flow of relief supplies that were coming in to Halifax on an hourly basis, much of it from Boston and other American locales.

After the last of the refugees left, Sean was able to start rebuilding the tannery.

Toni was helping out with injured children, mainly blinded younger ones, some of whom were orphans. She felt a kinship with the blind ones. She had narrowly escaped the same fate and felt it was her duty to help the doctors as a way to pay them back for what they had done for her.

Alan was working almost every day on the prevention of theft and looting from the destroyed shops and businesses. And also controlling the heavy volume of vehicles coming into the city. He and Toni rarely saw each other. Their wedding was brief but emotional. The reception and honeymoon would wait.

Because Peter knew Halifax well and also because of the prodigious work he had done saving lives after the initial explosion he was granted what was, effectively, permanent parole. This meant that he only had to check in at the Citadel once a day and spend the night there. The other PoWs had been relocated, which was a great relief to him because he couldn't relate to other German soldiers anymore. The number of military personnel in the city had grown after the disaster. There were now thousands of soldiers and sailors helping with the rebuilding efforts.

Peter felt that he had betrayed Halifax, the city that had taken him in during a desperate time in his life. He wanted to repay his self-imposed debt.

Sean, Morag, Toni and Alan all lived in Sean's house. Peter stayed there during the day too, there simply weren't any other spaces available. They had a dozen other people living on the property – people who had had their homes destroyed and who had all lost family members. A lot of them had been employees of the tannery, and Sean thought of them more as tenants now.

*
**

During the relocation of the remaining PoWs from the Citadel, one of the officers had escaped. His name was Hauptmann Karl von der Marwitz. After he escaped he went to ground and was thought to have found a way out of Canada.

Then, in early September 1918, a Canadian officer had his throat cut and, before any help came, he bled to death. At the time, it was just thought to be a random act of violence, a mugging gone wrong. There were some very desperate people in Halifax, so it was put down to that.

The following week a British naval officer was killed in the identical manner. Coincidence they thought. But after the third killing, this time a senior Canadian officer, a lieutenant colonel, was killed in the same manner the order came out that all officers would walk in pairs, at all times when away from their duty post.

That seemed to work because there were no more deaths for a fortnight. But then two subalterns were attacked at night by a knife-wielding mad man. That was the description given by the surviving man after his colleague had been killed by a stab wound to the chest. The man had run out of a side street holding a large hunting knife and wasted no time in attacking the two young lads who both panicked. By the time the second man had recovered his wits his friend was lying, bleeding, on the ground. The attacker had vanished as quickly as he had appeared.

He further described the attacker as a blond man, taller than average, wiry with medium length hair and, crucially, he was wearing a German officer's uniform – a bit battered and in disrepair but, unmistakably, an officer's uniform.

This was, of course, a perfect description of Karl von der Marwitz. Apparently, he had hidden in the city until the search for him had concluded before starting his killing spree. There was no indication that he was mad. All of his actions had been deliberate and well thought out. He only attacked officers, clearly this was premeditated.

All of the other captured officers who had been held with von der Marwitz were interviewed in their new camp outside of Halifax. They all said that he was a very intelligent man, quite personable but with an abject hatred of anything British.

He was one of the new German *Stoßtruppen,* or Stormtroopers, who had recently caused some grief in the trenches. They were mostly Prussians, and a large proportion of them were fanatics. Von der Marwitz had been sent to Canada because he was a member of a minor Prussian noble family, and a nephew of General Johannes Georg von der Marwitz, a prominent Prussian general.

Peter was also interviewed since they had been on the same ship. He confirmed that the man was a dangerous fanatic and that they hadn't liked each other from the start. Von der Marwitz was offended by the fact that a Jew had won the Blue Max and a handsome and younger Jew at that.

The men who interviewed Peter were senior British and Canadian officers, some of whom had experienced *Stoßtruppen* in France and could corroborate just how dangerous these men were. The consensus was that only someone as driven as he was would be able to track him down. Peter immediately volunteered; he thought that this would be his chance to redeem himself to Canada.

The colonels were taken aback, that's not where they were going with this at all. The thought of tracking down a fanatical German Stormtrooper using a German lieutenant colonel with a Pour le Mérite, was unsettling at best.

"Colonel Baum, I'm sure you can appreciate how unusual your request is," replied a British colonel, visibly squirming.

"Yes, sir, I do but I want nothing more than to repay this country for the way I betrayed her in 1914," he reasoned.

One of the Canadian colonels who had talked extensively with Peter and knew General Currie's plan replied. "Yes, we do Peter, but you must realise that allowing this could be construed as treason on our part. Employing an enemy combatant in this way is frowned upon at best."

"What if I were to formally defect to the Allied cause?" he continued, "then I would be fighting for my new allies."

"Hmm, we'll have to think about that," he replied.

The following day, von der Marwitz struck again, this time two visiting American naval officers were killed, one's throat was cut and the other was stabbed three times in the chest. Something needed to be done, and fast. They called Peter in for another interview.

"Colonel Baum, we've run out of options, we're willing to take the risk. It's definitely the lesser danger. How would you go about finding him?" the Canadian colonel asked. Colonel Derek Matheson was an experienced officer who had risen from 2nd Lieutenant to Colonel in France before being wounded at Passchendaele.

"I've thought about that. There are officers from every Allied country in Halifax right now, with a wide variety of uniforms."

"Go on," said Colonel Matheson.

"Would anyone, particularly a civilian, recognize my uniform as a German one?"

"Probably not, unless they'd seen one before. I think I see where you're going with this," Matheson said.

"Yes, if I wore my full uniform and walked around at night it may attract his attention. He would recognise me. He hated the fact that I had won the Pour le Mérite and he hadn't. Not to mention the fact that I'm a Jew, and he hates Jews," Peter reasoned.

"OK, how about this then, a counter offer if you will, you wear your dress uniform and I accompany you in mine. We would both be followed by a half dozen hand-picked soldiers who accompany us in the shadows. It might be too tempting a target for him to ignore."

They started that very night. Peter felt strange putting on his uniform again. The Blue Max seemed out of place now. His only consolation was that he hadn't been fighting Canadians when we won it.

The route they picked was due east from the Citadel to the harbour then northwest past the navy dockyard to the edge of the most devastated destruction zone and then roughly south and east back to the Citadel. This route took them about two hours but all they got was exercise. No sign of their quarry. Not that they had expected it to work that quickly.

They did the same thing every night for two weeks, changing the route slightly each time. On the fifteenth night as they were walking back to the Citadel up Queen Street, a man was suddenly standing right in front of them holding a small cavalry sword. He was clean shaven and had short hair. Clearly, he had been taking care of himself during his time on the run. His uniform though was showing some wear and tear.

"Hello, Karl," Peter greeted him in German. Von der Marwitz didn't speak English. "You're looking well, considering."

"Treasonous Jewish pig! How dare you wear the Pour le Mérite, only a Prussian is entitled to that!" he snarled.

"Well, there are some French soldiers who may not agree with you, Karl," Peter replied calmly. He knew that the soldiers accompanying them would be moving into place, so he had to keep von der Marwitz talking to give them time. "Let me introduce Colonel Derek Matheson of the Canadian Expeditionary Force, I understand it was one of his comrades who captured you." Peter was deliberately baiting him in order to provoke a reaction, all the while keeping a hand on his dagger. The Canadians allowed him to carry a dagger but drew the line at a pistol. He really missed his Mauser C96.

"He's nothing but a British lackey, and the British are a degenerate race!" he spat. "I'm not interested in him at all."

"What are you interested in then?" Peter casually replied.

"I would enjoy nothing more than cutting your stinking Jewish head off with this." He waved the sword around over his head. Peter spotted movement behind von der Marwitz. The men were almost in place.

"Well, why don't you then?" he felt rather than saw Colonel Matheson tensing himself. He now saw four soldiers moving up behind von der Marwitz and had to keep him focused elsewhere. He started to slowly draw his dagger.

Von der Marwitz spotted Peter's movement "Why don't you draw that thing then, pig? Then I can stick you properly." He was edging ever closer to the two men.

"I believe I will," said Peter as he simultaneously drew the dagger and lunged at von der Marwitz. The man foolishly swung his sword back, preparing to chop at Peter's head but Peter was quicker and rammed his dagger into von der Marwitz's chest right up to the hilt. Momentum carried the sword down and it bit into Peter's shoulder without causing any major damage.

Almost simultaneously three eighteen inch sword bayonets protruded from von der Marwitz's chest having entered from the back as the soldiers ran up and finished the job.

Colonel Matheson turned to Peter and said, "You have now completed your penance Colonel Baum. Welcome back to Canada, Peter!"

CHAPTER 20

FRANCE, AUGUST 1918

*
**

By August, the preparations for what was hoped to be the final offensive in this bloody and pointless war were ready. They had been delayed somewhat by the failed Jerry Spring Offensive but were now largely complete.

On August 8, they were in Amiens and that was where they kicked off from. They advanced so fast that they spent more time walking than fighting, and there was still plenty of that. The trenches were finally behind them, and good riddance too.

Ewan and his company spent the next three months chasing the once proud and fierce but now dispirited and demoralized, Imperial German Army almost all the way back to Germany. There didn't seem to be any formal strategy on the German's part, just pockets of hasty defences and a series of rear guard actions. These actions were no less fierce though because like cornered animals the Jerries knew they were fighting for their very lives. There was still some vicious fighting to be done and many good men died needlessly in the process but at least they could now taste victory.

The casualties were high but much lower when compared to previous years at any rate, but the odd thing was that while the earlier battles at Ypres, Vimy and Passchendaele had been brutal and horrific they were quite short, generally only a few days or weeks at the most. This time it went on day after day for weeks and names like Amiens, Arras, The Canal du Nord, Cambrai and Valenciennes came and went in a blood-tinged blur and were burned into their memories. The net effect was exhausting. If they weren't fighting they were walking. They slept, if at all, in barns and under wagons and in ditches.

It was gratifying though because they were liberating towns and villages all across northern France and Belgium. These soon to be forgotten places were intact, not in smithereens, and the people came out to greet them as they moved through them. It was very different from the four preceding years, which had been full of death and devastation, filling their eyes and their nostrils with unfathomable sights and smells. Now everything was green and as summer faded into fall the colours changed, and Ewan could almost imagine himself strolling through Fort William or Halifax simply enjoying the day.

Ewan and his men were fighting almost every day, but generally short, sharp actions, quickly resolved. Only once in those last few days was Ewan severely tested.

After three months of almost continuous fighting, on November 9 they entered the village of Bougnies on the outskirts of Mons where they encountered a hasty road block on the main road to Mons at a "Y" junction. They were accompanied by two Mark V tanks. This was the first time he'd worked directly with tanks, so he was interested in seeing what they could do.

Ewan sent Doug Crowfoot to have a look. "Doug, tak' half a dozen men an' tak' a look at yon barrier in the road up ahead."

"Righto, sir." And with that he was off.

He was back fifteen minutes later with a report. "Sir, we had a good look at the front of the barrier and saw three Spandaus poking their nasty little noses out the front."

"Well, that disnae sound sae bad, we can tak' those," Ewan said.

"Yeah, but the real surprise is in behind them. There are two, four-inch guns. They look like howitzers, in the courtyard of some buildings to the right of the main road," Doug Crowfoot added.

"Hmm, that sounds like a job for oor steel companions." Ewan went over to the two tanks, which were sitting in the front yard of a house right behind them waiting for their orders. One of them had big guns sticking out of two sponsons, one on each side, the other was bristling with machine guns. The one with the big guns had "Uncle Bob" painted on the side and the other one had "Auntie Mary".

"Oi, you in the tin can!" Ewan called out, banging on the side of the tank with his rifle butt. A head popped out of one of the side hatches. "I need a word if you please."

"Right, half a tick, sir, I'll be out in a jiffy," came the frustrated sounding reply.

Ewan heard some clanking and banging, then a muttered "Fook me!" then some more banging and then this very grubby man came out of the hatch and made his way over to Ewan. "Hullo sir! Sorry about the language, sir, I 'ad an argument with one of the fookin' engine manifolds, but I bloody *won!*" the man said with a Cheshire Cat grin. He was wearing a pair of coveralls, which were so filthy that Ewan couldn't tell what colour they had originally been. Grey he presumed. The man inside was no cleaner, it looked like he'd been using himself as a rag, "Cpl 'iggins sir, Tank Corps." The grin remained.

Despite the informality Ewan liked what he saw, he was no big fan of saluting or any other parade ground rubbish but was only interested in the vehicle itself. The good corporal was grubby and covered in oil but the tank itself was almost spotless, mud and dust notwithstanding.

"I'm new tae this whole tank game, Cpl Higgins, show me what ye've got. The five minute tour will do for now." Dale Higgins was one of the first men to transfer to tanks two years earlier, and he had been with them all through their first use on the Somme.

"Well, sir, these 'ere beasts are brand spanking new, just arrived from blighty last month." He was as proud as a new dad. "They're the very latest thing, one is a Male, which 'as two six pounders, one on either side, and three machine guns, the other is a Female which 'as five machine guns. The Males are called Male because they 'ave two ruddy great cocks, sir!" His grin got even broader.

"Aye, I can see that," Ewan smiled back. They were going to get along just fine. "Tell me how you use them." Ewan then got a quick explanation of the typical tactics used for tanks and was left with the impression that this lad knew what he was doing. "OK, come wi' me and we'll hatch a plan."

He called his platoon commanders around him.

"Cy, take your platoon and circle around the left of yon blockage and be prepared to stop any retreat past you. Mike, take your lads and come up the north road and take Cpl Higgins' Auntie Mary with you, use it as cover as well as the houses. Ed, I'll come wi' you and we'll go up the east road wi' Uncle Bob and use its guns to take out the Spandaus. Cpl Higgins, any comment?"

"No, that sounds good to me, sir!"

"Right then, let's be off. Mike, get tae the barrier five minutes before Ed," Ewan looked at his watch, it was 13:40. "Be there by 14:25 and Ed you be there by 14:30, that way Mike will distract the machine guns while you kill them. Any questions?" Ewan didn't expect any, these were all old hands by now, the addition of the tanks only made things easier.

There were none.

They gave Cy the promised half hour start and then set off. Mike also set off early because he had to get his men and their new toy around to the south end of the village.

Then Ed set off with Uncle Bob in the lead and the infantry spread out behind the tank, moving through the village very slowly.

The lead section spotted the roadblock first and Ewan went up to have a look. What he saw was a bit more than a hasty defence although he could see why Doug Crowfoot thought it was. There were four or five trestles spread across the intersection all wrapped in barbed wire and held down with any-thing heavy: sand bags, pieces of wood, bricks, wagons, the remains of a car, even a dead horse. He could see the machine guns with his binoculars, there was one at either end of the row of trestles and one in behind by the corner of a large shed to the right.

Just then a side hatch on the Male tank popped open and Dale Higgins poked his head out. "Let me take a crack at them, sir, this is a doddle, let me show you what one of these brutes can do."

"OK, but wait until your mate in Mary draws their fire." Ewan was still unsure about these new machines.

"Righto, sir." Higgins replied, his trademark grin firmly back in place.

They didn't have long to wait, they heard the grinding of tracks on cobble-stones a few minutes later. One advantage of this new swifter advance was that there was less cacophony of noise than in the trenches, so they could hear the tank approaching.

The Female tank hove into view on the right-hand side and immediately drew fire from the Jerry guns. Higgins said, "Wait 'ere sir, I shan't be long", and with that he started off towards the barrier. The Female opened up with the three machine guns that were facing the German guns, to distract them.

Higgins stopped about forty yards from the barrier and slewed the tank around, so it was facing straight into the intersection. Then he opened fire with his six pounders. Both guns fired at the same time and the two machine guns on the sides were annihilated. The third gun, the one in the middle, saw this and the crew immediately produced a white flag, which they obviously already had ready, and shouted, "*Kamerad, kamerad!*" then walked slowly and tentatively towards Higgins. They'd had enough.

Ewan banged on the hatch of Higgins' tank and when it opened said, "That was bloody amazing! I was looking at a frontal assault and taking casualties, we took that without a scratch!" he marvelled at this new machine.

"Aye, well it's not always that easy, we got lucky, that last bugger wanted to surrender and not die."

"Still, I'm bloody impressed!" Ewan enthused. "OK, let's see how ye are at takin' out artillery. The guns are behind yon building o'er there tae yer front."

"Don't worry, sir, Uncle Bob and I will deal with them in short order." He got out of his tank and ran over to the other tank to confer with L/Cpl Davies, its commander and then ran back to his own a couple of minutes later. "OK sir, that Welsh prat in Mary thinks he can take them both by himself if he can get behind them, which he can't so I told him no."

"What do ye want to do then?" Ewan asked, deferring to the expert.

"Well, they'll be pointed to the west, towards our lads so if I go past the building to the north and then enter the courtyard pointing south I should be able to take both before they can bring their guns to bear. Mary can guard the south approach."

"OK, my lads will be with you all the way in case there are any more infantry to deal with." Ewan agreed.

So, Higgins set off with Ed's platoon alongside and Ewan right along with them. He was only about ten yards from the right rear corner of Bob and well protected by the strange steel box moving at about three miles per hour right in front of him.

As he got close to the corner of the building Cpl Higgins slowed down and made ready to round the corner into the courtyard where the guns were. Ewan went to peek around the corner and see how the guns were oriented before they proceeded any further. He moved up to the corner and stuck his head around to have a look.

His worst fears were realised, the two guns were in line, one behind the other so Higgins wouldn't be able to take out both but, even worse, one of them was pointed directly at the corner. The Jerry gunners had anticipated the tank coming up that way and had moved one of the guns to cover it.

Ewan quickly moved around the tank to bang on the hatch where Higgins sat, to warn him.

Higgins didn't hear him nor did any of the other seven members of the crew. He was just moving to go around the front of the tank to wave at the driver when there was an almighty explosion as a 10.5 cm HE shell hit the front right corner of Bob causing the whole right side of the tank to separate from the hull, incinerating the crew in the process, including Higgins.

Ewan was blown onto his back into the street where he lay, stunned, for a few seconds. Miraculously no large pieces of metal had hit him, but he was bleeding from a dozen smaller wounds. Training, and experience kicked in once more, and he was on his feet again in less than a minute, ears ringing, bleeding all over but up and functioning. Pain he would deal with later.

The two German guns were still in service and Ewan now knew that there was at least a platoon of infantry guarding them. They must be dealt with, and fast because they were threatening the whole advance. Momentum was essential for success.

He sent a runner to bring up Cy and his platoon, and he brought together the platoon commanders as well as L/Cpl Davies, their new tank expert.

Ewan asked Davies what he could do. "Not too much, sir. A Female works in tandem with a Male and without the Male I'm just a mobile pillbox."

"My understanding is that Females were meant for infantry support," Ewan stated. "Not so?"

"Aye sir, absolutely, but not when there's only one."

Ewan thought for a few minutes and then, "OK, Cy you take your men and go through that building to the northeast, Mike, you do the same in the building immediately to the south, get into positions where you can provide harassing fire on the crews of those bloody guns and the infantry. Snipe them too if you can.

Ewan had a thought, "Davies, can yer machine go through buildings?" he asked.

L/Cpl Davies was a bright young lad and immediately knew what Ewan was asking. "Aye sir especially light metal buildings like those," he confirmed.

"Right then, Ed, you and Cpl Davies will move through that building to the west of the guns. Davies, only move until you can bring your guns to bear on the howitzers. One at a time if necessary."

"Right sir … um, I'm only a L/Cpl sir."

"Not if this works you're not!"

It took Cy and Mike about twenty-five minutes to get in place then Ewan heard sporadic rifle fire coming from the buildings. "Right lads, we'd better move sharpish because those buggers arnae goin' tae take too long resetting their guns and bringing the house doon on those lads."

"Got it, sir!" and "Aye, sir!" was heard at the same moment. They were on the ball.

Ewan stayed right behind the tank until it started to enter the building then he moved out of the way, so the roof wouldn't fall in on him.

L/Cpl Davies was a magician with the big brute of a tank. He broke through the outer wall without collapsing the roof and then proceeded to bulldoze his way from room to room, still with the roof intact. Two thirds of Ed's platoon was to his left and the remainder to the right – well out of the way if the roof did collapse. It seemed a miracle that it hadn't already.

Cy was able to get his men in position behind the two guns where he was able to snipe at the crews, bringing down several. Mike kept putting harassing fire down and kept the infantry busy.

This gave Cpl Davies time to get into position before the Jerries knew what was happening. Just as he broke through the last outer wall his luck ran out and the roof collapsed bringing the whole building down on top of him. Ewan thought he was done and that he'd have to find another way to deal with those guns. Just then he saw the tank slew around into a more favourable angle. Could nothing stop these things? They were able to bring two Vickers and a Hotchkiss to bear and made short work of the gun that had killed Higgins. Davies was only able to pin the crew of the other gun down though, not kill them. Ewan and Ed each took half of the platoon and worked around the sides of the first gun. Ed and his two sections put down covering fire with rifles, Lewis guns and Mills bombs.

Ewan then took the rest, twelve men or so, and worked his way behind the second gun. With Cy and Mike and half of Ed's men, not to mention the tank, providing withering covering fire, the remaining gun crew was trying to bury themselves under the building.

This made it very difficult to get at the Germans safely. Ewan had arranged a signal with his company commanders that meant cease fire: two sharp blasts of his whistle. He hoped they remembered the signal, and he also hoped that Cpl Davies was as smart as he seemed because he didn't know about the signal.

Ewan blew two piercing notes on his whistle. His men remembered and gradually fell silent. Davies too stopped firing, but he later said that he thought that meant that the guns were taken.

For what he earnestly hoped was the last time, Ewan yelled *"Fraoch Eilean!"* and he and his men charged into the midst of the gun crew. He tried to spare their lives, so he used the butt of his rifle and the hilt of his bayonet and ended up with seven prisoners, all wounded. The surviving infantry had melted away but would soon be captured.

They moved up towards Mons and spent yet another uncomfortable night in a barn. The next day was November 10. That day was like any other from the past three months, pursuing demoralized German soldiers through the beautiful French countryside. They moved into the ancient city of Mons that afternoon, still bearing the scars from 1914 but beautiful nonetheless. Once again, Ewan remarked on the stark contrast between now and a year ago in Passchendaele. Men were still dying, and things were still being destroyed but there was finally light at the end of the tunnel. The light of peace, the light of life.

The following day was November 11. Early in the morning, a despatch rider came from Division headquarters with an astounding message. The gist of the message was that there would be a cease fire at 11:00 a.m. Apparently an armistice would be signed, and the war would be over. This was too much to take in, no-one believed it at first, it was simply too big a concept to wrap the head around. While confirmation was being sought, the war carried on. They were ordered to continue the advance pending confirmation. They moved through Mons to the northeast, no resistance was encountered … could it be true? Did the Germans already know? Had they stopped fighting?

Confirmation came sometime later but, unbelievably, they were told to continue the advance right up to 11:00 a.m. This was the final straw for Ewan, he had seen many good men die for no apparently good reason. It had seemed to make some kind of sense at the time, but this was properly insane. The war would be over in a few hours, they knew it. There was, literally, no point in risking anyone's life anymore. He couldn't, in all conscience, be responsible for killing anyone anymore or of causing the deaths of any of his men when the war was won.

They continued advancing through Mons but slowly and carefully. There was still gunfire being heard, sporadic rifle fire from up ahead.

Turning a corner, a patrol from Cy's platoon came upon a group of German soldiers who were building a hasty defence in the front of a shop on the opposite side of a small courtyard or square. They came under fire from the Germans and two men were wounded. Instinctively they returned fire and killed one of the Jerries and wounded three more.

Everybody got under cover at that point. Cy sent a runner back to Ewan to tell him what was happening. Ewan had told his platoon commanders earlier to shoot only in self-defence.

"Bloody hell! Don't those buggers know the war is over?" he looked at his watch and saw that it was 10:23 a.m, the ceasefire was due to start in thirty-seven minutes, and he'd be damned if anyone else was going to die before then.

Ewan remembered passing a little café a block or so away, abandoned but relatively undamaged. He ran back to it, kicked in the door and found a small white tablecloth. He then returned to the corner and tied the cloth to his rifle. Maybe he could convince them to surrender? He raised the rifle as high as he could with the white truce flag hanging from it.

"*Deutches soldaten! Nicht schießen! Ich bin ein Freund!*" Ewan's German would, hopefully, help to save some lives for a change. "The war is over! In half an hour there will be a ceasefire … do you want to be the last men to die in this insanity?" he yelled across the square. Nothing happened so he repeated the message louder and waited again.

This time, after a pause, there was a tentative reply, "How do we know you aren't lying?"

"If I were lying would I do this?" He put his rifle down and then spread his arms and moved slowly into the open. He then started walking directly towards them. "See? I'm trusting that you men are smart enough tae realise the truth of what I'm telling you. My men will cut you to ribbons if ye shoot me."

There was a minute or so of hesitation but then one of them called out, "OK, we're coming out, don't shoot!" Then, one by one, the German soldiers raised their arms and walked out from behind the barrier. There were seven in all and two of whom were wounded.

Once they had all come out and been searched he asked one of the smokers to offer the Germans a cigarette.

Ewan had thought that all of them had come out from behind their hasty barricade. All, that is, except one who was hiding behind the barrier. He now stood up bringing his rifle to bear and shot Cy Gibson in the forehead, his skull split cleanly in two.

Ewan drew his pistol and fired, killing the man instantly.

Vibrating with fury at the sheer waste of it he barely restrained his men from killing their prisoners in cold blood.

He then glanced at his watch and saw that it was 11:01.

Then the overwhelming silence struck him. He had experienced silence in the trenches before but not as profound as this silence, this was the silence of peace.

And just like that, the Great War to end all wars was over.

$$\overset{*}{_{*\,*}}$$

Ewan couldn't believe it at first. He kept remembering all the men that he had served with who were no longer there, the men who had come from Halifax in 1915. Was that really only three years ago? It seemed like an eternity of eternities. The men who had come in as replacements who hadn't even lived long enough for him to meet them. The conscripts who had come over reluctantly but who had performed as well as the most experienced volunteer in the end.

The Germans whom he'd killed and whose faces were now permanently etched onto his brain.

The 25th could now rest for a while. The constant subcutaneous fear of being sent back to the front was over. The constant background noise of shelling and machine gun fire was no more. The prevalent sound now was birds. Where had they been all these years?

$$\overset{*}{_{*\,*}}$$

A week later, Ewan got his orders. They were moving into Germany itself, into the Rhineland. There was grumbling. Everyone thought they could now go home.

"OK, lads," Ewan said to the whole company as they were drawn up in front of him. "We're going intae Germany to make sure the natives don't get restless." A little laughter, which was encouraging, "But the Jerries surrendered because they were tired and had run out o' the necessary things tae run an army, or a country come tae that. We've been blockading their ports a' this time and supplies o' everything frae wood for airplanes and steel for weapons and vehicles tae flour and vegetables are below survival levels. The civilian population is done.

"We're going to go intae Germany as conquerors, but we're also going in as liberators because we've liberated the German people from their government who have kept them without food and without hope fer four lang years.

"When we go in, ye're not tae brag or show off tae the German people. This was not their fault. Imagine if the Germans had invaded your homes, would you like your families tae be treated poorly?

"The German army is finished but it's still largely intact so we must also be vigilant against any resentful remnants that we may come across.

"I'll get ye home as soon as I can, I promise."

The next day, they started moving towards Germany. The weather started out fine until towards the end of November, thereafter it rained at least a little every day. While they were marching through Belgium the villages and towns they marched through had, generally, friendly populations although some were heartily sick of soldiers of any flavour. Ewan could sympathize with that. Civilians in all the occupied areas had suffered under the Germans and were as relieved as his men were that it was all over.

On December 4, they reached the border between Belgium and Germany. A desultory rain greeted them and also a desultory population. The Germans weren't happy to see them, for obvious reasons, but nor were they hostile. They too had suffered much and were happy for it all to be over.

From there they spent the next ten days marching through the German countryside, which had been untouched by war. Ewan found it ironic that

Belgium and France had suffered as countries physically, but Germany had suffered as a people. He felt sorry for the wives and the fathers and mothers and brothers and sisters and sons and daughters of the young German men who would also not return home.

They were saying that this had been the last Great War. He passionately hoped they were right.

On December 13, they arrived at the Rhine and the beautiful old Westphalian city of Bonn, south of Cologne. It was a proud moment when they marched across the river on the old bridge. On the opposite side they passed a reviewing stand with General Currie taking the salute as the whole of the 2nd Division passed by him. It was raining the whole time, but no-one even noticed.

From there, the individual battalions and companies dispersed to their respective areas of responsibility for patrolling and keeping order. They had to guard German military depots in and around Bonn and control traffic in and out of the occupation zones. Not difficult work at all and they had nice comfy beds to retire to at night.

In comparison to the years of terror and suffering in the trenches this duty was heaven. But it wasn't Canada. The men wanted to go home. They wanted to see their loved ones, their wives, their mothers, their children.

The lightly veiled animosity displayed towards them by the German people was understandable but galling. They were constantly a little on edge. After having endured so much they needed to go home. They deserved to rest.

A few days later Ewan got word from the CO, Lt. Col. C.J. Mersereau, that he was being seconded to the Canadian Corps HQ because of his skill with the German language. He'd been expecting it, and with great anticipation, because it meant that he would soon be finding Peter's family. But only when it became real did he realise that he would have to say good-bye to his men. Men that he had fought with and bled with for three and a half years, men that he had promised he would bring home. He almost said no, because he had promised these men that he would bring as many of them home as possible. There weren't that many of the 1915 mob left. Most were either dead, wounded, PoW or missing. The thought of leaving his brothers left him tremendously conflicted. Should he leave Elsa to the mercies of the British bureaucracy and take his men home as he'd promised, or should he honour the promise he'd made to Peter and bring his family home?

In the end, as usual, there was no contest. Of course, he would find Elsa and the rest of her family and reunite them with his best friend, one to whom he was bound by friendship and now also by blood. His duty to his men was done. He'd made sure as many as possible had survived. There was nothing more he could do for them.

The day before he departed for Second Division HQ he brought his men together.

"Lads o' the MacKenzie Battalion! Well, the war is over, we've survived. Many didn't. Ye must always remember them and honour that memory. The war may be over, but the suffering isn't. The wounded will need our support as well as the love o' their families. You must promise that ye will look after yer injured brothers always.

"I know ye want to go home, and you will – as soon as the peace is secure. The rebuilding starts now. Treat the German civilians honourably and wi' dignity, as ye would have them treat your families. The CO tells me you'll be home as soon as transport can be made ready. That may take a while though, there are an awful lot of men who want tae go home. You'll have tae be patient and wait yer turn like everybody else.

"In the meantime every effort is being made tae keep ye busy. There will be sports and concerts. There will be school courses for those who wish it and loads of other activities tae keep the rest of you out o' trouble!

"I just want ye all to know that I'm proud tae have known every single one of you, and I couldn't have asked for better men, or better friends."

Turning to Sergeant Major Doug Crowfoot he said, "Doug, look after my boys please. They deserve to go home safely." He could barely hold back the tears.

He turned to Alex Tremblay, newly promoted to captain, "Alex, you'll take over after today. I know you love these bastards almost as much as I do. Please get them home."

With that Doug Crowfoot yelled, "Hip, Hip…"

"HOORAY!"

Ewan's company repeated that twice more and with that, Ewan moved on to fulfil his promise to Peter Baum.

CHAPTER 21

HALIFAX 1918

*
**

Peter's life got much easier after the incident with von der Marwitz. He had been granted almost permanent parole and had packed his uniform away for good. He still spent his nights at the Citadel but was free to roam around Halifax during the day. This was partly because he had proved his loyalty with von der Marwitz, partly because he had been so much help over the last year and partly because he was still working with Alan on recovery and rebuilding tasks. Alan was his escort ... officially. But he was also his good friend by now.

The last few months of 1918 were a mix of hardship and joy. Hardship because the reclamation of Halifax was carrying on and getting increasingly gruesome. Many bodies had not been recovered at the time and had suffered greatly over the summer. Joy because the war finally came to a grinding halt. Though the suffering continued, at least the carnage had stopped.

The Armistice of November 11, 1918 was just as much a surprise to the civilians as it was to the soldiers.

Morag was initially put out when she realised that Ewan wouldn't be home this Christmas either. The twins would be three before he was home! It simply wasn't fair. At least, though, he'd survived and was no longer in any danger.

She got a letter from him in early December, explaining to her why he had to stay for a while yet. He also said something rather cryptic:

Tell Peter that all three families will have a big reunion in Halifax in the spring.

She thought that was odd because she knew Peter was on his own and still a prisoner of war. He must have meant Alan and Toni as the third family, even though he hadn't met them yet.

Peter had settled into his current routine quite happily. Wake up in his cell in the Citadel, have breakfast in the Fort mess (he'd become a favourite of the guards), get picked up by Alan (his escort), spend the morning in Halifax helping him with the rebuilding efforts, have lunch with Morag, Toni and the twins and, sometimes, Sean, then the afternoon with Alan again for more of the same then back to the Citadel for supper and bed.

Compared to the three years of horror and deprivation he had endured it was heaven.

The only sour note was that he didn't have Elsa and his own child with him, but Ewan was seeing to that, so he wasn't too worried. Hopefully uncle Joe would come too.

Now, in December 1918, on the anniversary of the great explosion a small ceremony was held, and it was a sombre moment indeed. Peter, Morag, the twins, Alan, Toni, and Sean were all there.

"What a bloody mess," Morag stated, "why did this happen?" she continued, though they knew the physical answer by then.

"In a lot of ways, this was worse than the devastation in France," Peter observed.

"How so?" Sean asked.

"Because, although the destruction in France and Belgium was horrific, the population was largely spared," he noted, "here, I've pulled pieces of small children and old men and women from the shattered remains of their own houses."

"I suppose so, but it's all horrific however you look at it," Morag replied.

"I went to Germany to defend my Fatherland against the Russians but then went to fight the French instead. After they learned I spoke good English I went to fight the British. And, only by the sheerest chance was I captured by the Canadians, by my best friend in fact." He paused for a moment, "What right do these countries have making their citizens destroy each other when we should all be friends? Your general Currie, came to see me in a field hospital in France when he heard I had lived in Canada before the war.

"He understood this. That's why I'm here. He asked me if I would be an ambassador for a renewed friendship between Canada and Germany … whatever is left of it." Peter was very worked up about all this. "I agreed instantly. Whatever I can do to make amends for fleeing to Germany in 1914, and to stop this from happening again, I will."

"I'm just glad you're safe Peter. I hope Ewan contacts Elsa and arranges for her passage here." Morag was saddened by the whole process.

Peter wrapped his arms around her and then they both started crying. Sean and Toni got caught up in the emotion too and joined the pair in their grief. Alan hung on to Toni just as tightly; he had very nearly lost her in the explosion.

They stood like that for several minutes, spending their emotions like water, until Peter reiterated, "I vowed, after Verdun, that I would never let this happen again."

*
**

That afternoon, Peter and Alan went back into the harbour area where the damage had been the worst. Alan's primary task was to recover any bodies and prevent looting. Normally he hated looters, but in this case, he could almost understand their desperation. People had lost their homes, their families, and their livelihoods. Usually what he did, with Peter's help, was simply chase them off rather than try and arrest them. There simply were no adequate facilities for processing petty thieves. And no appetite for it either.

This day, though, there had been a report of an organized gang from south of Halifax somewhere – Bridgewater perhaps – who were stealing construction materials that were arriving by the trainload for the reconstruction effort.

This wasn't just petty looting, they were organized and had specific targets in mind. Plus, a night watchman had been killed during an earlier robbery and this gang were the likely culprits. They were after electrical cable, which was worth a small fortune on the black market. The Chief Constable himself had briefed them all on what to look out for, and they were on their way to the North Street Station which, though battered, was still functional. Sergeant Bancroft would be in charge, with Alan as his number two.

A gang of four men, possibly more, had been spotted after 2:00 a.m. on each of the last three nights. After that night watchman was stabbed two weeks ago, there were always at least three pairs of officers on the scene each night. Because they were so shorthanded, Alan had talked his superiors into letting Peter be his partner for this arrest.

"Right, Peter, these bastards are dangerous, they've already stabbed another night watchman at the station. He'll live but only because his relief caught them in the act. They buggered off without getting anything … this time," Alan explained.

Peter laughed, "I'm no stranger to danger, Alan!"

"No, I don't suppose you are," he laughed as well. "Sorry, I forgot who I was talking to. Still, there's no need to be careless."

"Halifax is my home now Alan, it's a pity it took a war for me to realise that." He was serious now. "I will do what I must to keep it safe."

Sergeant Geoffrey Bancroft picked his men, four teams of two. There were no others to spare. They went down to the railyard at last light. Alan wanted to be in position before the thieves got there. He picked a spot in full view of where the material was being unloaded from the train but also out of sight of anyone approaching that area. Lying down behind a partially destroyed wall, the waiting game began. He carried a shuttered lantern to be used as a signal to the other teams when they were ready to move in.

After six hours waiting in the bitter cold, and seeing nothing, Alan was almost ready to give up.

"We can't give up now, we've been here too long to pack up and go home." Peter was determined to see this through.

Four in the morning came and went and still nothing, even Peter was about done. Just as he too was finally thinking they should go home, he noticed a movement out of the corner of his eye, so he hunkered down to get a better look.

He had started to stand up, but stopped, "Alan, did you see that movement over by the train shed?" he whispered.

"No, nothing."

"Look closely at that brick wall to the right of the shed, there was something moving behind it," Peter added.

"Got 'em, six likely lads moving towards that stack of cable reels." With his binoculars Alan had seen three men approaching the stack of wiring. It was meant for replacement houses being built for the still too numerous, homeless victims of the explosion. Another three were staying back, probably as lookouts.

"Let's see what they do. When will the others signal us?"

"When we've caught the bastards red handed." He replied. "The moment they lift the reels onto their getaway vehicle we grab 'em."

After casing the reels of cable, two of the thugs then left to get their truck to make their haul. Ten minutes later, a blacked-out Ford Model TT truck, moved out of the darkness from down the line. They were very organized indeed. The Model TT was brand new and perfectly suited for the job. The truck had been stolen from the railway station. Alan could see two figures trussed up in the bed of the Ford. Apparently, the driver and his helper were hostages.

Peter then saw why Alan wanted to wait until they were loading the reels. They would need every man to lift the heavy bobbins, each one weighing up to a ton. Even with the block and tackle that they'd rigged up, it would be a tough go. That's what Alan was counting on. His sergeant had briefed him on the likely way the theft would be conducted and, so far, it was as expected.

Finally, the thieves had one reel off the ground and were just swinging it into place when Alan saw a brief flash of light from another lantern on the other side of the truck. "Right, that's our signal." Alan replied with a flash from his own lantern. The cable stealers were too busy to notice anything.

With that, they were off, and with less than fifty yards between them, they were on the thieves in seconds. Three other teams moved in from different directions and all four arrived within a few seconds of each other.

Armed only with truncheons, the police waded in. Then they were quickly met with a nasty surprise, several of the crooks had revolvers. They got off two quick, unaimed, shots. One killed one of the policemen and the other hit Alan in the leg, stopping him in his tracks. Peter stayed put long enough to see that Alan was not seriously hurt and then rushed in with the others.

A melee ensued, which resulted in two more policemen being shot, one of which was wounded but the other was Sergeant Bancroft. He died in Peter's arms. Two dead, now it was murder too.

Time to take stock. They decided to retreat and regroup behind some piles of lumber.

Peter, being the natural leader that he was and with three years of frontline experience under his belt, took the lead. The others just knew he had been wounded at Vimy Ridge … not which side he'd been on and accepted his leadership without question. Alan knew who Peter really was, of course, but Alan was still unconscious.

Quickly reassessing the situation and taking stock of the remaining men he realised that the thugs had the upper hand. Peter had cold cocked one of the gang with a punch to the side of the head, and another one had been knocked out by a well-aimed truncheon to the temple. That left four, of whom two had revolvers.

Of the eight policemen who had started, two were dead and two more were wounded badly enough that they would be of no further help, including Alan. So, both sides had four men but the crooks were armed. A frontal assault like at Verdun was not an option.

The only safe solution was to send one of the men for reinforcements.

"Jimmy, head back to town and bring as many men as you can get." Alan had come to, but he was still groggy. He couldn't move but he could issue orders.

"Right … I'll be back as quick as I can," Jim Davison replied.

Alan called out to the thugs, "Right you bastards, you'd best give up peacefully. You're not going anywhere!"

Silence.

"Did you hear me?" he yelled.

"Yes, we heard you, you fuckers, and you can go straight to hell!" That was the leader.

"Aye, well, we'll see who goes where soon enough!" Alan called back.

"Fuck you!"

Less than twenty minutes later, Jimmy returned with ten other men in tow. Short handed or not, Sgt Bancroft had been a popular man. Not to mention the need to save the hostages. This time they were armed. Four of them had Lee Enfields and the rest had revolvers.

Alan turned to Peter, "This is more your bailiwick, Peter, what do you suggest?"

Peter replied, "Right, the top priority has to be the driver and his comrade. They must be kept safe." Peter wouldn't risk civilian lives. Enough people had died in this war.

"Of course," Alan replied, "what can we do?"

"How much ammunition do you riflemen have?" he asked.

"We grabbed two bandoliers each," one of the constables replied.

"That should be more than enough," said Peter, "OK, you four with the rifles keep their heads down and I'll take three others, with revolvers, and we'll work our way around the back and take them from behind." Peter had done this too many times. But now it was in a good cause. He felt surprisingly calm. "Give us five minutes to get in position then start sniping at them, if you can hit one, so much the better but the idea is to keep them from looking too closely at what we're doing."

"Righto."

"Got it."

Five minutes later, Peter had worked his way behind the stack of reels and the truck to the point where he could see the hostages.

"You bastards better not be trying anything!" came a shout from the crooks. "We've got hostages, and we'll kill one if you try any funny business!"

"Wouldn't dream of it!" Alan replied.

Peter whispered to the three men who were accompanying him, "OK, we jump them as soon as the firing starts. You two run to the hostages and protect them. You, come with me." He said, pointing to the remaining man. They had gotten to within seventy-five yards of the Ford, which was where the hostages still were, though now under the truck.

Fortunately, the men with the rifles took this as a cue to start shooting. Peter's group dashed forward and got almost to them before they were spotted. One man spun on his heels and brought his revolver up and fired two quick shots at Peter, both missed, though one grazed his arm. Peter shot him in the stomach. A second man started for the truck to make good his threat to kill the hostages. One of Peter's companions tackled him just as he was aiming his revolver at the driver.

That left two men. Peter's other companion dealt with one of them while he faced the last man, the leader.

The others were opportunists who were just in it for a quick buck, but the ringleader was a hardened criminal who needed to be stopped. He charged at Peter with a Banshee howl and slammed into him before he could react, slamming his revolver into Peter's head. Peter dropped to his knees to shake the bees out of his ears.

The criminal adjusted his hold on the revolver quickly, shifting his aim, because one of the policemen was running at him. He got off a shot and hit the copper in the arm.

Peter got to his feet and found this crook facing to the right and kicked him in the back of the knee making him crumple to the floor with a scream of pain. Recovering quickly, he and Peter fought like tigers for several minutes.

The fight went back and forth for a while, then Peter's youth and conditioning started to tell. At one point, the man got his revolver to Peter's head only to have it smashed away again. Finally, Peter got behind the man and got him in a headlock. He got a firm grip on the man's head and twisted with a berserker's strength. The man's neck couldn't take the force and gave way with a loud crunch.

Peter sincerely hoped he had killed his last man.

By this time, the remaining criminals had been subdued and Alan had hobbled up to the scene. The last thing Peter expected was for Alan to burst out laughing when he saw the ringleader lying dead, at an unnatural angle, at Peter's feet.

Peter was huffing and puffing, breaking someone's neck is not a physically trivial thing to do. "Why is that funny?" he was genuinely surprised.

"Because, this bastard, my friend, is the man who tried to rape Toni!"

CHAPTER 22

HAMBURG AND HALIFAX 1919

***

The next morning, Ewan moved on to Div HQ in Bonn where he went to see his CO, Colonel Mersereau.

"Hello, Ewan, my lad, I'm so pleased to see you well." The colonel couldn't take his eyes off the little crimson ribbon with its miniature Victoria Cross in the centre on Ewan's chest. "I'm very glad you're safe."

Ewan snapped to attention but was beaten to the salute by the colonel who said, "No, lad, that gong of yours deserves a salute all by itself."

"Thank you sir," was Ewan's reply. He was starting to hate the attention that his medal brought him. But he was also smart enough to realise the benefit that it could have, the doors it could open.

Colonel Mersereau had a letter for him from the Mayor of Halifax. Ewan opened it, anticipating what he would find.

> *Dear Ewan:*
>
> *I hope you're in good health. Now that the war has been won,* (this must have been transcribed from a telegram, mail never arrived that quickly,) *you'll be happy to know that you may carry on with General Currie's instructions regarding Colonel Baum's family.*

Colonel Baum has provided his uncle's address. He assures me that his wife Elsa and Joseph Schulmann, and, presumably his child, live at 33 Paulinenplatz in Hamburg. Major General Burstall, who I believe is the commander of your division, has been apprised of the situation by General Currie so I think you'll find that every effort has been made to aid you in your mission.

When you find Mrs Baum, assure her that Colonel Baum sends his love. You are to secure transportation for as many of the members of Colonel Baum's family as would wish to come to Canada. Please use your discretion in this matter.

I believe General Burstall has further information for you.

Morag and your twins send their love to you.

God speed.

Peter Martin

Mayor of Halifax

The colonel then approached Ewan again and stuck out his hand. Ewan reached out to shake it. "Captain MacBride, in accordance with General Currie's wishes you are hereby promoted to the Brevet rank of Major. This is so you can more easily achieve your aim without the hassle of wading through staff at every stop. A major can open more doors than a captain and a major with a VC can open any door he damn well pleases!"

Once again, "Thank you, sir!"

Ewan immediately made an appointment to meet with General Burstall. The general, quite understandably, was a busy man and it was four full days before he could meet with Ewan.

He spent the time walking around Bonn and taking in the beautiful old city, the home of Beethoven. This was the first time he'd seen Germany properly. Since they'd marched across the border he hadn't had time to fully appreciate the beauty of the countryside. He now had the time to wonder again what the hell they had been doing these last four years. What the hell had it all been for? Had they achieved anything? Or was it just two outdated, overgrown and bloated empires thrashing out their death throes and taking millions of good men with them? Would they ever learn?

It had to end somewhere. Maybe it was here? But he'd heard it all before. How many times had he heard, "Don't worry it will all be over by Christmas"? Three Christmases he had spent in barns or ditches and in fear of his life. Now, with Christmas only four days away, this would be the fourth one away from Morag. He hadn't even met his children, who would be three years old before he did. Morag had sent him a photo of them last Christmas, and it was his most prized possession, second only to his photo of her.

*
**

Elsa was happy despite the desperation of the situation in Germany in December 1918. She was happy because she was watching her daughter, Ruth Morag Baum, now sixteen months old, running for the first time. She'd been walking on her own for several weeks now, but this was the first time she had run anywhere.

Mostly though she was happy because she had received a letter from Peter through the Red Cross. She hadn't heard from him since he had been captured in France in April last year.

She knew he was alive but nothing else. How he had got a letter to her she didn't know, and she didn't care. All she cared about was that Peter was alive and well.

What she read was, frankly, unbelievable. Peter was a VIP prisoner in Halifax! He was visiting with Morag and Sean and some other new friends on a regular basis and had been assured that Elsa and his son and his uncle Joe would be able to come to Canada when the war was over, regardless of who won.

The letter had been sent several months ago. Obviously, he never got her letter telling him he had a daughter. She wasn't surprised, the Red Cross had told her it was virtually impossible to get a letter to German prisoners of war, though they'd try. They didn't even know he was in Canada.

He wasn't able to say very much, just that he was well and back with friends again. To her, though, that spoke volumes. It meant that they'd be together again at some point very soon, and she was over the moon about it.

"Well, *liebchen,* what has you so happy?" Uncle Joe asked, pleased at her mood. She had been in and out of depression for months. Only Ruth had kept her going.

"Oh, uncle Joe, I just got the most wonderful letter … from Peter!" she couldn't hold back the tears anymore.

"That *is* wonderful!" he said, "How is he?"

"He's safe and well, uncle Joe, that's all that matters!" she couldn't stop smiling. "He's in Canada!" she told him.

"Canada? Why there?" he asked.

"I don't know. It is strange, but I don't care, I just know that he's well, that's all that matters," she replied.

Joe Schulmann was a patriot, but he was also a smart, practical man. He saw the writing on the wall. He knew that Germany was facing some hard and desperate times, and he wasn't a young man anymore. The cooperage had been extremely busy during the war, making barrels for the war effort. Most of his able-bodied men had been lost to the army but so many lightly wounded men had not been able to return to duty and were returning to Germany that he was able, just barely, to keep a strong workforce. He had, therefore, made a lot of money. A substantial amount of this money he had been wise enough to invest in Switzerland. And also some in America before they entered the war.

Elsa said, "He also said we'd be able to go to Canada after the war. How could he know that uncle Joe?"

"I don't know, *liebchen,* but it is an interesting thought."

The general sent for him the next morning. Major General Burstall had been the commander of 2ⁿᵈ Canadian Division since 1916. He had had a fairly distinguished career and had been one of the architects of the Canadian Artillery which had later played such a pivotal role at Vimy Ridge. He was not a frontline combat soldier however and was suitably impressed with Ewan's collection of ribbons.

Ewan went in, snapped to attention and saluted. "Good morning, sir!"

"Good morning, Major MacBride." General Burstall welcomed him, "this is an interesting situation you find yourself in, lad."

"Aye, sir, it is," he replied.

"If I didn't know better," he said pointing at Ewan's ribbons, "I might think you were a Hun lover." Ewan felt his dander start to rise, "don't worry lad, General Currie has apprised me of his plan and, although I feel it's a bit premature to try and start mending fences just yet, it's certainly not a bad course of action, and I'll do what I can to promote the idea."

"Thank you sir," was Ewan's tentative reply.

"What do you need? I understand that Colonel Baum's wife is in Hamburg."

"Yes sir, I have the address."

"Hamburg is not in the occupied zone. I can get you as far as Dortmund, which is on the northern edge. After that you'll be on your own. I cannot guarantee your safety beyond that point," Burstall said, hoping he'd give up at this point.

"Sir, I speak good German. I'll be fine. I'll go in civilian clothes," Ewan confidently replied.

"I can't authorize that."

"At this point, sir, the only way ye're going to stop me is to arrest me."

"Yes, I can see that, and I can't arrest the holder of the Empire's highest decoration." Burstall gave in. "So, what can I do to help?"

"Sir, I owe Peter Baum my life. If ye can clear any red tape I'll have tae go through to get tae Dortmund that would be a great help. My French is not as good as my German."

"Yes, I can do that." The general offered. "Sit down for God's sake, you make me nervous," he said, pointing to the settee in the corner.

Ewan sat down as ordered. In truth, he was glad to because his nerves were getting the better of him contemplating how hard it would be to retrieve Elsa and her family from newly defeated Germany. He felt as apprehensive as he did on the day the battle of Passchendaele started.

General Burstall was as good as his word, in less than half an hour he had a letter for Ewan. It read:

To whom it may concern.

This letter is to inform all authorities that this officer, Major Ewan MacBride, is on business under the direct auspices of General Arthur Currie, GOC, Canadian Corps.

He is to be allowed free passage through any and all Allied barriers throughout the occupied zones of Germany.

Signed

Henry Burstall

Major General, GOC, 2nd Canadian Division

"Thank you, sir." Ewan replied with feeling.

"This should get you to Dortmund at least but beyond that you are on your own. I strongly recommend that you do not pursue this course of action Major MacBride. I can see from those ribbons on your chest, however, that you're not a fan of pursuing safe courses of action."

"No, sir," Ewan responded with his customary wolfish grin.

*
**

Ewan went to the headquarters and asked to see some maps of Germany, old ones would do he said. He then plotted a course from Dortmund to Hamburg. First, he would find a nondescript transport to Lunen, he would then change into civilian clothes and make his way on foot out of the occupied zone. Next, he would get on a train bound for Hamburg and, with any luck, he'd be with Elsa by the next night. Joe Schulmann's house was only a few blocks from the railroad station, so he could walk from there. Then he'd play it by ear.

The next day, he bought a knapsack and a civilian suit from a local tailor who was eager to trade it for anything edible, his family were starving. He filled it with other foodstuffs that were in short supply in Germany, which was virtually everything, thinking they'd be useful as bribes once he got past Dortmund.

He also packed his bayonet and his FN pistol. There was no telling what he would encounter on this trip.

That afternoon, he caught a military train from Bonn, through Cologne, Dusseldorf, and Essen to Dortmund. The trip took the better part of two days because of the confusion caused by the movement of occupying French and Belgian soldiers, large numbers of German PoWs being moved around pending their repatriation and the general confusion of moving through a newly defeated and occupied country.

The trip to Dortmund was however, uneventful, movement problems notwithstanding. He had expected roadblocks, both paper and physical, at every stop and every turn. The French army controlled the areas he went through and, as General Burstall predicted, his uniform and rank got him through most areas and that letter got him through the rest.

The German railways were their usual efficient selves. But most of the railway workers were older and Ewan saw many with an empty sleeve or trouser leg, reminding him of his Da in Fort William.

Once he got to Dortmund he used his letter one more time. There was a young Belgian officer supervising the loading of several tons of German ammunition being transferred to a safe location where it would be destroyed. He was, quite understandably, very nervous. The poor lad was only about eighteen and had been in training when the war ended. Now, a month later, he was loading German war materiel onto trains heading to points west, he didn't even know where, for disposal.

He was positively spinning with confusion already and when Ewan showed him the letter he went into veritable convulsions. Seeing Ewan's rank and all those ribbons just about sent him over the edge. He didn't know what any of the ribbons were for but he, quite rightly, assumed that anyone with that many brightly coloured decorations, was someone to be respected.

Ewan told him he needed to get to the boundary of the occupied zone. The poor lad didn't even ask him why, he just asked a man driving a passing cart if he could take Ewan to Lunen, which was approximately ten miles northeast of Dortmund. The man was too tired and harried to object, so he sullenly agreed, and Ewan was on his way to Germany proper.

When he got to the outskirts of Lunen, he stopped the man, a baker by trade who had been delivering his wares to a shop in Dortmund and gave him a pound of sugar as thanks. The baker's scowl turned into a smile and then he left.

Ewan quickly looked to make sure no-one had seen him then he ducked into a nearby shed and quickly changed into the suit he had obtained. He then carefully packed his uniform into the knapsack.

Spending the night in the shed seemed like the safest thing to do because it was getting quite dark. He didn't think it wise to travel at night through what was, until six weeks ago, enemy territory. Sleeping in sheds was not a problem.

On leaving the shed the next morning, he noticed a pair of crutches propped against the wall and with a sudden inspiration he grabbed one on the theory that a fit looking man walking with a crutch was less likely to be a threat than one without. Plus, he'd have another weapon if he needed one.

Reaching the River Lippe, he crossed at the railway bridge to avoid being spotted. It was less than a mile from there to the railway station and from there he hoped to get a train to Hamburg.

Arriving at the station two hours later, he got nervous because he would have to talk to a stationmaster in order to get a ticket. He hadn't used his German on any locals yet. Ewan's German was quite good, but he had a Scots accent, so he didn't know if he could pull it off.

In the event he needn't have worried, the train started in Lunen since the route to Dortmund wasn't open yet due to the occupation. So, he simply got on the first eastbound train he saw and mumbled "Hamburg *bitte*," to the first conductor he met. Finding a seat as far away from anyone as he could possibly get he sat and enjoyed the ride. The conductor probably thought he was rude, but the crutch helped, eliciting sympathy from everyone else on the train. There were many other men with missing limbs or blinded or bandaged up, even some still in uniform, and he was extra careful around them.

The train passed through Munster and Bremen on the way, and Ewan could almost forget where he was and enjoy the scenery. Germany was an amazingly beautiful country, he could see why Germans were so willing to fight for her. He understood Peter's decision to leave his new home a little better now.

The train stopped at several small stations on the way. At every stop, Ewan saw the people trying to carry on with their normal lives. He saw from their body language that there was no spark in them, no life. They moved like automatons, going through the motions but not enjoying life.

They were going through the grieving process. They would bounce back in due course like any grieving parent, but it would take time. There were millions of grieving parents and wives and children in Germany going through the same process at this very moment. They too would eventually bounce back but their process was just beginning.

The train went through field after field of stunted or dead crops. The men who normally tended those crops were lying dead in France or Belgium or Russia or at the bottom of the North Sea.

They arrived in Hamburg six hours later and then Ewan got off. Just like that, he was in Peter's hometown.

Ewan had looked at a map of Hamburg while still in Bonn and had found that Joe Schulmann's house was only a few blocks from the railway station, so he decided to walk. It was only just above freezing, so a brisk walk would keep him warm. He got turned around a couple of times because of the twisty Hamburg streets but by the time the light was going he had arrived at 33 Paulinenplatz. He knocked on the door and waited.

After a short time, he heard two locks being drawn back and then the door opening tentatively revealing the second most beautiful woman in Halifax.

Elsa took one look at him then both eyes and her mouth opened wide and she fainted dead away. Ewan caught her before she fell and carried her gently into the sitting room through the open door to his right.

Ewan said with his cheeky wolfish grin fully in place, "Why do I always have that effect on women?"

Uncle Joe walked right up to Ewan and said, "You must be Ewan, I've heard much about you but how in God's name did you get here?" Joe was dumbfounded.

Ewan gave him the short version of events, the full explanation would come later. It was then that he noticed the highly-decorated Christmas tree in the corner of the room.

"A very Merry Christmas to you, lad!" It was Christmas Eve, Ewan was at least with family again.

Elsa came to a few minutes later and saw Ewan straight away. "Ewan, my god, Ewan, it is you!" She jumped to her feet, threw her arms around him and hugged him until he thought he was going to suffocate.

He was no less happy to see her and hugged back. "Aye, I'm not an illusion, it's really me."

"But how? How could you possibly be here? This is Germany! We're at war!"

"Well, actually we're not," he reminded her gently. "But that's why I'm in mufti, it's still not possible, nor safe, for non-Germans to travel freely in Germany. Particularly Allied soldiers."

"Then how?" Joe was just as interested as Elsa.

"Well this is all due to Peter," he said. "When he was captured he made a deal with General Currie that he would help the rebuilding process after the war, as long as he didn't have to betray his country during the fighting. In return, the general promised he'd do all he could to get you and his son, and possibly uncle Joe to Canada as soon as possible."

Elsa now had an enormous smile on her face. "Ah, well, there's a problem with that," she began.

Ewan had seen the crib in the background and assumed that's where the little lad was.

"Well, it's better to show you I think," she went over to the crib and picked up a little bundle from it. Ewan was immediately suspicious when he saw pink bows and ribbons all over the blanket that the babe was sleeping in. "Let me introduce you to Peter's son, *Miss* Ruth Morag Baum."

Ewan was taken aback for a second but then he burst out laughing, "Well I'll be jiggered!" he cried. "Peter was so sure it was a boy."

"You've seen him? How is he?" Elsa pressed.

"Actually, I'm the one who captured him!" Ewan explained. He saw the looks on both Elsa and Joe's faces. "'Twas last year at Vimy. It's a long story for another time. He was well when last I saw him. They sent him back tae Canada in fact. That's how this all came about. In addition tae the deal he made with General Currie he helped a lot after the explosion in Halifax last December."

"Explosion? What explosion? He's in Halifax?" Elsa needed to know.

"Aye, there was a massive explosion in the harbour, which destroyed most of the city from what I hear."

"Oh, *mein Gott!* Is Morag well?"

"Aye, Morag and our twins are well and so are her Da and two other new friends that she's made. I think there were some injuries but she's keeping that tae hersel'. Peter is being held in a PoW camp for VIP prisoners at the Citadel. He helped pull survivors out of the rubble from what I can gather. That's another reason why I'm here."

All Elsa heard was "Morag and the twins are well." Twins? They have twins? She had missed so much since leaving Canada. She said, "Yes, I got a letter from him just a few days ago from the Red Cross, but what you said fills in some gaps."

Ewan immediately fitted into Elsa's German family and, for a while at least, he could forget the last four years and have a family again. All that was missing was Morag.

They spent Christmas Day and Boxing Day reconnecting and bringing uncle Joe up to speed with all the goings on from the Canadian side.

*
**

Rudolph Schmidt was starving. When the war ended, so did his service in the army. Already relegated to a menial job due to his previous injury he had initially traded off that injury for sympathy amongst his peers. As the numbers of wounded soldiers in the army grew exponentially and the number of disastrous battles fought grew almost as fast he was able to claim that he had been wounded in France. No one bothered or had time, to check.

By 1918, there were so many wounded veterans that he just faded into the woodwork. He was not very bright and had an evil streak that did not endear him to his CO. This meant that he never rose very high in the ranks. He was still a private. But, so long as he was useful to the army, in however minor a role, he was able to feed, clothe, and house himself.

The Armistice of November 11 had changed all that. To all intents and purposes, the army no longer existed. Schmidt was out of a job. He was left roaming the streets, hunting for food like a street cur.

There were tens of thousands like him. Men who had been wounded and left to fend for themselves as best they could. What was left of the German government did not have the ability to look after her population of healthy citizens, let alone her wounded veterans.

Most were honourable men who had sincerely fought for the Fatherland. Through no fault of their own they were simply left destitute due to the virtual collapse of the German state. These men tried to keep society working to the best of their abilities. Germans are hardworking, resilient people who can endure much. The days ahead would test that resilience to the breaking point and beyond.

There were, however, a growing number who, like Schmidt, were at the bottom of society. Already not highly regarded, these people formed into gangs of like-minded thugs who wandered the streets of Germany like packs of increasingly ravenous, but toothless, dogs. Like the slowly congealing fat in a cold stew, these gangs were growing bigger and more desperate as their resources dwindled to nothing.

They followed many ideologies but the most common were the Nationalists and the Communists. The Communists were emboldened by their comrades in Russia who had overthrown the Tsars and were in the process of forming a communist government. They felt that the Imperialists loyal to the Kaiser had caused the war and the subsequent fall of Germany.

The Nationalists felt that the Fatherland had been betrayed and stabbed in the back by subversive elements spread throughout German society like a cancer. Chief among these elements, they felt, were the Communists and the Jews.

Clearly these two competing and diametrically opposed ideologies did not get along. Anger in this increasingly desperate and volatile situation was never far from the surface and was starting to boil over.

In the midst of all this, Rudolf Schmidt found a home with the Nationalists. In later years the SA and the Nazis would develop out of this increasingly fanatical ideology, but for now they were just one pack of street curs pitted against another.

Schmidt had honed his rabblerousing skills at the cooperage before the war where, among other things, he had successfully blamed a young Jewish boy for the death of his brother, even though he had later found out that it had been in a fight with another man over a girl or something. Occasionally, he wondered where Peter Baum had gone but he didn't really care. Good riddance to Jewish filth, he thought.

One thing that still rankled him, though, was how that other Jew, Joseph Schulmann had demoted him to the shipping area as a result of the incident.

It was time to settle that score.

*
**

On the morning of the twenty-ninth, Ewan sat down with Joe and Elsa to talk about the best way of leaving. "The tricky part is goin' tae be getting tae Allied lines. I came through Dortmund and then Lunen. When we get tae Lunen I'll put my uniform on again. I have a letter from General Currie authorizing me tae bring all three o' you back wi' me so after that it should be relatively plain sailing. Joe, any thoughts on how we would get there?"

Elsa piped up, "I will pretend to be your wife," she said, as if it was the obvious solution.

"I doubt that it would be that easy. Once we get tae the Allied side that will work, in fact that was my thought too, but getting that far could be difficult."

"Tosh," Joe said, "it will be no problem. I have many connections on the railways who will turn a blind eye … for a fee. As soon as it was obvious that the war was unwinnable, when the Americans entered, many people have been trying to figure ways to get to the Allied side, so they can escape from Germany, especially Jews. It will take many years before everything is right again here. If it ever is. There are several different political factions fighting for dominance, from the left and from the right, and it's already starting to get violent. Everybody is blaming everybody else for the defeat." Joe worried for the long-term future of his country.

"You won't be able tae tak' much wi' you, pack light," Ewan advised. "We'll leave tomorrow."

"Yes, I have some knapsacks we can use. We won't need much, I have been using Swiss and American banks to build up funds so all I will need is a little cash to get to Dortmund. Elsa, we need to pack." Then he and Elsa got to work preparing to leave Germany forever.

*
**

Schmidt knew where Joe Schulmann lived so he gathered two other men who had their own scores to settle, for real or imagined offences. They gathered up a few simple weapons. They each had a knife and Schmidt also had a large spanner, which he planned to use on Joe. He had been staking the house out for a few days now and saw that Joe had visitors. A woman and a baby. The baby was obviously no threat and the woman looked like she might be singled out for some "special" treatment. He would enjoy playing with that little whore!

The three thugs waited until three in the morning on the twenty-eighth. Everyone was staying inside as much as possible, people only left the safety of their homes if they absolutely had to.

They went around back to get in through the servants' entrance. One of the two extra thugs was a professional thief who had only been let out of gaol because Germany was desperate for men, and he had been given to the army. He was sent to the front after minimal training, but he had deserted before the train even left Hamburg. The other man was too unintelligent to function in society at all.

The three ruffians broke into the house quite easily. They were trying to be careful even though there was only one old man, a woman and a baby in the house. They didn't know about Ewan.

Joe and Elsa were sleeping upstairs in neighbouring bedrooms, and Ewan was sleeping in a third bedroom on the ground floor. As luck would have it, his room was in the opposite corner of the house from the back door. He didn't hear the trio slithering up the back stairs to Joe's room.

The first he knew of it was when he heard Elsa scream. Three years of trench warfare had made him able to react instantly to danger. Within a few seconds, he was on his feet and, after quickly grabbing his weapons, was bounding, three stairs at a time, up the front staircase. He heard scuffling in Joe's room and headed that way but then he heard Elsa scream again so he went straight to her room.

*
**

Joe was worried about the trip to Allied lines. He wasn't worried about himself, he was old and had had a good life so whatever would happen would happen. Elsa was young but was street wise, her early life had seen to that, so he wasn't too worried about her either. What he was worried about was his great-niece, she was just a little baby and didn't deserve to be going through this much hardship at the beginning of her young life.

As a result, he couldn't sleep so his mind started drifting. He almost missed the scratching outside his door. He knew better than to call out so he slipped quietly out of bed and grabbed the poker from the fireplace. He heard two voices whispering outside his door, so he waited for them to enter. Then Elsa screamed, and he rushed the door to get to her room.

Holding the poker at the ready he yanked open his door. The two thugs weren't expecting that so soon and lost their balance. Recovering quickly, they rushed into the room bowling the old man over.

Joe got a solid hit on one of the attackers with the poker before he found himself at the mercy of two angry bruisers. He recognized them as two men he had let go for stealing from the cooperage.

"Say good-bye, old man."

*
**

Schmidt made his way slowly up the stairs and headed for Elsa's room. He had given the other two instructions to grab the old Jew and bring him to the woman's room, so he could watch Schmidt enjoy her to the fullest. His plan was to kill the child in front of the woman and then rape and kill her while Schulmann watched. Only then would he have his revenge on the Jewish scum.

He got to Elsa's door and then slowly opened it, trying to be as quiet as he could. Then he went inside where he paused to let his eyes become accustomed to the dark. He spotted a bed in the corner and a shape on it, which he assumed was the woman.

*
**

Elsa had just gone back to bed after feeding Ruth and was still wide awake. She lay, staring at the ceiling, daydreaming about being reunited with Peter sooner than she had a right to hope for.

She was just enjoying the quiet when she heard a squeak outside her door. It sounded like a loose floor board, but she wasn't sure. She was about to ignore it, but then she heard a scratching sound, which perked her ears up. Staying absolutely still required a supreme act of will.

Reaching for a metal water jug on the nightstand, she tensed up preparing to react quickly.

If she hadn't been fully awake and listening intently she would have missed the almost perfectly silent door opening. As it was, the door opened very slowly, and she perceived, rather than saw, someone come through the gap. As the shape approached her bed she waited until it was right beside her and then with a scream she swung the jug and connected with something.

Thinking it was the attackers' head she jumped out of bed and went to turn the light on.

Schmidt gave out a painful yelp, clutching his shoulder where Elsa had hit him. When she turned the light on he saw where she was and charged towards her, grabbing her night dress and ripping it off. When he saw her pale but very womanly curves he was overcome with lust and charged her anew. Elsa screamed again and almost immediately Ewan ran into the room with his pistol in one hand and his bayonet in the other.

Seeing that Schmidt was preoccupied with pawing poor Elsa, Ewan pistol-whipped him in the face, stunning him momentarily. Pausing just long enough to tell Elsa to grab Ruth and run into the next room, he spun around just in time to catch Schmidt's fist full in his face.

Shaking his head and with tears in his eyes and a broken nose, Ewan went after Schmidt who was, by now, chasing after Elsa again. Ewan caught up to him quickly and leapt onto his back, smashing him in the face with his pistol. Enraged even further, Schmidt swung around and tried to hit Ewan with the spanner but almost missed, only hitting him with a glancing blow on his side.

With his combat reactions still sharp, Ewan dropped his pistol and transferred his bayonet to his good hand in one fluid motion. Schmidt managed to hit him in the side of the head with the spanner once more, another glancing blow, painful but nothing more. They rolled around on the floor for many seconds before Ewan's strength and fitness finally won out. They found themselves on their feet staring each other down. Schmidt rushed at Ewan in a wild charge, but his false leg finally gave way under the strain. Ewan deftly dodged the charge and as Schmidt passed him, he drove all eighteen inches of gleaming Sheffield steel into Schmidt's belly like a bullfighter making his first strike.

Screaming in agony, Schmidt fell to his knees and his last thought before the lights went dim was, "This is how my brother died," then fell on his face.

Quickly regaining his wits, he heard scuffling from Joe's room next door. After grabbing his pistol, he rushed into the room just in time to see one of the thugs slash Joe's neck with his knife.

The two men were having fun beating the old man with the legs of a chair that they had smashed into his back. Joe was fighting back as best he could, but he was over sixty and had been very sedentary in his later years and was definitely getting the worst of it.

He shot the one who had slashed Joe, in the back of the head, ending his days of thievery. The second man, seeing his friend die so dramatically, bellowed a primordial howl and came after Ewan with his knife.

Ewan tripped over the remains of the chair and fell on the floor, spinning onto his back just in time to see this thug come at him, knife first. Ewan was in a fight for his life, and he knew it.

The two wrestled on the floor for several seconds. Ewan was fitter, but the brute was much bigger and was starting to get the better of him. He had his hands around Ewan's throat and was starting to squeeze. As his strength started to ebb Ewan saw Morag's face in his mind's eye.

He felt himself start to black out and was staring into the thug's enraged face.

Suddenly the man's expression turned to surprise. Blood started pouring out of his mouth and Ewan felt the pressure around his throat ease. Then he noticed several inches of steel protruding from the man's throat. In a burst of adrenaline he pushed the man off and the first thing he saw was Elsa, in a berserker rage and covered in blood. Her shoulders and chest were heaving with exertion.

She had retrieved Ewan's bayonet from Schmidt's body and shoved it, almost to the hilt, into the man's neck.

Elsa then collapsed on top of Ewan, vibrating with fear and emotion. He wrapped his arms around her and held on like a drowning man. It was then that he noticed she was still naked and shivering.

But, remembering Joe, he let go of her and went to him.

Joe was sitting up at the foot of his bed, having dragged himself there out of the carnage around him. He was wracked by fits of coughing that were bringing bloody froth to his lips.

Ewan knew without even seeing the wounds that Joe had been stabbed in the chest and a lung had been irreparably damaged. He had seen too many similar wounds in France to have any hope.

Getting down on his knees, Ewan saw that Joe was trying to speak. He was in agony and had great difficulty making himself heard. Elsa knelt down beside him. She was crying.

"Ewan …" he coughed, "… Ewan, my boy, …" he coughed again. "… you must get Elsa away, to … to Canada …" coughing, "… to Peter …"

"You have my promise, Joe. Elsa is as precious to me as my own family is. Rest, we'll get help."

"No … no, I'm kaput, finished." Almost nonstop coughing now and blood pouring out of his mouth. "You must find … must find … Hans Schwarz … at the station … he can help you." And with one last fit of coughing, Joe slipped away.

Turning to Elsa with tears in his eyes, Ewan hugged her until she had stopped sobbing and vibrating. It seemed like hours. She was beyond devastated. Joe had been family, she had grown to love him as a favourite uncle, or as the father she had always wanted.

Now what were they going to do?

Ewan recovered quickly. They had to get moving, and soon. He didn't know if anyone had heard that shot but he didn't think it was a good idea to stick around to find out.

"Elsa, we have tae move, lass, we canna stay here." Fortunately, she was a level headed and practical girl, and she recovered her wits quickly. "Grab what you need for Ruth and your knapsack and we'll get out o' here. I'll grab Joe's bag, I know he had packed some documents we'll need. I'll sort through it later."

Elsa washed the blood off herself and put on her practical walking clothes that she and Peter used for their long hikes. She grabbed some cloths for nappies for Ruth and some extra clothes for herself and the baby. She was ready in less than ten minutes. Ewan was impressed, no wonder she and Morag had been such good friends.

They quickly slipped out the back door and made their way to the train station. Taking refuge in a shed across from the station they slept in each other's arms until first light. Ruth nestled comfortably between them.

Ewan took stock of what was in Joe's knapsack. He had indeed been well prepared. Inside, Ewan found enough cash to buy the train if need be. He also found paperwork allowing Peter to access Joe's money in Switzerland, and America too as it turned out. Enough to make Peter a wealthy man, assuming German money was still any good. There were also some family trinkets that Joe couldn't part with. A miniature of his wife, Inga, who had been a robust but pretty woman in her youth. Other photos and mementos of Joe's life. They were Peter's now. Everything else could be left behind.

Joe had also packed some of Peter's identification papers, ones that he'd left for safekeeping while he was in France – birth certificate and so on. Enough, Ewan felt, that he could pose as Peter Baum quite convincingly if necessary. So, they were now Mr and Mrs Peter Baum, of Hamburg, visiting relatives near Lunen.

They freshened up as best they could and went into the train station to look for Hans Schwarz. Ewan didn't know how he could help but Joe had seemed adamant that they talk to him. Elsa said, "Uncle Joe talked about a man at the station who arranged barrel shipments to several clients, breweries mostly, outside of Hamburg. I think he works in the cargo area."

"OK, we'll start there, I dinna want tae attract too much attention mind, so we'd best be careful."

"I think I had better do the talking," she said, "your German is good but it is not *that* good!" Elsa gave a weak smile.

"Righto." Ewan smiled back.

The cargo was organized at the back of the station, closest to the street. They heard a lot of activity there. This station was one of the major rail hubs in Hamburg.

Elsa found him in his office at the back. "Herr Schwarz, Joe Schulmann recommended you to us. Perhaps you can help with arrangements for travelling to Dortmund?"

"Yes, Joe and I are old friends, how can I help?" Hans was very accommodating. "But Dortmund … that's in the occupied zone, it's very difficult to pass into that area," he hedged.

"We know," Ewan added, "but we have friends there that we must see."

Hans Schwarz was originally John Black. He had moved to Germany fifteen years before, after meeting and falling in love with a German girl in Liverpool. He had spent the war chafing about not being able to help his homeland very much. Spending the war pretending he was from South West Africa, to explain his accent, was galling at best. Finally, he was able to help a fellow Briton. Ewan's accent didn't fool him at all, though he didn't cotton on to Ewan being a soldier. As far as he was concerned, they were Herr *und* Frau Baum of Hamburg and Ewan was in the same situation that he had been in.

"What sort of friends?" Hans replied, in English. With the war over he felt confident enough to reply in his mother tongue.

Realizing that he had been found out, Ewan reverted to English too. "You're English," not accusing, just stating a fact.

"Aye, I married a German girl, Traudl, who was studying in Liverpool. We got married and moved here, to her home in Hamburg in 1897. She is the love of my life ... or she was until she was butchered last year by some evil bastards simply because she was Jewish." Not even trying to hide his contempt. "Now that she's gone, I'll probably move back to England."

"I think that might be wise," Ewan said, "Life is going tae get much harder here soon what with the gangs startin' tae roam the streets, beating up people who don't conform to their made up standards."

"Aye, it was one of them right wing bastards that killed Traudl," he lamented, "I meant it, what can I do for you?"

"Well, as Ewan ... err ... I mean, Peter ... said, we need to get to Dortmund. It's very important." Elsa explained.

Hans ignored the slip of the tongue. "Aye, well, as I said, Dortmund is in the Allied zone ... bloody near impossible to get there."

"I came through there a few days ago at Lunen, heading here."

"Much easier from that side, nobody's heading north until things settle down ... and that might be years. South on the other hand ..." Hans explained.

"How close can we get?" Ewan asked.

"Hmm ... I can get you to Selm, no bother, from there you're only a few miles short. How did you get across the first time?" Hans/John asked.

"I slipped o'er the rail bridge in the wee hours o' the morning." Ewan said.

"Well, all right then, I know the station master at Selm, he's from a local farming family and would be willing to get you to Lunen. His name is Rudolf Bergmann. His family was beaten up too, and his daughter raped … for being Communists."

So, in the event they got tickets to the small town of Selm, a few miles north of Lunen. The Allied side of the occupation zone was only around six miles due south. Elsa was determined to crawl if necessary, if it would get her back to Peter sooner.

They got to Selm early that afternoon and went to find Rudolf Bergmann. They found him dealing with several wounded soldiers who were trying to get home to Bonn and found they couldn't get through the military checkpoints.

"Are you Herr Bergmann?" Elsa asked.

"Yes, what can I do for you two?"

"Herr Schwarz, in Hamburg, said we should talk to you. We need to get to Lunen, if possible."

They went through the same explanation that they'd given Hans and with roughly the same result. The upshot was that the next morning they were in a hay cart heading to Lunen and would be there before dark.

Rudolf didn't believe a word they were saying but who was he to hold back people trying to flee the remains of Germany?

The cart belonged to Heinrich Ludwig, an elderly, roly-poly Bavarian farmer who knew both Hans and Rudolf. He was a very cheerful fellow and didn't seem to have a care in the world.

Ewan helped Elsa into the cart and then handed Ruth up to her. "Here, bury yourselves in the hay, I'll sit up front with the driver," he said.

Elsa just nodded her head, she didn't trust her emotions enough to say anything. She couldn't decide whether to be frightened or excited or both.

Ewan went to the driver and introduced himself in German. "Thank you for what you're doing," he started.

"Ach, it's not a problem," he said, "I'm a good Bavarian beer drinker and no-one would question me. Everyone around here knows me! If anyone asks, you are my cousin from Berlin!"

"Still, thank you very much, things are probably going to get very strained around here shortly. I wouldn't want to make your life any harder because of me." He was seriously concerned for the man.

"As I said, everyone knows me. I have no Jewish relatives. No Communist friends. I'm just a good German!" he laughed a hearty Bavarian laugh.

Ewan wondered again why all this carnage had been necessary. People were just people all over the world. Heinrich was a good example of a man who he'd love to share a beer, or three, with. Someone he would have no problem being friends with in another life.

Certainly, there were nasty, evil Germans. That bastard who killed Joe, the men who killed Hans' wife. But they were the exception to the rule. He'd had a chance to talk with several PoWs when he was at the aid station with Peter on Vimy Ridge. They all turned out to be men exactly like his men: afraid for their lives, afraid for their friends' lives, sick and tired of the mud and blood and lice and rats and the other atrocities in the trenches. Why couldn't the governments find some other way to settle disputes?

Heinrich was no different, he just wanted to live his life, to drink good German beer and to eat good German sausages.

Ewan and Heinrich spent the trip in companionable silence with no animosity at all.

They arrived on the outskirts of Lunen a little after dark. That suited Ewan just fine. He wanted to find a place to lie up overnight and then cross the railway bridge before first light. "Elsa, we're here, we're at Lunen," he whispered into the back. There was no response. He got a little worried and lifted a layer of hay off of the two refugees in his charge.

What he saw made him chuckle. Elsa and Ruth were sound asleep with Ruth encircled by Elsa's arms and legs. The gentle swaying of the cart had put them to sleep. It was a perfect little nest, and he was reluctant to wake them up, but they had to keep moving.

Elsa shook her head, groggily, and opened her eyes slowly. She took a moment or two to wake up and orient herself. "We're in Lunen," Ewan repeated.

"Oh, good. Where next?" she asked, entirely trusting Ewan because what other choice did she have?

"We'll have tae make our way tae the river and cross at the same bridge I crossed at before. We'll lie up in the wood until just before first light and cross then. We should be in the occupied zone before it gets fully light." His confidence was infectious, and she was buoyed up by his calm manner. "Then

I'll put my uniform back on, and I have a letter that will get us all the way to Halifax!"

Ewan wasn't too worried. It was a very porous border zone and they weren't acting like smugglers or criminals. Would criminals have a baby?

They crossed the bridge when it was light enough to see where they were going. At this point, Ewan felt it was safe enough to wear his uniform again since they were now back in the occupied zone. They found a small cow shed where Ewan changed.

Elsa was suitably impressed, "I see you've had an interesting war too," she said.

"Just as Peter has. I think he and I are of the same mind now though. We must do whatever we can to stop this madness from happening again."

They hitched a ride in a farm cart that was heading to Dortmund with local produce. The farmer recognized his uniform as something unpleasant but inevitable and reluctantly gave them a lift. Ewan gave him a pound of flour for his trouble. Once there they simply went to the railway station and Ewan used General Currie's letter to secure passage to Bonn where they would meet with his CO again.

The man at the ticket office greeted them with, "Happy New Year."

Ewan realised that it was January 1, 1919.

*
**

On the evening of January 5, 1919, Morag received a telegram from the war office in Ottawa telling her that Ewan would be on the *HMHS Araguaya*, arriving in Halifax the following week. She couldn't believe it! Could it be true? The telegram went on to say that Colonel Baum's wife, Elsa and their daughter, Ruth, were with him.

Since this was Friday and Peter had already gone back to the Citadel to play Prisoner of War again, she had to wait until he came down the following morning to tell him. But she couldn't wait. She had to tell someone, so she sought out Toni and Sean.

They were in the tannery office helping to find transportation for the last of the refugees who had been living in their shipping area since the explosion.

Morag couldn't hold back her excitement, she rushed straight up to her Da crying, "Da … Da …. Ewan w … will be back next week! I … I can't believe it!" she was stuttering with joy.

"Calm yourself girl … what was that you said?" Sean thought he had heard wrong.

"Ewan will be back next week! And Elsa will be with him!!" Too excited to stop vibrating she clung to Sean for support.

Toni had overheard and she, too, was excited for her friend. She hadn't met either Ewan or Elsa, but it was like they were old friends already, Morag had told her so much about them both.

There was no way on God's little green Earth that anyone was getting any sleep that night … not even the twins.

"Yer Da's coming home, my babies! He'll be home next week! Yer finally going to meet yer Da" her excitement was infectious, they started laughing with excitement. Three and a half now they were able to understand what this meant and couldn't stop laughing and crying either.

The next morning, Alan brought Peter down from the Citadel in time for breakfast. Not just porridge and weak tea, he noticed, but bacon and eggs and toast as well. Sean had pulled in a lot of favours for this feast. Peter couldn't help but wonder what was up. There had to be something important in the works to warrant this largesse.

He didn't have long to wait, Morag had managed to keep a straight face right up to the point where he leaned over to give her a peck on the cheek. She couldn't resist throwing her arms around him and almost yelling, "Ewan will be home next week, and he's got Elsa with him!!"

He couldn't believe his ears! Could this be true? Could it all be over? He didn't dare hope. And yet he couldn't help himself. He returned Morag's hug, with interest, and then Sean and Toni and Alan got in on the act.

Ten minutes later, when they had all calmed down a little, Morag put her deadpan, serious face on again and said, "There's only one slight problem, Peter."

"Oh, what could possibly be wrong after all that?" he said.

"Elsa isn't bringing your son home with her." She was trying desperately to keep a straight face.

"What? But I thought …. What? What happened?" he was devastated, almost more important than Elsa coming home was that he would finally meet his son.

Morag saw how distressed he was and couldn't keep up the pretence. "She's not bringing your son home, because your son …" pausing for effect, "is a daughter, Ruth, I believe!"

The relief was almost comical to see, "Oh, thank God! … That was cruel Morag, don't scare me like that!" He was smiling and laughing when he said it though.

The next five days were agony. Waiting those last few days was almost worse than the previous three and a half years.

Then on January 12, she got a telegram from the Mayor of Halifax telling her that the *HMHS Araguaya* would be docking the following afternoon and she was to be at the harbour by 2:00 p.m.

Accordingly, all seven of them were at the pier by 10:00 a.m. sharp … Morag couldn't wait that long, somehow hoping that going early would make the ship come early.

Peter couldn't wait either. He knew this was largely a publicity stunt, especially when the same dignitaries that were present when he had arrived showed up again. But he couldn't care less. He was going to see Elsa again. Part of him had wondered if he ever would.

But then 2:00 p.m. came and went, as did 3:00 p.m., and then 4:00 p.m. Morag was starting to get nervous. "Why aren't they here yet?" she pleaded. "They have to be coming! They just have to be!"

"Trust me, if the military is only two, or even three, hours late then you are doing well!" Peter laughed.

Then Alan said, "Look, there, just entering the harbour, it's a ship!"

Sure enough it was a ship, and as it drew nearer, they all realised that it was the ship they were waiting for.

The *HMHS Araguaya*, had arrived.

*
**

Colonel Mersereau greeted them warmly. This was another box he could tick off. He didn't quite understand what General Currie's intent was but he'd done all right so far so who was he to cause waves?

"Frau Baum! What a pleasant surprise! I hope Major MacBride has treated you well?" he enquired.

"Yes, of course, Ewan and I are old friends," she replied.

"So I understand, he and your husband … Peter … is it?"

"That's right, sir," Ewan interjected, "we were business partners before the war. In Halifax," he added.

"Interesting," the Colonel replied. "Well, in the spirit of General Currie's intent I'd best get you back to Halifax as soon as I can. And who is this beautiful young lady?" he was looking at Ruth.

"This is our daughter, Ruth, she and Peter have not yet met."

They spent the next three days exploring Bonn. It was a beautiful old city, parts of it dating back to Roman times. All the while waiting on tenterhooks because they were both desperate to bring their respective families together again, Ewan ever mindful of the fact that he hadn't met his children either.

On the fourth day the colonel sent for them. "Well, I've got good news and better news! The good news is that I have secured passage for you on a hospital ship bound for Halifax. The better news is that it leaves in a week, from France."

"Thank you, sir." Ewan replied. "Will I be going wi' her?" he asked, somewhat tentatively. He didn't want to raise his hopes prematurely.

"Of course! You will be her escort."

After that it was a whirlwind. Ewan secured the rest of his kit – surprisingly little for almost four years in Europe. Elsa, of course, had nothing except Ruth, and she, of course, was everything anyway.

Colonel Mersereau's last act was to arrange for space to get them on a train heading to Brest in France where they would board His Majesty's Hospital Ship *Araguaya* bound for Halifax.

And, just like that, they were on their way back to Canada. No longer requiring convoys, they were able to travel faster, thus they arrived on January 13, 1919 – almost four years since Ewan had left in 1915. He was both more, and less, the man he had been in that heady time of excitement.

*
**

From the moment they spotted the Cape Race lighthouse off their starboard bow they knew they were home. Ewan was under no illusions now.

This was home. He was Canadian, through and through. He had shed too much blood and seen too many friends die, Canadians all, to think of himself in any other way.

Likewise, Elsa knew she was home too. It was simpler for her, though, it was because Peter was here and home was wherever he was.

It was still a few hours before they got to Halifax though, so they stayed on the deck, as close to the bow as they could get, until they docked. Orderlies would come by periodically with tea and sandwiches. They also brought up a suitable basket for Elsa to put Ruth in, though Ruth was just as excited as her mother. All three of them were wrapped in blankets in the brisk January cold as they approached Halifax harbour.

Then, when they passed to the left of McNabs Island, Ewan finally let himself believe he was home. In the back of his mind, there had been this nagging doubt that this was all a dream and that he would wake up any moment in a cold sweat having had a horrible nightmare. But the island sealed it for him. They were home.

They were spared a view of the devastation that had been wrought in Halifax the previous year. It was largely repaired but still obvious. Instead, they would berth at precisely the same spot that Ewan had left for France from in May 1915.

He didn't see any of that though. His eyes were fixated on the most beautiful shock of red hair he could imagine. They were far too far away to see clearly, but he was absolutely sure that hair belonged to Morag. He could smell it and feel it and taste it, even from here.

Almost two, interminable, hours later they docked.

They were home.

It took three more hours before the wounded were all unloaded and they could take their turn.

As they were coming down the ramp, Ewan was still staring at that beautiful red hair and oblivious to all else.

*
**

The ship was taking forever to dock and when it finally did they had to wait several more hours for them to unload the wounded.

From the moment the ship was tied up though, Peter spotted the bright straw-coloured hair of his beautiful bride, Elsa. He didn't wave, though, because he was afraid that if it wasn't her and that if he waved at the wrong person, Elsa wouldn't come.

Morag had also spotted Ewan. She didn't know how she knew it was him amidst all those other khaki clad figures, she just knew. Maybe she did have second sight? She didn't know. All she knew was that her man was home and would be in her arms again soon.

*
**

As Ewan got closer to the familiar group waiting for him, he started to slow down. He wanted to savour the moment. He wanted this moment to be one of the lasting images of the war. Not of men exploding into a pink mist in front of him or of friends gurgling out their last or of piles of corpses so mutilated he couldn't even tell what uniform they had been wearing, or a million other equally horrifying memories. This was the moment he wanted to remember most.

Elsa had no such reservations. As soon as she was sure it was Peter she broke into a run and met him half way, as he sprinted towards her, gammy leg forgotten for the moment.

After crushing her to him for what seemed like forever he stared at his equally beautiful daughter and started weeping. Tears of utter happiness streamed down his cheeks. He fell to his knees in joy!

Ewan finally got the courage to approach Morag. She was equally tentative, also wanting to savour the moment. Then, as they stood less than a foot apart, she said, "You're late, you said you'd be home by Christmas."

"Aye, but I didn't say which one!"

And with that they fell into each other's arms.

CPSIA information can be obtained
at www.ICGtesting.com
Printed in the USA
LVHW091922271118
598388LV00008B/202/P